# MYTH ALLIANCES

# MYTH ALLIANCES

*MYTH-ING PERSONS*

*LITTLE MYTH MARKER*

*M.Y.T.H. INC. LINK*

## by Robert Lynn Asprin

Nelson Doubleday, Inc.     Garden City, New York

# Contents

# MYTH-ING PERSONS

# Chapter I

*"Reputations are fine up to a point. After that they become a pain!"*
**—D. Juan**

**T**HERE is something sinfully satisfying about doing something you know you aren't supposed to. This was roughly my frame of mind as I approached a specific nondescript tent at the Bazaar at Deva with my breakfast under my arm . . . guilty, but smug.

"Excuse me, young sahr!"

I turned to find an elderly Deveel waving desperately at me as he hurried forward. Normally I would have avoided the encounter, as Deveels are always selling something and at the moment I wasn't buying, but since I wasn't in a hurry I decided to hear what he had to say.

"I'm glad I caught you in time," he said, struggling to catch his breath. "While I don't usually meddle, you really don't want to go in there!"

"Why not? I was just. . . ."

"Do you know who lives there?"

"Well, actually I thought. . . ."

"That is the dwelling of the Great Skeeve!"

Something about this busybody irritated me. Maybe it was the way he never let me finish a sentence. Anyway, I decided to string him along for a while.

"The Great Skeeve?"

"You never heard of him?" The Deveel seemed genuinely shocked. "He's probably the most powerful magician at the Bazaar."

My opinion of the busybody soared to new heights, but the game was too much fun to abandon.

"I've never had too much faith in magicians," I said with studied casualness. "I've found for the most part their powers are overrated."

The oldster rolled his eyes in exasperation.

"That may be true in most cases, but not when it comes to the Great Skeeve! Did you know he consorts with Demons and has a dragon for a familiar?"

I favored him with a worldly smile.

"So what? Deva is a crossroads of the dimensions. Dimension travelers, or Demons as you call them, are the norm around here. As a Deveel, your main livelihood comes from dealing with Demons. As for the dragon, there's a booth not eight rows from here that sells dragons to anyone with the price."

"No, no! You don't understand! Of course we all deal with Demons when it comes to business. The difference is that this Skeeve is actually *friends* with them . . . invites them into his home and lives with them. One of his permanent house guests is a Pervert, and I don't know of a single Deveel who would stoop that low. What's more, I've heard it said that he has underworld connections."

The game was growing tiresome. Any points the Deveel had made with his tribute to the Great Skeeve had been lost with interest when he started commenting on Demons.

"Well, thank you for your concern," I said, holding out my hand for a handshake. "I promise you I'll remember everything you've said. What was your name again?"

The Deveel grabbed my hand and began pumping it vigorously.

"I am Aliman, and glad to be of assistance," he said with an ingratiating smile. "If you really want to show your gratitude, remember my name. Should you ever be in need of a *reputable* magician, I have a nephew who's just getting started in the business. I'm sure we could arrange some discount prices for you. Tell me, what is *your* name so I can tell him who to watch for?"

I tightened my grip slightly and gave him my widest smile. "Well, my friends call me Skeeve."

"I'll be sure to tell . . . SKEEVE?"

The Deveel's eyes widened, and his complexion faded from red to a delicate pink.

"That's right," I said, retaining my grip on his hand. "Oh, and for your information Demons from Perv are called Pervects, not Perverts . . . and he's not my house guest, he's my partner."

The Deveel was struggling desperately now, trying to free his hand.

"Now then, how many customers have you scared away from my business with your tales about what a fearsome person I am?"

The Deveel tore loose from my grip and vanished into the crowds, sounding an incoherent scream of terror as he went. In short, Aliman left. Right?

I watched him go with a certain amount of mischievous satisfaction. I wasn't really angry, mind you. We literally had more money than we could use right now, so I didn't begrudge him the customers. Still, I had never really paused to consider how formidable our operation must look from the outside. Viewing it now through a stranger's eyes, I found myself more than a little pleased. Considering the dubious nature of my beginning, we had built ourselves quite a reputation over the last few years.

I had been serious when I told Aliman that I didn't have much faith in magicians. My own reputation was overrated to say the least, and if I was being billed as a powerful magician, it made the others of my profession more than a little suspect in my eyes. After several years of seeing the inside of the magic business, I was starting to wonder if *any* magician was really as good as people thought.

I was so wrapped up in these thoughts as I entered our humble tent that I had completely forgotten that I was supposed to be sneaking in. I was reminded almost immediately.

The reminder came in the form of a huge man who loomed up to block my path. "Boss," he said in a squeaky little voice that was always surprising coming from such a huge body, "you shouldn't ought to go out alone like that. How many times we got to tell you. . . ."

"It's all right, Nunzio," I said, trying to edge around him. "I just ducked out to get some breakfast. Want a bagel?"

Nunzio was both unconvinced and undaunted in his scolding.

"How are we supposed to be your bodyguards if you keep sneaking off alone every chance you get? Do you know what Don Bruce would do to us if anything happened to you?"

"C'mon, Nunzio. You know how things are here at the Bazaar. If the Deveels see me with a bodyguard, the price of everything goes through the ceiling. Besides, I like being able to wander around on my own once in a while."

"You can afford the higher prices. What you can't afford is to set yourself up as a target for every bozo who wants the rep of bagging the Great Skeeve."

I started to argue, but my conversation with Aliman flashed across my mind. Nunzio was right. There were two sides to having a reputation. If anyone believed the rumors at the Bazaar and still meant me harm, they would muster such firepower for the attempt that my odds for survival would be nonexistent.

"Nunzio," I said slowly, "you may be right, but in all honesty what could you and Guido do to stop a magical attack on me?"

"Not a thing," he said calmly. "But they'd probably try to knock off your bodyguards first, and that might give you time to get away or hit them yourself before they could muster a second attack."

He said it easily, like you or I might say "The sun rises in the east," but it shook me. It had never really occurred to me how expendable bodyguards are, or how readily they accept the dangers of their profession.

"I'll try to remember that in the future," I said with a certain degree of grave humility. "What's more, I think I owe you and Guido an apology. Where is Guido, anyway?"

"Upstairs arguing with His Nibs," Nunzio grinned. "As a matter of fact, I was looking for you to break it up when I found you had snuck out again."

"Why didn't you say so in the first place?"

"What for? There's no rush. They'll be arguing until you get there. I figured it was more important to convince you to quit going out alone."

I groaned a little inside, but I had learned long ago the futility of arguing priorities with Nunzio.

"Well, thanks again for the advice, but I'd better get upstairs before those two kill each other."

With that I headed across the courtyard for the fountain stairs to our offices. . . .

Courtyard? Fountain stairs?

What happened to the humble tent I was walking into a minute ago?

*Weelll* . . . I said I was a magician, didn't I? Our little stall at the Bazaar is bigger on the inside than it is on the outside. Lots bigger. I've lived in royal palaces that weren't as big as our "humble tent." I can't take any credit for this particular miracle, though, other than the fact that it was my work that helped earn us our current residence. We live here rent-free courtesy of the Devan Merchants Association as partial payment for a little job we did for them a while back. That's also how I got my bodyguards . . . but that's another story.

Devan Merchants Association, you ask? Okay. For the uninitiated,

I'll go over this just once. The dimension I'm currently residing in is Deva, home of the shrewdest deal-drivers in all the known dimensions. You may have heard of them. In my own home dimension they were called devils, but I have since learned the proper pronunciation is Deveels. Anyway, my gracious living quarters are the result of my partner and I beating the Deveels at their own game . . . which is to say we got the better of them in a deal. Don't tell anyone, though. It would ruin their reputation and maybe even cost me a cushy spot. You see, they still don't know they've been had.

Anyway, where was I? Oh, yes. Heading for the offices. Normally after sneaking out I would stop by the stables to share breakfast with Gleep, but with a crisis on my hands I decided to forgo the pleasure of my pet's company and get to work. Gleep. He's the dragon Aliman was talking about . . . and I'm *not* going to try to condense *that* story. It's just too complicated.

Long before I reached the offices I could hear their voices raised in their favorite "song." The lyrics changed from time to time, but I knew the melody by heart.

"Incompetent bungler!"

"Who are you calling an incomplete bungler?"

"I stand corrected. You are a *complete* bungler!"

"You better watch your mouth! Even if you are the boss's partner, one more word and I'll. . . ."

"You'll what? If you threw a punch the safest place to be would be where you're aiming."

"Izzat so?"

It sounded like I had arrived in the nick of time. Taking a deep breath, I casually strolled into the teeth of the fracas.

"Hi, guys." I pretended to be totally unaware of what was going on. "Anyone want a bagel?"

"No, I don't want a bagel!" came the sneering response from one combatant. "What I want is some decent help."

". . . and while you're at it see what you can do about getting me a little respect!" the other countered.

The latter comment came from Guido, senior of my two bodyguards. If anything, he's bigger and nastier than his cousin Nunzio.

The former contribution came from Aahz. Aahz is my partner. He's also a demon, a Pervect to be exact, and even though he's slightly shorter than I am, he's easily twice as nasty as my two bodyguards put together.

My strategy had worked in that I now had their annoyance focused on me instead of each other. Now, realizing the potential devastation of their respective temperaments individually, much less collectively, I had cause to doubt the wisdom of my strategy.

"What seems to be the trouble?"

"The trouble," Aahz snarled, "is that your ace bodyguard here just lost us a couple of clients."

My heart sank. I mentioned earlier that Aahz and I have more money than we know what to do with, but old habits die hard. Aahz is the tightest being I've ever met when it comes to money, and, living at the Bazaar at Deva, that's saying something! If Guido had really lost a potential customer, we'd be hearing about it for a long time.

"Ease up a minute, partner," I said more to stall for time than anything else. "I just got here, remember? Could you fill me in on a few of the details?"

Aahz favored Guido with one more dark stare.

"There's not all that much to tell," he said. "I was in the middle of breakfast . . ."

"He was drinking another meal," Guido translated scornfully.

". . . when mush-for-brains here bellows up that there are some customers waiting downstairs in reception. I called back that I'd be down in a few, then finished my meal."

"He kept them waiting at least half an hour. You can't expect customers to. . . ."

"Guido, could you hold the editorial asides for one round? Please?" I interceded before Aahz could go for him. "I'm still trying to get a rough idea of what happened, remember? Okay, Aahz. You were saying?"

Aahz took a deep breath, then resumed his account.

"Anyway, when I got downstairs, the customers were nowhere to be seen. You'd think your man here would be able to stall them or at least have the sense to call for reinforcements if they started getting twitchy."

"C'mon, Aahz. Guido is supposed to be a bodyguard, not a receptionist. If some customers got tired of waiting for you to show up and left, I don't see where you can dodge the blame by shifting it to. . . ."

"Wait a minute, Boss. You're missing the point. They didn't leave!"

"Come again?"

"I left 'em there in the reception room, and the next thing I know Mr. Mouth here is hollerin' at me for losing customers. They never came out! Now, like you say, I'm supposed to be a bodyguard. By my figuring we've got some extra people wandering the premises, and all this slob wants to do is yell about whose fault it is."

"I know whose fault it is," Aahz said with a glare. "There are only two ways out of that reception room, and they didn't come past me!"

"Well they didn't come past *me!*" Guido countered.

I started to get a very cold feeling in my stomach.

"Aahz," I said softly.

"If you think I don't know when. . . ."

"AAHZ!"

That brought him up short. He turned to me with an angry retort on his lips, then he saw my expression.

"What is it, Skeeve? You look as if. . . ."

"There are more than two ways out of that room."

We stared at each other in stunned silence for a few moments, then we both sprinted for the reception room, leaving Guido to trail along behind.

The room we had selected for our reception area was one of the largest in the place, and the only large room with easy access from the front door. It was furnished in a style lavish enough to impress even those customers spoiled by the wonders of the Bazaar who were expecting to see the home office of a successful magician. There was only one problem with it, and that was the focus of our attention as we dashed in.

The only decoration that we had kept from the previous owners was an ornate tapestry hanging on the north wall. Usually I'm faster than Aahz, but this time he beat me to the hanging, sweeping it aside with his arm to reveal a heavy door behind it.

Our worst fears were realized.

The door was unlocked and standing ajar.

# Chapter II

*"Success often hinges on choosing a*
*reliable partner."*
**—Remus**

**"W**HAT'S that?" Guido demanded, taking advantage of our
stunned silence.

"It's a door," I said.

"An open door, to be specific," Aahz supplied.

"I can see that for myself!" the bodyguard roared. "I meant what is it
doing here?"

"It would look pretty silly standing alone in the middle of the street
now, wouldn't it?" Aahz shot back.

Guido purpled. As I've said, these two have a positive talent for
getting under each other's skins.

"Now look, all I'm askin'. . . ."

"Guido, could you just hang on for a few minutes until we decide
what to do next? Then we'll explain, I promise."

My mind was racing over the problem, and having Aahz and Guido
going at each other did nothing for my concentration.

"I think the first thing we should do, partner," Aahz said thoughtfully, "is to get the door closed so that we won't be . . . interrupted while
we work this out."

Rather than answer, I reached out a cautious toe and pushed the door shut. Aahz quickly slipped two of the bolts in place to secure it.

That done, we leaned against the door and looked at each other in silence.

"Well? What do you think?" I asked at last.

"I'm in favor of sealing it up again and forgetting the whole thing."

"Think it's safe to do that?"

"Don't know, really. Not enough information."

We both turned slowly to level thoughtful stares at Guido.

"Say, uh, Guido, could you tell us a little more about those customers who came in this morning?"

"Nothing doin'." Guido crossed his arms. "You're the guys who insist on 'information for information.' Right? Well, I'm not telling you anything more until somebody tells me about that door. I mean, I'm supposed to be your bodyguard and nobody bothers to tell me there's another way into this place?"

Aahz bared his teeth and started forward, but I caught him by the shoulder.

"He's right, partner. If we want his help, we owe him an explanation."

We locked eyes again for a moment, then he shrugged and retreated.

"Actually, Guido, the explanation is very simple. . . ."

"That'll be a first," the bodyguard grumbled.

In a bound, Aahz was across the room and had Guido by the shirt front.

"You wanted an explanation? Then SHUT UP AND LET HIM EX-PLAIN!"

Now Guido is no lightweight, and he's never been short in the courage department. Still, there's nothing quite like Aahz when he's really mad.

"O—Okay! Sorry! Go ahead, Boss. I'm listening."

Aahz released his grip and returned to his place by the door, winking at me covertly as he went.

"What happened is this," I said, hiding a smile. "Aahz and I found that door when we first moved in here. We didn't like the looks of it, so we decided to leave it alone. That's all."

"That's all? A back door that even you admit looks dangerous and all you do is ignore it? And if that wasn't bad enough, you don't even bother to tell your bodyguards about it? Of all the lamebrained, half. . . ."

Aahz cleared his throat noisily, and Guido regained control of himself . . . rapidly.

"Aahh . . . what I mean to say is . . . oh well. That's all behind us now. Could you give *me* a little more information now that the subject's out in the open? What's on the other side of that door, anyway?"

"We don't know," I admitted.

"YOU DON'T KNOW?" Guido shrieked.

"What we *do* know," Aahz interrupted hastily, "is what *isn't* on the other side. What isn't there is any dimension we know about."

Guido blinked, then shook his head. "I don't get it. Could you run that past me again . . . real slow?"

"Let me try," I said. "Look, Guido, you already know about dimensions, right? How we're living in the dimension Deva, which is an entirely different world than our own home dimension of Klah? Well, the people here, the Deveels, are masters of dimension travel to a point where they build their houses across the dimension barriers. That's how come this place is bigger on the inside than it is on the outside. The door is in Deva, but the rest of the house is in another dimension. That means if we go through that door, the back door that we've just shown you, we'd be in another world . . . one we know nothing about. That's why we were willing to leave it sealed up rather than stick our noses out into a completely unknown situation."

"I still think you should have checked it out," the bodyguard insisted stubbornly.

"Think again," Aahz supplied. "You've only seen two dimensions. Skeeve here has visited a dozen. I've been to over a hundred myself. The Deveels you see here at the Bazaar, on the other hand, know over a thousand different dimensions."

"So?"

"So we think they gave us this place because it opens into a dimension that *they* don't want . . . 'don't want' as in 'scared to death of'. Now, you've seen what a Deveel will brave to turn a profit. Do *you* want to go exploring in a world that's too mean for *them* to face?"

"I see what you mean."

"Besides," Aahz finished triumphantly, "take another look at that door. It's got more locks and bolts than three ordinary bank vaults."

"*Somebody* opened it," Guido said pointedly.

That took some of the wind out of Aahz's sails. Despite himself, he shot a nervous glance at the door.

"Well . . . a good thief with a lockpick working from this side. . . ."

"Some of these locks weren't picked, Aahz."

I had been taking advantage of their discussion to do a little snooping, and now held up one of my discoveries for their inspection. It was a padlock with the metal shackle snapped off. There were several of them scattered about, as if someone had gotten impatient with the lockpick and simply torn the rest of them apart with his hands.

Guido pursed his lips in a silent whistle. "Man, that's strong. What kind of person could do that?"

"That's what we've been trying to get you to tell us," Aahz said nastily. "Now, if you don't mind, what were those customers like?"

"Three of them . . . two men and a woman . . . fairly young-looking, but nothing special. Klahds by the look of 'em. Come to think of it, they did seem a bit nervous, but I thought it was just because they were coming to see a magician."

"Well, now they're on the other side of the door." Aahz scooped up one of the undamaged locks and snapped it into place. "I don't think they can pick locks, or break them if they can't reach 'em. They're there, which is their problem, self-inflicted I might add, and we're here. End of puzzle. End of problem."

"Do you really think so, Aahz?"

"Trust me."

Somehow that phrase struck a familiar chord in my memory, and the echoes weren't pleasant. I was about to raise this point with Aahz when Nunzio poked his head in the door.

"Hey, Boss. You got visitors."

"See?" my partner exclaimed, beaming. "I told you things could only get better! It's not even noon and we've got more customers."

"Actually," Nunzio clarified, "it's a delegation of Deveels. I think it's the landlord."

"The landlord?" Aahz echoed hollowly.

"See how much better things have gotten?" I said with a disgusted smirk. "And it's not even noon."

"Shall I run 'em off, Boss?" Guido suggested.

"I think you'd better see 'em," Nunzio advised. "They seem kind'a upset. Something about us harboring fugitives."

Aahz and I locked gazes in silence, which was only natural as there was nothing more to be said. With a vague wave that bordered on a nervous tic, I motioned for Nunzio to show the visitors in.

As expected, it was the same delegation of four from the Devan Chamber of Commerce who had originally hired us to work for the Bazaar, headed by our old adversary, Hay-ner. Last time we dealt with him, we had him over a barrel and used the advantage mercilessly. While he had agreed to our terms, I always suspected it had hurt his Devan pride to cut such a generous deal and that he had been waiting ever since to pay us back. From the smile on his face as he entered our reception room, it appeared he felt his chance had finally come.

"Aahh, Master Skeeve," he said. "How good of you to see us so promptly without an appointment. I know how busy you are, so I'll come right to the point. I believe there are certain individuals in residence here that our organization is *most* anxious to speak with. If you would be so kind as to summon them, we won't trouble you further."

"Wait a minute, Hay-ner," Aahz put in before I could respond. "What makes you think the people you're looking for are here?"

"Because they were seen entering your tent less than an hour ago and haven't come out yet," said the largest of Hay-ner's back-up team.

I noticed that unlike Hay-ner, he wasn't smiling. In fact, he looked down-right angry.

"He must mean the ones who came in earlier," Nunzio suggested helpfully. "You know, Boss, the two guys with the broad."

Aahz rolled his eyes in helpless frustration, and for once I was inclined to agree with him.

"Umm, Nunzio," I said, staring at the ceiling, "why don't you and Guido wait outside while we take care of this?"

The two bodyguards trooped outside in silence, though I noticed that Guido glared at his cousin with such disdain that I suspected a stern dressing-down would take place even before I could get to him myself. The Mob is no more tolerant than magicians of staff members who say more than they should in front of the opposition.

"Now that we've established that we all know who we're talking about and that they're here," Hay-ner said, rubbing his hands together, "call them out and we'll finish this once and for all."

"Not so fast," I interrupted. "First of all, neither of us have laid eyes on those folks you're looking for, because, second of all, they aren't here. They took it on the lam out the back door before we could meet them."

"Somehow, I don't expect you to take our word for it," Aahz added. "So feel free to search the place."

The Deveel's smile broadened, and I was conscious of cold sweat breaking out on my brow.

"That won't be necessary. You see, whether I believe you or not is of little consequence. Even if we searched, I'm sure you would be better at hiding things than we would be at finding them. All that really matters is that we've established that they did come in here, and that makes them *your* responsibility."

I wasn't sure exactly what was going on here, but I *was* sure that I was liking it less and less with each passing moment.

"Wait a minute, Hay-ner," I began. "What do you mean 'We're responsible'? Responsible for what?"

"Why, for the fugitives, of course. Don't you remember? When we agreed to let you use this place rent-free, part of the deal was that if anyone of this household broke any of the Bazaar rules, and either disappeared off to another dimension or otherwise refused to face the charges, that you would personally take responsibility for their actions. It's a standard clause in any Bazaar lease."

"Aahz," I said testily, "you cut the deal. Was there a clause like that in it?"

"There was," he admitted. "But I was thinking of Tananda and Chumley at the time . . . and we'll stand behind them anytime. Massha, too. It never occurred to me that they'd try to claim that anyone who walked through our door was a member of our household. I don't see how they can hope to prove. . . ."

"We don't have to prove that they're in your household," Hay-ner smiled. "You have to prove they aren't."

"That's crazy," Aahz exploded. "How can we prove. . . ."

"Can it, Aahz. We can't prove it. That's the point. All right, Hay-ner. You've got us. Now what exactly have these characters done that we're responsible for and what are our options? I thought one of the big sales points of the Bazaar was that there weren't any rules here."

"There aren't many," the Deveel said, "but the few that do exist are strictly enforced. The specific rule your friends broke involves fraud."

He quickly held up a hand to suppress my retort.

"I know what you're going to say. Fraud sounds like a silly charge with all the hard bargaining that goes on here at the Bazaar, but to us it's a serious matter. While we pride ourselves in driving a hard bargain, once the deal is made you get the goods you were promised. Sometimes there are specific details omitted in describing the goods, but anything actually *said* is true. That is our reputation and the continued success of the Bazaar depends on that reputation being scrupulously maintained. If a trader or merchant sells something claiming it to be magical and it turns out to have no powers at all, that's fraud . . . and if the perpetrators are allowed to go unpunished, it could mean the end of the Bazaar as we know it."

"Actually," I said drily, "all I was going to do was protest you billing them as our friends, but I'll let it go. What you haven't mentioned is our options."

Hay-ner shrugged. "There are only three, really. You can pay back the money they took falsely plus a twenty-five percent fine, accept permanent banishment from the Bazaar, or you can try to convince your fr—aahh, I mean the fugitives to return to the Bazaar to settle matters themselves."

"I see . . . Very well. You've had your say. Now please leave so my partner and I can discuss our position on the matter."

Aahz took care of seeing them out while I plunged into thought as to what we should do. When he returned, we both sat in silence for the better part of an hour before either of us spoke.

"Well," I said at last, "what do you think?"

"Banishment from the Bazaar is out!" Aahz snarled. "Not only would it destroy our reputations, I'm not about to get run out of the Bazaar *and* our home over something as idiotic as this!"

"Agreed," I said grimly. "Even though it occurs to me that Hay-ner is bluffing on that option. He wants us to stick around the Bazaar as much as we want to stay. He was the one who hired us in the first place, remember? I think he's expecting us to ante up and pay the money. That way he gets back some of the squeeze he so grudgingly parted with. Somehow the idea of giving in to that kind of pressure really galls me."

Aahz nodded. "Me too."

There followed several more minutes of silence.

"Okay," Aahz said finally, "who's going to say it?"

"We're going to have to go after them." I sighed.

"Half right," Aahz corrected. "*I'm* going to have to go after them. Partner or not, we're talking about hitting a totally new dimension here, and it's too dangerous for someone at your level of magical skill."

"*My* level? How about you? You don't have any powers at all. If it's too dangerous for me, what's supposed to keep you safe?"

"Experience," he said loftily. "I'm used to doing this, and you aren't. End of argument."

" 'End of argument' nothing! Just how do you propose to leave me behind if I don't agree?"

"That's easy," Aahz grinned. "See who's standing in the corner?"

I turned to look where he was pointing, and that's the last thing I remembered for a long time.

# Chapter III

*"Reliable information is a must for successful planning."*
**—C. Columbus**

"**H**EY! Hot stuff! Wake up!! You okay?"

If I led a different kind of life, those words would have been uttered by a voluptuous vision of female loveliness. As it was, they were exclaimed by Massha.

This was one of the first things that penetrated the fogginess of my mind as I struggled to regain consciousness. I'm never at my best first thing in the morning, even when I wake up leisurely of my own accord. Having wakefulness forced upon me by someone else only *guarantees* that my mood will be less than pleasant.

However groggy I might be feeling, though, there was no mistaking the fact that it was Massha shaking me awake. Even through unfocused eyes, her form was unmistakable. Imagine, if you will, the largest, fattest woman you've ever met. Now expand that image by fifty percent in all directions, top it off with garish orange hair, and false eyelashes and purple lipstick, and adorn it with a wheelbarrow load of gaudy jewelry. See what I mean? I could recognize Massha a mile away on a dark night . . . blindfolded.

"Of course I'm okay, *apprentice!*" I snarled. "Don't you have any lessons you're supposed to be practicing or something?"

"Are you *sure?*" she pressed mercilessly.

"Yes, I'm sure. Why do you ask? Can't a fellow take a little nap without being badgered about it?"

"It's just that you don't usually take naps in the middle of the reception room floor."

That got my attention, and I forced my eyes into focus. She was right! For some reason I was sprawled out on the floor. Now what could have possessed me to. . . .

Then it all came back! Aahz! The expedition into the new dimension!

I sat bolt upright . . . and regretted it immediately. A blinding headache assaulted me with icepick intensity, and my stomach flipped over and landed on its back with all the grace of a lump of overcooked oatmeal.

Massha caught me by the shoulder as I started to list.

"Steady there, High Roller. Looks like your idea of 'okay' and mine are a little out of synch."

Ignoring her, I felt the back of my head cautiously and discovered a large, tender lump behind my ear. If I had had any doubts as to what had happened, they were gone now.

"That bloody Pervert!" I said, flinching at the new wave of pain brought on by the sound of my own voice. "He must have knocked me out and gone in alone!"

"You mean Aahz? Dark, green, and scaly himself? I don't get it. Why would your own partner sucker-punch you?"

"So he could go through the door without me. I made it very clear that I didn't want to be left behind on this caper."

"Door? What door?" Massha said with a frown. "I know you two have your secrets, Boss, but I think you'd better fill me in on a few more details as to exactly what's going on around here."

As briefly as I could, I brought her up to date on the day's events, including the explanation as to why Aahz and I had never said anything about the house's mysterious back door. Being a seasoned dimension traveler herself, she grasped the concept of an unlisted dimension and its potential dangers much more rapidly than Guido and Nunzio.

"What I don't understand is even if he didn't want you along, why didn't he take *someone* else as a backup?"

"Like who?" I said with a wry grimace. "We've already established that you're *my* apprentice and he doesn't give you orders without clearing them through me. He's never been impressed with Guido and Nunzio. Tananda and Chumley are off on their own contracts and aren't due back for several days. Even Gus is taking a well-earned vacation with Berfert. Besides, he knows good and well that if he started building a team and excluded me, there'd be some serious problems before the dust settled. I wouldn't take something like that lying down!"

"Don't look now, but you just did," my apprentice pointed out dryly, "though I have to admit he sort of forced it on you."

With that, she slid a hand under each of my armpits and picked me up, setting me gently on my feet.

"Well, now what? I supposed you're going to go charging after him with blood in your eye. Mind if I tag along? Or are you bound and determined to be as stupid as he is?"

As a matter of fact, that was exactly what I had been planning to do. The undisguised sarcasm in her voice combined with the unsettling wobbliness of my legs, however, led me to reconsider.

"No," I said carefully. "One of us blundering around out there is enough . . . or one too many, depending on how you count it. While I still think I should have gone along, Aahz has dealt this hand, so it's up to him to play it out. It's up to me to mind the store until he gets back."

Massha cocked an eyebrow at me.

"That makes sense," she said, "though I'll admit I'm a little surprised to hear you say it."

"I'm a responsible businessman now." I shrugged. "I can't afford to go off half-cocked like a rash kid anymore. Besides, I have every confidence in my partner's ability to handle things."

Those were brave words, and I meant them. Two days later, however, this particular "responsible businessman" was ready to go off *fully* cocked. Guido and Nunzio ceased to complain about my sneaking off alone . . . mostly because I didn't go out at all! In fact, I spent most of my waking hours and all of my sleeping hours (though I'll admit I didn't sleep much) in the reception room on the off-chance that I could greet Aahz on his triumphant return.

Unfortunately, my vigil went unrewarded.

I did my best to hide my concern, but I needn't have bothered. As the hours marched on, my staff's worries grew until most of my time was spent telling them, "No, he isn't back yet. When he gets here, I'll let you know." Even Guido, who never really got along with Aahz, took to stopping by at least once an hour for a no-progress report.

Finally, as a salve for my own nerves, I called everyone into the reception room for a staff meeting.

"What I want to know is how long are we just going to sit around before we admit that something's gone wrong?" Guido muttered for the fifth time.

"How long do you figure it takes to find a fugitive in a strange dimension?" I shot back. "How long would it take you to find them if they were on Klah, Guido? We've got to give him some time."

"How much time?" he countered. "It's already been two days. . . ."

"Tananda and Chumley will be back any time now," Massha interrupted. "Do you think they'll just sit around on their hands when they find out that Aahz is out there all alone?"

"I thought *you* were the one who thought that going after him was a stupid idea?"

"I still do. Now do you want to know what I think of the idea of doing *nothing?*"

Before I could answer, a soft knock sounded at the door . . . the back door!

"See!" I crowed triumphantly. "I told you he would be back!"

"That doesn't sound like his knock," Guido observed suspiciously.

"And why should he knock?" Massha added. "The door hasn't been locked since he left."

In my own relief and enthusiasm, their remarks went unnoticed. In a flash I was at the door, wrenching it open while voicing the greeting I had been rehearsing for two days.

"It's about time, part . . . ner."

It wasn't Aahz.

In fact, the being outside the door didn't look anything at all like Aahz. What was doubly surprising, though, was that I recognized her!

We had never really met . . . not to exchange names, but shortly after meeting Aahz I had been strung up by an angry mob while impersonating her, and I had seen her in the crowd when I successfully "interviewed" for the job of court magician at Possiltum.

What I had never had a chance to observe first-hand was her radiant complexion framed by waves of sun-gold hair, or the easy grace with which she carried herself, or the . . . .

"It's the Great Skeeve, right? Behind the open mouth?"

Her voice was so musical it took me a few moments to zero in on what she had said and realize that she was expecting an answer.

"Aahh . . . yes. I mean, at your service."

"Glad to finally meet you face-to-face," she said briskly, glancing at Guido and Massha nervously. "I've been looking for an excuse for a while, and I guess this is it. Got some news for you . . . about your apprentice."

I was still having problems focusing on what she was saying. Not only was her voice mesmerizing, she was easily the loveliest woman I had ever met . . . well, girl actually. She couldn't have been much older than me. What's more, she seemed to like me. That is, she kept smiling hesitantly and her deep blue eyes never left mine. Now, I had gotten respect from my colleagues and from beings at the Bazaar who knew my reputation, but never from anyone who looked like . . . .

Then her words sank in.

"My apprentice?"

I stole an involuntary glance at Massha before I realized the misunderstanding.

"Oh, you mean Aahz. He's not my apprentice any more. He's my partner. Please come in. We were just talking about him."

I stood to one side of the door and invited her in with a grand sweeping gesture. I'd never tried it before, but I had seen it used a couple of times while I was working the court at Possiltum, and it had impressed me.

"Umm—Boss? Could I talk to you for a minute?"

"Later, Guido."

I repeated the gesture, and the girl responded with a quick smile that lit up the room.

"Thanks for the invite," she said, "but I'll have to take a rain check. I really can't stay. In fact, I shouldn't be here at all. I just thought that someone should let you know that your friend . . . Aahz is it? Anyway, your friend is in jail."

That brought me back to earth in a hurry.

"Aahz? In jail? For what?"

"Murder."

"MURDER!" I shrieked, dropping all attempts to be urbane. "But Aahz wouldn't. . . ."

"Don't shout at me! Oh, I knew I shouldn't have come. Look, I know he didn't do it. That's why I had to let you know what was going on. If you don't do something, they're going to execute him . . . and they know how to execute demons over here."

I spun around to face the others.

"Massha! Go get your jewelry case. Guido, Nunzio! Gear up. We're going to pay a little call on our neighbors."

I tried to keep my voice calm and level, but somehow the words came out a bit more intense than I had intended.

"Not so fast, Boss," Guido said. "There's something you oughta know first."

"Later. I want you to. . . ."

"NOW, Boss. It's important!"

"WHAT IS IT!"

Needless to say, I was not eager to enter into any prolonged conversations just now.

"She's one of 'em."

"I beg your pardon?"

"The three that went out through the back door. The ones your partner is chasing. She's the broad."

Thunderstruck, I turned to the girl for confirmation, only to find the doorway was empty. My mysterious visitor had disappeared as suddenly as she had arrived.

"This could be a trap, you know," Massha said thoughtfully.

"She's right." Guido nodded. "Take it from someone who's been on the lam himself. When you're running from the law and there are only a couple of people who can find you, it gets real tempting to eliminate that link. We've only got her word that your partner's in trouble."

"It wouldn't take a mental giant to figure out that you and Aahz are the most likely hunters for the Deveels to hire. After all, they knew whose house they were cutting through for their getaway," Massha added.

Guido rose to his feet and started pacing.

"Right," he said. "Now suppose *they've* got Aahz. Can you think of a better way to bag the other half of the pair than by feeding you a line about your partner being in trouble so you'll come charging into whatever trap they've laid out? The whole set-up stinks, Boss. I don't know about strange dimensions, but I *do* know about criminals. As soon as you step through that door, you're gonna be a sitting duck."

"Are you *quite* through?"

Even to my ears my voice sounded icy, but for a change I didn't care.

Guido and Massha exchanged glances, then nodded silently.

"Very well. You may be right, and I appreciate your concern for my well-being. HOWEVER . . ."

My voice sank to a deadly hiss.

". . . what if you're wrong? What if our fugitive *is* telling the truth? You've all been on my case about not doing anything to help Aahz. Do you really think I'm just going to sit here while my partner AND friend burns for a crime he didn't commit . . . on the off-chance that getting involved *might* be dangerous to me?"

With great effort I forced my tones back to normal.

"In ten minutes I'm going through that door after Aahz . . . and if I'm walking into a trap, it had better be a good one. Now do any of you want to come with me, or am I going it alone?"

# Chapter IV

*"It's useless to try to plan for the unexpected
. . . by definition!"*
**—A. Hitchcock**

**A**CTUALLY, it was more like an hour before we were really ready to go, though for me it seemed like a lot longer. Still, even I had to admit that not taking the proper preparations for this venture would not only be foolish, it would be downright suicidal!

It was decided that Nunzio would stay behind so there would be someone at our base to let Tananda and Chumley know what was going on when they returned. Needless to say, he was less than thrilled by the assignment.

"But I'm supposed to be your bodyguard!" he argued. "How'm I supposed to guard you if I'm sittin' back here while you're on the front lines?"

"By being sure our support troops get the information they need to follow us," I said.

As much as I disliked having to argue with Nunzio, I would rather dig in my heels against half a dozen Mob-type bodyguards than have to explain to Tananda and Chumley why they weren't included in this rescue mission.

"We could leave a note."

"No."

"We could. . . ."

"NO! I want you *here*. Is that plain enough?"

The bodyguard heaved a heavy sigh. "Okay, Boss. I'll hang in here until they show up. Then the three of us will. . . ."

"No!" I said again. "Then Tananda and Chumley will come in after us. You're going to stay here."

"But Boss. . . ."

"Because if Hay-ner and his crew show up again, someone has to be here to let them know we're on the job and that we haven't just taken off for the tall timber. Assuming for the moment that we're going to make it back, we need our exit route, and you're going to be here making sure it stays open. All we need is for our hosts to move in a new tenant while we're gone . . . say, someone who decides to brick up this door while we're on the other side."

Nunzio thought this through in silence.

"What if you don't come back?" he asked finally.

"We'll burn that bridge when we come to it," I sighed. "But remember, we aren't that easy to kill. At least one of us will probably make it back."

Fortunately, my mind was wrenched away from that unpleasant train of thought by the arrival of Guido.

"Ready to go, Boss."

Despite the desperateness of the situation and the haunting time pressures, I found myself gaping at him.

"What's that?" I managed at last.

Guido was decked out in a long dark coat and wearing a wide-brimmed hat and sunglasses.

"These? These are my work clothes," he said proudly. "They're functional as well as decorative."

"They're what?"

"What I mean is, not only do people find 'em intimidating, the trench coat has all these little pockets inside, see? That's where I carry my hardware."

"But. . . ."

"Hi, Hot Stuff. Nice outfit, Guido."

"Thanks! I was just telling the Boss here about it."

Massha was dressed . . . or should I say undressed in *her* work clothes. A brief vest struggled to cover even part of her massive torso, while an even briefer bottom was on the verge of surrendering its battle completely.

"Ummm . . . Massha?" I said carefully. "I've always meant to ask. Why don't you . . . ummm . . . wear more?"

"I like to dress cool when we're going into a hot situation," she winked. "You see, when things speed up, I get a little nervous . . . and the only thing worse than havin' a fat broad around is havin' a *sweaty* fat broad around."

"I think it's a sexy outfit," Guido chimed in. "Reminds me of the stuff my old man's moll used to wear."

"Well thanks, Dark and Deadly. I'd say your old man had good taste . . . but I never tasted him."

I studied them thoughtfully as they shared a laugh over Massha's joke. Any hope of a quiet infiltration of this unknown dimension was rapidly disintegrating. Either Guido or Massha alone was eye-catching, but together they were about as inconspicuous as a circus parade and an army maneuver sharing the same road. Then it occurred to me that, not knowing what things were like where we were heading, they might fit in and *I* would stand out. It was a frightening thought. If everybody there looked like this. . . .

I forced the thought from my mind. No use scaring myself any more than I had to before there was information to back it up. What was important was that my two assistants were scared. They were trying hard not to show it, but in doing so, each was dropping into old patterns, slipping behind old character masks. Guido was playing his "tough gangster" bit to the hilt, while Massha was once more assuming her favorite "vamp" character with a vengeance. The bottom line, though, was that, scared or not, they were willing to back my move or die trying. It would have been touching, if it weren't for the fact that it meant they were counting on me for leadership. That meant I had to stay calm and confident . . . no matter how scared I felt myself. It only occurred to me as an afterthought that, in many ways, leadership was the mask *I* was learning to slip behind when things got tight. It made me wonder briefly if *anyone* ever really knew what they were doing or felt truly confident, or if life was simply a mass game of role-playing.

"Okay. Are we ready?" I asked, shrugging off my wandering thoughts. "Massha? Got your jewelry?"

"Wearing most of it, and the rest is right here," she said, patting the pouch on her belt.

While I will occasionally make snide mental comments about my apprentice's jewelry, it serves a dual purpose. Massha's baubles are in reality a rather extensive collection of magical gimmicks she has accumulated over the years. How extensive? Well, before she signed on as my apprentice to learn real magic, she was holding down a steady job as the magician for the city-state of Ta-hoe on the dimension of Jahk solely on the strength of her collected mechanical "powers." While I agreed with Aahz that real magic was preferable to mechanical in that it was less likely to malfunction (a lesson learned from first-hand experience) I sure didn't mind having her arsenal along for back-up.

"You know that tracking ring? The one you used to find the king? Any chance there's an extra tucked away in your pouch?"

"Only have the one," she said, waggling the appropriate finger.

I cursed mentally, then made the first of what I feared would be many unpleasant decisions on this venture.

"Give it to Nunzio. Tananda and Chumley will need it to find us."

"But if we leave it behind, how are we going to find your partner?"

"We'll have to figure out something, but we can't afford to divide our forces. Otherwise, even if we get Aahz, we could still end up wandering around out there trying to find the other half of the rescue team."

"If you say so, Hot Stuff," she grimaced, handing over the ring, "but I hope you know what you're doing."

"So do I, Massha, so do I. Okay, gang, let's see what our backyard is *really* like!"

\* \* \*

From the outside, our place looked a lot more impressive than the side that showed in the Bazaar. It really did look like a castle . . . a rather ominous one at that, squatting alone on a hilltop. I really didn't study it too close, though, beyond being able to recognize it again for our trip out. As might be expected, my main attention was focused on the new dimension itself.

"Kinda dark, ain't it."

Guido's comment was more statement than question, and he was right.

Wherever we were, the lighting left a lot to be desired. At first I thought it was night, which puzzled me, as so far in my travels all dimensions seemed to be on the same sun-up and sun-down schedule. Then my eyes adjusted to the gloom and I realized the sky was simply heavily overcast . . . to a point where next to no light at all penetrated, giving a night-like illusion to the day.

Aside from that, from what I could see, this new land seemed pretty much like any of the others I had visited: Trees, underbrush, and a road leading to or from the castle, depending on which way you were facing. I think it was Tananda who was fond of saying "If you've seen one dimension, you've seen them all." Chumley, her brother, argued that the reason for the geologic similarities was that all the dimensions we traveled were different realities off the same base. This always struck me as being a bit redundant . . . "They're all alike because they're the same? C'mon Chumley!", but his rebuttals always left me feeling like I'd been listening to someone doing readings in another language, so of late I've been tending to avoid the discussions.

"Well, Hot Stuff, what do we do now?"

For a change, I had an answer for this infuriating question.

"This road has to go somewhere. Just the fact that it exists indicates we aren't alone in this dimension."

"I thought we already knew that," Guido said under his breath. "That's why we're here."

I gave him my best dark glare.

"I believe there was *some* debate as to whether or not we were being lied to about Aahz being held prisoner. If there's a road here, it's a cinch that neither my partner nor the ones he was chasing built it. That means we have native types to deal with . . . possibly hostile."

"Right," Massha put in quickly. "Put a sock in it, Guido. I want to hear our plan of action, and I don't like being kept waiting by hecklers."

The bodyguard frowned, but kept his silence.

"Okay. Now, what we've got to do is follow this road and find out where it goes. Hug the side of the road and be ready to disappear if you hear anybody coming. We don't know what the locals look like, and until I have a model to work from, it's pointless for me to try to disguise us."

With those general marching orders, we made our way through the dark along the road, moving quietly to avoid tipping our hand to anyone ahead of us. In a short time we came up to our first decision point. The road we were on ended abruptly when it met another, much larger thoroughfare. My assistants looked at me expectantly. With a shrug I made the arbitrary decision and led them off to the right down this new course. As we went, I reflected with some annoyance that even though both Massha and Guido knew that I was as new to this terrain as they were, it somehow fell to me to choose the path.

My thoughts were interrupted by the sound of voices ahead, coming our way. The others heard it too, and without word or signal we melted into the underbrush. Squatting down, I peered through the gloom toward the road, anxious to catch my first glimpse of the native life forms.

I didn't have long to wait. Two figures appeared, a young couple by the look of them, talking and laughing merrily as they went. They looked pretty normal to me, which was a distinct relief, considering the forms I had had to imitate in some of the other dimensions. They were humanoid enough to pass for Klahds . . . or Jahks, actually, as they were a bit pale. Their dress was not dissimilar from my own, though a bit more colorful. Absorbing all this in a glance, I decided to make my first try for information. I mean, after all my fears, they were so familiar it was almost a letdown, so why not bull ahead? Compared with some of the beings I've had to deal with in the past, this looked like a piece of cake.

Signaling the others to stay put, I stepped out onto the road behind my target couple.

"Excuse me!" I called. "I'm new to this area and in need of a little assistance. Could you direct me to the nearest town?"

Translation pendants were standard equipment for dimension travel, and as I was wearing one now, I had no fear of not being understood.

The couple turned to face me, and I was immediately struck by their eyes. The "whites" of their eyes glowed a dark red, sending chills down my spine. It occurred to me that I might have studied the locals a bit longer before I tried to pass myself off as a native. It also occurred to me that I had already committed myself to this course of action and would have to bluff my way through it regardless. Finally, it occurred to me that I was a suicidal idiot and that I hoped Massha and Guido were readying their back-up weapons to save me from my own impatience.

Strangely enough, the couple didn't seem to notice anything unusual about my appearance.

"The nearest town? That would be Blut. It's not far, we just came from there. It's got a pretty wild night life, if you're into that kind of thing."

There was something about his mouth that nagged at the edges of my mind. Unfortunately, I couldn't look at it directly without breaking eye contact, so, buoyed by my apparent acceptance, I pushed ahead with the conversation.

"Actually, I'm not too big on night life. I'm trying to run down an old friend of mine I've lost touch with. Is there a post office or a police station in Blut I could ask at?"

"Better than that," the man laughed. "The one you want to talk to is the Dispatcher. He keeps tabs on everybody. The third warehouse on your left as you enter town. He's converted the whole second floor into an office. If he can't help you, nobody can."

As vital as the information was, I only paid it partial attention. When the man laughed, I had gotten a better look at his mouth. His teeth were. . . .

"Look at his teeth!" the girl gasped, speaking for the first time.

"My teeth?" I blinked, realizing with a start that she was staring at me with undisguised astonishment.

Her companion, in the meantime, had paled noticeably and was backing away on unsteady legs.

"You . . . you're . . . Where did you come from?"

Trying my best to maintain a normal manner until I had figured out what was going on, I moved forward to keep our earlier conversational distance.

"The castle on the hill back there. I was just. . . ."

"THE CASTLE!?!"

In a flash the couple turned and sprinted away from me down the road.

"Monster!! Help!! MONSTER!!!"

I actually spun and looked down the road behind me, trying to spot the object of their terror. Looking at the empty road, however, it slowly began to sink in. They were afraid of *me!* Monster?

Of all the reactions I had tried to anticipate for our reception in this new land, I had never in my wildest imaginings expected this.

Me? A monster?

"I think we've got problems, High Roller," Massha said as she and Guido emerged from the brush at my side.

"I'll say. Unless I'm reading the signs all wrong, they're afraid of me."

She heaved a great sigh and shook her head.

"That's not what I'm talking about. Did you see their teeth?"

"I saw his," I said. "The canines were long and pointed. Pretty weird, huh?"

"Not all that weird, Hot Stuff. Think about it. My bet is that you were just talking to a couple of vampires!"

# Chapter V

*"To survive, one must be able to adapt to changing situations."*
**—Tyrannosaurus Rex**

"**V**AMPIRES," I said carefully.

"Sure. It all fits." Massha nodded. "The pale skin, the sharp fangs, the red eyeliner, the way they turned into bats. . . ."

"Turned into bats?"

"You missed it, Boss," Guido supplied. "You were lookin' behind you when they did it. Wildest thing I ever saw. One second they was runnin' for their lives, and the next they're flutterin' up into the dark. Are all the other dimensions like this?"

"Vampires. . . ."

Actually, my shock wasn't all that great. Realizing the things Aahz and I had run into cruising the so-called "known and safe" dimensions, I had expected something a bit out of the ordinary in this one. If anything, I was a bit relieved. The second shoe had been dropped . . . and it really wasn't all that bad! That is, it could have been worse. (If hanging around with Aahz had taught me anything, it was that things could always be worse!) The repetitive nature of my conversational brilliance was merely a clever ploy to cover my mental efforts to both digest this new bit of information and decide what to do with it.

"Vampires are rare in any dimension," my apprentice replied, stepping into the void to answer Guido's question. "What's more, they're pretty much feared universally. What I can't figure out is why those two were so scared of Skeeve here."

"Then again," I said thoughtfully, "there's the question of whether or not we can safely assume the whole dimension is populated with beings like the two we just met. I know it's a long shot, but we might have run into the only two vampires in the place."

"I dunno, High Roller. They acted pretty much at home here, and they sure didn't think you'd find anything unusual about *their* appearance. My guess is that they're the norm and we're the exceptions around here."

"Whatever," I said, reaching a decision at last, "they're the only two examples we have to work with so far, so that's what we'll base our actions on until proven different."

"So what do we do against a bunch of vampires?"

As a bodyguard, Guido seemed a bit uneasy about our assessment of the situation.

"Relax," I smiled. "The first order of business is to turn on the old reliable disguise spell. Just a few quick touch-ups and they won't be able to tell us apart from the natives. We could walk through a town of vampires and they'd never spot us."

With that, I closed my eyes and went to work. Like I told the staff, this was going to be easy. Maintain everyone's normal appearance except for paler skin, longer canines, and a little artful reddening of the eyes, and the job was done.

"Okay," I said, opening my eyes again. "What's next?"

"I don't like to quote you back at yourself, Hot Stuff," Massha drawled, "but didn't you say something about disguises being the first thing before we went any further?"

"Of course. That's why I just . . . wait a minute. Are you trying to say we still have the same appearance as before I cast the spell?"

One of the problems with casting a disguise spell is that as the caster, I can never see the effects. That is, I see people as they really are whether the spell is on or not. I had gotten so used to relying on the effects of this particular spell that it had never occurred to me that it might not work.

Massha and Guido were looking at each other with no small degree of concern.

"Ummm . . . maybe you forgot."

"Try again."

"That's right! This time remember to. . . ."

"Hold it, you two," I ordered in my most commanding tone. "From your reactions, I perceive that the answer to my questions is 'yes.' That is, that the spell didn't work. Now just ease up a second and let me think. Okay?"

For a change they listened to me and lapsed into a respectful silence. I might have taken a moment to savor the triumph if I wasn't so worried about the problem.

The disguise spell was one of the first spells I had learned, and until now was one of my best and most reliable tools. If it wasn't working, something was seriously wrong. Now I knew that stepping through the door hadn't lessened my knowledge of that particular spell, so that meant that if something was haywire, it would have to be in the. . . .

"Hey, Hot Stuff! Check the force lines!"

Apparently my apprentice and I had reached the conclusion simultaneously. A quick magical scan of the sky overhead and the surrounding terrain confirmed my worst fears. At first I thought there were no force lines at all. Then I realized that they were there, but so faint that it took nearly all of my reserve power just to detect them.

"What's all this about force lines?" Guido demanded.

Massha heaved an impatient sigh.

"If you're going to run with this crowd, Dark and Deadly, you'd best start learning a little about the magic biz . . . or at least the vocabulary. Force lines are invisible streams of energy that flow through the ground and the air. They're the source of power we tap into when we do our bibbity-bobbity-boo schtick. That means that in a land like this one, where the force lines are either non-existent or very weak. . . ."

". . . you can't do squat," the bodyguard finished for her. "Hey, Boss! If what she says is true, how come those two you just met could still do that bat-trick?"

"By being very, *very* good in the magic department. To do so much with so little means they don't miss a trick . . . pardon the pun . . . in tapping and using force lines. In short, they're a lot better than either Massha or me at the magic game."

"That makes sense." Massha nodded. "In any dimension I've been in that had vampires, they were some of the strongest magic-slingers around. If this is what they have to train on, I can see why they run hog-wild when they hit a dimension where the force lines are both plentiful and powerful."

I rubbed my forehead, trying desperately to think and to forestall the headache I felt coming on. Right on schedule, things were getting worse!

"I don't suppose you have anything in your jewelry collection that can handle disguises, do you?"

Despite our predicament, Massha gave a low laugh.

"Think about it, High Roller. If I had anything that could do disguises, would I walk around looking like this?"

"So we get to take on a world of hot-shot magic types with our own cover fire on low ammo," Guido summarized.

"Okay. So it'll be a little tougher than I thought at first. Just remember my partner has been getting along pretty well these last few years without any powers at all."

"Your partner is currently sitting in the hoosegow for murder," Guido said pointedly. "That's why we're here in the first place. Remember?"

"Besides," I continued, ignoring his comment (that's another skill I've learned from Aahz), "it's never been our intention 'to take on the whole world.' All we want to do is perform a quick hit and run. Grab Aahz and get back out with as little contact with the natives as possible. All this means is that we've got to be a little more careful. That's all."

"What about running down the trio we started out to retrieve?"

I thought briefly about the blonde who had warned us of Aahz's predicament.

"That's part of being more careful," I announced solemnly. "If . . . I mean, *when* we get Aahz out of jail, we'll head for home and count ourselves as lucky. So we . . . pay off the Deveels. It's a . . . cheap price to . . . pay for. . . ."

I realized the staff was looking at me a little askance. I also realized that my words had been gradually slowing to a painful broken delivery as I reached the part about paying off the Deveels.

I cleared my throat and tried again.

"Ummm, let's just say we'll reappraise the situation once we've reached Aahz. Okay?"

The troops still looked a little dubious, so I thought it would be best if I pushed on to the next subject.

"As to the opposition, let's pool our knowledge of vampires so we have an idea of what we're up against. Now, we know they can shapechange into bats or dogs. . . ."

". . . or just into a cloud of mist," Massha supplied.

"They drink blood," Guido said grimly.

"They don't like bright light, or crosses. . . ."

". . . and they can be killed by a stake through their heart or. . . ."

"They drink blood."

"Enough with the drinking blood! Okay, Guido?"

I was starting to get more than a little annoyed with my bodyguard's endless pessimism. I mean, none of us was particularly pleased by the way things were going, but there was nothing to be gained by dwelling on the negatives.

"Sorry, Boss. I guess looking on the dark side of things gets to be a habit in my business."

"Garlic!" Massha exclaimed suddenly.

"What's that?"

"I said 'garlic'," she repeated. "Vampires don't like garlic!"

"That's right! How about it, Guido? Do you have any garlic along?" The bodyguard actually looked embarrassed.

"Can't stand the stuff," he admitted. "The other boys in the Mob used to razz me about it, but it makes me break out in a rash."

Terrific. We probably had the only Mob member in existence who was allergic to garlic. Another brilliant idea shot to hell.

"Well," I said, heaving a sigh, "now we know what we're up against."

"Ummm . . . say, Hot Stuff?" Massha said softly. "All kidding aside. Aren't we a little overmatched on this one? I mean, Dark and Deadly here can hold up his end on the physical protection side, but I'm not sure my jewelry collection is going to be enough to cover us magically."

"I appreciate the vote of confidence," Guido smiled sadly, "but I'm not sure my hardware is going to do us a lick of good against vampires. With the Boss out of action on the magic side. . . ."

"Don't count me out so fast. My magic may not be at full power, but I can still pull off a trick or two if things really get rough."

Massha frowned. "But the force lines. . . ."

"There's one little item I've omitted from your lessons so far, apprentice," I said with a smug little grin. "It hasn't really been necessary what with the energy so plentiful on Deva . . . as a matter of fact, I've kind of gotten out of the habit myself. Anyway, what it boils down to is that you don't always tap into a force line to work magic. You can store the energy internally like a battery so that it's there when you need it. While we've been talking, I've been charging up, so I can provide a bit of magical cover as needed. Now, I won't be able to do anything prolonged like a constant disguise spell, and what I've got I'll want to use carefully because it'll take a while to recharge after each use, but we won't be relying on your jewelry completely."

I had expected a certain amount of excitement from the staff when they found out I wasn't totally helpless. Instead, they looked uncomfortable. They exchanged glances, then looked at the sky, then at the ground.

"Ummm . . . does this mean we're going on?" Guido said at last.

"That's right," I said, lips tight. "In fact, I probably would have gone on even if my powers were completely gone. Somewhere out there my partner's in trouble, and I'm not going to back away from at least *trying* to help him. I'd do the same if it was one of you, but we're talking about Aahz here. He's saved my skin more times than I care to remember. I can't just. . . ."

I caught myself and brought my voice back under control.

"Look," I said, starting again. "I'll admit we never expected this vampire thing when we started out, and the limited magic handicap is enough to give anyone pause. If either or both of you want to head back, you can do it without hard feelings or guilt trips. Really. The only reason I'm pushing on is that I know me. Whatever is up ahead, it can't be any worse than what I would put myself through if I left Aahz alone to die without trying my best to bail him out. But that's me. If you want out, go ahead."

"Don't get your back up, Hot Stuff," Massha chided gently. "I'm still not sure how much help I'm going to be, but I'll tag along. I'd probably have the same problem if anything happened to you and I wasn't there, that you'd have if anything happened to Aahz. I *am* your apprentice, you know."

"Bodyguarding ain't much, but it's all I know," Guido said glumly. "I'm supposed to be guardin' that body of yours, so where it goes, I go. I'm just not wild about the odds, know what I mean?"

"Then it's settled," I said firmly. "All right. As I see it, our next stop is Blut."

"Blut," Massha echoed carefully.

"That's right. I want to look up this Dispatcher character and see what he has to say. I mean, a town is a town, and we've all visited strange towns before. What we really need now is information, and the nearest source seems to be Blut."

"The Dispatcher," Massha said without enthusiasm.

"Blut," Guido repeated with even less joyful anticipation.

It occurred to me that while my assistants were bound and determined to stay with me on this caper, if I wanted wholehearted support, I'd better look for it from the natives . . . a prospect I didn't put much hope in at all.

# Chapter VI

*"An agent is a vampire with a telephone!"*
**—Any Editor**

**R**EMEMBER how I said that if you've seen one town, you've seen 'em all? Well, forget it. Even though I've visited a lot of dimensions and seen a lot of towns, I had to admit that Blut looked a little strange.

Everything seemed to be done to death in basic black. (Perhaps "done to death" is an unfortunate turn of a phrase. Whatever.) Mind you, when I say everything, I mean *everything*. Cobblestones, walls, roof tiles, everything had the same uninspired color scheme. Maybe by itself the black overtones wouldn't have seemed too ominous, if it weren't for the architectural decorations that seemed to abound everywhere you looked. Stone dragons and snakes adorned every roof peak and ledge, along with the inescapable gargoyles and, of course, bats. I don't mean "bats" here, I mean "BATS"!!! Big bats, little bats, bats with their wings half open and others with their wings spread wide . . . BATS!!! The only thing they all seemed to have in common (besides being black) was mouths full of needle-sharp teeth . . . an image which did nothing to further the confidence of my already nervous party. I myself felt the tension increasing as we strode down the street under the noses of those fierce adornments. One almost expected the stone figures to come to life and swoop down on us for a pint or two of dinner.

"Cheerful sort of place, isn't it?" Massha asked, eyeing the rooftops.

"I don't like to complain, Boss," Guido put in, lying blatantly, "but I've been in friendlier-looking graveyards."

"Will you both keep your mouths shut!" I snarled, speaking as best I could through tightly pressed lips. "Remember our disguises."

I had indeed turned on my disguise spell as we entered town, but in an effort to conserve magical energy, I had only turned our eyes red. If any of the others on the street, and there were lots of them, happened to spot our non-vampirish teeth, the balloon would go up once and for all. Then again, maybe not. We still hadn't figured out why the couple we met on the road had been so afraid of me, but I wasn't about to bank the success of our mission on anything as flimsy as a hope that the whole town would run at the sight of our undisguised features.

Fortunately, I didn't have to do any magical tinkering with our wardrobe. If anything, we were a little drab compared to most of the vampires on the street. Though most of them appeared rather young, barely older than me, they came in all shapes and sizes, and were decked out in some of the most colorful and outrageous garb it has ever been my misfortune to encounter as they shouted to each other or wove their way in and out of taverns along the street.

It was night now, the clouds having cleared enough to show a star-studded night sky, and true to their billing, vampires seemed to love the night life.

"If everybody here is vampires," Guido said, ignoring my warning, "how do they find anybody to bite for blood?"

"As far as I can tell," Massha answered, also choosing to overlook the gag order, "they buy it by the bottle."

She pointed to a small group of vampires sitting on a low wall merrily passing a bottle of red liquid back and forth among themselves. Despite our knowledge of the area, I had subconsciously assumed they were drinking wine. Confronted by the inescapable logic that the stuff they were drinking was typed, not aged, my stomach did a fast roll and dip to the right.

"If you two are through sightseeing," I hissed, "let's try to find this Dispatcher character before someone invites us to join them for a drink."

With that, I led off my slightly subdued assistants, nodding and waving at the merrymaking vampires as we went. Actually, the goings on looked like a lot of fun, and I might have been tempted to join in, if it weren't for the urgency of our quest . . . and, of course, the fact that they *were* vampires.

Following the instructions I had gleaned from the couple on the road before their panicky flight, we found the Dispatcher's place with no problem. Leaving Guido outside as a lookout, Massha and I braved the stairs and entered the Dispatcher's office.

As strange as Blut had appeared, it hadn't prepared me for the room we stepped into.

There were hundreds of glass pictures lining the walls, pictures which depicted moving, living things much like looking into a rack of fishbowls. What was more, the images being displayed were of incredible violence and unspeakable acts being performed on seemingly helpless victims. The overall effect was neither relaxing nor pleasant . . . definitely not something I'd want on the wall at home.

I was so entranced by the pictures, I almost missed the Dispatcher himself until he rose from his desk. Perhaps "rose" is the wrong description. What he actually did was hop down to the floor from his chair which was high to begin with, but made higher by the addition of a pillow to the seat.

He strode forward, beaming widely, with his hand extended for a handshake.

"Hi there Vilhelm's the name Your problem is my problem Don't sit down Standing problems I solve for free Sitting problems I charge for Reasonable rates Just a minor percentage off the top What can I do for you?"

That was sort of all one sentence in that he didn't pause for breath. He did, however, seize my hand, pump it twice, then repeated the same procedure with Massha, then grabbed my hand again . . . all before he stopped talking.

All in all, it was a little overpowering. I had a flash impression of a short, stocky character with plump rosy cheeks and a bad case of the fidgets. I had deliberately tried not to speculate on what the Dispatcher would look like, but a cherub vampire still caught me a little off-guard.

"I . . . ummm . . . how did you know I have a problem?"

That earned me an extra squeeze of the hand and a wink.

"Nobody comes in here unless they've got a problem," he said, finally slowing down his speech a bit. "I mean, I could always use a bit of help, but does anyone leap forward to lend a hand? Fat chance. Seems like the only time I see another face in the flesh is when it means more work for me. Prove me wrong . . . please! Tell me you came in here to take over for an hour or so to let me duck out for a bite to drink."

"Well, actually, we've got a problem and we were told. . . ."

"See! What did I tell you? All right. What have you got? A standing or a sitting problem? Standing problems I handle for. . . ."

He was off again. In a desperate effort to keep our visit short, I interrupted his pitch.

"We're looking for a friend who. . . ."

"Say no more! A friend! Just a second!"

With that he vaulted back into his chair, grabbed the top off a strange-looking appliance on his desk, diddled with it briefly, then started talking into it.

"Yea Darwin? Vilhelm. I need . . . sure. . . ."

Leaning back in his chair, he tucked the gadget under one side of his head and grabbed another.

"This is Vilhelm. Is Kay around? . . . Well, put her on when she's done. . . ."

The second gadget slid in under the same ear as the first and he reached for yet another.

"I know I shouldn't ask this," I murmured to Massha, "but what's he doing?"

"Those are telephones," she whispered back as a fourth instrument came into play. "You talk into one end of it and whoever's at the other end can hear you and talk back. It beats running all over town to find an answer."

By this time, the little vampire had so many instruments hung from his shoulders and arms he looked like he was being attacked by a nest of snakes. He seemed to be handling it well, though, talking first into one, then another, apparently keeping multiple conversations going at once like a juggler handles a basket full of balls.

"Gee, that's kind of neat!" I exclaimed. "Do you think we could get some of these for our place at the Bazaar?"

"Believe me, they're more trouble than they're worth," Massha said. "In nothing flat you find you're spending all your time on the phone talking to people and not accomplishing anything. Besides, ever since they broke up the corporation. . . ."

"I think I've got it!" Vilhelm announced, jumping down to floor-level again. "I've got one friend for you definite, but to be honest with you he's only so-so. I've got call-backs coming on two others, so let's see what they're like before you commit on the definite. Okay?"

"Ummm . . . I think there's some kind of mistake here," I said desperately, trying to stop the madness before it progressed any further. "I'm not trying to find a *new* friend. I'm trying to locate a friend I already have who may be here in town."

He blinked several times as this news sank in. He started to turn back to his phones in an involuntary motion, then waved a hand at them in disgusted dismissal.

"Heck with it," he said with a sigh. "If they can come up with anything, I can always fob 'em off on someone else for a profit. Now then, let's try this again. You're looking for someone specific. Are they a townie or a transient? It *would* help if you gave me a little something to go on, you know."

He seemed a little annoyed, and I would have liked to do or say something to cheer him up. Before I could think of anything, however, my apprentice decided to join the conversation.

"This is quite a layout you've got, Fast Worker. Mind if I ask exactly what it is you do?"

As always, Massha's "people sense" proved to be better than mine. The little vampire brightened noticeably at the compliment, and his chest puffed out as he launched into his narration.

"Well, the job was originally billed as Dispatcher . . . you know, as in Dispatcher of Nightmares. But anyway, like any job, it turned out to involve a lot of things that aren't on the job description. Now it's sort of a combination of dispatcher, travel agent, lost and found, and missing persons bureau."

"Nightmares?" I questioned, unable to contain myself.

"Sure. Anything that comes out of Limbo, be it dreams or the real thing, comes through here. Where're you from that you didn't know that?"

Obviously, I wasn't wild about continuing on the subject of our place of origin.

"Ahhh, can you really help us find our friend? He's new in town, like us."

"That's right. You're looking for someone. Sorry. I get a little carried away sometimes when I talk about my work. New in town, hmmm? Shouldn't be that hard to locate. We don't get that many visitors."

"He might be in jail," Massha blurted out before I realized what she was going to say.

"In jail?" The vampire frowned. "The only outsider in jail right now is. . . . Say! Now I recognize you! The eyes threw me for a minute. You're Skeeve, aren't you?"

"Screen 97B!" he declared proudly, gesturing vaguely over his shoulder. "There's someone a dozen dimensions over from here, runs a hot dog stand, who features you in his most frequent nightmares. You, a dragon, and a Pervert. Am I correct in assuming that the current resident in our fair jail is none other than your sidekick Aahz?"

"To be correct, that's Pervect, not Pervert . . . but except for that you're right. That's my partner you've got locked up there, and we aim to get him out."

I was probably talking too much, but being recognized in a dimension I'd never heard of had thrown me off balance. Then again, the Dispatcher didn't seem all that hostile at the discovery. More curious than anything else.

"Well, well. Skeeve himself. I never expected to meet you in person. Sometime you must tell me what you did to that poor fellow to rate the number-one slot on his hit parade of nightmares."

"What about Aahz?" I said impatiently.

"You know he's up for murder, don't you?"

"Heard it. Don't believe it. He's a lot of things, but a murderer isn't one of them."

"There's a fair amount of evidence." Vilhelm shrugged. "But tell me. What's with the vampire getup. You're no more a vampire than I'm a Klahd."

"It's a long story. Let's just say it seemed to be the local uniform."

"Let's not," the dispatcher grinned. "Pull up a chair . . . free of charge, of course. I've got time and lots of questions about the other dimensions. Maybe we can trade a little information while you're here."

# Chapter VII

*"I don't see anything thrilling about it!"*
**—M. Jackson**

**"I** really don't see how you can drink that stuff," I declared, eyeing Vilhelm's goblet of blood.

"Funny," he smiled in return, "I was about to say the same thing. I mean, you know what W. C. Fields said about water!"

"No. What?"

"Now let me get this straight," Guido interrupted before I could get any answer. "You're sayin' you vampire guys don't really drink blood from people?"

"Oh, a few do," the Dispatcher said with a shrug. "But it's an acquired taste, like steak tartare. Some say it's a gourmet dish, but I could never stand the stuff myself. I'll stick with the inexpensive domestic varieties any night."

We were all sprawled around the Dispatcher's office at this point, sipping our respective drinks and getting into a pretty good rap session. We had pulled Guido in off door watch and I had dropped our disguises so my energy reserve wasn't being drained.

The Dispatcher had played with his phones, calling from one to the other. Then he put them all down and announced that he had them on "hold," a curious expression since it was the first time in half an hour he hadn't been holding one.

Vilhelm himself was turning out to be a priceless source of information, and, as promised, had a seemingly insatiable curiosity about otherworldly things.

"Then how do you account for all the vampire legends around the other dimensions," Massha said skeptically.

The Dispatcher made a face.

"First of all, you've got to realize who you're dealing with. Most of the ones who do extensive touring outside of Limbo are 'old money' types. We're talking about the idle rich . . . and that usually equates to bored thrill-seekers. Working stiffs like me can't afford to take that kind of time away from our jobs. Heck, I can hardly manage to get my two weeks each year. Anyway, there are a lot more of us around the dimensions than you might realize. It's just that the level-headed ones are content to maintain a low profile and blend with the natives. They content themselves with the blood of domestic livestock, much the way we do here at home. It's the others that cause the problems. Like any group of tourists, there's always a few who feel that just because they're in another world or city, the rules don't apply . . . and that includes common manners and good taste. They're the ones who stir up trouble by getting the locals up in arms about 'bloodsucking monsters.' If it makes you feel any better, you human types have a pretty bad rep yourselves here in Limbo."

That caught my attention.

"Could you elaborate on that last point, Vilhelm? What problem could the locals have with us?"

The Dispatcher laughed.

"The same one you humans have with us vampires. While humans aren't the leading cause of death in vampires any more than vampires are a leading cause of death in humans, it's certainly one of the more publicized and sensational ways to go."

"Is that why the first locals we met took off like bats out of hell . . . if you'll pardon the expression?" Massha asked.

"You've got it. I think you'll find that the citizens of Blut will react the same way to you that you would if you ran into a vampire in your home dimension."

"I don't notice you bein' particularly scared of us," Guido said suspiciously.

"One of the few advantages of this job. After a few years of monitoring the other dimensions, you get pretty blasé about demons. As far as I can tell, most of 'em are no worse than some of the folks we've got around here."

This was all very interesting, but I was getting a little fidgety about our mission.

"Since you know we aren't all evil or on a permanent vampire hunt, what can you tell us about the mess Aahz is in? Can you give us any help there?"

"I dunno," the Dispatcher said, rubbing his jaw thoughtfully. "Until I found out who he was, I was ready to believe he was guilty as sin. There's an awful lot of evidence against him."

"Such as?" I pressed.

"Well, he was caught with a stake and mallet in his hand, and there are two eyewitnesses who say they saw him kill one of our citizens and scatter his dust to the winds."

"Wait a minute. You mean you ain't got no *corpus delecti?*" Guido said, straightening in his chair. "Sorry to interrupt, Boss, but you're playin' in my alley now. This is somethin' I know a little about. You can't go on trial for murder without a corpse, know what I mean?"

"Maybe where you come from," Vilhelm corrected, "but things get a little different when you're dealing with vampires. If we *had* a body, or even just the pile of dust, we could revive him in no time flat. As it is, the problem is when there's *no* body . . . when a vampire's been reduced to dust and the dust scattered. That's when it's impossible to pull 'em back into a functional mode."

"But if there isn't a body, how do you know the victim is dead at all?" I asked.

"There's the rub," Vilhelm agreed. "But in this case, there's a matter of two eyewitnesses."

"Two of 'em, eh?" Massha murmured thoughtfully. "Would you happen to have descriptions of these two peepers?"

"Saw 'em myself. They were both off-worlders like yourselves. One was a young girl, the blonde and innocent type. The other was a pretty sleazy-looking guy. It was her who sold us on the story, really. I don't think anyone would have believed him if he said that werewolves were furry."

My heart sank. I had wanted very badly to believe the girl who had warned us of Aahz's danger was somehow an innocent bystander in the proceedings. Now it looked as if. . . .

"Do the descriptions sound familiar, Hot Stuff? Still think Guido and I were being paranoid when we said this might be a set-up? Sounds like they framed your partner, then came back after you to complete the set."

I avoided her eyes, staring hard at the wall monitors.

"There might be another explanation, you know."

My apprentice gave out a bark of laughter.

"If there is, I'm dying to hear it. Face it, High Roller, any way you look at it the situation stinks. If they cooked up a frame that tight on Green and Scaly on such short notice, I'm dying to see what kind of a trap they've got waiting for you now that they've had time to get ready *before* inviting you to step in."

It occurred to me that I had never been that mouthy when I was an apprentice. It also occurred to me that now I understood why Aahz had gotten so angry on the rare occasions when I had voiced an opinion . . . and the rarer times when I was right.

"I think I missed a lap in this conversation somewhere." Vilhelm frowned. "I take it you know the witnesses?"

Massha proceeded to bring the Dispatcher up to date, with Guido growling counterpoint to the theme. For once I was glad to let them do the talking. It gave me a chance to collect my scattered thoughts and try to formulate a plan. When they finished, I still had a long way to go on both counts.

"I must admit, viewed from the light of this new information, the whole thing does sound a little suspicious," the vampire said thoughtfully.

"A *little* suspicious!" Massha snorted. "It's phonier than a smiling Deveel!"

"Tell ya what," Guido began, "just give us a few minutes alone with these witnesses of yours and we'll shake the truth out of 'em."

"I'm afraid that will be a little difficult," the Dispatcher said, eyeing the ceiling. "You see, they haven't been around for a while. Disappeared right after the trial."

"The trial!?" I snapped, abandoning my efforts to collect my wits. "You mean the trial's already been held?"

The vampire nodded.

"That's right. Needless to say, your friend was found guilty."

"Why do I get the feeling he didn't get a suspended sentence for a first offense?" Guido growled under his breath.

"As a matter of fact, he's been slated for execution at the end of the week," Vilhelm admitted.

That got me out of my seat and pacing.

"We've got to do something," I said needlessly. "How about it, Vilhelm? Can you help us out at all? Any chance of getting the verdict reversed or at least a stay of execution?"

"I'm afraid not. Character witnesses alone wouldn't change anything, and as for new evidence, it would only be your word against the existing witnesses . . . and you've already admitted the defendant is a friend of yours. Mind you, *I* believe you, but there are those who would suspect you'd say anything or fabricate any kind of tale to save your partner."

"But can you *personally* give us a hand?"

"No, I can't," the vampire said, turning away. "You all seem like real nice folks, and your friend is probably the salt of the earth, but I have to live here and deal with these people for a long time. If I sided with outsiders against the town legal system, my whole career would go down the drain whether I was right or not. It's not pretty and I don't like it, but that's the way things are."

"We could fix it so you like it a lot less!" Guido said darkly, reaching into his coat.

"Stop it, Guido," I ordered. "Let's not forget the help Vilhelm's *already* given us. It's a lot more than we expected to get when we first came into this dimension, so don't go making enemies out of the only friend we've got locally. Okay?"

The bodyguard sank back into his chair, muttering something I was just as glad I didn't hear, but his hand came out of his coat empty and stayed in sight.

"So what do we do now, Hot Stuff?" Massha sighed.

"The only thing I can think of is to try to locate those witnesses before the execution date," I said. "What I can't figure is how to go about looking without getting half the town down on our necks."

"What we really need is a bloodhound," Guido grumbled.

"Say, that's not a bad idea!" Vilhelm exclaimed, coming to life. "Maybe I can help you after all!"

"You got a bloodhound?" the bodyguard said, raising his eyebrows.

"Even better," the vampire declared. "I don't know why I didn't think of it before. The ones you need to get in touch with are the Woof Writers."

I studied him carefully to see if this were some kind of joke.

"The Woof Writers?" I repeated at last.

"Well, that's what we in Blut call them behind their backs. Actually, they're a husband-wife team of werewolves who are on a big crusade to raise sympathy for humans."

"Werewolves," I said carefully.

"Sure. We got all kinds here in Limbo. Anyway, if anyone in this dimension will be willing to stick their necks out for you, they're the ones. They do their own thing and don't really give a hang what any of the other locals think about it. Besides, werewolves are second to none when it comes to sniffing out a trail."

"Werewolves."

Vilhelm cocked his head at me curiously.

"Am I imagining things, Skeeve, or didn't you just say that?"

"What's more," Massha smiled sweetly, "he'll probably say it again. It bears repeating."

"Werewolves," I said again, just to support my apprentice.

"Boss," Guido began, "I don't want to say this, but nobody said anything about werewolves when we. . . ."

"Good," I interrupted brusquely. "You don't want to say it, and I don't want to hear it. Now that we're in agreement, let's just pass on it and. . . ."

"But Boss! We can't team up with werewolves."

"Guido, we just went over this. We're in a tight spot *and* in a strange dimension. We can't afford to be choosy about our allies."

"You don't understand, Boss. I'm allergic to 'em!"

I sank down into a chair and hid my face in my hands.

"I thought you were allergic to garlic," I said through my fingers.

"That, too," the bodyguard said. "But mostly I'm allergic to furry things like kitties or fur coats or. . . ."

". . . or werewolves," Massha finished for him. "Frankly, Dark and Deadly, one starts to wonder how you've been able to function effectively all these years."

"Hey, it doesn't come up all that often, know what I mean?" Guido argued defensively. "How many times have *you* been attacked by somethin' furry?"

"Not as often as I'd like!" Massha leered.

"Enough, you two," I ordered, raising my head. "Guido, have you ever actually been near a werewolf?"

"Well, no. But. . . ."

"Then until we know for sure, we'll assume you're *not* allergic to them. Okay? Vilhelm, exactly where do we find these Woof Writers of yours?"

# Chapter VIII

*"First, let's decide who's leading and
who's following."*
**—F. Astaire**

"**B**OSS, just where the hell *is* Pahkipsee?"

I found myself wondering if all bodyguards spent most of their time complaining, or if I had just gotten lucky.

"Look, Guido. You were there and heard the same instructions I did. If Vilhelm was right, it should be just up the road here a couple more miles."

". . . 'a rather dead bedroom community, fit only for those not up to the fast-lane life-style of the big city,' " Massha quoted in a close imitation of the vampire's voice.

Guido snickered rudely.

"Why do I get the feeling you didn't particularly warm to Vilhelm, Massha?" I suppressed a grin of my own.

"Maybe it's because he's the only guy we've met she hasn't made a pass at?" Guido suggested.

Massha favored him with an extended tongue and crossed eyes before answering.

"Oh, Vilhelm's okay," she said. "Kinda cute, too . . . at least the top of his head was. And he did admit that in general vampires were more partial to cities and parties while werewolves preferred the back-to-nature atmosphere of rural living. I just didn't like the crack, that's all. I grew up on a farm, you know. Country breakfasts have a lot to do with my current panoramic physique. Besides, something inside says you shouldn't trust a smiling vampire. . . . or at least you shouldn't trust him too far."

I had been about to mention the fact that I had grown up on a farm, too, but withheld the information. Obviously, farm food hadn't particularly affected my physique, and I didn't want to rob my apprentice of her excuse.

"If he had wanted to do us harm, all he would have had to do was blow the whistle on us while we were still in town," I pointed out. "Let's just take things at face value and assume he was really being as nice as he seemed . . . for all our peace of minds."

I wished I was as confident as I sounded. We were a long way out in the boondocks, and if Vilhelm had wanted to send us off on a wild goose chase, he couldn't have picked a better direction to start us off in.

"Yeah, well I'd feel a lot better if we weren't being followed," Guido grumbled.

I stopped in my tracks. So did Massha . . . in her tracks, that is. The bodyguard managed to stumble into us before bringing his own forward progress to a halt.

"What is it, Boss? Something wrong?"

"For a minute there, I thought I heard you say that we were being followed."

"Yeah. Since we left the Dispatcher's. Why does . . . you mean you didn't know?"

I resisted an impulse to throttle him.

"No, Guido. I didn't know. You see, my bodyguard didn't tell me. He was too busy complaining about the road conditions to have time to mention anything as trivial as someone following us."

Guido took a few shaky steps backward.

"Hey! C'mon, Boss. Don't be like that. I thought you knew! Honest. Whoever's back there isn't doin' such a hot job of hiding the fact that they're dogging our trail. Any idiot could've spotted . . . I mean. . . ."

"Keep going, Dark and Deadly," Massha urged. "You're digging yourself in further with every word, in case you hadn't noticed."

With great effort I brought myself back under control.

"Whatever," I said. "I don't suppose you have any idea who it is?"

"Naw. There's only one of 'em. Unless. . . ."

His voice trailed off into silence and he looked suddenly worried.

"Out with it, Guido. Unless what?"

"Well, sometimes when you're getting *really* tricky about tailing someone, you put one real clumsy punk out front so's they can be spotted while you keep your real ace-hitter hidden. I hadn't stopped to think of that before. This turkey behind us could be a decoy, know what I mean?"

"I thought you used decoys for ducks, not turkeys," Massha scowled.

"Well, if that's what's happening, then *we're* sitting ducks, if it makes you feel any better."

"Could both of you just be quiet for a few minutes and let me think?" I said, suddenly impatient with their banter.

"Well, maybe it isn't so bad," Guido said in a doubtful voice. "I'm pretty sure I would have spotted the back-up team if there was one."

"Oh sure," Massha sneered. "Coming out of a town full of vampires that can change themselves into mist whenever they want. Of course you'd spot them."

"Hey. The Boss here can chew on me if he wants, but I don't have to take that from you. You didn't even spot the turkey, remember?"

"The only turkey I can see is. . . ."

"Enough!" I ordered, having arrived at a decision despite their lack of cooperation. "We have to find out for sure who's behind us and what they want. This is as good a place as any, so I suggest we all retire into the bushes and wait for our shadow to catch up with us. . . . No, Massha. I'll be over here with Guido. You take the other side of the road."

That portion of my plan had less to do with military strategy than with an effort on my part to preserve what little was left of my nerves. I figured the only way to shut the two of them up was to separate them.

"I'm sorry, Boss," Guido whispered as we crouched side by side in the brush. "I keep forgettin' that you aren't as into crime as the boys I usually run with."

Well, I had been half right. Massha on the other side of the road was being quiet, but as long as he had someone to talk to, Guido was going to keep on expressing his thoughts and opinions. I was starting to understand why Don Bruce insisted on doing all the talking when the bodyguards were around. Encouraging employees to speak up as equals definitely had its drawbacks.

"Will you keep your voice down?" I tried once more. "This is supposed to be an ambush."

"Don't worry about that, Boss. It'll be a while before they catch up, and when they do, I'll hear 'em before. . . ."

"Is that you, Skeeve?"

The voice came from the darkness just up the road.

I gave Guido my darkest glare, and he rewarded it with an apologetic shrug that didn't look particularly sincere to me.

Then it dawned on me where I had heard that voice before.

"Right here," I said, rising from my crouch and stepping onto the road. "We've been waiting for you. I think it's about time we had a little chat."

Aside from covering my embarrassment over having been discovered, that had to be my best understatement in quite a while. The last time I had seen this particular person, she was warning me about Aahz's imprisonment.

"Good." She stepped forward to meet me. "That's why I've been following you. I was hoping we could. . . ."

Her words stopped abruptly as Guido and Massha rose from the bushes and moved to join us.

"Well, look who's here," Massha said, flashing one of her less pleasant smiles.

"If it isn't the little bird who sang to the vampires," Guido leered, matching my apprentice's threatening tone.

The girl favored them with a withering glance, then faced me again.

"I was hoping we could talk alone. I've got a lot to say and not much time to say it. It would go faster if we weren't interrupted."

"Not a chance, Sweetheart," Guido snarled. "I'm not goin' to let the Boss out of my sight with you around."

". . . besides which, I've got a few things to tell you myself," Massha added, "like what I think of folks who think frames look better on people than on paintings."

The girl's eyes never left mine. For all her bravado, I thought I could detect in their depths an appeal for help.

"Please," she said softly.

I fought a brief skirmish in my mind, and, as usual, common sense lost.

"All right."

"WHAT! C'mon, Boss. You can't let her get you alone! If her pals are around. . . ."

"Hot Stuff, if I have to sit on you, you aren't going to. . . ."

"Look!" I said, wrenching my eyes away from the girl to confront my mutinous staff. "We'll only go a few steps down the road there, in plain sight. If anything happens you'll be able to pitch in before it gets serious."

"But. . . ."

". . . and you certainly can't think *she's* going to jump me. I mean, it's a cinch she isn't carrying any concealed weapons."

That was a fact. She had changed outfits since the last time I saw her, probably to fit in more with the exotic garb favored by the party-loving vampires. She was wearing what I've heard referred to as a "tank top" which left her midsection and navel delightfully exposed, and the open-sided skirt (if you can call two flaps of cloth that) showed her legs up past her hips. If she had a weapon with her, she had swallowed it. Either that, or. . . .

I dragged my thoughts back to the argument.

"The fact of the matter is that she isn't going to talk in front of a crowd. Now, am I going to get a chance to hear another viewpoint about what's going on, or are we going to keep groping around for information with Aahz's life hanging in the balance?"

My staff fell silent and exchanged glances, each waiting for the other to risk the next blast.

"Well, okay," Massha agreed at last. "But watch yourself, Hot Stuff. Remember, poison can come in pretty bottles."

So, under the ever-watchful glares of my assistants, I retired a few steps down the road for my first words alone with. . . .

"Say, what *is* your name, anyway?"

"Hmmm? Oh. I'm Luanna. Say, thanks for backing me up. That's a pretty mean-looking crew you hang around with. I had heard you had a following, but I hadn't realized how nasty they were."

"Oh, they're okay once you get to know them. If you worked with them on a day-to-day basis, you'd find out that they . . . heck, none of us are really as dangerous or effective as the publicity hype cuts us out to be."

I was suddenly aware of her eyes on me. Her expression was strange . . . sort of a bitter half-smile.

"I've always heard that *really* powerful people tended to understate what they can do, that they don't have to brag. I never really believed it until now."

I really didn't know what to say to that. I mean, my reputation had gotten big enough that I was starting to get used to being recognized and talked about at the Bazaar, but what she was displaying was neither fear nor envy. Among my own set of friends, admiration or praise was always carefully hidden within our own brand of rough humor or teasing. Faced with the undiluted form of the same thing, I was at a loss as to how to respond.

"Ummm, what was it you wanted to talk to me about?"

Her expression fell and she dropped her eyes.

"This is so embarrassing. Please be patient with me, Skeeve . . . is it all right if I call you Skeeve? I haven't had much experience with saying 'I'm sorry' . . . heck, I haven't had much experience with people at all.

Just partners and pigeons. Now that I'm here, I really don't know what to say."

"Why don't we start at the beginning?" I wanted to ease her discomfort. "Did you really swindle the Deveels back at the Bazaar?"

Luanna nodded slowly without raising her eyes.

"That's what we do. Matt and me. That and running, even though I think sometimes we're better at running than working scams. Maybe if we were better at conning people, we wouldn't get so much practice at running."

Her words thudded at me like a padded hammer. I had wanted very badly to hear that she was innocent and that it had all been a mistake. I mean, she was so pretty, so sweet, I would have bet my life that she was innocent, yet here she was openly admitting her guilt to me.

"But why?" I managed at last. "I mean, how did you get involved in swindling people to begin with?"

Her soft shoulders rose and fell in a helpless shrug.

"I don't know. It seemed like a good idea when Matt first explained it to me. I was dying to get away from the farm, but I didn't know how to do anything but farmwork for a living . . . until Matt explained to me how easy it was to get money away from people by playing on their greed. 'Promise them something for nothing,' he said, 'or for so little that they think *they're* swindling *you.*' When he put it that way, it didn't seem so bad. It was more a matter of being smart enough to trick people who thought they were taking advantage of you."

". . . by selling them magical items that weren't." I finished for her. "Tell me, why didn't you just go into the magic trade for real?"

Her head came up, and I caught a quick flash of fire in her sad blue eyes.

"We didn't know any magic, so we had to fake it. You probably can't understand that, since you're the real McCoy. I knew that the first time I saw you at Possiltum. We were going to try to fake our way into the Court Magician spot until you showed up and flashed a bit of real magic at the crown. Even Matt had to admit that we were outclassed, and we kind of faded back before anyone asked us to show what we could do. I think it was then that I. . . ."

She broke off, giving me a startled, guilty look as if she had been about to say something she shouldn't.

"Go on," I urged, my curiosity piqued.

"It's nothing, really," she said hastily. "Now it's your turn. Since I've told you my story, maybe you won't mind me asking how you got started as a magician."

That set me back a bit. Like her, I had been raised on a farm. I had run away, though, planning to seek my fortune as a master thief, and it was only my chance meeting with my old teacher Garkin and eventually Aahz that had diverted my career goals toward magic. In hindsight, my motives were not discernibly better than hers, but I didn't want to admit it just now. I kind of liked the way she looked at me while laboring under the illusion that I was someone noble and special.

"That's too long a tale to go into just now," I said brusquely. "There are still a few more answers I'd like from you. How come you used our place as a getaway route from Deva?"

"Oh, that was Vic's idea. We teamed up with him just before we started working our con at the Bazaar. When it looked like the scam was starting to turn sour, he said he knew a way-off dimension that no one would be watching. Matt and I didn't even know it was your place until your doorman asked if we were there to see you. Matt was so scared about having to tangle with you that he wanted to forget the whole thing and find another way out, but Vic showed us the door and it looked so easy we just went along with him."

"Of course, it never occurred to you that we'd get stuck with the job of trying to bring you back."

"You better believe it occurred to us. I mean, we didn't think you'd *have* to do it. We expected you'd be mad at us for getting you involved and come after us yourself. Vic kept saying that we shouldn't worry, that if you found us here in Limbo he could fix it so you wouldn't be able to take us back. I didn't know he was thinking about setting up a frame until he sprang it on your partner."

I tried to let this console me, but it didn't work.

"I notice that once you found out that Aahz was being framed, you still went along with it."

"Well . . . I didn't want to, but Vic kept saying that if you two were as good as everyone said, that your partner could get out of jail by himself. We figured that he'd escape before the execution, but with the whole dimension hunting him as a fugitive that he'd be too busy running for home to bother about catching us."

I was starting to get *real* anxious to meet this guy Vic. It also occurred to me that of all the potential problems our growing reputation could bring down on us, this was one we had never expected.

"And you believed him?"

Luanna made a face, then shrugged.

"Well . . . you're supposed to be able to do some pretty incredible things, and I don't want you to think I don't believe in your abilities, but I was worried enough that I sneaked back to let you know what was going on . . . just in case."

It was almost funny that she was apologizing for giving us the warning. Almost, but not quite. My mind kept running over what might have happened if she *had* believed in me completely.

"I guess my only other question is who is this citizen that Aahz is supposed to have killed?"

"Didn't anybody tell you?" she blinked. "It's Vic. He's from this dimension . . . you know, a vampire. Anyway, he's hiding out until the whole thing's resolved one way or another. I don't think even Matt knows where he is. Vampires are normally suspicious, and after I sneaked out the first time, he's even gotten cagey around us. He just drops in from time to time to see how we're doing."

Now I *knew* I wanted to meet friend Vic. If I was lucky, I'd meet him before Aahz did.

"Well, I do appreciate you filling me in on the problem. Now, if you'll just come back to Blut with us and explain things to the authorities, my gratitude will be complete."

Luanna started as if I had stuck her with a pin.

"Hold on a minute! Who said anything about going to the authorities? I can't do that! That would be doublecrossing *my* partners. I don't want to see you or your friends get hurt, but I can't sacrifice my own to save them."

An honest crook is both incongruous and infuriating. Aahz had often pointed this out to me when some point in my ethic kept me from going along with one of his schemes, and now I was starting to understand what he was talking about.

"But then why are you here?"

"I wanted to warn you. Vic has been thinking that you might come into Limbo after your partner, and he's setting up some kind of trap if you did. If he was right, I thought you should know that you're walking into trouble. I figured that if you came, you'd look up the Dispatcher, so I waited there and followed you when you showed up. I just wanted to warn you is all. That and. . . ."

She dropped her eyes again and lowered her voice until I could hardly hear her.

". . . I wanted to see you again. I know it's silly, but. . . ."

As flattering as it was, this time I was unimpressed.

"Yeah, sure." I interrupted. "You're so interested in me you're willing to let my partner sit on a murder rap just so you can watch me go through my paces."

"I already explained about that," she said fiercely, stepping forward to lay a hand on my arm.

I stared at it pointedly until she removed it.

"Well," she said in a small voice. "I can see that there's nothing more I can say. But, Skeeve? Promise me that you won't follow me when I leave? You or your friends? I took a big risk finding you. Please don't make me regret it."

I stared at her for a long moment, then looked away and nodded.

"I know you're disappointed in me, Skeeve," came her voice, "but I can't go against my partners. Haven't you ever had to do something you didn't want to do to support your partner?"

That hit home . . . painfully.

"Yes, I have," I said, drawing a ragged breath. "I'm sorry, Luanna. I'm just worried about Aahz, that's all. Tell you what. Just to show there're no hard feelings, can I have a token or something? Something to remember you by until I see you again?"

She hesitated, then pulled a gossamer-thin scarf from somewhere inside her outfit. Stepping close, she tucked it into my tunic, then rose on her tiptoes and kissed me softly.

"It's nice of you to ask," she said. "Even if I don't mean anything to you at all, it's nice of you to ask."

With that, she turned and sprinted off down the road into the darkness.

I stared after her.

"You're letting her go!?"

Suddenly Massha was at my side, flanked by Guido.

"C'mon, Boss. We gotta catch her. She's your partner's ticket off death row. Where's she goin'?"

"To meet up with her partners in crime," I said. "Including a surprisingly lively guy named Vic . . . surprising since he's the one that Aahz is supposed to have killed."

"So we can catch 'em all together. Nice work, Hot Stuff. Okay, let's follow her and. . . ."

"No!"

"Why not?"

"Because I promised her."

There was a deathly silence as my assistants digested this information.

"So she walks and Green and Scaly dies, is that it?"

"You're sellin' out your partner for a skirt? That musta been some kiss."

I slowly turned to face them, and, mad as they were, they fell silent.

"Now listen close," I said quietly, "because I'm not going to go over it again. If we tried to follow her back to their hideout, and she spotted us, she'd lead us on a wild goose chase and we'd never catch up with them . . . and we need that so-called corpse. I don't think her testimony alone will swing the verdict."

"But Boss, if we let her get away. . . ."

"We'll find them," I said. "Without us dogging her footsteps, she'll head right back to her partners."

"But how will we. . . ."

In answer, I pulled Luanna's scarf from my tunic.

"Fortunately, she was kind enough to provide us with a means to track her, once we recruit the necessary werewolf."

Guido gave my back a slap that almost staggered me.

"Way to go, Boss," he crowed. "You really had me goin' for a minute. I thought that chickie had really snowed you."

I looked up to find Massha eyeing me suspiciously.

"That *was* quite a kiss, Hot Stuff," she said. "If I didn't know better, I'd think that young lady is more than a little stuck on you . . . and you just took advantage of it."

I averted my eyes, and found myself staring down the road again.

"As a wise woman once told me," I said, "sometimes you have to do things you don't like to support your partner. . . . Now, let's go find these Woof Writers."

# Chapter IX

*"My colleagues and I feel that independents like ElfQuest are nothing but sheep in wolves' clothing!"*

—S. Lee

**T**HE Woof Writers turned out to be much more pleasant than I had dared hope, which was fortunate as my werewolf disguises were some of the shakiest I'd ever done. Guido was indeed allergic to werewolves as feared (he started sneezing a hundred yards from their house) and was waiting outside, but even trying to maintain two disguises was proving to be a strain on my powers in this magic-poor dimension. I attempted to lessen the drain by keeping the changes minimal, but only succeeded in making them incredibly unconvincing even though my assistants assured me they were fine. No matter what anyone tells you, believe me, pointy ears alone do not a wolf make.

You might wonder why I bothered with disguises at all? Well, frankly, we were getting a little nervous. Everyone we had talked to or been referred to in this dimension was so *nice!* We kept waiting for the other shoe to drop. All of our talks and discussions of possible traps had made us so skittish that we were now convinced that there was going to be a double-cross somewhere along the way. The only question in our minds was when and by whom.

With that in mind, we decided it would be best to try to pass ourselves off as werewolves until we knew for sure the Woof Writers were as well-disposed toward humans as Vilhelm said they were. The theory was that if they weren't, the disguises might give us a chance to get out again before our true nature was exposed. The only difficulty with that plan was that I had never seen a werewolf in my life, so not only was I working with a shortage of energy, I was unsure as to what the final result should look like. As it turned out, despite their knowledgeable advice, my staff didn't know either.

While we're answering questions from the audience, you might ask, if neither I nor my assistants knew what a werewolf looked like, how I knew the disguises were inadequate? Simple. I deduced the fact after one look at real werewolves. That and the Woof Writers told me so. Didn't I tell you they were great folks? Of course, they let us sweat for a while before admitting that they knew we were poorly disguised humans all along, but I myself tend to credit that to their dubious sense of humor. It's Massha who insists it was blatant sadism. Of course, she was the one who had to eat a bone before they acknowledged the joke.

Anyway, I was talking about the Woof Writers. It was interesting in that I had never had much opportunity to watch a husband-wife team in action before (my parents don't count). The closest thing to the phenomenon I had witnessed was the brother-sister team of Tananda and Chumley, but they spent most of their conversational time trying to "one-down" each other. The Woof Writers, in contrast, seemed to take turns playing "crazy partner-sane partner." They never asked my opinion, but I felt that she was much better at playing the crazy than he. He was so good at playing the straight that when he did slip into crazy mode, it always came as a surprise.

"Really, dear," Idnew was saying to Massha, "wouldn't you like to slip out of that ridiculous disguise into something more comfortable? A werewolf with only two breasts looks so silly."

"Idnew," her husband said sternly, "you're making our guests uncomfortable. Not everyone feels as easy about discussing their bodies as you do."

"It's the artist in me," she returned. "And besides, Drahcir, who was it that set her up to eat a bone?—and an old one at that. If you were a little more conscientious when you did the shopping instead of stocking up on junk food. . . ."

"Oh, don't worry about me, Hairy and Handsome," Massha interceded smoothly, dropping into her vamp role. "I've got no problems discussing my body, as long as we get equal time to talk about yours. I've always liked my men with a lot of facial hair, if you get my drift."

I noticed Idnew's ears flatten for a moment before returning to their normal upright position. While it may have been nothing more than a nervous twitch, it occurred to me that if we were going to solicit help from these two, it might not be wise to fan any embers of jealousy that might be lying about.

"Tell me," I said hastily, eager to get the subject away from Massha's obvious admiration of Drahcir, "What got you started campaigning for better relationships between humans and werewolves?"

"Well, there were many factors involved," Drahcir explained, dropping into the lecturer mode I had grown to know so well in such a short time. "I think the most important thing to keep in mind is that the bad reputation humans have is vastly overrated. There is actually very little documented evidence to support the legends of human misconduct. For the most part, werewolves tend to forget that, under the proper conditions, we turn into humans. Most of them are afraid or embarrassed and hide themselves away until it passes, but Idnew and I don't. If anything we generally seize the opportunity to go out and about and get the public used to seeing harmless humans in their midst. Just between us, though, I think Idnew here likes to do it because it scares the hell out of folks to be suddenly confronted by a human when they aren't expecting it. In case you haven't noticed, there's a strong exhibitionist streak in my wife. For myself, it's simply a worthy cause that's been neglected for far too long."

"The other factor, which my husband has neglected to mention," Idnew put in impishly, "is that there's a lot of money in it."

"There is?" I asked.

My work with Aahz had trained me to spot profit opportunities where others saw none, but this time the specific angle had eluded me.

"There . . . umm . . . are certain revenues to be gleaned from our campaign," Drahcir said uneasily, shooting a dark glance at his wife. "T-shirts, bumper stickers, lead miniatures, fan club dues, greeting cards, and calendars, just to name a few. It's a dirty job, but somebody's got to do it. Lest my wife leave you with the wrong impression of me, however, let me point out that I'm supporting this particular cause because I *really* believe in it. There are lots of ways to make money."

". . . and he knows them all, don't you dear?" Idnew said with a smile.

"Really?" I interrupted eagerly. "Would you mind running over a few? Could I take notes?"

"Before you get carried away, High Roller," Massha warned, "remember why we came here originally."

"Oh! Right! Thanks, Massha. For a minute there I . . . Right!"

It took me a few seconds to rechannel my thoughts. While Aahz's training has gotten me out of a lot of tight spots and generally improved my standard of living, there are some unfortunate side effects.

Once I got my mind back on the right track, I quickly filled the werewolves in on our current problem. I kept the details sketchy, both because I was getting tired of going back and forth over the same beginning, and to keep from having to elaborate on Luanna's part in causing our dilemma. Still, the Woof Writers seemed quite enthralled by the tale, and listened attentively until I was done.

"Gee, you're really in a spot," Idnew said when I finally ground to a halt. "If there's anything we can do to help. . . ."

"We can't," Drahcir told us firmly. "You're behind on your deadlines, Idnew, and I've got three more appearances this month . . . not to mention answering the mail that's piled up the last two weekends I've been gone."

"Drahcir. . . ." Idnew said, drawing out his name.

"Don't look at me like that, dear," her husband argued before she had even started her case, "and don't cock your head, either. Someone's liable to shove a gramophone under it. Remember, *you're* the one who keeps pointing out that we have to put more time into our work."

"I was talking about cutting back on your personal appearances," Idnew argued. "Besides, this is important."

"So's meeting our deadlines. I'm as sympathetic to their problem as you are, but we can't let the plight of one small group of humans interfere with our work on the big picture."

"But *you're* the one who insists that deadlines aren't as important as. . . ."

She broke off suddenly and semaphored her ears toward her husband.

"Wait a minute. Any time you start talking about 'big pictures' and 'grand crusades' . . . is our bank account low again?"

Drahcir averted his eyes and shifted his feet uncomfortably.

"Well, I was going to tell you, but I was afraid it might distract you while you were trying to work. . . ."

"All right. Let's have it," his wife growled, her hackles rising slightly. "What is it you've invested our money in this time?"

I was suddenly very uncomfortable. Our little discussion seemed to be dissolving into a family fight I felt I had no business being present for. Apparently Massha felt the same thing.

"Well, if you can't help us, that's that," she said, getting to her feet. "No problem. A favor's not a favor if you have to be argued into it. C'mon, Hot Stuff. We're wasting our time *and* theirs."

Though in part I agreed with her, desperation prompted me to make one last try.

"Not so fast, Massha. Drahcir is right. Time's money. Maybe we could work out some kind of a fee to compensate them for their time in helping us. Then it's not a favor, it's a business deal. Face it, we *really* need their help in this. The odds of us finding this Vic character on our own are pretty slim."

Aahz would have fainted dead away if he had heard me admitting how much we needed help *before* the fee was set, but that reaction was nothing compared to how the Woof Writers took my offer.

"What did you say?" Drahcir demanded, rising to all fours with his ears back.

"I said that maybe you'd help us if we offered to pay you," I repeated, backing away slightly. "I didn't mean to insult you. . . ."

"You can't insult Drahcir with money," his wife snapped. "He meant what did you say about Vic?"

"Didn't I mention him before?" I frowned. "He's the vampire that Aahz is supposed to have. . . ."

There was a sudden loud flapping sound in the rafters above our heads, like someone noisily shaking a newspaper to scare a cat off a table. It worked . . . not on the cat (I don't think the werewolves owned one) but on Massha and me. My apprentice hit the floor, covering her head with her hands, while I, more used to sudden danger and being more svelte and agile, dove beneath the coffee table.

By the time we recovered from our panicky . . . excuse me, our shrewd defensive maneuvers, there was nothing to see except the vague shape of someone with huge wings disappearing out the front door.

"This one's all yours, dear," Drahcir said firmly, his posture erect and unmoved despite the sudden activity.

"Come on, honey," his wife pleaded. "You're so much better at explaining things. You're supposed to help me out when it comes to talking to people."

"It's a skill I polished at those personal appearances you're so critical of," he retorted stiffly.

"Would *somebody* tell me what's going on?" I said in tones much louder than I usually use when I'm a guest in someone's home.

Before I could get an answer, the door burst open again utterly destroying what little was left of my nervous system.

"Hey, Boss! Did you s—se—Wha—wa. . . ."

"Outside, Guido!" I ordered, glad to have someone I could shout at without feeling guilty. "Blow your nose . . . and I'm *fine,* thanks! Nice of you to ask!"

By the time my bodyguard had staggered back outside, his face half buried in a handkerchief, I had managed to regain most of my composure.

"Sorry for the interruption," I said as nonchalantly as I could, "but my colleague *does* raise an interesting question. What *was* that?"

"Scary?" Massha suggested.

Apparently she had recovered her composure a little better than I had. I closed my eyes and reflected again on the relative value of cheeky apprentices.

*"That,"* Drahcir said loftily, barely in time to keep me from my assistant's throat, "was Vic . . . one of my wife's weird artist friends who dropped in unannounced for a prolonged stay *and,* unless I miss my guess, the criminal you're looking for who framed your partner."

"He wasn't really a friend of mine," Idnew put in in a small voice. "Just a friend of a friend, really. Weird artist types tend to stick together and pass around the locations of crash spaces. He was just another charity case down on his luck who. . . ."

". . . who is currently winging his way back to his accomplice with the news that we're on their trail," I finished with a grimace.

"Isn't that 'accomplices' as in plural?" Massha asked softly.

I ignored her.

"Oh, Drahcir," Idnew said, "now we have to help them. It's the only way we can make up for having provided a hideout for the very person they were trying to find."

"If I might point out," her husband replied, "we've barely met these people. We don't really owe them an explanation, much less any help. Besides, you still have a deadline to meet and. . . ."

"Drahcir!" Idnew interrupted. "It could get real lonely sleeping in the old kennel while I work day and night on a deadline, if you catch my meaning."

"Now, dear," Drahcir said, sidling up to his wife, "before you go getting into a snit, hear me out. I've been thinking it over and I think there's a way we can provide assistance without biting into our own schedules. I mean, we *do* have a friend . . . one who lives a little north of here . . . who's temporarily between assignments and could use the work. I'm sure he'd be willing to do a little tracking for them at a fraction of the fee that we'd charge for the same service."

He was obviously talking in the veiled references partners use to communicate or check ideas in front of strangers, as his words went completely over my head, but drew an immediate reaction from Idnew.

"Oh, Drahcir!" she exclaimed excitedly, all trace of her earlier anger gone. "That's perfect! And he'll just *love* Massha."

"There's still the question of whether or not we can get him here in time," her husband cautioned. "And of course I'll want a percentage off the top as a finder's fee. . . ."

"WHAT!" I exclaimed.

"I agree," Idnew said firmly. "A finder's fee is totally. . . ."

"No! Before that," I urged. "What did you say about there not being enough time? I thought the execution wasn't scheduled until the end of the week!"

"That's right," Drahcir said. "But the end of the week is tomorrow. Your friend is slated to be executed at high midnight."

"C'mon, Massha," I ordered, heading for the door. "We're heading back to Blut."

"What for?" she demanded. "What can we do without a tracker?"

"We've tried being nice about this, and it isn't working," I responded grimly. "Now we do it the other way. You wanted action, apprentice? How do you feel about giving me a hand with a little jailbreak?"

# Chapter X

*"What's wrong with a little harmless crime once in a while?"*

**—M. Blaise**

"**B**UT I'm telling you, Boss, jailbreak is a bad rap. With you operating at only half power in the magic department, there's no tellin' what can go wrong, and then. . . ."

"Before we get all worked up about what can go wrong, Guido," I said, trying to salvage something constructive out of the conversation, "could you give me a little information on exactly how hard it is to break someone out of jail? Or haven't you been involved in any jailbreaks, either?"

"Of course I've been along on some jailbreaks," the bodyguard declared, drawing himself up proudly. "I've been an accomplice on *three* jailbreaks. What kind of Mob member do you take me for, anyway?"

With a heroic effort I resisted the temptation to answer that particular rhetorical question.

"Okay. So how about a few pointers? This is my first jailbreak, and I want it to go right."

I was all set to settle in for a fairly lengthy lecture, but instead of launching into the subject, Guido looked a bit uncomfortable.

"Umm . . . actually, Boss, I don't think you'd want to use any of the plans I followed. You see, all three of 'em were busts. None of 'em worked, and in two of the capers, the guy we were tryin' to save got killed. That's how I know about what a bad rap a jailbreak is, know what I mean?"

"Oh, swell! Just swell! Tell me, *Mister* bodyguard, with your allergies and zero-for-three record at jailbreak, did you ever do *anything* for the Mob that worked?"

A gentle hand fell on my shoulder from behind.

"Hey! Ease up a little, High Roller," Massha said softly. "I know you're worried about your partner, but don't take it out on Guido . . . or me, either, for that matter. We may not be much, but we're here and trying to help as best we can when we'd both just as soon be back at the Bazaar. You're in a bad enough spot without starting a two-front war by turning on your allies."

I started to snap at her, but caught myself in time. Instead, I drew a long ragged breath and blew it out slowly. She was right. My nerves were stretched to the breaking point . . . which served me right for not following my own advice.

We were currently holed up at the Dispatcher's, the only place I could think of for an in-town base of operations, and as soon as we had arrived, I had insisted that both Massha and Guido grab a bit of sleep. We had been going nonstop ever since stepping through the door into Limbo, and I figured that the troops would need all the rest they could get before we tried to spring Aahz. Of course, once I had convinced them of the necessity of racking out, I promptly ignored my own wisdom and stayed up thinking for the duration.

The rationalization I used for this insane action was that I wanted some extra time uninterrupted to recharge my internal batteries, so whatever minimal magic I had at my disposal would be ready for our efforts. In actuality, what I did was worry. While I had indeed taken part in several criminal activities since teaming up with Aahz, they had all been planned by either Aahz or Tananda. This was my first time to get involved in masterminding a caper, and the stakes were high. Not only Aahz's but Massha's and Guido's futures were riding on my successful debut, and my confidence level was at an all-time low. After much pondering, I had decided to swallow my pride and lean heavily on Guido's expertise, which was why it hit me so hard when I discovered that he knew even less about successful jailbreaks than I.

"Sorry, Guido," I said, trying to restructure my thinking. "I guess I'm more tired than I realized. Didn't mean to snap at you."

"Don't worry, Boss," the bodyguard grinned. "I've been expectin' it. All the big operators I've worked with get a little crabby when the heat's on. If anything, your temper gettin' short is the best thing I've seen since we started this caper. That's why I've been so jumpy myself. I wasn't sure if you weren't taking the job seriously, or if you were just too dumb to know the kind of odds we were up against. Now that you're acting normal for the situation, I feel a lot better about how it's goin' to come out in the end."

Terrific! Now that I was at the end of my rope, our eternal pessimist thought things were going great.

"Okay," I said, rubbing my forehead with one finger, "we haven't got much information to go on, and what we do know is bad. According to Vilhelm, Aahz is being held in the most escape-proof cell they have, which is the top floor of the highest tower in town. If we try to take him from the inside, we're going to have to fool or fight every guard on the way up *and* down. To me, that means our best bet is to spring him from the outside."

My assistants nodded vigorously, their faces as enthusiastic as if I had just said something startlingly original and clever.

"Now, with my powers at low ebb, I don't think I can levitate that far *and* spring the cell. Massha, do you have anything in your jewelry collection that would work for rope and climbing hooks?"

"N—no," she said hesitantly, which surprised me. She usually had a complete inventory of her nasty pretties on the tip of her tongue.

"I saw a coil of rope hangin' just inside the door," Guido supplied.

"I noticed it, too," I acknowledged, "but it isn't nearly long enough. We'll just have to use up my power getting up to the cell and figure some other way of opening the window."

"Ummm . . . you don't have to do that, High Roller," Massha said with a sigh. "I've got something we can use."

"What's that?"

"The belt I'm wearing with all my gear hung on it. It's a levitation belt. The controls aren't horribly reliable, but it should do to get us to the top of the tower."

I cocked an eyebrow at my apprentice.

"Wait a minute, Massha. Why didn't you mention this when I asked?"

She looked away quickly.

"You didn't ask about a belt. Only about rope and climbing hooks."

"Since when do I have to ask you specific questions . . . or any questions, for that matter, to get your input?"

"All right," she sighed. "If you really want to know, I was hoping we could find a way to do this without using the belt."

"Why?"

"It embarrasses me."

"It what?"

"It embarrasses me. I look silly floating around in the air. It's okay for skinny guys like you and Guido, but when I try it, I look like a blimp. All I'd need is Goodyear tattooed on my side to make the picture complete."

I closed my eyes and tried to remember that I was tired and that I shouldn't take it out on my friends. The fact that Massha was worried about appearances while I was trying to figure out a way to get us all out of this alive wasn't really infuriating. It was . . . flattering! That was it! She was so confident of my abilities to get us through this crisis that she had time to think about appearances! Of course, the possibility of betraying that confidence set me off in another round of worrying. Wonderful.

"You okay, Boss?"

"Hmmm? Yeah. Sure, Guido. Okay. Now Massha floats up to the window, which leaves you and me free to. . . ."

"Hold it, Hot Stuff," Massha said, holding up a hand. "I think I'd better explain a little more about this belt. I bought it in an 'as-is' rummage sale, and the controls are not all they should be."

"How so?"

"Well, the 'up' control works okay, but the 'altitude' is shaky so you're never sure how much you can lift or how high it will go. The real problem, though, is the 'down' control. There's no tapering-off effect, so it's either on or off."

I was never particularly good at technical jargon, but flying was something I knew so I could almost follow her.

"Let me see if I've got this right," I said. "When you go up, you aren't sure how much power you'll have, and when you land. . . ."

". . . it ain't gentle," she finished for me. "Basically, you fall from whatever height you're at to the ground."

"I don't know much about this magic stuff," Guido commented dryly, "but that doesn't sound so good. Why would you use a rig like that, anyway?"

"I don't . . . at least not for flying," Massha said. "Remember, I told you I think it makes me look silly? All I use it for is a utility belt . . . you know, like Batman? I mean, it's kind of pretty, and it isn't easy to find belts in my size."

"Whatever," I said, breaking into their fashion discussion. "We're going to use it tonight to get up to the cell even if it means rigging some kind of ballast system. Now all we need to figure out is how to open the cell window and a getaway plan. Guido, it occurs to me that we might pick up a few lessons on jailbreaks from your experiences even if they *were* unsuccessful. I mean, negative examples can be as instructive as positive examples. So tell me, in your opinion what went wrong in the plans you followed in the past?"

The bodyguard's brow furrowed as it took on the unaccustomed exercise of thought.

"I dunno, Boss. It seems that however much planning was done, something always came up that we hadn't figured on. If I had to hang our failures on any one thing, I'd say it was just that . . . overplanning. I mean, after weeks of lectures and practice sessions, you get a little overconfident, so when something goes wrong you're caught flatfooted, know what I mean?"

Nervous as we were, that got a laugh from both Massha and me.

"Well, that's one problem we won't have to worry about," I said. "Our planning time is *always* minimal, and for this caper we're going to have to put it together in a matter of hours."

"If you take hours, you'll never pull it off," Vilhelm said, entering our planning room just in time to hear my last comment.

"What's that supposed to mean?" Massha growled.

"Say, are you *sure* you guys are on the level?" the vampire said, ignoring my apprentice. "It occurs to me that I've only got your word on all this . . . that Vic is still alive and all. If you're taking advantage of my good nature to get me involved in something crooked. . . ."

"He's alive," I assured him. "I've seen him myself since we were here last . . . but you didn't answer the question. What was that you were saying about what would happen if we took hours to plan the jailbreak?"

The Dispatcher shrugged.

"I suppose you guys know what you're doing and I should keep my mouth shut, but I was getting a little worried. I mean, it's sundown already, and if you're going to make your move before the execution, it had better be soon."

"How do you figure that?" I frowned. "The action isn't slated until high midnight. I had figured on waiting a while until it was dark and things quieted down around town a little."

"Are you kidding?" the vampire said with a start, his eyebrows going up to his hairline. "That's when . . . oh, I get it. You're still thinking in terms of your off-dimension timetables. You've got to . . . umm, you might want to be sitting down for this, Skeeve."

"Lay it on me," I said, rubbing my forehead again. "What have I overlooked now? Even without the blindfold and the cigarette I'd just as soon take the bad news standing up."

"Well, you've got to remember that you're dealing with a city of vampires here. Sundown is the equivalent of dawn to us. That's when things *start* happening, not when they start winding down! That means. . . ."

". . . that high midnight is a major traffic time and the longer we wait, the more people there will be on the street," I said, trying to suppress a groan.

Once the basic oversight had been pointed out, I could do my own extrapolations . . . with all their horrible consequences. Trying to fight back my own panic, I turned to my assistants.

"Okay, troops. We're on. Guido, grab that rope you saw. We may need it before this is over."

The bodyguard's eyes widened with astonishment.

"You mean we're going to start the caper right now? But Boss! We haven't planned. . . ."

"Hey, Guido," I said, flashing a grin that was almost sane. "You were the one who said that overplanning was a problem. Well, if you're right, this should be the most successful jailbreak ever!"

# Chapter XI

*"Nice jail. Looks strong."*
—H. Houdini

**V**ILHELM was right about one thing. The streets were nowhere nearly as crowded as they had been the times we navigated their length well after sundown. Only a few stray beings wandered here and there, mostly making deliveries or sweeping down the sidewalks in front of their shops prior to opening. Except for the lack of light, the streets looked just like any town preparing for a day's business . . . that and the red eyes of the citizens.

We hugged the light as we picked our way across town. . . .

That's right. I said "hugged the light." I try to only make the same mistake a dozen times. In other dimensions, we would have "hugged the dark" to avoid being noticed or recognized. Here, we "hugged the light." Don't laugh. It worked.

Anyway, as we picked our way through the streets of Blut, most of my attention was taken up with the task of trying to map a good getaway route. Getting Aahz out of jail I would deal with once we got there. Right now I was worried about what we would do once we had him out . . . a major assumption, I know, but I had so little optimism that I clung to what there was with all fours.

The three of us looked enough like vampires in appearance to pass casual inspection. There was no way, however, that we could pass off my scaly green partner as a native without a disguise spell, and I wasn't about to bet on having any magical energy left after springing Aahz. As such, I was constantly craning my neck to peer down sidestreets and alleys, hoping to find a little-traveled route by which we could spirit our fugitive colleague out of town without bringing the entire populace down on our necks. By the time we reached our destination, I was pretty sure I could get us back to the Dispatcher's by the route we were following, and *positively* sure that if I tried to take us there by the back routes, I would get us totally and helplessly lost.

"Well, Boss. This is it. Think we can crack it?"

I don't think Guido really expected an answer. He was just talking to break the silence that had fallen over us as we stood looking at our target.

The Municipal Building was an imposing structure, with thick stone walls and a corner tower that stretched up almost out of sight into the darkness. It didn't look like we could put a dent in it with a cannon . . . if we had a cannon, which we didn't. I was used to the tents of the Bazaar or the rather ramshackle building style of Klah. While I had been gradually getting over being overawed by the construction prevalent here in Blut, this place intimidated me. I'd seen shakier looking mountains!

"Well, one thing's for certain," I began, almost under my breath.

"What's that?"

"Staring at it isn't going to make it any weaker."

Neither of my assistants laughed at my joke, but then again, neither did I.

Shaking off a feeling of foreboding, I turned to my staff.

"All right, Guido. You stay down here and keep watch. Massha? Do you think that belt of yours can lift two? It's time I went topside and took a good look at this impregnable cell."

My apprentice licked her lips nervously and shrugged.

"I don't know, Hot Stuff. I warned you that the controls on this thing don't work right. It could lift us right into orbit for all I know."

I patted her shoulder in what I hoped was a reassuring way.

"Well, give it a try and we'll find out."

She nodded, wrapped one arm around my chest, and used her other hand to play with the jewels on her belt buckle.

There was a sparkle of light, but beyond that nothing.

"Not enough juice," she mumbled to herself.

"So turn it up already," I urged.

Even if the vampires tended to avoid light, we were lit up like a

Christmas tree and bound to attract attention if we stayed at ground level much longer.

"Cross your fingers," she said grimly and touched the jewels again.

The light intensified and we started up fast . . . too fast.

"Careful, Boss!" Guido shouted and grabbed my legs as they went past him.

That brought our progress to a halt . . . well, almost. Instead of rocketing up into the night, we were rising slowly, almost imperceptibly.

"That's got it, High Roller!" Massha exclaimed, shifting her grip to hang onto me with both arms. "A little more ballast than I had planned on, though."

I considered briefly telling Guido to let go, but rejected the thought. If the bodyguard released his grip, we'd doubtless resume our previous speed . . . and while a lot of folks at the Bazaar talked about my meteoric rise, I'd just as soon keep the phrase figurative. There was also the minor detail that we were already at a height where it would be dangerous for Guido to try dropping back to the street. There was that, and his death-grip on my legs.

"Don't tell me, let me guess," I called down to him. "You're acrophobic, too?"

The view of Blut that was unfolding beneath us was truly breathtaking. Truly! My life these days was so cluttered with crises and dangers that a little thing like looking down on buildings didn't bother me much, but even I was finding it hard to breathe when confronted up close with sheer walls adorned with stone creatures. Still, until I felt his fingernails biting into my calves, it had never occurred to me that such things might upset a rough-and-tumble guy like Guido.

"Naw. I got nothin' against spiders," he replied nervously. "It's heights that scare me."

I let that one go. I was busy studying the tower, which could be viewed much more clearly from this altitude. If anything, it looked stronger than the portion of the building that was below us. One feature captured my attention, though. The top portion of the tower, the part I assumed was Aahz's cell, was shaped like a large dragon's head. The window I had been expecting was actually the creature's mouth, with its teeth serving as bars.

I should have anticipated something like that, realizing the abundance of stone animals on every other building in town. Still, it came as a bit of a surprise . . . but a pleasant surprise. I had been trying to figure a way to get through iron bars, but stone teeth might be a bit easier. Maybe with

Aahz working from the inside and us working from the outside, we could loosen the mortar and. . . .

I suddenly realized that in a few moments we would be level with the cell . . . and that a few moments after that we'd be past it! Unless something was done, and done fast, to halt our upward progress, we'd only have time for a few quick words with Aahz before parting company permanently. With time running out fast, I cast about for a solution.

The wall was too far away to grab onto, and there was no way to increase our weight, unless. . . .

When Aahz first taught me to fly, he explained the process as "levitation in reverse." That is, instead of using the mind to lift objects, you push against the ground and lift yourself. Focusing my reservoir of magical energy, I used a small portion to try *flying* in reverse. Instead of pushing up, I pushed down!

Okay. So I was desperate. In a crisis, I'll try anything, however stupid. Fortunately, this stupid idea worked!

Our upward progress slowed to a halt with me hanging at eye-level with the cell's dragon mouth.

Trying not to show my relief, I raised my voice.

"Hey, Aahz! When are visiting hours?"

For a moment there was no response, and I had a sudden fear that we were hanging a hundred feet in the air outside an empty cell. Then my partner's unmistakable countenance appeared in the window.

"Skeeve?" he said in a skeptical voice. "Skeeve! What are you doing out there?"

"Oh, we were just in the neighborhood and thought we'd drop in," I replied in my best nonchalant voice. "Heard you were in a bit of trouble and thought we'd better get you out before it got serious."

"Who's we?" my partner demanded, then he focused on my assistants. "Oh no! Those two? Where are Tananda and Chumley? C'mon, Skeeve. I need a rescue team and you bring me a circus act!"

"It's the best I could do on short notice," I shot back, slightly annoyed. "Tananda and Chumley aren't back from their own work yet, but I left a message for them to catch up with us if they could. Of course, I'm not sure how much help they'll be. In case you're wondering why I'm being carried by my apprentice instead of flying free, this particular dimension is exceptionally low on force lines to tap in to. If anything, I think I'm pretty lucky that I brought 'these two' along instead of ending up with a whole team of for-real magicians who are too proud to use gimmicks. It's thanks to 'these two' that I made it this far at all. Now, do you want our help, or do you want to wait for the next team to float past? I mean, you're in no rush, are you?"

"Now don't get your back up, partner," Aahz said soothingly. "You caught me a little off-guard is all. So tell me, just how do you figure to get me out of here?"

That brought me back to earth . . . or as close to it as I could get while suspended in mid-air.

"Umm . . . actually, Aahz, I was kinda hoping *you* might have a few ideas on the subject. You're usually pretty good at coming up with plans to get us out of tight spots."

"What I want to know," Guido snarled, turning slightly in the wind, "is how come your partner hasn't figured a way out of there all by himself, if he's so all-fired smart?"

I started to rebuke my bodyguard, but slowly his words sank in. That was a good question! Aahz was strong . . . I mean STRONG! By rights he should have been able to rip the stone teeth out of the window all by himself. What *was* keeping him here?

"Oh, I'm having so much fun in here I just couldn't bear to leave," Aahz barked back. "I'm in here because I can't get out, that's why. What's more, if any of you have any ideas about how to get me out, I think now's a real good time to share them with the rest of us."

"Wait a minute, Aahz," I said. "*Why* can't you get out . . . and how did they catch you in the first place?"

"I was framed," my partner retorted, but I noticed his voice was a bit more subdued.

"We already know that," I pressed. "What I want to know is why you didn't just bust a few heads and sprint for home? You've never been particularly respectful of local authority before."

To my surprise, Aahz actually looked embarrassed.

"I was drugged," he said in a disgusted tone. "They put something in my drink, and the next thing I knew I had a stake and mallet in my hands and a room full of officials. Whatever it was they used, it kept me groggy all the way through the trial . . . I mean I couldn't walk straight, much less defend myself coherently, and after that I was in *here!*"

"The old Mickey Finn trick!" Massha snorted, rocking our entire formation. "I'm surprised someone as off-worldly as you could get caught by such a corny stunt."

"Yeah. It surprised me, too!" Aahz admitted. "I mean, that gag is so old, who would really expect anyone to try it at all?"

"Only if you figured the mark was louder than he was smart," Guido sneered.

"Is that so!" my partner snapped, ready to renew their old rivalry. "Well, when I get out of here, you and me can. . . ."

"Stop it, you two," I ordered. "Right now the problem is to get us *all* out of here before the balloon goes up . . . no offense, Massha. Now spill, Aahz. What's so special about this cell that's keeping you bottled up?"

My partner heaved a great sigh.

"Take another look at it, Skeeve. A *close* look."

I did. It still looked the same to me: a tower room in the shape of a dragon's head.

"Yeah. Okay. So?"

"So remember where we are. This thing was built to hold *vampire* criminals. You know, beings with superhuman strength that can change into mist?"

My gaze flew back to the dragon's head.

"I don't get it," I admitted. "How can any stone cell hold beings like that?"

"That's the point." Aahz winced. "A stone cell *can't!* This thing is made of *living* stone. If whoever's inside tries to bust out, it swallows them. If they try to turn into mist, it inhales them."

"You mean. . . ."

"Now you're getting the picture."

He flashed his toothy grin at me despite his obvious depression.

"The cell is alive!"

Startled by this revelation, I looked at the tower top cell again. As if it had been waiting for the right cue, the dragon's head opened its eyes and looked at me.

# Chapter XII

*"For the right person, the impossible is easy!"*

**—Dumbo**

To everyone's surprise, particularly my own, I didn't find the revelation about the true nature of Aahz's confinement at all discouraging. If anything, I was doubly pleased. Not only did I have an immediate idea for how to beat the problem, I had arrived at it before my knowledgeable partner . . . well before, as a matter of fact, as he had been pondering his dilemma for days whereas I had only just received the information. Of course, he was probably not in a position to see the easy solution that I could.

"What are you grinning at?" he demanded. "If there's anything funny about this, it eludes me completely."

Unlike my own amiable self, Aahz tends to show his worry by getting mad. Come to think of it, he tends to express almost any emotion by getting mad. Well, at least he's consistent.

"Tell me," I said, eyeing the dragon's head, "you say this thing's alive. How alive is it?"

"What do you mean, 'how alive is it'?" Aahz scowled. "It's alive enough to swallow me if it gets it into its head. That's alive enough for me."

"I mean, can it hear and see?"

"Who cares?" my partner said, in a dazzling display of charm and curiosity that makes him so lovable. "I hadn't planned on asking it out for a date."

I stared thoughtfully at the beast.

"I was just wondering if it could hear me . . . say, if I said that I thought it was the ugliest building decoration I've seen here in town?"

The dragon's head rewarded me by narrowing its eyes into an evil glare.

"I think it can hear you, Boss," Guido said, shifting his grip nervously. "It doesn't look like it liked that last comment."

"Oh, swell!" Aahz grumbled. "Tell you what, partner. Why don't *you* come in here and sit on this thing's tongue instead of me before you start getting it all riled up?"

"I was just checking." I smiled. "To tell the truth, I think it's the most incredible thing I've seen since I started traveling the dimensions. I just said that other to test its reactions."

The dragon stopped glaring, but it still looked a little bit suspicious and wary.

"Well, find some other reaction to test, okay?" my partner snapped. "For some obscure reason, I'm a little nervous these days, and every time this thing moves its tongue I age a few centuries."

I ignored his grumbling and shook one of my legs.

"Hey, Guido! Are you still paying attention down there?"

His grip tightened fiercely.

"Of course I'm paying attention, you little . . . I mean, yeah, Boss. There's not much else to do while we're hangin' here, know what I mean? And quit jerking your leg around . . . please?"

I found his verbal slip rather interesting, but now wasn't the time to investigate further.

"Well, listen up," I said. "Here's what I want you to do. I want you to let go with one hand and pass the rope up to me. . . ."

"No way, Boss! Have you seen how far down it is? I'm not lettin' go no matter what you. . . ."

". . . because if you don't," I continued as if he hadn't interrupted, "I'm going to start squirming around until either you lose your grip with both hands or Massha loses her grip on me. Whichever way it goes, you'll fall. Get my drift? Now for once could you just follow orders without a lot of back-talk? We don't have much time to pull this off."

There was a stricken silence below as Guido absorbed my ultimatum and weighed the possibilities.

"Pull what off?" Aahz demanded. "Why doesn't anybody tell me anything? If this master plan of yours is riding on that sorry excuse for a bodyguard, you might as well give up right now. I've told you all along that he was too lily-livered to be any good at. . . ."

"Who's lily-livered?!" Guido shouted. "Look, Big Mouth, as soon as we get you out of there, you and me are going to settle this once and. . . ."

"First, we've got to get him out, Guido," I interrupted. "The rope."

"Right, Boss. One rope coming up. We'll see who's lily-livered. The last person who called me that was my mom, and by the time I got done with her. . . ."

Our whole formation began to rock dangerously as he fumbled through his coat one-handed in search of the rope. For a minute, I was afraid he was mad enough to let go with both hands to speed his search.

"Easy there, Guido," I cautioned. "We can. . . ."

"Here it is, Boss!" he said, flipping the rope up so violently that it almost whacked me in the face. "I hope you can use it to hang the son of a. . . ."

"Hanging isn't enough!" Aahz taunted. "It takes more than a piece of rope to do me in."

"Yeah. It takes a little girl with blue eyes and a spiked drink," my bodyguard sneered back. "If you think I'm going to let you live *that* one down. . . ."

I forced myself to ignore them. While it was tempting to rally to Luanna's defense, there were other more pressing matters to attend to.

Moving as carefully as I could, I looped one end of the rope up and around Massha's waist. It took a couple of tries and a lot more rope than I would have liked, but finally I managed to catch the dangling end and tie it off securely.

"What's with the rope, Hot Stuff?" Massha said calmly, the only one of our group who had managed to keep her cool through the entire proceedings.

"Well, with any luck, in a little while we're going to be heading down . . . with Aahz," I explained. "Even though I know you're strong, I don't think your hands are strong enough to keep a grip on all three of us while we make the trip. This is to be sure we don't lose anyone *after* we spring the cell."

"Speaking of that," Aahz called, "I'm still waiting to hear how you're going to get me out of this thing. You might even say I'm *dying* to find out."

He wasn't the only one. The dragon's head was watching my every movement through slitted eyes. I'm not sure how much pride it took in its job, but it was obvious the beast wasn't getting ready to overwhelm us with its cooperation.

Everything was as ready as I could make it, so I decided it was time to play my trump card.

"There's nothing to it, really," I told my partner with a smile. "Talk to me."

It isn't often I catch my old mentor totally by surprise . . . I get him upset on a fairly regular basis, but total surprise was a real rarity. This was one of those golden times.

"Say WHAT?" Aahz exclaimed loudly.

"Trust me, Aahz," I insisted. "I know what I'm doing. Just talk to me. Tell me a story. How did you first meet Garkin?"

"Oh, that," he said, rolling his eyes expressively. "Well, we were at the same boring cocktail party, see . . . you know, one of those dreary affairs where the crowd has you pinned against the wall and you get stuck talking to whatever the tide washes up against you? Anyway, he was trying to impress some little bit of fluff with his magic, which really wasn't all that hot in those days . . . let me tell you, partner, anytime you start getting depressed with your lack of progress in the magic business, remind me to tell you what your old teacher Garkin was like when we first met. But, as I was saying, out of respect for the craft, I just had to wander over and show them what the *real* stuff looked like . . . not that I had any interest in her myself, mind you. . . ."

I felt Guido tugging on my pantleg.

"Say, Boss," he complained. "What is this? I thought we were in a hurry."

"This is what we needed the time for," I whispered back.

"For *this?*" he grumbled. "But Boss, if we don't get started. . . ."

"We're started," I answered. "Now pay attention to what he's saying."

I was afraid our side comments might have distracted Aahz, but I needn't have worried. As per normal, once my partner got on a verbal roll, he wasn't that easy to stop.

". . . so there we were, just the three of us, mind you, and remember, our clothes were five floors away at this point. . . ."

"What's going on, Hot Stuff?" Massha hissed from her position above me. "I *know* you've heard this story before. Heck. *I've* heard it four times myself."

"Keep your eye on the dragon," I advised her. "And be ready to act fast."

I was going through the motions of reacting to Aahz's story and fielding the impatient questions of my assistants as best I could, but my real attention was focused on the dragon's head. My strategy was already working. Aahz's droning account of past glories was starting to take effect.

The dragon's eyes were definitely starting to glaze.

". . . of course, after all that, I just *had* to take her home with me. It was the least I could do for the poor thing under the circumstances."

Aahz was winding up his story already! I had to keep him going just a little bit longer.

"Was that the party where you met Tananda?" I said, deliberately feeding him another cue.

"Tananda? No. That's another story completely. I met her when I was sitting in on a cut-throat game of dragon poker over at the Geek's. We had a real pigeon on the line, the kind of idiot who would bet a busted Corp's a' Corp's into a Unicorn Flush showing, you know? Well, I was a little low on funds just then, so. . . ."

Guido was getting restless again.

"Boss, how much longer are we gonna. . . ."

"Not much longer," I interrupted. "Get hold of the rope. We're about to move."

". . . now I was holding Ogres back-to-back . . . or was it Elves? No, it was Ogres. I remember because Tananda had Elves wrapped up. Of course, we didn't know that until the end of the hand. Anyway, as soon as the Geek opened, I bumped him back limit, and Tananda . . ."

That did it. I should have known a hand-by-hand, bet-by-bet description of dragon poker would do the trick.

Without any warning at all, the dragon yawned . . . long and wide.

Aahz broke off his narration, a momentous event in itself, and blinked his surprise.

"Quick, Aahz! Jump for it!"

Bewildered as he was, there was nothing wrong with my partner's reflexes. He was out of the dragon's mouth in a flash, diving through the air to catch the rope below Guido.

As soon as his hands closed on our lifeline, several things happened at the same time.

With the extra weight on Massha's levitation belt, our whole formation started to sink at an alarming rate . . . my apprentice lost her grip on me, giving me minor rope burns as I clutched madly for the rope, almost too late to follow the advice I had been so freely giving to everyone else . . . and the dragon closed his mouth.

I caught one last glimpse of the beast before we sank from sight, and I honestly don't think he even knew we were gone. His eyelids were at half-mast, and the eyes themselves were out of focus from boredom. Aahz's stories tended to have that effect on even vaguely-intelligent beings. I had simply found a practical application for the phenomenon.

"I've gotta change the controls, Hot Stuff!" Massha called, alerting me once more to our current situation.

The ground was rushing up to meet us with frightening speed.

I remembered the faulty controls that held all of us at their mercy.

"No! Wait, Massha! Let me try. . . ."

Exerting my last ounce of reserve power, I worked at levitating our whole crew. Under normal circumstances, I could lift three people easily and four or five in a pinch. Here in Limbo, using everything I had with Massha's belt assisting me, I barely managed to slow our descent to a moderate crawl.

"What happened there, partner?" Aahz called. "How did you know that thing was going to yawn?"

"Call it a lucky guess," I grunted, still concentrating on keeping us from crashing. "I'll explain later."

"Check the landing zone," Guido warned.

I sneaked a peek.

We had been at our task longer than I thought. The sidewalk below was crowded with vampires strolling here and there as Blut's legendary nightlife fired up.

"I don't think we can bluff our way through this one," Aahz said calmly. "Any chance you can steer us around the corner into the alley? There doesn't seem to be as much of a crowd there."

Before I could answer, something flashed past us from above with a flutter of leather wings.

"JAILBREAK!" it screamed, banking around the corner. "Murderer on the loose! JAILBREAK!"

# Chapter XIII

*"I've never seen so damn many Indians."*
—G. A. Custer

THE words of alarm had an interesting effect on the crowd below. After a brief glance to see us descending into their midst, to a man they turned and ran. In a twinkling, the street was empty.

"What's going on?" I called to Aahz, unable to believe our good fortune.

"Beats me!" my partner shouted back. "I guess none of the normal citizenry want to tangle with an escaped murderer. Better get us down fast before they figure out how badly outnumbered we are."

I didn't have to be told twice. Our escape had just gotten an unexpected blessing, but I wasn't about to make book on how long it would last. I cut my magical support, and we dropped swiftly toward the pavement.

"What was that that blew the whistle on us?" Massha said, peering up into the darkness where our mysterious saboteur had disappeared.

"I think it was that Vic character," Guido answered from below me. "I got a pretty good look at him when he bolted past me back at the Woof Writer."

"Really?" I asked, half to myself, twisting around to look after the departed villain. "That's one more we owe him."

"Later," Aahz commanded, touching down at last. "Right now we've got to get out of here."

Guido was beside him in a second. I had to drop a ways, as with the extra weight removed from the rope, we had ceased to sink.

"C'mon, Massha!" I called. "Cut the power in that thing. It's not that far to fall."

"I'm trying!" she snapped back, fiddling with the belt buckle once more. "The flaming thing's malfunctioning again!"

The belt setting had changed. Holding the rope, I could feel that there was no longer an upward pull. Unfortunately, Massha wasn't sinking, either. Instead, she hovered in mid-air about fifteen feet up.

"Hey, Boss! We got company!"

I followed my bodyguard's gaze. There was a mob forming down the street to our left, and it didn't look happy. Of course, it was hard to tell for sure, but I had the definite impression that their eyes were glowing redder than normal, which I was unable to convince myself was a good sign.

"Maasshhhha!" I nagged, my voice rising uncontrollably as I tugged on the rope.

"It's jammed!" she whimpered. "Go on, take off, Hot stuff. No sense in all of us getting caught."

"We can't just leave you here," I argued.

"We don't have time for a debate," Aahz snarled. "Guido! Get up there ahead of us and keep the street open. We can't afford to get cut off. Okay, let's go!"

With that, he snatched the rope out of my hand and took off running down the street away from the crowd with Guido out front in point position and Massha floating over his head like a gaudy balloon. For once, I didn't object to him giving orders to my bodyguard. I was too busy sprinting to keep up with the rest of my group.

If the watching mob was having any trouble deciding what to do, the sight of us fleeing settled it. With a howl, they swarmed down the street in pursuit.

When I say "with a howl," I'm not speaking figuratively. As they ran, some of the vampires transformed into large, fierce-looking dogs, others into bats, presumably to gain more speed in the chase. While Aahz and I had been chased by mobs before, this was the first pack of pursuers who literally bayed at our heels. I must say I didn't care much for the experience.

"Where are we going, Aahz?" I panted.

"Away from them!" he called back.

"I mean, eventually," I pressed. "We're heading the wrong way to get back to our hideout."

"We can't hole up until we've shaken our fan club," my partner insisted. "Now shut up and run."

I had certain doubts about our ability to elude our pursuers while towing Massha overhead to mark our position, but I followed Aahz's instructions and pumped the pavement for all I was worth. For one thing, if I pointed out this obvious fact to my partner, he might simply let go of the rope and leave my apprentice to fend for herself. Then again, the option to running was to stand firm and face the mob. All in all, running seemed like a *real* good idea.

Guido was surprisingly good at clearing a path for us. I had never really seen my bodyguard in action, but with his constant carping and allergy problems throughout this venture, I was tending to discount his usefulness. Not so. The vampires we encountered in our flight had not heard the alarm and were unprepared for the whirlwind that burst into their midst. Guido never seemed to break stride as he barreled into victim after victim, but whatever he did to them was effective. None of the fallen bodies which marked his progress attempted to interfere with Aahz or me . . . heck, they didn't even move.

"River ahead, Boss!" he called over his shoulder.

"What's that?" I puffed, realizing for the first time how out of shape I had grown during my prosperous stay at the Bazaar.

"A river!" he repeated. "The street we're on is going to dead-end into a river in a few blocks. I can see it from here. We're going to have to change direction or we'll get pinned against the water."

I wondered whether it wouldn't be a good idea for us to just plunge into the river and put some moving water between us and the vampires, as I seemed to recall a legend that that was one of the things that could stop them. Then it occurred to me that my bodyguard probably couldn't swim.

"Head right!" Aahz shouted. "There! Up that alley."

Guido darted off on the indicated course with my partner and I pounding along about fifteen paces behind him. We had built up a bit of a lead on our pursuers, though we could still hear their cries and yelps a block or so back, and for the first time I started to have the hope that we might actually elude them. Now that we were out of their line of sight. . . .

"Look out. . . ."

There was a sudden cry from above, and Massha came crashing to the ground, gaining the dubious distinction of being the first person I've ever witnessed doing a belly-flop on dry land. I'm sure the ground didn't actually shake, but the impact was enough to leave that impression. I experienced a quick flash of guilt, realizing that my first thought was not for the well-being of my apprentice, but rather unbridled relief that she hadn't landed on one of us.

"I think the controls just came unstuck," Aahz said, rather unnecessarily to my thinking.

"Are you all right, Massha?" I said, crouching over her.

"Wha—ha . . ." came the forced reply.

"Of course, she's not all right," Aahz snapped, assuming translator duties. "At the very least she's got the wind knocked out of her."

Whatever the exact extent of the damages suffered from her fall, my apprentice wasn't even trying to rise. I would have liked to give her a few minutes recovery time, but already the sounds of our pursuers were drawing closer.

"Can you carry her, Aahz?"

"Not on my best day," my partner admitted, eyeing Massha's sizable bulk. "How about you? Have you got enough juice left to levitate her?"

I shook my head violently.

"Used it all supervising our aerial maneuvers back at the jail."

"Hey, Boss!" Guido hissed, emerging from the shadows behind us. "The alley's blocked. This is the only way out!"

And that was that. Even if we got Massha up and moving, all it meant was that we'd have to retrace our steps right back into the teeth of the mob. We had run our race . . . and were about to lose it rather spectacularly.

The others knew it, too.

"Well, it's been nice working with you, Guido," Aahz said with a sigh. "I know I've gotten on your case a couple of times, but you're a good man to have around in a pinch. You did some really nice crowd work getting us this far. Sorry about that last turn call."

"No hard feelings," my bodyguard shrugged. "You gave it your best shot. This alley would have been my choice, too, if I'd been workin' alone. Boss, I warned you I was a jinx when it came to jailbreaks. I gotta admit, though, for a while there I really thought we were goin' to pull this one off."

"It was a long shot at best." I grinned. "At least you can't say that *this* one suffered from over-planning."

Aahz clapped a hand on my shoulder.

"Well, partner?" he said. "Any thoughts on how to play this one? Do we try to surrender peacefully, or go down swinging?"

I wasn't sure the crowd would give us a choice. They were almost at our alley, and they didn't sound like they cared much for talking.

"NOT THIS WAY! THEY'RE DOUBLING BACK TOWARD THE JAIL!"

This unexpected cry came from the street near the mouth of our alley.

I couldn't believe it, but apparently the mob did. There were curses and shouted orders, but from their fast-fading manner it was plain that the crowd had turned and was now heading back the way they had come.

"What was that?" Massha managed, her voice returning at last.

I motioned her to be silent and cocked an eyebrow at Aahz, silently asking the same question.

He answered with an equally silent shake of the head.

Neither of us knew for sure what was going on, but we both sensed that the timely intervention was neither accidental nor a mistake. Someone had deliberately pulled the crowd off our backs. Before we celebrated our good fortune, we wanted to know who and why.

A pair of figures appeared at the mouth of the alley.

"You can come out now," one of them called. "Sorry to interfere, but it looked like so much fun we just *had* to play, too."

I'd know that voice anywhere, even if I didn't recognize the figure as well as the unmistakable form of her brother.

"Tananda! Chumley!" I shouted, waving to pinpoint our position. "I was wondering when you'd show up."

The sister-brother team of Trollop and Troll hastened to join us. For all their lighthearted banter, I can think of few beings I'd rather have on or at my side when things get tight.

"Are you all right?" Tananda asked, stopping to help Massha to her feet.

"Really never had much dignity," my apprentice responded, "and what little I did have is shot to hell. Except for that I'm fine. I'm starting to see why you Big Leaguers are so down on mechanical magic."

Chumley seized my hand and pumped it vigorously.

"Now don't be too rough on your little gimmicks, ducks," he advised. "That little ring you left us was just the ticket we needed to get here in time for the latest in our unbroken string of last-minute rescues. Except for the typical hash you've made of your end-game, it looks like you've done rather well without us. We've got all present and accounted for, including Aahz, who seems remarkably unscathed after yet one more near-brush with disaster. Seems like all that's left is a hasty retreat and a slow celebration . . . eh, what?"

"That's about the size of it," I agreed. "It's great having the two of you along to ride shotgun on our exit, though. Speaking of which, can you find the castle from here? I've gotten a little turned around. . . ."

"Hold it right there!" Aahz broke in. "Before we get too wrapped up in congratulating each other, aren't there a few minor details being over-looked?"

The group looked at each other.

"Like what?" Tananda said at last.

"Like the fact that I'm still wanted for murder, for one," my partner glared. "Then again, there's the three fugitives we're supposed to be bringing back to Deva with us."

"Oh, come on, Aahz," the Trollop chided, poking him playfully in the ribs. "With the reputation you already have, what's a little thing like a murder warrant?"

"I didn't do it," Aahz insisted. "Not only didn't I kill this Vic charac-ter, nobody did. He's still around somewhere laughing down his sleeve at all of us. Now while I'll admit my reputation isn't exactly spotless, it doesn't include standing still for a bum rap . . . or letting someone get away with making a fool of me!"

"Of course, saving the money for paying the swindlers' debts plus the fines involved has nothing to do with it, eh, Aahz?" Chumley said, winking his larger eye.

"Well . . . that, too," my partner admitted. "Isn't it nice that we can take care of both unpleasant tasks at the same time?"

"Maybe we could settle for just catching Vic and let the others go," I murmured.

"How's that again, partner?"

"Nothing, Aahz," I said with a sigh. "It's just that . . . nothing. C'mon everybody. If we're going to go hunting, it's going to require a bit of planning, and I don't think we should do it out here in the open."

# Chapter XIV

*"Relax, Julie. Everyone will understand."*
**—Romeo**

**F**ORTUNATELY, Massha's elevated position during our flight had given her an excellent view of our surroundings, and we were able to find our way back to the Dispatcher's without being discovered by the aroused populace. Now that our numbers had increased, however, Vilhelm's greeting was noticeably cooler.

"I'm starting to believe what everybody says," the little vampire complained. "Let one demon in, and the next thing you know the neighborhood's crawling with them. When I decided to talk to you folks instead of blowing the whistle on you, I didn't figure on turning my office into a meeting place for off-worlders."

"C'mon, Vilhelm," I said, trying to edge my foot into the doorway. "We don't have any place else to go in town. There aren't *that* many of us."

"We could always just wait out on the street until the authorities come by," Aahz suggested. "I don't imagine it would take much to convince them that this guy has been harboring fugitives."

"Can it, Green and Scaly," Massha ordered, puffing herself up to twice her normal size. "Vilhelm's been nice to us so far, and I won't listen to anyone threaten him, even you. Just remember that you'd still be cooling your heels in the slammer if it weren't for him. Either he helps of his own free will, or we look elsewhere."

Aahz gave ground before her righteous indignation.

"Are you going to let your apprentice talk to me that way?" he demanded.

"Only when she's right." I shrugged.

"I say, Aahz," Chumley intervened. "Could you possibly curb your normally vile manners for a few moments? We don't really need one more enemy in this dimension, and I, for one, would appreciate the chance to extend my thanks to this gentleman before he throws us out."

When he's working, Chumley goes by the name of Big Crunch and does a Neanderthal that's the envy of half the barbarians at the Bazaar. On his own time, however, his polished charm has solved a lot of problems for us . . . almost as many as Aahz's bluster has gotten us into.

"Oh, come on in," the Dispatcher grumbled. "Enter freely and of your own accord and all that. I never could turn my back on somebody in trouble. Guess that's why I've never traveled the other dimensions myself. They'd eat me alive out there."

"Thanks, Vilhelm," I said, slipping past him into the office before he could change his mind. "You'll have to forgive my partner. He really isn't always like this. Being on death row hasn't done much for his sense of humor."

"I guess I'm a little edgy myself," the vampire admitted. "Strange as it sounds, I've been worried about you folks . . . and your motor-mouthed friend who's been keeping me company hasn't helped things much."

I did a quick nose count of our troop.

"Wait a minute," I frowned. "Who's been waiting for us?"

Now it was Vilhelm's turn to look surprised.

"Didn't one of you send out for a werewolf? He said he was with you."

"Aahh! But I am! My friends, they do not know me yet, but I shall be their salvation, no?"

With that, I was overwhelmed by a shaggy rug. Well, at least that's what I thought until it came off the floor and threw itself into my arms with the enthusiasm of a puppy . . . a very large puppy.

"What's *that*?!" Aahz said, his eyes narrowing dangerously. "Skeeve, can't I leave you alone for a few days without you picking up every stray in any given dimension?"

"That," in this case, was one of the scroffiest-looking werewolves I'd ever seen . . . realizing, of course, that until this moment I'd only seen two. He had dark bushy eyebrows (if you'll believe that on a werewolf) and wore a white stocking cap with a maple leaf on the side. His whiskers were carefully groomed into a handlebar mustache, and what might have been a goatee peered from beneath his chin. Actually, viewed piecemeal, he was very well-groomed. It's just when taken in its entirety that he looked scroffy. Maybe it was the leer. . . .

"Honest, Aahz," I protested, trying to untangle myself. "I've never seen him before in my life!"

"Oh, but forgive me," the beast said, releasing me so suddenly I almost fell. "I am so stupeed, I forget to introduce. So! I am an artist extraordinaire, but also, I am ze finest track-air in ze land. My friends, the Woof Writers, they have told me of your pro-blem and I have flown like ze wind to aid you. No? I am Pepe Le Garou A. and I am at your service."

With that, he swept into a low bow with a flourish that if I hadn't been so flabbergasted I would have applauded. It occurred to me that now I knew why the Woof Writers had snickered when they told us they knew of someone who could help.

"Boss," Guido said, his voice muffled by his hand, which he was holding over his nose and mouth. "Shall I wait outside?"

Tananda cocked an eyebrow at him.

"Allergy problems? Here, try some of this. No dimension traveler should be without it."

She produced a small vial and tossed it to my bodyguard. "Rub some onto your upper lip just below your nose."

"Gee, thanks," Guido said, following her instructions. "What is it?"

"It's a counter-allergenic paste." She shrugged. "I think it has a garlic base."

"WHAT?" my bodyguard exclaimed, dropping the vial.

Tananda favored him with one of her impish grins.

"Just kidding. Nunzio was worried about you and told us about your allergies . . . all of them."

Her brother swatted her lightly on the rump.

"Shame on you, little sister," he said, smiling in spite of himself. "After you get done apologizing to Guido, I suggest you do the same for our host. I think you nearly gave him a heart attack with that last little joke."

This was, of course, just what I needed while stranded in a hostile dimension. A nervous vampire, a melodramatic werewolf, and now my teammates decide it's time to play practical jokes on each other.

"Ummm . . . tell me, Mr. A.," I said, ignoring my other problems and turning to the werewolf. "Do you think you can. . . ."

"No, non," he interrupted. "Eet is simply Pepe, eh?"

"Pepe A.," I repeated dutifully.

"Zat's right," he beamed, apparently delighted with my ability to learn a simple phrase. "Now, before we . . . how you say, get down to ze business, would you do me ze hon-air of introducing me to your colleagues?"

"Oh. Sorry. This is my partner, Aahz. He's. . . ."

"But of course! Ze famous Aahz! I have so long wished to meet you."

If there's anything that can coax Aahz out of a bad mood, it's flattery . . . and Pepe seemed to be an expert in that category.

"You've heard of me?" he blinked. "I mean . . . what exactly have you heard? There have been so many adventures over the years."

"Do you not remem-bair Piere? I was raised from a pup on his tales of your fight with Isstvan."

"Piere? You know Piere?"

"Do I know him? He is my uncle!"

"No kidding. Hey, Tananda! Did you hear that? Pepe here's Piere's nephew. Wait'll we tell Gus."

I retired from the conversation, apparently forgotten in the reunion.

"Say, Skeeve," Vilhelm said, appearing at my side. "It looks like this could take a while. Should I break out the wine?"

That got my attention.

"Wine? You've got wine?"

"Stocked up on it after your last visit," the vampire admitted with a grin. "Figured it might come in handy the next time you came through. I may gripe a bit, but talking to you and your friends is a lot more fun than watching the tubes."

"Well bring it out . . . but I get the first glass. Unless you've got lots there won't be much left after my partner there gets his claws on it."

I turned back to the proceedings just in time to see Pepe kissing my apprentice's hand.

"Do not be afraid, my little flow-air," he was saying. "Here is one who truly appreciates your beauty, as well as . . . how should I say it, its quantity?"

"You're kinda cute," Massha giggled. "But I never did go in much for inter-species dating, if you get my drift."

I caught Aahz's attention and drew him away from the group.

"Could you take over for a while here, partner?" I said. "I've been running nonstop since the start of this thing and could use a little time by myself to recharge my batteries before we fire up again."

"No problem," he nodded, laying a hand on my shoulder. "I figure we won't be moving before sunup . . . and Skeeve? I haven't had a chance to say it, but thanks for the bail-out."

"Don't mention it," I grinned weakly. "Tell me you wouldn't do the same for me."

"Don't know," he retorted. "You've never suckerpunched me at the beginning of a caper."

"Now *that* I still owe you for."

Just then, Vilhelm appeared with the wine, and Aahz hurried away to rejoin the group.

I managed to snag a goblet and retired to a secluded corner while the party went into high gear. Pepe seemed to be fitting in well with the rest of the team, if not functioning as a combination jester and spark plug, but somehow I felt a bit distant. Sipping my wine, I stared off into the distance at nothing in particular, letting my thoughts wander.

"What's the trouble, handsome?"

"Hmmm? Oh. Hi, Tananda. Nothing in particular. Just a little tired, that's all."

"Mind if I join you?" she said, dropping to the floor beside me before I could stop her. "So. Are you going to tell me about it? Who is she?"

I turned my head slowly to look at her directly.

"I beg your pardon?"

She kept her eyes averted, idly running one finger around the rim of her goblet.

"Look," she said, "if you don't want to talk about it, just say so . . . it's really none of my business. Just don't try to kid me or yourself that there's nothing bothering you. I've known you a long time now, and I can usually tell when there's something eating you. My best guess right now, if I'm any judge of the phenomenon, is that it's a girl."

Ever since I'd met Tananda, I'd had a crush on her. With her words, though, I suddenly realized how badly I wanted someone to talk to. I mean, to Guido and Massha I was an authority figure, and I wasn't about to open up to Aahz until I was sure he'd take the problem seriously and not just laugh, and as for Chumley . . . how do you talk about woman problems with a troll?

"Okay. You got me," I said, looking back into my wine. "It's a girl."

"I thought so," Tananda smiled. "Where have you been keeping her? Tell me, is she beautiful and sensitive?"

"All that and more." I nodded, taking another drink from my goblet. "She's also on the wrong side."

"Whoops," Tananda said, straightening up. "You'd better run that one past me again."

I filled her in on my encounters with Luanna. I tried to keep it unbiased and informative, but even I could tell that my tones were less controlled than I would have liked.

Tananda sat in silence for a few moments after I'd finished, hugging her legs and with her chin propped up on her knees.

"Well," she said at last, "from what you say, she's an accomplice at best. Maybe we can let her go after we get them all rounded up."

"Sure."

My voice was flat. Both Tananda and I knew that once Aahz got on his high horse there was no telling how merciful or vicious he would be at any given point.

"Well, there's always a chance," she insisted. "Aahz has always had a soft spot where you're concerned. If you intercede for her, and if she's willing to abandon her partners. . . ."

". . . and, if a table had wings, we could fly it back to the Bazaar." I frowned. "No, Tananda. First of all, she won't give up her partners just because they're in a crunch. That much I know. Besides, if I put that kind of pressure on her, to choose between me and them, I'd never know for sure if she really wanted me or if she was just trying to save her own skin."

Tananda got to her feet.

"Don't become so wise that you're stupid, Skeeve," she said softly before she left. "Remember, Luanna's already chosen you twice over her partners. Both times she's risked her life and their getaway to pass you a warning. Maybe all she needs is what you haven't yet given her—an invitation for a chance at a new life with a new partner. Don't be so proud or insecure that you'd throw a genuine admirer to the wolves rather than run the risk of making a mistake. If you did, I don't think I'd like you much . . . and I don't think you would either."

I pondered Tananda's advice after she'd gone. There was one additional complication I hadn't had the nerve to mention to her. Whatever Luanna's feelings for me were, how would they change when she found out I'd used her scarf . . . her token of affection, to guide a pack of hunters to their target?

# Chapter XV

*"Everybody needs a career manager!"*
**—Lady Macbeth**

**"S**O where is he?" Aahz grumbled for the hundredth time . . . in the last five minutes.

The sun had been up for hours, or at least as up as it seemed to get in this dimension. Since my arrival in Limbo, I had never seen what I am accustomed to thinking of as full sunlight. Whether the constant heavy overcast condition which seemed to prevail during daylight hours was the result of magic or some strange meteorologic condition I was never sure, but it did nothing to alleviate the air of gloom that clung to the town of Blut like a shroud.

The whole team was impatient to get started, but Aahz was the only one who indulged himself in expressing his feelings as often . . . or as loudly. Of course, it might have been simply that he was making so much of a fuss that the others were willing to let him provide the noise for all of them rather than letting their own efforts get constantly upstaged.

"Just take it easy, partner," I said soothingly, struggling to keep from snapping at him in my own nervous impatience. "There aren't that many all-day stores in this dimension."

"What do you expect, dealing with a bunch of vampires," he snapped.

"I still don't like this idea. Nonmagical disguises seem unnatural somehow."

I heaved a quiet sigh inside and leaned back to wait, propping my feet up on a chair. This particular quarrel was old before Vilhelm had left on his shopping trip, and I was tired going over it again and again.

"Be reasonable, Aahz," Tananda said, taking up the slack for me. "You know we can't wander around town like this . . . especially you with half the city looking for you. We need disguises, and without a decent power source, Skeeve here can't handle disguises for all of us. Besides, it's not like we're using mechanical magic. We won't be using magic at all."

"That's what everybody keeps telling me," my partner growled. "We're just going to alter our appearances without using spells. That sounds like mechanical magic to me. Do you know what's going to happen to our reputations if word of this gets back to the Bazaar? Particularly with most of the competition looking for a chance to splash a little mud on the Great Skeeve's name? Remember, we're already getting complaints that our prices are too high, and if this gets out. . . ."

The light dawned. I could finally see what was eating at Aahz. I should have known there was money at the bottom of this.

"But Aahz," I chimed in, "our fees *are* overpriced. I've been saying that for months. I mean, it's not like we need the money. . . ."

". . . and I've been telling you for months that it's the only way to keep the riff-raff from draining away all your practice time," he shot back angrily. "Remember, your name's supposed to be the Great Skeeve, not the Red Cross. You don't do charity."

Now we were on familiar ground. Unlike the disguise thing, this was one argument I never tired of.

"I'm not talking about charity," I said. "I'm talking about a fair fee for services rendered."

"Fair fee?" my partner laughed, rolling his eyes. "You mean like that deal you cut with Watzisname? Did he ever tell you about that one, Tananda? We catch a silly bird for this Deveel, see, and my partner charges him a flat fee. Not a percentage, mind you, a flat fee. And how much of a flat fee? A hundred gold pieces? A thousand. No. TEN. Ten lousy gold pieces. And half an hour later the Deveel sells his 'poor little bird' for over a hundred thousand. Nice to know we don't do charity, isn't it?"

"C'mon, Aahz," I argued, writhing inside. "That was only five minutes' work. How was I supposed to know the silly bird was on the endangered species list? Even *you* thought it was a good deal until we heard what the final sale was. Besides, if I had held out for a percentage and the

Deveel had been legit and never sold the thing, we wouldn't have even gotten ten gold pieces out of it."

"I never heard the details from your side," Tananda said, "but what I picked up on the streets was that everybody at the Bazaar was really impressed. Most folks think that it's a master-stroke of PR for the hottest magician at the Bazaar to help bring a rarity to the public for a mere fraction of his normal fees. It shows he's something other than a cold-hearted businessman . . . that he really cares about people."

"So what's wrong with being a cold-hearted businessman?" Aahz snorted. "How about the other guy? Everybody thinks he's a villain, and he's crying all the way to the bank. He retired on the profit from that one sale alone."

"Unless Nanny misled me horribly when she taught me my numbers," Chumley interrupted, "I figure your current bankroll could eat that fellow's profit and still have room for lunch. Any reason you're so big on squirreling away so much gold, Aahz? Are you planning on retiring?"

"No, I'm not planning on retiring," my partner snapped. "And you're missing the point completely. Money isn't the object."

"It isn't?"

I think everybody grabbed that line at the same time . . . even Pepe, who hadn't known Aahz all that long.

"Of course not. You can always get more gold. What can't be replaced is time. We all know Skeeve here has a long way to go in the magic department. What the rest of you keep forgetting is how short a life span he has to play with . . . maybe a hundred years if he's lucky. All I'm trying to do is get him the maximum learning time possible . . . and that means keeping him from using up most of his time on nickel-and-dime adventures. Let the smalltime operators do those. My partner shouldn't have to budge away from his studies unless the assignment is something *really* spectacular. Something that will advance his reputation and his career."

There was a long silence while everybody digested that one, especially me. Since Aahz had accepted me as a full partner instead of an apprentice, I intended to forget his role as my teacher and career manager. Thinking back now, I could see he had never really given up the work, just gotten sneakier. I wouldn't have believed that was possible.

"How about this particular nickel-and-dime adventure?" Tananda said, breaking the silence. "You know, pulling your tail out of a scrape? Isn't this a little lowbrow for the kind of legend you're trying to build?"

The sarcasm in her voice was unmistakable, but it didn't faze Aahz in the least.

"If you'll ask around, you'll find out that I didn't want him along on this jaunt at all. In fact, I knocked him cold trying to keep him out. A top-flight magician shouldn't have to stoop to bill collecting, especially when the risk is disproportionately high."

"Well, it all sounds a little cold-blooded for my taste, Aahz," Chumley put in. "If you extend your logic, our young friend here is only going to work when the danger is astronomically high, and conversely if the advancement to his career is enough, no risk is too great. That sounds to me like a sure-fire way to lose a partner *and* a friend. Like the Geek says, if you keep bucking the odds, sooner or later they're going to catch up with you."

My partner spun to confront the troll nose-to-nose.

"Of course it's going to be dangerous," he snarled. "The magic profession isn't for the faint of heart, and to hit the top he's going to have to be hair-triggered and mean. There's no avoiding that, but I can try to be sure he's ready for it. Why do you think I've been so dead-set against him having bodyguards? If he starts relying on other people to watch out for him, he's going to lose the edge himself. *That's* when he's in danger of walking into a swinging door."

That brought Guido into the fray.

"Now let me see if I've got this right," my bodyguard said. "You don't want me and my cousin Nunzio around so that the Boss here can handle all the trouble himself? That's crazy talk, know what I mean? Now listen to me, 'cause this time I know what I'm sayin'. The higher someone gets on the ladder, the more folks come huntin' for his head. Even if they don't do nothin' they got people gunning for them, 'cause they got power and respect and there's always somebody who thinks they can steal it. Now I've seen some of the Big Guys who try to act just like you're sayin' . . . they're so scared all the time they don't trust nothin' or nobody. The only one they can count on is themselves, and everybody else is suspect. That includes total strangers, their own bodyguards, their friends, *and* their partners. Think about *that* for a minute."

He leaned back and surveyed the room, addressing his next comments to everyone.

"People like that don't last long. They don't trust nobody, so they got nobody. Ya can't do everything alone and sooner or later they're lookin' the wrong way or asleep when they should be watchin' and it's all over. Now I've done a lot of jobs as a bodyguard, and they were just jobs, know what I mean? The Boss here is different, and I'm not just sayin' that. He's the best man I've met in my whole life because he likes people and ain't afraid to show it. More important, he ain't afraid to risk his neck to help somebody even if it *isn't* in his best interest. I work double hard for him because I don't want to see anything happen to him . . . and if that means comin' along on weird trips like this, then that's the way it is. Anybody that wants to hurt him is gonna have to come through me . . . and that includes fightin' any of you if you want to try to turn him into somethin' he isn't and doesn't want to be."

Massha broke in with a loud clapping of her hands.

"Bravo, Guido," she said. "I think your problem, Green and Scaly, is that your idea of success is out of step with everyone else's. We all want to see good things happen for Skeeve, here, but we also like him just the way he is. We've got enough faith in his good sense to back him in whatever move he makes in his development . . . without trying to frog-march or trick him up a specific path."

Aahz not only gave ground before this onslaught of protest, he seemed to shrink in a little on himself.

"I like him too," he mumbled. "I've known him longer than any of you, remember? He's doing fine, but he could be so much more. How can he choose a path if he can't see it? All I'm trying to do is set him up to be bigger than I . . . than *we* could ever think of being ourselves. What's wrong with that?"

Despite my irritation at having my life discussed as if I weren't in the room, I was quite touched, by my friends' loyal defense of me, and most of all by Aahz.

"You know, partner," I said softly, "for a minute there, you sounded just like my father. He wanted me to be the best . . . or more specifically, to be better than he was. My mom always tried to tell me that it was because he loved me, but at that time it just sounded like he was always being critical. Maybe she was right . . . I'm more inclined to believe it today than I was then, but then again, I'm older now. If nothing else, I've had to try to tell people I love them when the words just won't come . . . and gotten upset with myself when they couldn't see it when I tried to show them.

"Aahz, I appreciate your concern and I want your guidance. You're right, there are paths and options I can't even comprehend yet. But I also have to choose my own way. I want to be better eventually than I am today, but not necessarily the best. I think Guido's right, there's a big price tag attached to being at the top, and I'd want to think long and hard if I wanted to pay it . . . even if I was convinced I could, which I'm not. I *do* know that if it means giving up the trust I have in you and everybody else in this room, I'll settle for being a nickel-and-dime operator. *That* price I'll never pay willingly."

Silence started to descend again as each of us retreated into his or her own thoughts; then the werewolf bounded into the middle of the assemblage.

"But what is this, eh?" he demanded. "Surely this cannot be ze great team of Aahz and Skeeve, ze ones who can laugh at any dan-gair?"

"You know, Pepe," Aahz said warningly, "you've got a great future as a stuffed head."

"My head?" The werewolf blinked. "But she is not . . . oohh. I see now. You make ze joke, eh? Good. Zat is more like it."

". . . and as far as laughing at danger goes," I joined in, determined to hold up my end of the legend, "the only danger I see here is dying of boredom. Where *is* Vilhelm anyway?"

"I know you and Aahz are fond of each other, Skeeve," Chumley yawned, "but you've *got* to spend more time with other people. You're starting to sound like him. Maybe you can tag along the next time I have an assignment."

"Over my dead body," my partner said. "Besides, what could he learn from a troll that I couldn't teach him myself?"

"I could teach him not to catch birds for Deveels for ten gold pieces," the troll grinned, winking at his sister. "That seems to be a part of his education you've neglected."

"Izzat so!" my partner bristled. "You're going to teach him about price setting? How about the time you set your own sister up to steal an elephant without bothering to check. . . ."

And they were off again. As I listened, I found myself reflecting on the fact that while it was nice to know the depths of my friends' feelings about me, it was far more comfortable when they managed to conceal it under a cloak of banter. For the most part, open sincerity is harder to take than friendly laughter.

# Chapter XVI

*"Don't be fooled by appearances."*
—**Malloy**

THINGS were pretty much back to normal by the time Vilhelm returned with our disguises . . . which was a good thing as the process of masking-up proved to be a test of everybody's sense of humor.

Until I had hooked up with Aahz, I had never had occasion to pretend I was anyone but myself. As such, I had no way of knowing how long it took to don a physical disguise without resorting to magic. By the time we were done, I had a new respect for the skills I had learned, not to mention a real longing for a dimension . . . any dimension with a strong force line to work with.

Tananda was a major help; her experiences with the assassin's guild came into play and she took the lead in trying to coach us in our new roles.

"Guido, straighten up!" she commanded, exasperation creeping into her voice. "You walk like a gangster."

"I am a gangster!" my bodyguard snarled back. "Besides, what's wrong with the way I walk? It got us to the jail, didn't it?"

"Half the town wasn't looking for you then," Tananda argued. "Besides, then you could pick your own route. We don't know where the opposition's holed up. We're going to have to walk through crowds on this hunt, and that walk just doesn't make it. Ninety percent of costuming is learning to move like the character you're trying to portray. Right now you move like you're looking for a fight."

"Try walking like Don Bruce," I suggested. "He's a gangster, too."

That earned me a black look, but my bodyguard tried to follow my instructions, rising up on the balls of his feet and mincing along.

"Better," Tananda said, leaving Guido prancing up and down the room with a scowl on his face.

"How are we doing?"

"Lousy," she confided in me. "This is taking a lot longer than it should. I wish there were more mirrors in this place . . . heck, any mirrors would be nice."

It hadn't been until we started gearing up that we realized that Dispatcher had no mirrors at all. He claimed they weren't popular or necessary among vampires. This left us with the unenviable job of checking each other's make-up and costumes, a chore which would have been Homeric even if less sensitive egos were involved.

"How're my teeth?" Massha demanded, sticking her head in front of me and opening her mouth.

It was like staring into the depths of an underground cave.

"Umm . . . the left side is okay, but you're still missing a few on the right. Hang on a second and I'll give you a hand."

Teeth were turning out to be a special problem. We had hoped to find some of the rubber fangs so prevalent in the Bazaar novelty stores to aid in our disguises. Unfortunately, none of the shops in Blut had them. The closest thing they had in stock, according to Vilhelm, were rubber sets of human teeth designed to fit over fangs. The vampire assured us that locally they were considered quite frightening. Faced by this unforeseen shortage, we were resorting to using tooth-black to blacken all our teeth except the canines for a close approximation of the vampires we were trying to imitate. When we tried it out, it wasn't a bad effect, but the actual application was causing countless problems. When one tried to apply the stuff on oneself without a mirror, it was difficult to get the right teeth, and if one called on one's friends for assistance, one rapidly found that said friend was soon possessed by an overpowering impulse to paint one's tongue black instead of the teeth.

"I don't like this cloak," Guido announced, grabbing my arm. "I want to wear my trench coat."

"Vampires don't wear trench coats," I said firmly. "Besides, the cloak really looks great on you. Makes you look . . . I don't know, debonair but menacing."

"Yeah?" he retorted skeptically, craning his neck to try to see himself.

"You think you've got problems?" Massha burst in. "Look at what I'm supposed to wear! I'll trade your cloak for this rig any day."

As you might have noticed, the team was having more than a little difficulty adapting to their disguises. Massha in particular was rebelling against her costume.

After having been floated over our escape like a balloon over a parade, we feared that she would be one of the most immediately recognizable of our group. As such, we not only dyed her garish orange hair, we insisted that her new costume cover as much of her as possible. To this end, Vilhelm had found a dress he called a "moo-moo," a name which did nothing toward endearing the garment to my apprentice.

"I mean, *really*, High Roller," she said, backing me toward a corner. "Isn't it bad enough that half the town's seen me as a blimp? Tell me I don't have to be a *cow* now."

"Honest, Massha," Vilhelm put in. "The style is fairly popular here in Blut. A lot of the ladies wear it who are . . . that is, are a bit. . . ."

"Fat!?"

She loomed over the little vampire.

"Is that the word you're groping for, Short and About To Become Extinct?"

"Let's face it, dear," Tananda said, coming to the rescue. "You *are* carrying a little extra weight there. Believe me, if there's one time you can't kid yourself about your body, it's when you're donning costumes. If anything, that outfit makes you look a little slimmer."

"Don't try to kid a kidder, sweetie," Massha sighed. "But you're right about the costuming thing. This thing is so *drab*, though. First I'm a blimp, and now I'm an army tent."

"Now *that* I'll agree with," Tananda nodded. "Trust a man to find a drab mu-mu. Tell you what. There's a scarf I was going to use for a belt, but maybe you could wear it around your neck."

I was afraid that last crack would touch off another explosion, but Massha took it as a helpful suggestion and the two of them went off in search of other possible adornments.

"Got a minute, partner?"

From the tone of Aahz's voice, I knew the moment I had been dreading had arrived.

Chumley didn't have to worry about a disguise at all, as trolls were not uncommon in this dimension. Tananda also insisted that she looked enough like a vampire to pass with only minimal modifications. I hadn't seen any vampires with green hair, but she claimed that she had, so, as always, I yielded to her greater experience in these matters. I was also on the "minimal disguise" list, everyone agreeing that no one in Blut had gotten enough of a look at me to fix the image in their mind. While I wasn't wild about being so unmemorable, I went along with it . . . especially when I saw what Guido and Massha were going through. The problems with those two notables have already been mentioned: troublesome, but not insurmountable. Then there was Aahz. . . .

"Is there something wrong?" I asked innocently.

"You bet your dragon there's something wrong!" my partner snarled. "And don't try to play innocent with me! It didn't work when you were my apprentice, and it sure isn't going to work now."

Aahz's disguise had presented us with some knotty problems. Not only was he the most wanted member of our party, he was also easily the most distinctive. After the trial and his time in jail, it was doubtful that there was a single citizen of Blut who wouldn't recognize him on sight. I mean, there just aren't that many scaly green demons wandering around any dimension . . . except possibly his home dimension of Perv. It was therefore decided . . . almost unanimously . . . that not only would we change my partner's color with make-up, but that it would also be necessary to change his sex.

"Does this, perchance, have something to do with your disguise?" I inquired, trying to keep a straight face.

"Yes, it has something to do with my disguise," he mimicked, "and, so help me, partner or no, if you let that smile get away, I'll punch your lights out. Understand?"

With a great effort I sucked my cheeks in and bit my lower lip.

"Seriously, though," he said, almost pleading, "a joke's a joke, but you don't really expect me to go out in public looking like *this*, do you?"

In addition to the aforementioned make-up, Aahz's disguise required a dress and a wig. Because of the size of his head (a problem Vilhelm had wisely down-played as much as possible) the selection of wigs available had been understandably small. In fact, the only available in his size was a number called "Lady Go-GoDiva," which involved a high blonde beehive style offset by a long ponytail that hung down to his knees. Actually, the ponytail turned out to be a blessing in disguise, as the dark blue dress Vilhelm had selected for my partner turned out to have an exceptionally low neckline, and the hair draped over his shoulder helped hide the problem we had had finding ample or suitable material to stuff his bosom with.

"As my wise old mentor once told me when I was faced with a similar dilemma," I said sagely, "what does it matter what people think of you? They aren't supposed to know it's you, anyway. That's the whole idea of a disguise."

"But this get-up is humiliating!"

"My words precisely when someone else I could name deemed it necessary for *me* to dress up as a girl, remember?"

"You're enjoying this, aren't you?" Aahz glowered, peering at me suspiciously.

"Well, there are a couple of other options," I admitted.

"That's more like it!" he grinned, reaching for his wig.

"You could stay behind. . . ."

His hand stopped just short of its mission.

". . . or we could forget the whole thing and pay the fine ourselves."

The hand retreated as my partner's shoulders sagged in defeat. I felt no joy at the victory. If anything, I had been half hoping he would be embarrassed enough to take me up on my suggestion of abandoning the project. I should have known better. When there's money involved, it takes more than embarrassment to throw Aahz off the scent . . . whether the embarrassment is his own or someone else's.

"All right, everybody," I called, hiding my disappointment. "Are we ready to go?"

"Remember your sunglasses!" Tananda added.

That was the final touch to our disguises. To hide our non-red eyes, each of us donned a pair of sunglasses. Surveying the final result, I had to admit that aside from Tananda and Chumley, we didn't look like us. Exactly what we *did* look like I wouldn't venture to say, but we sure didn't look like *us!*

"Okay," Aahz chimed in, his discomfort apparently behind him. "Does everyone have their marching orders? Vilhelm? Are you sure you can track us on that thing?"

"No problem," the little vampire nodded. "When things get slow around here I use this rig to do a little window peeking right here in town. Covering the streets is even easier."

"Remember," I told him, "watch for our signal. When we catch up with this Vic character, we're going to want you to get some responsible local witnesses there chop-chop."

"Well now," Aahz grinned evilly, "you don't have to be *too* quick about it. I wouldn't mind having a little time alone with him before we turn him over to the authorities."

My heart sank a little. Aahz sounded determined to exact a bit of vengeance out of this hunt, and I wasn't at all sure he would restrict himself to Vic when it came time to express his ire.

I think Tananda noticed my concern.

"Ease up a little, Aahz," she said casually. "I don't mind helping you out of a tight spot, but count me out when it comes to excessive force for the sake of vengeance. It lacks class."

"Since when did you worry about excessive violence?" Aahz growled, then shrugged his acceptance. "Okay. But maybe we'll get lucky. Maybe he'll resist arrest."

I was still worried, but realized that that was about the most restraint I would get out of my partner.

"Now that that's settled," I said, producing Luanna's scarf, "Pepe, take a whiff of this."

"Enchanting," he smiled, nuzzling the piece of cloth. "A young lady, no? Eef ze body is as good as ze aroma, I will follow her to the end of ze world whether you accompany me or not."

I resisted an impulse to wrap the scarf around his neck and pull.

"All right, everybody," I said, retrieving the scarf and tucking it back into my tunic in what I hoped was a casual manner. "Let's go catch us a renegade vampire."

# Chapter XVII

*"The trail's got to be 'round here somewhere!"*
**—D. Boone**

**I**T was only a few hours short of sunset as we set out on our quest, a nagging reminder of exactly how long our efforts at physical disguise had taken. We had agreed to avoid following Pepe as a group so as not to attract attention. Instead, we moved singly or in groups of two, using both sides of the street and deliberately walking at different paces. The faster walkers averaged their progress with the slower by occasionally stopping to look into shop windows, thereby keeping our group together without actually appearing to. Tananda pointed out that not only would this procedure lessen our chances of being noticed, but also that it would maximize our chances for at least some of the group's escape if one of us should be discovered . . . a truly comforting thought.

Even though Luanna had claimed to have been watching for us at the Dispatcher's, it had been so long ago I fully expected her scent would have long since dissipated or at least been masked by the passage of numerous others. As such, I was moderately surprised when the werewolf signaled almost immediately that he had found the trail and headed off with a determined air. Either her scent was stronger than I had thought, or I had grossly underestimated Pepe's tracking ability.

The trail wound up and down the cobblestoned streets, and we followed as quickly as we could without abandoning our pretense of being casual strollers who did not know each other. For a while, our group made up the majority of the beings visible, causing me to doubt the effectiveness of our ruse, but soon the vampires began to emerge to indulge their taste for the nightlife and we became much less obvious.

I was paired up with Chumley, but the troll was strangely quiet as we made our way along. At first I thought he was simply concentrating on keeping the werewolf in sight, but as time wore on, I found the silence somehow unnerving. I had always respected Chumley as being one of the saner, leveler heads among our motley assemblage, and I was starting to have an uneasy impression that he was not wholeheartedly behind this venture.

"Is there something bothering you, Chumley?" I asked at last.

"Hmmm? Oh. Not really, Skeeve. I was just thinking."

"About that?"

The troll let out a small sigh.

"I was just contemplating our adversary, this Vic fellow. You know, from what's been said, he's quite resourceful in a devious sort of way."

That took me a little aback. So far I had considered our vampire foe to be everything from an annoyance to a nemesis. The idea of studying his methods had never entered my mind.

"What leads you to that conclusion?"

The troll pursed his lips as he organized his thoughts.

"Consider what he's accomplished so far. The entire time we've known of him, he's been on the run . . . first from the Deveels, and then from Aahz, who's no slouch at hunting people once he sets his mind to it. Now, assuming for the moment that Vic is actually the brains of the group, he was quick enough to take advantage of being left alone in your waiting room to escape out the back door. He couldn't have planned that in advance, even knowing about the door. He probably had some other plan in mind, and formulated this new course of action on the spot."

We paused for a moment to let a small group of vampires cross the intersection in front of us.

"Now, that would have sufficed for an escape in most instances, but they happened to pick an exit route that left you and Aahz responsible, which set your partner on their trail," Chumley continued. "With nothing to go on but your reputations, Vic not only correctly deduced that he would be followed, but he also managed to spot Aahz's weakness and exploit it to frame him and make it stick . . . again, not the easiest task, particularly realizing it involved convincing and coaching his two accomplices in their roles."

All of this was doing nothing for my peace of mind. I was having enough difficulty forcing myself to believe that we were really hunting a vampire, the sort of creature I normally avoid at all costs, without having to deal with the possibility that he was shrewd and resourceful as well. Still, I had learned that ignoring unpleasant elements of a caper was perhaps the worst way to prepare for them.

"Keep going," I urged.

"Well," the troll sighed, "when you stumbled on his hiding place at the Woof Writers, he didn't panic. He waited to hear as much of your plans as possible, all the while taking advantage of the opportunity to assess you first-hand, then timed his escape so as to catch you all flat-footed."

I digested this distasteful addition to the rapidly growing data file. "Do you really think he was sizing me up?"

"There's no doubt in my mind. Not only was he gauging your skills and determination, he was successful enough at second-guessing you, based on the results of his studies, to be waiting to sound the alarm when you busted Aahz out of jail. . . . a particularly bold move when one realizes that he was running the risk of being recognized, which would have blown his frame-up of your partner."

"Bold or desperate," I said thoughtfully. "That's probably why he waited until we had actually sprung Aahz and were on the way down before he blew the whistle. If we had gotten away unscathed, then the frame would be useless, so at that point he really wasn't risking anything."

"Have it your way," the troll shrugged. "The final analysis remains that we have one tough nut to crack. One can only wonder what he will do when we catch up with him this time."

"If he's performing up to par, it could be rough on us."

Chumley shot me a sidelong glance.

"Actually, I was thinking it could be rough on your lady fair . . . if he has managed to observe the feelings you have for her."

I started to protest, then the impact of his theory hit me and my embarrassment gave way to concern.

"Is it really that apparent? Do you think he could spot it? If so, he might already have done something to Luanna for having contacted us."

"It stands out all over you to anyone who knows you," Chumley said, shaking his head. "As for someone watching you for the first time . . . I just don't know. He'd be more likely to deduce it from the information you had . . . such as his name. That kind of data had to come from somewhere, though there's an outside chance that with your current reputation he'll assume that you gleaned it by some magical source."

I barely heard him. My mind was focused on the possibility that

Luanna might be hurt, and that I might indirectly have been the cause. A black well of guilt was rising up to swallow me, when I felt a hand on my shoulder.

"Don't tune out now, Skeeve," Chumley was saying, shaking me slightly. "First of all, we're going to need you shortly. Secondly, even if Vic's figured out that you're in love with her, I don't think he'll have hurt her. If anything, he'll save her for a trump card to use against us."

I drew a deep ragged breath.

". . . and he'll be just the bastard to do it, too," I said. "I don't know what I'll be able to do, for us or for her, but I'll be ready to try. Thanks, Chumley."

The troll was studying me closely.

"Actually, I wasn't thinking that he was such a blighter," he said. "More like a clever, resourceful person who's gotten in over his head and is trying his best to ad-lib his way out. Frankly, Skeeve old boy, in many ways he reminds me of you. You might think about that when attempting to appraise his likely courses of action and how to counter them."

I tried again to weigh what he was saying, but all I could think about was what the consequences of this hunt could mean to Luanna. It was difficult enough for me to accept that we would have to force Luanna and her cohorts to answer to the authorities for their indiscretions, but the thought of placing her in physical danger was unbearable.

I looked around for Aahz, fully intending to put an end to this hunt once and for all. To my surprise, the rest of the group was assembled on the corner ahead, and my partner was beckoning us to join them.

"What's going on?" I asked, almost to myself.

"Just off-hand," Chumley replied, "I'd say we've reached our destination."

A cold wave of fear washed over me, and I hurried to the rendezvous with Chumley close behind.

"We're in luck," Aahz announced as I arrived. "Guido here says he saw Vic entering the building just as we got here. It's my guess they're all inside right now."

"Aahz, I—I want us to quit right now," I blurted, painfully aware of how weak it sounded.

"Oh?" my partner said, cocking an eyebrow at me. "Any particular reason?"

I licked my lips, feeling the eyes of the whole group on me.

"Only one. I'm in love with one of the fugitives . . . the girl."

"Yeah. Now tell me something I didn't know," Aahz smirked, winking at me.

"You knew?"

"All of us knew. In fact, we were just discussing it. Remember, we all know you . . . and me probably best of all. It's already been pretty much decided to let your love-light go. Think of it as a present from us to you. The other two are ours."

Five minutes ago, that would have made me deliriously happy. Now, it only seemed to complicate things.

"But Chumley was just saying that there's a chance they might hurt her if they find out she helped us," I explained desperately. "Can't we just let them all go?"

"Not a chance, partner," Aahz said firmly. "In addition to our original reasons, you've just mentioned the new one. Your girlfriend could be in trouble, and the only way to be sure she's safe is to remove her partners . . . Fast."

"Believe him, Skeeve," Tananda urged. "It may not be nice, but it's the best way."

"Really, Boss," Guido said quietly. "Unless we finish this thing here and now, you're never goin' to know if she's safe, know what I mean?"

That almost made sense, but I was still worried. "I don't know, Aahz. . . ."

"Well I do," my partner snapped. "And the longer we stand down here, the more chance there is that they'll either get away or set up a trap. If you're uncertain, stay down here . . . in fact, that's not a bad idea. Massha, you stay down here with him in case they try to bolt out this way. While you're waiting, watch for the witnesses that Vilhelm's supposed to be sending along. Tananda, you and Chumley and Guido come along with me. This is a job for experienced hard-cases. Pepe, we appreciate your help, but this isn't really your fight."

"But of course." The werewolf grinned. "Besides, I am a lo-var, not a figh-tar. I will wait here to see the finale, eh?"

"But Aahz. . . ."

"Really, partner, you'll be more help down here. This isn't your kind of fight, and we need someone to deal with the witnesses. You're good at that kind of thing."

"I was going to ask if you had given the signal to Vilhelm."

"Signal?" Aahz blinked. "How's this for a signal?!"

With that, he tore off his wig and threw it on the ground, followed closely by his dress.

"Think he'll get the message? Besides, no way am I going to try to fight in that get-up."

"Now you're talkin'!" Guido crowed.

In a flash he had discarded his cloak and was pulling on his now-familiar trench coat.

"Where did that come from?" I demanded.

"Had it with me all the time," the bodyguard said smugly. "It would have been like leaving an old friend behind."

"Well, if you and your old friend are ready," Tananda murmured, "we'd better get started."

"Itching for action?" Aahz grinned.

"No. More like eager to get off the street," she said. "Since you boys have shown your true colors, we're starting to draw a crowd."

Sure enough, the vampires on the street had ceased whatever they had been doing before and were gathering in knots, whispering together and pointing at our group.

"Umm . . . we'd better finish this fast," Aahz said, shooting a nervous glance around. "All right, gang. Let's go for the gusto!"

"Go for the what?" I asked, but they were already on their way into the building.

I noticed they were all moving faster than normal. I also noticed that Massha, Pepe, and I were the only ones left on the street . . . and now the crowd was pointing at us!

# Chapter XVIII

*"I didn't come all this way to sit out the fight!"*

**—R. Balboa**

"**W**HAT'S going on?"

I looked around to find that one of the vampires had detached himself from his group of friends and was addressing me directly.

"Beats me," Massha interceded. "A bunch of off-worlder types just took off into that building with blood in their eyes. I'm waiting to see what happens next."

"Far out," the vampire breathed, peering toward the structure. "I haven't seen that many off-worlders in one place except in the flickers. Wasn't one of them that escaped murderer, Aahz?"

I really didn't want this character to join our little group. While our disguises seemed to be holding up under casual inspection, I was pretty sure that prolonged close scrutiny would reveal not only the nonlocal nature of Massha and myself, but also the fact that we were trying to hide it.

"You may be right," I said, playing a hunch. "If so, it's a good thing you happened along. We're going to need all the help we can get."

"Help? Help for what?"

"Why to catch the murderer, of course. We can't let him get away again. I figure it's our duty to stop him ourselves or at least slow him up until the authorities arrive."

"We? You mean the three of you? You're going to try to stop a murderer all by yourselves?"

"Four of us now that you're here."

The vampire started backing away.

"Ummm . . . actually I've got to get back to my friends. We're on our way to a party. Sorry I can't help, but I'll spread the word that you're looking for volunteers, okay?"

"Hey, thanks," I called as if I believed him. "We'll be right here."

By the time I had finished speaking, he had disappeared into the crowd. Mission accomplished.

"Nicely done, my friend," Pepe murmured. "He does not, how you say, want to get involved, no?"

"That's right," I said, my eyes on the building again. "And to tell you the truth, I'm not too wild about the idea either. What do you think, Massha? It's awfully quiet in there."

"I'll say," my apprentice agreed. "I'm just trying to figure out if that's a good or a bad sign. Another ten minutes and I'm heading in there to check it out myself."

I nodded my consent, even though I doubted she saw it. We both had our eyes glued to the building, memorizing its every detail.

It was a four-story structure . . . or it would be if it weren't for the curved peak that jutted out from the roof fully half-again as high as the main building. It looked as if the builder had suddenly added the adornment in a last-minute attempt to have his work stand as tall or taller than its neighbors. From the number of windows in the main structure, I guessed it was an apartment building or a hotel or something. In short, it looked like it had a lot of little rooms. I found myself wondering exactly how our strike force was supposed to locate their target without kicking in every door in the place . . . a possibility I wouldn't put past Aahz.

I was about to express this fear to Massha when a loud crash sounded from within.

"What was that?" I demanded of no one in particular.

"Sounded like a loud crash," my apprentice supplied helpfully.

I forced myself to remember that no one out here knew any more about what was going on inside than I did.

After the crash, everything was quiet once more. I tried to tell myself that the noise might have nothing at all to do with the strike force, but I didn't believe it for a minute. The crowd was talking excitedly to each other and straining to see the various windows. They seemed quite confident that something else would happen soon, much more than I, but then again, maybe as city dwellers they were more accustomed to such vigils than I.

Suddenly, Tananda appeared in the doorway.

"Did they come out this way?" she called.

"No one's been in or out since you went in," I responded.

She swore and started to re-enter the building.

"What happened?" I shouted desperately.

"We nailed one of them, but Vic got away. He's loose in the building somewhere, and he's got the girl with him."

With that, she disappeared before I could make any further inquiries. Terrific.

"Exciting, eh?" Pepe said. "I tell you, I could watch such a chase for hours."

"Well, I can't," I snapped. "I've had it with sitting on the sidelines. Massha? I'm going in there. Want to come?"

"I dunno, Hot Stuff. I'd like to, but somebody should be here to plug this escape route."

"Fine. You wait here, and I'll. . . ."

I turned to enter the building and bumped headlong into Vilhelm.

"What are you doing here?" I demanded, not really caring.

The Dispatcher shook his head slightly to clear it. Being smaller, he had gotten the worse of our collision.

"I'm here with the witnesses, remember? I was supposed to bring them."

"You were supposed to *send* them. Oh well, where are they?"

"Right here," he said, gesturing to a sullen group of vampires standing behind him. "This is Kirby, and Paul, and Richard, and Adele, and Scott . . . some of the most respected citizens in town. Convince them and you're home free."

Looking at the group, I suddenly realized how Aahz had ended up on death row. If the jury had been anything like these specimens, they would have hung their own mothers for jaywalking. While I didn't relish the thought of trying to convince them of anything, I found myself being very glad I didn't have to deal with them on a regular basis.

"Okay. So we're here," the one identified as Kirby growled. "Just what is it we're supposed to be witnessing? If this is one of your cockamamie deals, Vilhelm. . . ."

I interrupted simply by taking my sunglasses off and opening my eyes wide, displaying their whites. The bad reputation of humans in this dimension was sufficient to capture their undivided attention.

"Perhaps you recall a certain murder trial that took place not too long ago?" I said, trying to work the toothblack off with my tongue. "Well, the convicted murderer who escaped is my partner, and right now he's inside that building. He and a few of our friends are about to show you one surprisingly lively corpse . . . specifically the fellow that my partner is supposed to have killed. I trust that will be sufficient to convince you of his innocence?"

While the vampires were taken aback by my presence in their midst, they recovered quickly. Like I said, they were real hard cases and didn't stay impressed very long.

"So how much time is this going to take?" Kirby said impatiently. "I'm giving up my sleep for this, and I don't get much of it."

That was a good question, so, not having an answer, I stalled.

"You sleep nights? I thought. . . ."

"I'm a day owl," the vampire waved. "It's easier to get my work done when the phone isn't ringing every five minutes . . . which usually means waiting until everyone else is asleep. But we're getting off the subject. The bottom line is that my time is valuable, and the same holds true for my colleagues. If you think we're going to just stand around here until. . . ."

There was a sudden outcry from the crowd, and we all looked to find them talking excitedly and pointing up at the roof.

A figure had emerged, fighting to pick his way across the steeply sloped surface while dragging a struggling girl by one arm.

Vic!

This was the first time I had gotten a clear look at my foe, and I was moderately surprised. He was younger than I had expected, barely older than myself, and instead of a menacing cloak, he was sporting a white turtleneck and sunglasses. It suddenly occurred to me that if sunglasses enabled me to pass for a vampire, that they would also let a vampire pass undetected among humans.

The vampire suddenly stopped as his path was barred by Tananda, who appeared as if by magic over the edge of the roof. He turned to retrace his steps, only to find that the trio of Aahz, Guido, and Chumley had emerged behind him, cutting off his retreat.

"I believe, gentlemen and lady, that up there is the elusive body that started this whole thing," I heard myself saying. "If you can spare a few more moments, I think *my* colleagues will have him in custody so that you might interrogate him at your leisure."

"Don't be too sure of that, High Roller," Massha cautioned. "Look!"

His chosen routes of escape cut off, Vic was now scrabbling up the roof peak itself, Luanna hanging in his grip. While I had to admire his strength, I was at a loss to understand what he was trying to accomplish with the maneuver. It was obvious that he had been exposed, so why didn't he just give it up?

The answer became apparent in the next few moments. Reaching the apex of the roof, the vampire underwent a chilling metamorphosis. Before the strike force could reach him, he hunched forward and huge batwings began to grow and spread from his back. His plans gone awry, he was getting ready to escape.

In immediate response to his efforts, Tananda and Guido both produced projectile weapons and shouted something to him. Though the distance was too great to make out the words clearly, it was obvious to me that they were threatening to shoot him down if he tried to take to the air.

"We may have a murder case yet," Kirby murmured, squinting to watch the rooftop drama unfold.

"Murder?" I exclaimed, turning on him. "How can you call it murder if they're only trying to keep him from escaping *your* justice?"

"That wasn't what I meant," the vampire said, never taking his eyes from the action. "Check it out."

I looked . . . and my heart stood still.

Aahz had been trying to ease up the roof peak closer to Vic and his hostage. Vic must have seen him, because he was now holding Luanna out over the drop as he pointed an angry finger at my partner. The threat was unmistakable.

"You know, eet is people like zat who give ze vampires a bad name, eh?" Pepe said, nudging me.

I ignored him, lost in my own anxiety and frustration at the stalemated situation. A noticeably harder jab from Massha broke my reverie, however.

"Hey, Hot Stuff. Do you see what I see?"

I tore my gaze away from the confrontation and shot a glance her way. She was standing motionless, her brow furrowed with concentration and her eyes closed.

It took me a few moments to realize what she was doing, then I followed suit, scarcely daring to hope.

There it was! A force line! A big, strong, beautiful, glorious force line.

I had gotten so used to not having any magical energy at my disposal in this dimension that I hadn't even bothered to check!

I opened myself to the energy, relished it for a fleet moment, then rechanneled it.

"Excuse me," I said with a smile, handing my sunglasses to Kirby. "It's about time I took a hand in this directly."

With that, I reached out with my mind, pushed off against the ground, and soared upward, setting a course for the cornered vampire on the roof.

# Chapter XIX

*"All right, pilgrim. This is between you and me!"*

**—A. Hamilton**

I had hoped to make my approach unobserved, but as I flew upward, the crowd below let out a roar that drew the attention of the combatants on the roof. Terrific! When I wanted unobtrusive, I got notoriety.

Reaching a height level with that of the vampire, I hovered at a discreet distance.

"Put away the nasties," I called to Tananda and Guido. "He's not getting away by air."

They looked a bit rebellious, but followed the order.

"What's with the Peter Pan bit, partner?" Aahz shouted. "Are you feeling your Cheerioats, or did you finally find a force line?"

"Both." I waved back, then turned my attention to Vic.

Though his eyes were obscured by his sunglasses, I could feel his hateful glare burning into me to the bone.

"Why don't you just call it quits?" I said in what I hoped was a calm, soothing tone. "It's over. We've got you outflanked."

For a moment he seemed to waver with indecision. Then, without warning, he threw Luanna at Aahz.

"Why can't you all just leave me alone!" he screamed, and dove off the roof.

Aahz somehow managed to snag the girl's hurtling form, though in the process he lost his balance and tumbled backward down the roof peak, cushioning the impact with his own body.

I hesitated, torn between the impulse to check on Luanna's welfare and the desire to pursue Vic.

"Go get him!" my partner called. "We're fine!"

That was all the encouragement I needed. Wheeling to my right, I plunged after the fleeing vampire.

What followed was one of the more interesting experiences of my limited magical career. As I mentioned before, my form of flying magically isn't really flying . . . it's controlled levitation of oneself. This made enthusiastic pursuit a real challenge to my abilities. To counterbalance the problem, however, Vic couldn't really fly either . . . at least he never seemed to flap his wings. Instead, he appeared content to soar and bank and catch an occasional updraft. This forced him to continually circle and double back through roughly the same area time and time again. This suited me fine, as I didn't want to wander too far away from my energizing force line now that I had found it. The idea of running out of power while suspended fifty feet in the air did not appeal to me at all.

Anyway, our aerial duel rapidly became a curious matching of styles with Vic's swooping and circling in his efforts to escape and my vertical and horizontal maneuverings to try to intercept him. Needless to say, the conflict was not resolved quickly. As soon as I would time a move that came close enough to an interception to justify attempting it again, Vic would realize his danger and alter his pattern, leaving me to try to puzzle out his new course.

The crowd loved it.

They whooped and hollered, their words of encouragement alternately loud and faint as we changed altitude. It was impossible to tell which of us they were cheering for, though for a while I thought it was me, considering the approval they had expressed when I first took off to join the battle. Then I noticed that the crowd was considerably larger than it had been when I entered the fray, and I realized that many of them had not been around to witness the beginning of the conflict. To them, it probably appeared that a monster from another dimension was chasing one of their fellow beings through the sky.

That thought was disquieting enough that I spared some of my attention to scan the surrounding rooftops on the off-chance that a local sniper might be preparing to help his fellow countryman. It turned out to be the wisest decision I had made.

As I was looking over my shoulder, I plowed full force into Vic, who had doubled back on his own path. The feint would have probably worked if I had seen it, but as it was we collided at maximum speed, the impact momentarily stunning us both. I managed to grab a double handful of the vampire's turtleneck as we fell about ten feet before I adjusted my levitation strength to support us both.

"What's the matter with you!" I demanded, trying to shake him, which succeeded only in moving us both back and forth in the air. "Running away won't help."

Then I realized he was crying.

Somehow, this struck me as immensely unfair. I mean, how are you supposed to stay mad at a villain that cries? Okay. So I'm a soft tough. But the crying really did make a difference.

"I can't fight you all!" he sobbed, tears streaming down his cheeks. "Maybe if I knew some magic I could take one of you with me . . . but at least you're going to have to work for your kill!"

With that he tore loose from my grasp and swooped away.

His words stunned me so much I almost let him escape. Fortunately, I had the presence of mind to call out to him.

"Hey, dummy! Nobody's trying to kill you!"

"Yeah, sure," he shouted back. "You're up here just for the fun of it."

He was starting to bank toward the street, and I knew I'd only have time for one more try.

"Look! Will you stop running if I quit chasing you? I think there's a major misunderstanding here."

He glanced back over his shoulder and saw that I was still where I was when we collided. Altering his course slightly, he flared his wings and landed on a carved gargoyle ornament jutting out from the side of the building.

"Why should you want to talk?" he called, wiping his face with one hand. "I thought nothing I could say would change your mind."

"You'd be surprised," I shouted back. "Say, do you mind if I land on that ledge near you? I feel pretty silly just hanging here."

He glanced at the indicated ledge, and I could see his wings flex nervously.

"C'mon," I urged. "I'll be further away from you there than I was when we started this chase back on the roof. You'll still have a clean shot at getting away if I try anything."

He hesitated, then nodded his consent.

Moving slowly so as not to alarm him, I maneuvered my way to my new perch. Truth to tell, I was glad to get something solid under my feet again. Even using magic, flying can take a lot out of you, and I was relieved to get a chance to rest. Now that I was closer, I could see that Vic was breathing heavily himself. Apparently his form of flying was no picnic either.

"All right," I said in a much more conversational tone. "Let's take this thing from the top. Who says we're trying to kill you?"

"Matt does," the vampire responded. "He's the one who filled me in on you and your pet demon. To be honest with you, I had never even heard of you until Matt explained whose home we had stumbled into."

"Matt?" I frowned.

Then I remembered. Of course. The third member of the fugitive party. Luanna's old con artist partner who nobody had been paying attention to at all. A germ of an idea began to form in my head.

"And he says we're out to kill you?"

"That's right. According to him nobody crosses the Great Skeeve or makes a fool of him and lives . . . and using your house as an escape route definitely qualifies."

The reputation thing again. I was beginning to realize why so many magicians preferred to lead the lives of recluses.

"That's crazy, Vic," I said. "If I tried to kill everybody who's made a fool of me, I'd be armpit-deep in corpses."

"Oh yeah?" he shot back. "Well, if you aren't out to kill me, why did you send your pet demon after us?"

Despite my resolve to settle this thing amicably, I was starting to get annoyed.

"First of all, he's not my pet demon. He's my partner and his name is **Aahz**. Secondly, I didn't send him. He knocked me out cold and came himself. Third and final, he was never out to kill you. He was trying to bring you and your cohorts back to Deva so we wouldn't get stuck paying off the people you swindled plus a hefty fine. Are you getting all this, or am I going too fast for you?"

"But I didn't swindle anybody," the vampire protested. "Those two offered me a job helping them sell magic charms. I didn't know they weren't genuine until Matt said the customers were mad and we had to run. I suggested we hide out here because it's the only place I know besides the Bazaar."

"Uh-huh," I said, studying the sky. "Next you'll be saying you didn't frame my partner *or* sound the alarm on us when we tried to spring him."

Vic's wings dropped as he hung his head.

"That much I can't deny . . . but I was scared! I framed the demon because it was the only way I could think of to get him off our trail for a while. I really thought he could get loose on his own, and when I saw you at the Woof Writers', I knew he was going to get away. I sounded the alarm hoping you would all get caught and be detained long enough to give us a head start. Looking back on it, they were pretty ratty things to do, but what would *you* do if you had a pack of killer demons on your trail?"

Now *that* I could identify with. Chumley's words about Vic and I being alike echoed in my ears. I had had to improvise in some pretty hairy situations myself.

"Wait a minute!" I growled. "Speaking of killer demons, what was that bit with you dangling Luanna over the edge of the building back there?"

"I was bluffing," the vampire shrugged. "Your friends were threatening to shoot me if I tried to fly away, and it was the only thing I could think of to try to get them to back off. I wouldn't deliberately hurt anyone . . . especially Luanna. She's sweet. That's why I was trying to help her escape with me after they caught Matt."

That brought me to the question that had been nagging at my mind since I started this wild chase.

"If you don't mind me asking, why didn't you just change into mist and drift away? We could never have caught you then."

Vic gave a short, bitter laugh.

"Do you know how rough it is to turn into mist? Well, you're a magician. Maybe you do know. Anyway, you might as well know the truth. I'm not much in the magic department . . . in fact, I'm pretty much a bust as a vampire. I can't even change all the way into a bat! These wings are the best I've been able to do. That's why I was looking for a new life in the Bazaar. I'd rather be a first-class anything than a third-rate vampire. I mean, I don't even like blood!"

"You should meet my bodyguard." I grinned despite myself. "He's a gangster who's allergic to garlic."

"Garlic? I love garlic."

I opened my mouth to offer him Guido's job, then shut it rapidly. If this character was half as desperate as he sounded, he'd probably take the offer seriously and accept, and then where would I be? All we needed to complete our menagerie was a magic-poor vampire.

"Well," I said instead, "I guess that answers all my questions except one. Now that you know we aren't trying to kill you, are you ready to quit running and face the music?"

The vampire gnawed his lower lip as he thought.

"You're sure it will be all right?"

"I can't say for sure until I talk to my partner," I admitted, "but I'm pretty sure things will be amenable. The main problem is to get the murder charges against him dropped . . . which I think we've already accomplished. As for you, I think the only thing they could have against you is false arrest, and there's no way Aahz will press charges on that one."

"Why not?"

I gave him my best grin.

"Because if he did, we couldn't take you back to Deva to deal with the swindling charge. Believe me, if given a chance between revenge and saving money, you can trust Aahz to be forgiving every time."

Vic thought about it for a few more moments, then shrugged.

"Embarrassment I'm used to dealing with, and I think I can beat the swindling rap. C'mon, Skeeve. Let's get this thing over with."

Having finally reached a truce, however temporary, we descended together to face the waiting crowd.

# Chapter XX

*"There's no accounting for taste!"*
—Colonel Sanders

"**B**UT Skeeve. . . ."
BANG!
". . . I told you before. . . ."
BANG! BANG!
". . . I could never abandon Matt. . . ."
BANG!
". . . he's my partner!"
BANG! BANG!
"But Lu. . . ."
BANG!
". . . excuse me. HEY, PARTNER! COULD YOU KNOCK OFF THE HAMMERING FOR A MINUTE? I'M TRYING TO HAVE A CONVERSATION HERE!"

"Not a chance," Aahz growled around his mouthful of nails. "I'm shutting this door permanently before anything else happens. But tell you what, I'll try to hammer quietly."

If you deduce from all this that we were back at our place on Deva, you're right. After some long, tense conversations with the citizens of Blut and fond farewells to Vilhelm and Pepe, our whole crew, including our three captives, had trooped back to the castle and through the door without incident.

I had hoped to have a few moments alone with Luanna, but, after several attempts, the best I had been able to manage was this conversation in the reception room under the watchful eyes of Aahz and Matt.

Matt, incidentally, turned out to be a thoroughly unpleasant individual with a twisted needle-nose, acne, a receding hairline, and the beginnings of a beer-belly. For the life of me, I couldn't figure out what Luanna saw in him.

"But that was when you thought he was in a jam," I said, resuming the argument. "Aahz and I have already promised to help defend him *and* Vic when they go before the Merchants Association. There's no need to stand by him yourself."

"I don't understand you, Skeeve," Luanna declared, shaking her head. "If I wouldn't leave Matt when he was in trouble, why should I leave him when things look like they're going to turn out okay? I know you don't like him, but he's done all right by me so far . . . and I still owe him for getting me away from the farm."

"But we're making you a good offer," I tried again desperately. "You can stay here and work for Aahz and me, and if you're interested we could even teach you some real magic so you don't have to. . . ."

She stopped me by simply laying a hand on my arm.

"I know it's a good offer, Skeeve, and it's nice of you to make it. But for the time being I'm content to stay with Matt. Maybe sometime in the future, when I have a little more to offer you in return, I'll take you up on it . . . if the deal's still open."

"Well," I sighed, "if that's really what you want. . . ."

"Hey! Don't take it so hard, buddy," Matt laughed, clapping his hand on my shoulder. "You win some, you lose some. This time you lost. No hard feelings. Maybe you'll have better luck with the next one. We're both men of the world, and we know one broad's just like any other."

"Matt, *buddy,*" I said through clenched teeth, "get that hand off my shoulder before it loses a body."

As I said, even on our short trip back from Limbo I had been so underwhelmed by Matt that I no longer even bothered trying to be polite or mask my dislike for him. He could grate on my nerves faster than anyone I had ever met. If he was a successful con artist, able to inspire trust from total strangers, then I was the Queen of May.

"Matt's just kidding," Luanna soothed, stepping between us.

"Well I'm not," I snarled. "Just remember you're welcome here any time you get fed up with this slug."

"Oh, I imagine we'll be together for quite some time," Matt leered, patting Luanna lightly on her rump. "With you big shots vouching for us we should be able to beat this swindling rap . . . and even if we lose, so what? All it means is I'll have to give them back their crummy twenty gold pieces."

Aahz's hammering stopped abruptly . . . or maybe it was my heart. I tried vainly to convince myself that I hadn't heard him right.

"Twenty gold pieces?" I said slowly.

"Yeah. They caught on to us a lot quicker here at the Bazaar than I thought they would. It wasn't much of a haul even by my standards. I can't get over the fact that you big shots went through so much trouble to drag us back here over a measly twenty gold pieces. There must be more to this principle thing than I realized."

"Ummm . . . could I have a word with you, partner?" Aahz said, putting down his hammer.

"I was about to ask the same thing," I admitted, stepping to the far side of the room.

Once we were alone, we stared at each other, neither wanting to be the first to speak.

"You never did get around to asking Hay-ner how much was at stake, did you?" Aahz sighed absently.

"That's the money side of negotiations and I thought you covered it," I murmured. "Funny, we both stood right there the whole time and heard every word that was said, and neither of us caught that omission."

"Funny. Right. I'm dying." My partner grimaced.

"Not as much as you will if word of this gets out," I warned. "I vote that we give them the money to pay it off. I don't want to, but it's the only way I can think of to keep this thing from becoming public knowledge."

"Done." Aahz nodded. "But let me handle it. If Matt the Rat there gets wind of the fact that the whole thing was a mistake on our part, he'd probably blackmail us for our eyeteeth."

"Right," I agreed.

With that, we, the two most sought-after, most highly-paid magicians at the Bazaar, turned to deal with our charges, reminded once more why humility lies at the core of greatness.

# LITTLE MYTH MARKER

# Chapter I

*"The difference between an inside
straight and a blamed fool is callin'
the last bet!"*

**B. Maverick**

"**C**ALL!"

"Bump."

"Bump again."

"Who're you trying to kid? You got elf-high nothing!"

"Try me!"

"All right! Raise you limit."

"Call."

"Call."

"Elf-high nothing bumps you back limit."

"Fold."

"Call."

For those of you starting this book at the beginning (Bless you! I hate it when readers cheat by reading ahead!), this may be a little confusing. The above is the dialogue during a game of dragon poker. What is dragon poker, you ask? Well, it's reputed to be the most complicated card game ever invented . . . and here at the Bazaar at Deva, they should know.

The Bazaar is the biggest shopping maze and haggling spot in all the dimensions, and consequently gets a lot of dimension travelers (demons) passing through. In addition to the shops, stalls, and restaurants (which really doesn't do justice to the extent or variety of the Bazaar) there is a thriving gambling community in residence here. They are always on the lookout for a new game, particularly one that involves betting, and the more complicated the better. The basic philosophy is that a complicated game is more easily won by those who devote full time to its study than by the tourists who have dabbled in it or are trying to learn it as the game goes on. Anyway, when a Deveel bookie tells me that dragon poker is the most complicated card game ever, I tend to believe him.

"Fold."

"Call."

"Okay, Mr. Skeeve the Grater. Let's see you beat this! Dragons full!"

He exposed his hole cards with a flourish that bordered on a challenge. Actually, I had been hoping he would drop out of the hand. This particular individual (Grunk, I think his name was) was easily two heads taller than me and had bright red eyes, canines almost as long as my forearm, and a nasty disposition. He tended to speak in an angry shout, and the fact that he had been losing steadily had not mellowed him in the slightest.

"Well? C'mon! What have you got?"

I turned over my four hole cards, spread them next to the five already face up, then leaned back and smiled.

"That's it?" Grunk said, craning his neck and scowling at my cards. "But that's only . . ."

"Wait a minute," the player on his left chimed in. "It's Tuesday. That makes his unicorns wild."

"But it's a month with an 'M' in it!" someone else piped up. "So his ogre is only half of face value!"

"But there's an even number of players. . . ."

I told you it was a complicated game. Those of you who know me from my earlier adventures (blatant plug!) may wonder how it is I understand such a complex system. That's easy. I don't! I just bet, then spread the cards and let the other players sort out who won.

You may wonder what I was doing sitting in on a cutthroat game of dragon poker when I didn't even know the rules. Well, for once, I have an answer. I was enjoying myself on my own for a change.

You see, ever since Don Bruce, the Mob's fairy godfather, supposedly hired me to watch over the Mob's interests at the Bazaar and assigned me two bodyguards, Guido and Nunzio, I've rarely had a moment to myself. This weekend, however, my two watchdogs were off making their yearly report to Mob Central, leaving me to fend for myself. Obviously, before they left, they made me give my solemn promise to be careful. Also obviously, as soon as they were gone, I set out to do just the opposite.

Even aside from our percentage of the Mob's take at the Bazaar, our magic business had been booming, so money was no problem. I filched a couple thousand in gold from petty cash and was all set to go on a spree when an invitation arrived to sit in on one of the Geek's dragon poker games at his club, the Even-Odds.

As I said before, I know absolutely nothing about dragon poker other than the fact that at the end of a hand you have five cards face up and four face down. Anytime I've tried to get my partner, Aahz, to teach me more about the game, I've been lectured about "only playing games you know" and "don't go looking for trouble." Since I was already looking for mischief, the chance to defy both my bodyguards *and* my partner was too much to resist. I mean, I figured the worst that could happen was that I'd lose a couple thousand in gold. Right?

"You're all overlooking something. This is the forty-third hand and Skeeve there is sitting in a chair facing north!"

I took my cue from the groans and better-censored expressions of disgust and raked in the pot.

"Say, Geek," Grunk said, his red eyes glittering at me through half-lowered eyelids. "Are you *sure* this Skeeve fellow isn't using magic?"

"Guaranteed," responded the Deveel who was gathering the cards and shuffling for the next hand. "Any game I host here at the Even-Odds is monitored against magic *and* telepathy."

"Weelll, I don't normally play cards with magicians, and I've heard that Skeeve here is supposed to be pretty good in that department. Maybe he's good enough that you just can't catch him at it."

I was starting to get a little nervous. I mean, I wasn't using magic . . . and even if I was going to, I wouldn't know how to use it to rig a card game. The trouble was that Grunk looked perfectly capable of tearing my arms off if he thought I was cheating. I began racking my brain for some way to convince him without admitting to everyone at the table just how little I knew about magic.

"Relax, Grunk. Mr. Skeeve's a good player, that's all. Just because he wins doesn't mean he's cheating."

That was Pidge, the only other human-type in the game. I shot him a grateful smile.

"I don't mind someone winning," Grunk muttered defensively, "But he's been winning all night."

"I've lost more than you have," Pidge said, "and you don't see me griping. I'm tellin' you Mr. Skeeve is *good.* I've sat in on games with the Kid, and I should know."

"The Kid? You've played against him?" Grunk was visibly impressed.

"And lost my socks doing it," Pidge admitted wryly. "I'd say that Mr. Skeeve here is good enough to give him a run for his money, though."

"Gentlemen? Are we here to talk or to play cards?" the Geek interrupted, tapping the deck meaningfully.

"I'm out," Pidge said, rising to his feet. "I know when I'm outclassed —even if I have to go in the hole before I'll admit it. My marker still good, Geek?"

"It's good with me if nobody else objects."

Grunk noisily slammed his fist down on the table, causing several of my stacks of chips to fall over.

"What's this about markers?" he demanded. "I thought this was a cash-only game! Nobody said anything about playing for IOUs."

"Pidge here's an exception," the Geek said. "He's always made good on his marker before. Besides, you don't have to worry about it, Grunk. You aren't even getting all of *your* money back."

"Yeah. But I lost it betting against somebody who's betting markers instead of cash. It seems to me . . ."

"I'll cover his marker," I said loftily. "That makes it personal between him and me, so it doesn't involve anyone else at the table. Right, Geek?"

"That's right. Now shut up and play, Grunk. Or do you want us to deal you out?"

The monster grumbled a bit under his breath but leaned back and tossed in another chip to ante for the next hand.

"Thanks, Mr. Skeeve," Pidge said. "And don't worry. Like the Geek says, I always reclaim my marker."

I winked at him and waved vaguely as he left, already intent on the next hand as I tried vainly to figure out the rules of the game.

If my grand gesture seemed a little impulsive, remember that I'd been watching him play all night, and I knew how much he had lost. Even if all of it was on IOUs, I could cover it out of my winnings and still show a profit.

You see, Grunk was right. I had been winning steadily all night . . . a fact made doubly surprising by my ignorance of the game. Early on, however, I had hit on a system which seemed to be working very well: Bet the players, not the cards. On the last hand, I hadn't been betting that I had a winning hand, I was betting that Grunk had a losing hand. Luck had been against him all night, and he was betting wild to try to make up for his losses.

Following my system, I folded the next two hands, then hit them hard on the third. Most of the other players folded rather than question my judgment. Grunk stayed until the bitter end, hoping I was bluffing. It turned out that I was (my hand wasn't all that strong), but that his hand was even weaker. Another stack of chips tumbled into my hoard.

"That does it for me," Grunk said, pushing his remaining chips toward the Geek. "Cash me in."

"Me too."

"I should have left an hour ago. Would have saved myself a couple hundred."

The Geek was suddenly busy converting chips back to cash as the game broke up.

Grunk loitered for a few minutes after receiving his share of the bank. Now that we were no longer facing each other over cards, he was surprisingly pleasant.

"You know, Skeeve," he said, clapping a massive hand on my shoulder, "it's been a long time since I've been whipped that bad at dragon poker. Maybe Pidge was right. You're slumming here. You should try for a game with the Kid."

"I was just lucky."

"No. I'm serious. If I knew how to get in touch with him, I'd set up the game myself."

"You won't have to," one of the other players put in as he started for the door. "Once word of this game gets around, the Kid will come looking for you."

"True enough," Grunk laughed over his shoulder. "Really, Skeeve. If that match-up happens, be sure to pass the word to me. That's a game I'd like to see."

"Sure, Grunk," I said. "You'll be one of the first to know. Catch you later."

Actually, my mind was racing as I made my goodbyes. This was getting out of hand. I had figured on one madcap night on my own, then calling it quits without anyone else the wiser. If the other players started shooting their mouths off all over the Bazaar, there would be no hope of keeping my evening's adventure a secret . . . particularly from Aahz! The only thing that would be worse would be if I ended up with some hotshot gambler hunting me down for a challenge match.

"Say, Geek," I said, trying to make it sound casual. "Who is this 'Kid' they keep talking about?"

The Deveel almost lost his grip on the stack of chips he was counting. He gave me a long stare, then shrugged.

"You know, Skeeve, sometimes I don't know when you're kidding me and when you're serious. I keep forgetting that as successful as you are, you're still new to the Bazaar . . . and to gambling specifically."

"Terrific. Who's the 'Kid'?"

"The Kid's the current king of the dragon poker circuit. His trademark is that he always includes a breath mint with his opening bet for each hand . . . says that it brings him luck. That's why they call him the 'Sen-Sen Ante Kid.' I'd advise you to stay away from him, though. You had a good run tonight, but the Kid is the best there is. He'd eat you alive in a head-to-head game."

"I hear that." I laughed. "I was only curious. Really. Just cash me in and I'll be on my way."

The Geek gestured at the stacks of coins on the table.

"What's to cash?" he said. "I pulled mine out the same time I cashed the others' out. The rest is yours."

I looked at the money and swallowed hard. For the first time I could understand why some people found gambling so addictive. There was easily twenty thousand in gold weighing down the table. All mine. From one night of cards!

"Um . . . Geek? Could you hold on to my winnings for me? I'm not wild about the idea of walking around with that much gold on me. I can drop back by later with my bodyguards to pick it up."

"Suit yourself," the Geek shrugged. "I can't think of anyone at the Bazaar who would have nerve enough to jump you, with your reputation. Still, you might run into a stranger. . . ."

"Fine," I said, heading for the door. "Then I'll be . . ."

"Wait a minute! Aren't you forgetting something?"

"What's that?"

"Pidge's marker. Hang on and I'll get it."

He disappeared before I could protest, so I leaned against the wall to wait. I had forgotten about the marker, but the Geek was a gambler and adhered more religiously to the unwritten laws of gambling than most folks obeyed civil law. I'd just have to humor him and . . .

"Here's the marker, Skeeve," the Deveel announced. "Markie, this is Skeeve."

I just gaped at him, unable to speak. Actually, I gaped at the little blond-headed moppet he was leading by the hand. That's right. A girl. Nine or ten years old at the most.

I experienced an all-too-familiar sinking feeling in my stomach that meant I was in trouble . . . lots of it.

# Chapter II

*"Kids? Who said anything about kids?"*
**Conan**

**T**HE little girl looked at me through eyes that glowed with trust and love. She barely stood taller than my waist and had that wholesome, healthy glow that young girls are all supposed to have but so few actually do. With her little beret and matching jumper, she looked so much like an oversized doll that I wondered if she'd say "Mama" if you turned her upside down, then right-side up again.

She was so adorable that it was obvious that anyone with a drop of paternal instinct would fall in love with her on sight. Fortunately, my partner had trained me well; any instincts I had were of a more monetary nature.

"What's that?" I demanded.

"It's a little girl," the Geek responded. "Haven't you ever seen one before?"

For a minute, I thought I was being baited. Then I remembered some of my earliest conversations with Aahz and controlled my temper.

"I realize that it's a little girl, Geek," I said carefully. "What I was really trying to ask is a) who is she? b) what is she doing here? and c) what has this got to do with Pidge's marker? Do I make myself clear?"

The Deveel blinked his eyes in bewilderment.

"But I just told you. Her name is Markie. She's Pidge's marker . . . you know, the one you said you would cover personally?"

My stomach bottomed out.

"Geek, we were talking about a piece of paper. You know, 'IOU, etc.'? A marker! Who leaves a little girl for a marker?"

"Pidge does. Always has. C'mon, Skeeve. You know me. Would I give anyone credit for a piece of paper? I give Pidge credit on Markie here because I know he'll be back to reclaim her."

"Right. *You* give him credit. I don't deal in little girls, Geek."

"You do now," he smiled. "Everyone at the table heard you say so. I'll admit I was a little surprised at the time."

". . . But not surprised enough to warn me about what I was buying into. Thanks a lot, Geek old pal. I'll try to remember to return the favor someday."

In case you didn't notice, that last part was an open threat. As has been noted, I've been getting quite a reputation around the Bazaar as a magician, and I didn't really think the Geek wanted to be on my bad side.

Okay. So it was a rotten trick. I was getting desperate.

"Whoa. Hold it," the Deveel said quickly. "No reason to get upset. If you don't want her, I'll give you cash to cover the marker and keep her myself . . ."

"That's better."

". . . at the usual terms, of course."

I knew I was being suckered. *Knew* it, mind you. But I had to ask anyway.

"What terms?"

"If Pidge doesn't reclaim her in two weeks, I sell her into slavery for enough money to cover her father's losses."

Check and mate.

I looked at Markie. She was still holding the Geek's hand, listening solemnly while we argued out her fate. As our eyes met, she said her first words since she had entered the room.

"Are you going to be my new daddy?"

I swallowed hard.

"No, I'm not your daddy, Markie. I just . . ."

"Oh, I know. It's just that every time my *real* daddy leaves me with someone, he tells me that they're going to be my pretend daddy for a while. I'm supposed to mind them and do what they tell me just as if they were my real daddy until my real daddy comes to get me. I just wanted to know if you were going to be my new pretend daddy?"

"Ummm . . ."

"I hope so. You're nice. Not like some of the scumbags he's left me with. Will you be my new daddy?"

With that, she reached out and took hold of my hand. A small thrill ran through me like an autumn shiver. She was so vulnerable, so trusting. I had been on my own for a long time, first alone, then apprenticed to Garkin, and finally teamed with Aahz. In all that time, I had never really been responsible for another person. It was a funny feeling, scary and warming at the same time.

I tore my eyes away from her and glared at the Geek again.

"Slavery's outlawed here at the Bazaar."

The Deveel shrugged. "There are other dimensions. As a matter of fact, I've had a standing offer for her for several years. That's why I've been willing to accept her as collateral. I could make enough to cover the bet, the cost of the food she's eaten over the years, and still turn a tidy profit."

"That's about the lowest . . ."

"Hey! The name's 'the Geek,' not 'the Red Cross'! I don't do charity. Folks come to me to bet, not for handouts."

I haven't thrown a punch at anyone since I started practicing magic, but I was sorely tempted to break that record just this once. Instead, I turned to the little girl.

"Get your things, Markie. Daddy's taking you to your new home."

\* \* \*

My partner and I were currently basing our operations at the Bazaar at Deva, which is the home dimension of the Deveels. Deveels are reputed to be the sharpest merchants, traders, and hagglers in all the known dimensions. You may have heard of them in various folk tales in your own home dimension. Their fame lingers even in dimensions they have long since stopped trading in.

The Bazaar is the showcase of Deva . . . in fact, I've never seen a part of Deva that wasn't the Bazaar. Here the Deveels meet to trade with each other, buying and selling the choicest magics and miracles from all the dimensions. It's an around-the-clock, over-the-horizon sprawl of tents, shops, and barter blankets where you can acquire anything your imagination can conjure as well as a lot of things you never dreamed existed . . . for a price. Many inventors and religious figures have built their entire career from items purchased in one trip to the Bazaar. Needless to say, it is devastating to the average budget . . . even if the holder of the purse-strings has above-average sales resistance.

Normally I enjoy strolling through the booths, but tonight, with Markie beside me, I was too distracted to concentrate on the displays. It occurred to me that, fun as it is for adults, the Bazaar is no place to raise a child.

"Will we be living by ourselves, or do you have a girlfriend?"

Markie was clinging to my hand as we made our way through the Bazaar. The wonders of the stalls and shops dispensing magic reached out to us as they always do, but she was oblivious to them, choosing instead to ply me with questions and hanging on my every word.

" 'No' to both questions. Tananda lives with me, but she isn't my girlfriend. She's a free-lance assassin who helps me out on jobs from time to time. Then there's Chumley, her brother. He's a troll who works under the name of Crunch. You'll like them. They're nice . . . in a lot of ways they're nicer than I am."

Markie bit her lip and frowned. "I hope you're right. I've found that a lot of nice people don't like little kids."

"Don't worry," I said, with more confidence than I felt. "But I'm not done yet. There's also Guido and Nunzio, my bodyguards. They may seem a little gruff, but don't let them scare you. They just act tough because it's part of their job."

"Gee. I've never had a daddy who had bodyguards before."

"That's not all. We also have Buttercup, who's a war unicorn, and Gleep, who's my very own pet dragon."

"Oh, lots of people have dragons. I'm more impressed by the bodyguards."

That took me aback a little. I'd always thought that having a dragon was rather unique. I mean, nobody else I knew had a dragon. Then again, nobody else I knew had bodyguards, either.

"Let's see," Markie was saying. "There's Tananda, Chumley, Guido, Nunzio, Buttercup, and Gleep. Is that all?"

"Well, there's also Massha. She's my apprentice."

"Massha. That's a pretty name."

Now, there are lots of words to describe my apprentice, but unfortunately "pretty" isn't one of them. Massha is huge, both in height and breadth. There are large people who still manage to look attractive, but my apprentice isn't one of them. She tends toward loud, colorful clothes which invariably clash with her bright orange hair, and wears enough jewelry for three stores. In fact, the last time she got into a fight here at the Bazaar was when a nearsighted shopper mistook her for a display tent.

"Aahh . . . you'll just have to meet her. But you're right. Massha is a pretty name."

"Gee, you've got a lot of people living with you."

"Well . . . umm . . . there *is* one more."

"Who's that?"

"His name is Aahz. He's my partner."

"Is he nice, too?"

I was torn between loyalty and honesty.

"He . . . aah . . . takes getting used to. Remember how I told you not to be scared of the bodyguards even if they were a little gruff?"

"Yes."

"Well, it's all right to be scared of Aahz. He gets a little upset from time to time, and until he cools down it's best to give him a lot of room and not leave anything breakable—like your arm—within his reach."

"What gets him upset?"

"Oh, the weather, losing money, not making money . . . which to him is the same as losing money, any one of a hundred things that I say . . . and you! I'm afraid he's going to be a little upset when he meets you, so stay behind me until I get him calmed down. Okay?"

"Why would he be upset with me?"

"You're going to be a surprise to him, and he doesn't like surprises. You see, he's a very suspicious person and tends to think of a surprise as a part of an unknown plot against him . . . or me."

Markie lapsed into silence. Her brow furrowed as she stared off into nothingness, and it occurred to me that I was scaring her.

"Hey, don't worry," I said, squeezing her hand. "Aahz will be okay once he gets over being surprised. Now tell me about yourself. Do you go to school?"

"Yes. I'm halfway through Elemental School. I'd be further if we didn't keep moving around."

"Don't you mean Elementary School?" I smiled.

"No. I mean . . ."

"Whoops. Here we are. This is your new home, Markie."

I gestured grandly at the small tent that was our combination home and headquarters.

"Isn't it a little small for all those people?" she frowned, staring at the tent.

"It's bigger inside than it is outside," I explained. "C'mon. I'll show you."

I raised the flap for her and immediately wished I hadn't.

"Wait'll I get my hands on him!" came Aahz's booming voice from within. "After all the times I've told him to stay away from dragon poker!"

It occurred to me that maybe we should wait for a while before introducing Markie to my partner. I started to ease the flap down, but it was too late.

"Is that you, partner? I'd like to have a little chat, if you don't mind!"

"Remember. Stay behind me," I whispered to Markie, then proceeded to walk into the lion's den.

# Chapter III

*"I'm doing this for your own good!"*
**any establishment executioner . . .**
**or any parent**

$A$S I told Markie, our place at the Bazaar was bigger on the inside than on the outside . . . lots bigger! I've been in smaller palaces . . . heck, I've lived and worked in smaller palaces than our current domicile. Back when I was court magician at Possiltum, to be exact.

Here at the Bazaar, the Deveels think that any display of wealth will weaken their position when they haggle over prices, so they hide the size of their homes by tucking them into 'unlisted dimensions.' Even though our home looked like just a humble tent from the street, the inside included multiple bedrooms, a stable area, a courtyard and garden, etc., etc. You get the picture.

Unfortunately for me, at the moment it also included my partner, Aahz.

"Well, if it isn't the Bazaar's own answer to War, Famine, Death, and Pestilence! Other dimensions have the Four Horsemen, but the Bazaar at Deva has the Great Skeeve!"

Remember my partner, Aahz? I mentioned him back in Chapter One and again in Chapter Two. Most of my efforts to describe him fail to prepare people for the real thing. What I usually forget to mention to folks is that he's from the dimension Perv. For those of you unfamiliar with dimension travel, that means he is green and scaly with a mouth big enough for any other three beings and teeth enough for a school of sharks . . . if shark's teeth got to be four inches long, that is. I don't deliberately omit things from my descriptions. It's just that after all these years I've gotten used to him.

"Have you got anything at all to say for yourself? Not that there's any acceptable excuse, mind you. It's just that tradition allows you a few last words."

Well . . . I've *almost* gotten used to him.

"Hi, Aahz. Have you heard about the card game?"

"About two hours ago," Massha supplied from a nearby chair where she was entrenched with a book and a huge box of chocolates. "He's been like this ever since."

"I see you've done your usual marvelous job of calming him down."

"I'm just an apprentice around here," she said with a shrug. "Getting between you two in a quarrel is not part of my game plan for a long and prosperous life."

"If you two are *quite* through," Aahz growled, "I'm still waiting to hear what you have to say for yourself."

"What's to say? I sat in on a game of dragon poker. . . ."

"WHO'S BEEN TEACHING YOU TO PLAY DRAGON POKER? That's what there is to say! Was it Tananda? Chumley? How come you're going to other people for lessons all of a sudden? Aren't I good enough for the Great Skeeve any more?"

The truth of the situation suddenly dawned on me. Aahz was my teacher before he insisted that I be elevated to full partner status. Even though we were theoretically equals, old habits die hard and he still considered himself to be my exclusive teacher, mentor, coach, and all-around nudge. What the *real* problem was was that my partner was jealous of someone else horning in on what he felt was his private student! Perhaps this problem would be easier to deal with than I thought.

"No one else has been teaching me, Aahz. Everything I know about dragon poker, I learned from you."

"But I haven't taught you anything."

"Exactly."

That stopped him. At least, it halted his pacing as he turned to peer suspiciously at me with his yellow eyes.

"You mean you don't know anything at all about dragon poker?"

"Well, from listening to you talk, I know about how many cards are dealt out and stuff like that. I still haven't figured out what the various hands are, much less their order . . . you know, what beats what."

"*I* know," my partner said pointedly. "What I don't know is why you decided to sit in on a game you don't know the first thing about."

"The Geek sent me an invitation, and I thought it would be sociable to . . ."

"The Geek? You sat in at one of the Geek's games at the Even-Odds to be sociable?" He was off again. "Don't you know that those are some of the most cutthroat games at the Bazaar? They eat amateurs alive at those tables. And you went there to be sociable?"

"Sure. I figured the worse that could happen would be that I lost a little money. The way things have been going, we can afford it. Besides, who knows, I might get lucky."

"Lucky? Now I know you don't know anything about dragon poker. It's a game of skill, not luck. All you could do was throw your money away . . . money we've both risked our lives for, I might add."

"Yes, Aahz."

"And besides, one of the first things you learn playing any kind of poker is that the surest way to lose is to go in *expecting* to lose."

"Yes, Aahz."

Out of desperation, I was retreating behind my strongest defense. I was agreeing with everything he said. Even Aahz has trouble staying mad at someone who's agreeing with him.

"Well, what's done is done and all the shouting in the world won't change it. I just hope you've learned your lesson. How much did it cost you, anyway?"

"I won."

"Okay. Just to show you there're no hard feelings, we'll split it. In a way it's my fault. I should have taught you . . ."

There was a sudden stillness in the room. Even Massha had stopped with a bonbon halfway to her mouth. Very slowly, Aahz turned to face me.

"You know, Skeeve, for a minute there, I thought you said . . ."

"I won," I repeated, trying desperately not to smile.

"You won. As in 'better than broke even' won?"

"As in 'twenty thousand in gold plus' won," I corrected.

"But if you didn't know how the game was played, how could you . . ."

"I just bet the people, not the cards. It seemed to work out pretty well."

I was in my glory now. It was a rare time indeed that I managed to impress my partner, and I was going to milk it for all it was worth.

"But that's crazy!" Aahz scowled. "I mean, it could work for a while, but in the long run . . ."

"He was great!" Markie announced, emerging from behind me. "You should have seen it. He beat everybody."

My "glory" came tumbling down around my ears. With one hand I shoved Markie back behind me and braced for the explosion. What I really wanted to do was run for cover, but that would have left Markie alone in the open, so I settled for closing my eyes.

Nothing happened.

After a few moments, I couldn't stand the suspense any more and opened one eye to sneak a peek. The view I was treated to was an *extreme* close-up of one of Aahz's yellow eyes. He was standing nose to nose with me, apparently waiting until I was ready before launching into his tirade. It was obvious that *he* was ready. The gold flecks in his eyes were shimmering as if they were about to boil . . . and for all I knew, they were.

"Who . . . is . . . that?"

I decided against trying to play dumb and say "Who is what?" At the range he was standing, Aahz would have bitten my head off . . . literally!

"Umm . . . remember I said that I won twenty thousand plus? Well, she's the plus."

"YOU WON A KID IN A CARD GAME!?!!"

The force of my partner's voice actually knocked me back two steps. I probably would have gone farther if I hadn't bumped against Markie.

"ARE YOU OUT OF YOUR MIND?? DON'T YOU KNOW THE PENALTY FOR SLAVERY IS . . ."

He disappeared in mid-sentence behind a wall of flesh and tasteless color. Despite her earlier claims of valuing self-preservation, Massha had stepped between us.

"Just cool down a minute, Green and Scaly."

Aahz tried to get around her.

"BUT HE JUST . . ."

She took a half step sideways and blocked him by leaning against the wall.

"Give him a chance to explain. He *is* your partner, isn't he?"

From the sound of his voice, Aahz reversed his field and tried for the other side.

"BUT HE . . ."

Massha took two steps and leaned against the other wall, all the while talking as if she wasn't being interrupted.

"Now either he's an idiot . . . which he isn't, or you're a lousy teacher . . . which you aren't, or there's more to this than meets the eye. Hmmm?"

There were several moments of silence, then Aahz spoke again in a voice much more subdued.

"All right, *partner*. Let's hear it."

Massha relinquished her spot and I could see Aahz again . . . though I almost wished I couldn't. He was breathing hard, but whether from anger or from the exertion of trying to get around Massha I couldn't tell. I could hear the scales on his fingers rasp as he clenched and unclenched his fists, and I knew that I'd better tell my story fast before he lost control again.

"I didn't win *her*," I said hastily. "I won her father's marker. She's our guarantee that he'll come back and make his losses good."

Aahz stopped making with the fists, and a puzzled frown creased his features.

"A marker? I don't get it. The Geek's games are always on a cash-and-carry basis."

"Well, he seems to have made an exception in Pidge's case."

"Pidge?"

"That's my daddy," Markie announced, stepping from behind me again. "It's short for Pigeon. He loses a lot . . . that's why everyone is always so happy to let him sit in on a game."

"Cute kid," Aahz said drily. "It also might explain why you did so well in the game tonight. One screwball can change the pace of an entire game. Still, when the Geek *does* take markers, he usually pays the winners in cash and handles the collecting himself."

"He was willing to do that."

"Then why . . ."

". . . and if Markie's father didn't show up in two weeks, he was going to take her off-dimension and sell her into slavery himself to raise the money."

From her chair, Massha gave a low whistle.

"Sweet guy, this Geek."

"He's a Deveel." Aahz waved absently, as if the statement explained everything. "Okay, okay. I can see where you felt you had to accept custody of the kid here instead of leaving her with the Geek. Just answer me one question."

"What's that?"

"What do *we* do with her if her father doesn't show up?"

Sometimes I like it better when Aahz is ranting than when he's thinking.

"Aahh . . . I'm still working on that one."

"Terrific. Well, when you come up with an answer, let me know. I think I'll stay in my room until this whole thing blows over."

With that he strode out of the room, leaving Massha and me to deal with Markie.

"Cheer up, Hot Stuff," my apprentice said. "Kids aren't all that much of a problem. Hey, Markie. Would you like a piece of chocolate?"

"No, thank you. It might make me fat and ugly like you."

I winced. Up until now, Massha had been my ally on the subject of Markie, but this might change everything. She was very sensitive about her weight, so most of us tended to avoid any mention of it. In fact, I had gotten so used to her appearance that I tended to forget how she looked to anyone who didn't know her.

"Markie!" I said sternly. "That wasn't a very nice thing to say."

"But it's true!" she countered, turning her innocent eyes on me.

"That's why it's not nice," Massha laughed, though I noticed her smile was a little forced. "C'mon, Markie. Let's hit the pantry and try to find you something to eat . . . something low-calorie."

The two of them trooped out, leaving me alone with my thoughts. Aahz had raised a good question. What *were* we going to do if Markie's father didn't come back? I had never been around kids before. I knew that having her around would cause problems, but how many problems? With everything else we had handled as a team, surely Aahz and I could handle a little girl. Of course, Aahz was . . .

"There you are, Boss! Good. I was hopin' you were still up."

I cleared my mind to find one of my bodyguards entering the room.

"Oh. Hi, Guido. How did the report go?"

"Couldn't be better. In fact, Don Bruce was so happy he sent you a little present."

In spite of my worries, I couldn't help smiling. At least *something* was going right.

"That's great," I said. "I could use a little cheering up just now."

"Then I've got just the thing. Hey, Nunzio! Bring her in here!"

My smile froze. I tried desperately not to panic. After all, I reasoned, people refer to a lot of things as "her." Boats, for example, or even . . .

"Boss, this is Bunny. Don Bruce sends her with his compliments on a job well done. She's going to be your moll."

The girl they were escorting into the room bore no resemblance at all to a boat.

# Chapter IV

*"A doll is a doll is a doll."*
**F. Sinatra**

**B**UNNY was a top-heavy little redhead with her hair in a pixie cut and a vacant stare a zombie would envy. She was vigorously chewing something as she rubbernecked, trying to take in the entire room at once.

"Gee. This is quite a place you guys've got here. It's a lot nicer than the last place I was at, ya know?"

"This is just the waitin' room," Nunzio said with pride. "Wait'll you see the rest of the layout. It's bigger'n any hangout I've ever worked, know what I mean?"

"What'sa matter with you two?" Guido barked. "Ain't ya got no manners? First things first. Bunny, this is the Boss. He's the one you're goin' to be workin' under."

Bunny advanced toward me holding out her hand. From the way her body moved under her tight-fitting clothes, there was little doubt what she was wearing under them . . . or not wearing, as the case may be.

"Pleased ta meetcha, Boss. The pleasure's mutual," she said brightly.

For once, I knew exactly what to say.

"No."

She stopped, then turned toward Guido with a frown.

"He means not to call him 'Boss' until you get to know him," my bodyguard assured her. "Around here he's just known as Skeeve."

"Gotcha," she winked. "Okay, *Skeeve* . . . ya know, that's kinda cute."

"No," I repeated.

"Okay. So it's not cute. Whatever you say. You're the Boss."

"NO!"

"But . . ."

I ignored her and turned directly to Guido.

"Have you lost your marbles? What are you doing bringing her in here like this?"

"Like I said, Boss, she's a present from Don Bruce."

"Guido, lots of people give each other presents. Presents like neckties and books . . . not girls!"

My bodyguard shrugged his shoulders helplessly. "So Don Bruce ain't lots of people. He's the one who assigned us to you in the first place, and he says that someone with your standin' in the Mob should have a moll."

"Guido . . . let's talk. Excuse us a minute, Bunny."

I slipped an arm around my bodyguard's shoulders and drew him off into a corner. That may sound easy until you realize I had to reach *up* to get to his shoulders. Both Guido and Nunzio are considerably larger than me.

"Now look, Guido," I said. "Remember when I explained our setup to you?"

"Sure, Boss."

"Well, let's walk through it again. Don Bruce hired Aahz and me on a non-exclusive basis to watch over the Mob's interests here at the Bazaar. Now, he did that because the ordinary methods he employs weren't working. . . . Right?"

"Actually, he hired *you* and included your partner. Except for that . . . right."

"Whatever. We also explained to you that the reason the Mob's usual methods weren't working was that the Bazaar merchants had hired us to chase the Mob out. Remember?"

"Yeah. That was really a surprise when you told us. You really had us goin', know what I mean?"

"Now that brings us to the present. The money we're collecting from the Bazaar merchants and passing on to Don Bruce, the money he thinks they're paying the Mob for protection, is actually being paid to us to keep the Mob away from the Bazaar. Get it?"

"Got it."

"Good. Then, understanding the situation as you do, you can see why I don't want a moll or anyone else from the Mob hanging around. If word gets back to Don Bruce that we're flim-flamming him, it'll reopen the whole kettle of worms. That's why you've got to get rid of her."

Guido nodded vigorously.

"No," he said.

"Then all you have to . . . what do you mean, 'no'? Do I have to explain it all to you again?"

My bodyguard heaved a great sigh.

"I understand the situation, Boss. But I don't think *you* do. Allow me to continue where you left off."

"But I . . ."

"Now, whatever you are, Don Bruce considers you to be a minor chieftain in the Mob running a profitable operation. Right?"

"Well . . ."

"As such, you are entitled to a nice house, which you have, a couple of bodyguards, which you have, and a moll, which you don't have. These things are necessary in Don Bruce's eyes if the Mob is to maintain its public image of rewarding successful members . . . just as it finds it necessary to express its displeasure at members who fail. Follow me?"

"Public image," I said weakly.

"So it is in the interests of the Mob that Don Bruce has provided you with what you have failed to provide yourself . . . namely: a moll. If you do not like this one, we can take her back and get another, but a moll you must have if we are to continue in our existing carefree manner. Otherwise . . ." He paused dramatically.

"Otherwise . . . ?" I prompted.

"If you do not maintain the appearance of a successful Mob member, Don Bruce will be forced to deal with you as if you were unsuccessful . . . know what I mean?"

I suddenly felt the need to massage my forehead. "Terrific."

"My sentiments exactly. Under the circumstances, however, I thought it wisest to accept his gift in your name and hope that you could find an amicable solution to our dilemma at a later date."

"I suppose you're . . . Hey! Wait a minute. We already have Massha and Tananda in residence. Won't they do?"

Guido gave his sigh again. "This possibility did indeed occur to me as well. Then I said to myself: 'Guido, do you really want to be the one to hang the label of moll on either Massha or Tananda, knowing those ladies as you do? Even if it will only be bantered around the Mob?' Viewed in that light, it was my decision to go along with Don Bruce's proposal and leave it to you to make the final decision . . . *Boss.*"

I shot a sharp glance at him for that last touch of sarcasm. Despite his affected speech patterns and pseudo-pompous explanations, I occasionally had the impression that Guido was far more intelligent than he let on. At the moment, however, his face was a study in innocence, so I let it ride.

"I see what you mean, Guido. If either Massha or Tananda are going to be known as 'molls,' I'd rather it was their choice, not mine. Until then, I guess we're stuck with . . . what's her name? Bunny? Does she wiggle her nose or something?"

Guido glanced across the room at the other two, then lowered his voice conspiratorily. "Just between you and me, Boss, I think you would be well advised to accept this particular moll that Don Bruce has personally selected to send. Know what I mean?"

"No, I don't." I grimaced. "Excuse me, Guido, but the mind's working a little slow just now. If you're trying to tell me something, you're going to have to spell it out."

"Well, I did a little checkin' around, and it seems that Bunny here is Don Bruce's niece, and . . ."

"HIS N . . ."

"Ssshh. Keep it down, Boss. I don't think we're supposed to know that."

With a supreme effort, I suppressed my hysteria and lowered my voice again. "What are you trying to do to me? I'm trying to keep this operation under wraps and you bring me Don Bruce's niece?"

"Don't worry . . ."

"DON'T . . ."

"Sshh! Like I said, I've been checking around. It seems the two of them don't get along at all. Wouldn't give each other the time of day. The way I hear it, he doesn't want her to be a moll, and she won't go along with any other kind of work. They fight over it like cats and dogs. Anyway, if you can trust any moll to not feed Don Bruce the straight scoop, it's her. That's why I was sayin' that you should keep this one."

My headache had now spread to my stomach.

"Swell. Just swell. Well, at least . . ."

"The one thing I couldn't find out, though," Guido continued with a frown, "is why he wants her with you. I figure that it's either that he thinks that you'll treat her right, or that he expects you to scare her out of bein' a moll. I'm just not sure which way you should play it."

This was not turning out to be a good night for me. In fact, it had gone steadily downhill since I won that last hand of dragon poker.

"Guido," I said. "Please don't say anything more. Okay? Please? Every time I think that things might not be so bad, you drag out something else that makes them worse."

"Just tryin' to do my job," he shrugged, obviously hurt, "but if that's what you want . . . well, you're the Boss."

"And if you say that one more time, I'm liable to forget you're bigger than me and pop you one in the nose. Understand? Being the 'Boss' implies a certain degree of control, and if there's one thing I don't have right now, it's control."

"Right, B . . . Skeeve," my bodyguard grinned. "You know, for a minute there you sounded just like my old B . . . employer. He used to beat up on Nunzio and me when he got mad. Of course, we had to stand there and take it. . . ."

"Don't give me any ideas," I snarled. "For now, let's just concentrate on Bunny."

I turned my attention once more to the problem at hand, which was to say Bunny. She was still staring vacantly around the room, jaws working methodically on whatever it was she was chewing, and apparently oblivious to whatever it was Nunzio was trying to tell her.

"Well, uh . . . Bunny," I said, "it looks like you're going to be staying with us for a while."

She reacted to my words as if I had hit her "on" switch.

"Eeoooh!" she squealed, as if I had just told her that she had won a beauty pageant. "Oh, I know I'm just goin' to *love* workin' under you, Skeevie."

My stomach did a slow roll to the left.

"Shall I get her things, Boss?" Nunzio said. "She's got about a mountain and a half of luggage outside."

"Oh, you can leave all that," Bunny cooed. "I just know my Skeevie is going to want to buy me a whole new wardrobe."

"Hold it! Time out!" I ordered. "House rules time. Bunny, some things are going to disappear from your vocabulary *right now*. First, forget 'Skeevie.' It's Skeeve . . . just Skeeve, or if you must, the Great Skeeve in front of company. Not Skeevie."

"Gotcha," she winked.

"Next, you do not work *under* me. You're . . . you're my personal secretary. Got it?"

"Why sure, sugar. That's what I'm always called."

Again with the wink.

"Now then, Nunzio. I want you to get her luggage and move it into . . . I don't know, the pink bedroom."

"You want I should give him a hand, Boss?" Guido asked.

"*You* stay put." I smiled, baring all my teeth. "I've got a special job for you."

"Now just a darn minute!" Bunny interrupted, her cutie-pie accent noticeably lacking. "What's this with the 'pink bedroom'? Somehow you don't strike me as the kind that sleeps in a pink bedroom. Aren't I moving into your bedroom?"

"*I'm* sleeping in my bedroom," I said. "Now isn't it easier for you to move into one of our spares than for me to relocate just so you can move into mine?"

As I said, it had been a long night, and I was more than a little slow. Lucky for me, Bunny was fast enough for both of us.

"I thought we was goin' to be sharin' a room, Mr. Skeeve. That's the whole idea of my bein' here, ya know? What's wrong? Ya think I got bad breath or sumpin'?"

"Aahh . . . ummm . . ." I said intelligently.

"Hi, Guido . . . Nunzio. Who's . . . oh wow!"

That last witty line didn't come from me. Massha had just entered the room with Markie in tow and lurched to a halt at the sight of Bunny.

"Hey, Boss! What's with the kid?"

"Guido, Nunzio, this is Markie . . . our *other* house guest. Massha, Markie, this is Bunny. She's going to be staying with us for a while . . . in the *pink* bedroom."

"Now I get it!" Bunny exclaimed. "You want we should play it cool because of the kid! Well, you can count on me. Discretion is Bunny's middle name. The pink bedroom it is!"

I could cheerfully have throttled her. If her meaning was lost on Markie, it certainly hadn't gotten past Massha, who was staring out at me from under raised eyebrows.

"Whatever!" I said rather than take more drastic action. "Now, Nunzio, you get Bunny set up in the pink bedroom. Massha, I want you to get Markie settled in the blue bedroom next to mine . . . and knock it off with the eyebrows. I'll explain everything in the morning."

"*That* I want to hear," she snorted. "C'mon, kid."

"I'm not tired!" Markie protested.

"Tough!" I countered. "I am."

"Oh," she said meekly and followed Massha.

Whatever kind of a crumb her father might be, somewhere along the line she had learned when adults could be argued with and when it was best to go with the flow.

"What do you want me to do, Boss?" Guido asked eagerly.

I favored him with my evilest grin.

"Remember that special assignment I said I had for you?"

"Yeah, Boss?"

"I'll warn you, it's dangerous."

That appealed to his professional pride, and he puffed out his chest. "The tougher the better. You know me!"

"Fine," I said. "All you have to do is go upstairs and explain Bunny to Aahz. It seems my partner isn't talking to me just now."

# Chapter V

*"Such stuff dreams are made of."*
**S. Beauty**

LUANNA was with me. I couldn't remember when she arrived or how long she had been here, but I didn't care. I hadn't seen her since we got back from the jailbreak on Limbo, and I had missed her terribly. She had left me to stay with her partner, Matt, and a little piece of me went with her. I won't be so cornball as to say it was my heart, but it was in that general vicinity.

There was so much I wanted to tell her . . . wanted to ask her, but it didn't really seem necessary. We just lay side by side on a grassy hill watching the clouds, enjoying each other's company in silence. I could have stayed like that forever, but she raised herself on one elbow and spoke softly to me.

"If you'll just skootch over a little, Skeevie, we can both get comfy."

This was somehow jarring to my serenity. She didn't sound like Luanna at all. Luanna's voice was musical and exciting. She sounded like . . .

"BUNNY!"

I was suddenly sitting bolt upright, not on a grassy knoll, but in my own bed.

"Ssshh! You'll wake up the kid!"

She was perched on the edge of my bed wearing something filmy that was even more revealing than the skin-tight outfit she had had on last night.

"What are you doing in my room!?"

I had distinct memories of stacking several pieces of furniture in front of the door before I retired, and a quick glance confirmed that they were still in place.

"Through the secret passageway," she said with one of her winks. "Nunzio showed it to me last night."

"Oh, he did, did he?" I snarled. "Remind me to express my thanks to him for that little service."

"Save your thanks, sugar. You're goin' to need them when I get done with you."

With that she raised the covers and slid in next to me. I slid out the other side of the bed as if a spider had just joined me. Not that I'm afraid of spiders, mind you, but Bunny scared me stiff.

"Now what's wrong?" she whined.

"Um . . . ah . . . look, Bunny. Can we talk for a minute?"

"Sure," she said, sitting up in bed and bending forward to rest her elbows on her knees. "Anything you say."

Unfortunately, her current position also gave me an unrestricted view of her cleavage. I promptly forgot what I was going to say.

"Aaah . . . I . . . um . . ."

There was a knock at the door.

"Come in!" I said, grateful for the interruption.

That is beyond a doubt the dumbest thing I have ever said.

The door opened, sweeping the stacked furniture back with amazing ease, and Chumley walked in.

"I say, Skeeve, Aahz has just been telling me the most remarkable . . . Hal-lo?"

I mentioned before that Chumley is a troll. What I didn't say was that he could blush . . . probably because I didn't know it myself until just now. Of all the sights I've seen in several dimensions, a blushing troll is in a category all its own.

"You must be Chumley!" Bunny chirped. "The boys told me about you."

"Umm . . . quite right. Pleased to make your acquaintance and all that," the troll said, trying to avert his eyes while still making polite conversation.

"Yeah. Sure, Chum. Don't you have somethin' else to do . . . like leavin'?"

I clutched at his arm in desperation.

"No! I mean . . . Chumley always comes by first thing in the morning."

"Ahh . . . Yes. Just wanted to see if Skeeve was ready for a spot of breakfast."

"Well, I got here first," Bunny bristled. "If Skeevie wants something to nibble on, he can . . ."

"Good morning, Daddy!"

Markie came bounding into the room and gave me a hug before any of us knew she was around.

"Well, well. You must be Skeeve's new ward, Markie," the troll beamed, obviously thankful to have something to focus on other than Bunny.

"And you're Chumley. Hi, Bunny!"

"Hiya, kid," Bunny responded with a noticeable lack of enthusiasm as she pulled the covers up around her neck.

"Are you up, Skeeve?"

The voice wafting in from the corridor was immediately identifiable as Tananda.

Chumley and I had rarely worked together as a team, but this time no planning or coordination was necessary. I scooped Markie up and carried her into the hall while Chumley followed, slamming the door behind him with enough force to crack the wood.

"Pip pip, little sister. Fine day, isn't it?"

"Hi, Tananda! What's new?"

Our cordial greetings, intended to disarm the situation, succeeded only in stopping our colleague in her tracks.

Tananda is quite attractive—if curvaceous, olive-skinned, green-haired women are your type. Of course, she looks a lot better when she isn't pursing her lips and narrowing her eyes suspiciously.

"Well, for openers, I'd say the little girl under your arm is new," she said firmly. "I may not be the most observant person, but I'm sure I would have noticed her if she had been around before."

"Oh. Well, there are a few things I've got to brief you on," I smiled weakly. "This is one of them. Her name is Markie, and . . ."

"Later, Skeeve. Right now I'm more curious about what my big brother's up to. How 'bout it, Chumley? I've seen you slam doors on the way *into* bedrooms before, but never on the way out."

"Ummm . . . that is . . ." the troll mumbled awkwardly.

"Actually," I assisted, "it's more like . . . you see . . ."

"Exactly what I had in mind," Tananda declared, slipping past us and flinging the bedroom door open.

My room was mercifully empty of occupants. Apparently Bunny had retreated through whatever secret panel she had emerged from. Chumley and I exchanged unnoted glances of relief.

"I don't get it," Tananda frowned. "You two acted like you were trying to hide a body. There's nothing here to be so secretive about."

"I think they didn't want you to see the girl in my daddy's bed," Markie supplied brightly.

I wanted to express my thanks to Markie but decided that I had enough problems without adding murder to the list.

"Well, Skeeve?" Tananda said, her eyebrows almost reaching her hairline.

"Ummm . . . actually, I'm not really her daddy. That's one of the things I wanted to brief you about."

"I meant about the girl in your room!"

"That's the other thing I wanted to . . ."

"Cut him some slack! Huh, Tananda? It's uncivilized to beat up on someone before breakfast."

That was Aahz, who for once had approached our gathering without being seen . . . or heard. He's usually not big on quiet entrances.

For that matter, I had never known him to be at all reluctant about beating up on someone—say, for example, me—before breakfast. Still, I was grateful for his intervention.

"Hi, Aahz. We were just . . ."

"Do you know what your partner is doing!?" Tananda said in a voice that could freeze wine. "He *seems* to be turning our home into a combination day-care center and . . ."

"I know all about it," Aahz interrupted, "and so will you if you'll just cool down. We'll explain everything over breakfast."

"Well . . ."

"Besides," Markie piped up, "it's not *your* home. It's my daddy's. He just lets you live here. He can do anything he wants in *his* house!"

I released my hold on her, hoping to dump her on her head. Instead, she twisted in midair and landed on her feet like a cat, all the while sneering smugly.

Tananda had stiffened as if someone had jabbed her with a pin.

"I suppose you're right, Markie," she said through tight lips. "If the 'Great Skeeve' wants to romp with some bit of fluff, it's none of my business. And if I don't like it, I should just go elsewhere."

She spun on her heel and started off down the hall.

"What about breakfast?" Aahz called after her.

"I'll be eating out . . . permanently!"

We watched her departure in helpless silence.

"I'd better go after her," Chumley said at last. "In the mood she's in, she might hurt someone."

"Could you take Markie with you?" Aahz requested, still staring after Tananda.

"Are you kidding?" the troll gaped.

"Well, at least drop her off in the kitchen. I've got to have a few words with Skeeve in private."

"I want to stay here!" Markie protested.

"Go," I said quietly.

There must have been something in my voice, because both Markie and Chumley headed off without further argument.

"Partner, you've got a problem."

"Don't I know it. If there was any way I could ship her back to Don Bruce, I'd do it in a minute, but . . ."

"I'm not talking about Bunny!"

That stopped me.

"You aren't?"

"No. Markie's the problem, not Bunny."

"Markie? But she's just a little girl."

Aahz heaved a small sigh and put one hand on my shoulder . . . gently, for a change.

"Skeeve, I've given you a lot of advice in the past, some of it better than others. For the most part, you've done pretty well at winging it in unfamiliar situations, but this time you're in over your head. Believe me, you don't have the vaguest idea of the kind of havoc a kid can cause in your life . . . especially a little girl."

I didn't know what to say. My partner was obviously sincere in his concern, and for a change was expressing it in a very calm, low-key manner. Still, I couldn't go along with what he was saying.

"C'mon, Aahz. How much trouble can she be? This thing with Tananda happened because of Bunny . . ."

". . . after Markie started mouthing off at the wrong time. I already had Tananda cooling off when Markie put her two cents in."

It also occurred to me that Markie was the one who had spilled the beans to Tananda in the first place. I shoved that thought to the back of my mind.

"So she doesn't have enough sense to keep her mouth shut. She's just a kid. We can't expect her to . . ."

"That's my point. Think about our operation for a minute, partner. How many times in one day can things go sour if someone says the wrong thing at the right moment? It's taken us a year to get Guido and Nunzio on board . . . and they're adults. Bringing a kid into the place is like waving a torch around a fireworks factory."

As much as I appreciated his efforts to explain a problem to me, I was starting to weary a bit of Aahz's single-minded pursuit of his point.

"Okay. So I haven't had much experience around kids. I may be underestimating the situation, but aren't you being a bit of an alarmist? What experience are you basing *your* worries on?"

"Are you kidding?" my partner said, laughing for the first time in our conversation. "Anyone who's been around as many centuries as I have has had more than their share of experience with kids. You met my nephew Rupert? You think he was born an adult? And he's only one of more nieces, nephews, and grandchildren than I can count without being reduced to a nervous wreck by the memories."

And I thought I couldn't be surprised by Aahz any more.

"Really? Grandchildren? I never even knew you had kids."

"I don't like to talk about it. That in itself should be a clue. When someone who likes to talk as much as I do totally avoids a subject, the memories have got to be less than pleasant!"

I was starting to get a bit worried. Realizing that Aahz usually tends to minimize danger, his warnings were starting to set my overactive imagination in gear.

"I hear what you're saying, Aahz. But we're only talking about one kid here. How much trouble can one little girl be?"

My partner's face suddenly split into one of his infamous evil grins. "Remember that quote," he said. "I'm going to be tossing it back at you from time to time."

"But . . ."

"Hey, Boss! There's someone here to see you!"

Just what I needed! I had already pretty much resolved not to take on any more clients until after Markie's father had reclaimed her. Of course, I didn't want to say that in front of Aahz, especially considering our current conversation.

"I'm in the middle of a conference, Guido!" I called. "Tell them to come back later."

"Suit yourself, Boss!" came the reply. "I just thought you'd want to know, seein' as how it's Luanna. . . ."

I was off like a shot, not even bothering to excuse myself. Aahz would understand. He knew I'd had a thing for Luanna since our expedition into Limbo.

On my way to the waiting room, I had time to speculate as to whether or not this was one of my bodyguard's little pranks. I decided that if it was, I would study hard until I knew enough magic to turn him into a toad.

My suspicions were groundless. She was there. My beautiful blond goddess. What really made my heart leap, though, was that she had her luggage with her.

"Hi, Luanna. What are you doing here? Where's Matt? How have things been? Would you like something to drink? Could I . . ."

I suddenly realized that I was babbling and forced myself to pause.

"Aahh . . . what I'm trying to say is that it's good to see you."

That got me the slow smile that had haunted my dreams. "I'm glad, Skeeve. I was afraid you'd forgotten about me."

"Not a chance," I said, then realized I was leering. "That is, no, I haven't forgotten a thing about you."

Her deep blue eyes locked with mine, and I felt myself sinking helplessly into their depths.

"That's good," she said in that musical voice of hers. "I was worried about taking you up on your offer after all this time."

That got through the fog that was threatening to envelop my mind. "Offer? What offer?"

"Oh, you don't remember! I thought . . . oh, this is embarrassing."

"Wait a minute!" I cried. "I haven't forgotten! It's just that . . . let me think . . . it's just . . ."

Like a beam of sunlight in a swamp the memory came to me. "You mean when I said that you could come to work for Aahz and me? That's it? Right?"

"That's what I was talking about!" The sun came from behind the clouds as she smiled again. "You see, Matt and I have split, and I thought . . ."

"Do you want any breakfast, Daddy? You said . . . oh! Hello."

"DADDY!!??"

Markie and Luanna stared at each other.

I revised my plans rapidly. I would study hard and turn *myself* into a toad.

"I can explain, Luanna . . ." I began.

"I think you should keep this one, Daddy," Markie said, never taking her eyes off Luanna. "She's a lot prettier than the other one."

"THE OTHER . . . Oh! You mean Tananda."

"No, I mean . . ."

"MARKIE!" I interrupted desperately. "Why don't you wait for me in the kitchen. I'll be along in a minute after I finish talking to . . ."

"Skeevie, are we going to go shopping?" Bunny slithered into the room. "I need . . . who's that!?"

"Me? I'm nobody." Luanna responded grimly. "I never realized until just now how much of a nobody I am!"

"Well, the job's already taken, if that's what you're here for," Bunny smirked.

"Wait a minute! It's a different job! Really! Luanna, I can . . . Luanna??"

Sometime during my hysteria, the love of my life had gathered up her bags and left. I was talking to empty air.

"Gee, Skeevie. What're you talkin' to her for when you got me? Aren't I . . ."

"Daddy. Can I . . ."

"SHUT UP! BOTH OF YOU! Let me think!"

Try as I might, the only thought that kept coming to me was that maybe Aahz was right. Maybe kids were more trouble than I thought.

# Chapter VI

*"Bring the whole family . . . but
leave the kids at home!"*
**R. McDonald**

"**R**EALLY, Hot Stuff. Do you think this is such a great idea?"

"Massha, please! I'm trying to think things out. I couldn't get my thoughts together back at Chaos Central with Aahz nattering at me, and I won't be able to do it now if you start up. Now, are you going to help or not?"

My apprentice shrugged her massive shoulders. "Okay. What do you want me to do?"

"Just keep an eye on those two and see that they don't get into any trouble while I think."

"Keep them out of trouble? At the Bazaar at Deva? Aren't Guido and Nunzio supposed to . . ."

"Massha!"

"All right. All right. I want it noted, though, that I'm taking this assignment under protest."

I'm *sure* I didn't give Aahz this much back talk when I was apprenticed to him. Every time I say that out loud, however, my partner bursts into such gales of laughter that now I tend to keep the thought to myself, even when he isn't around.

After some resistance, I had agreed to take Bunny and Markie on a stroll through the Bazaar. As I said to Massha, this was more to get a bit of time away from Aahz than it was giving in to Bunny's whining, though that voice was not easy to ignore.

In acknowledgment of Aahz's repeated warnings of trouble, I had recruited my apprentice to accompany us so I'd have a backup if things went awry. Guido and Nunzio were along, of course, but they were more concerned with things coming at me than with anything anyone in our party might do to the immediate environment.

All in all, we made quite a procession. Two Mob bodyguards, a woman-mountain disguised as a jewelry display, a moll, a kid, and me! For a change, I wasn't the "kid" of the party. There was something to be said for having an honest-to-goodness child traveling with you. It automatically made one look older and somehow more responsible.

We had been in residence at the Bazaar for some time now, and the neighborhood merchants were pretty much used to us. That is, they knew that if I was interested, I'd come to them. If I wasn't, no amount of wheedling or cajoling would tempt me into buying. That might seem a little strange to you, after all my glowing accounts of the wonders for sale at the Bazaar, but I had fallen into the pattern quite naturally. You see, if you just visit the Bazaar once in a while, it's all quite impressive, and you feel compelled to buy just to keep from losing out on some really nifty bargains. If you live there, on the other hand, there's no real compulsion to buy anything right now. I mean, if I need a plant that grows ten feet in a minute, I'll buy it . . . when I need it. Until then, the plant can stay in its shop three doors from our tent, and my money can stay in my pocket.

That's how things were, normally. Of course, my situation today was anything but normal. I had known this all along, of course, but I hadn't really stopped to think through all the ramifications of my current state of affairs.

Okay. So I was dumb. Remember, I was taking this stroll to try to get a chance to think. Remember?

Maybe I hadn't zeroed in on what my party looked like, but the Deveels spotted the difference before we had gone half a block.

Suddenly, every Deveel who hadn't been able to foist off some trinket on me for the last two years was out to give it one more try.

"Love potions! Results guaranteed!"

"Snake necklaces! Poisonous and non!"

"Special discounts for the Great Skeeve!"

"Special discounts for any *friend* of the Great Skeeve!"

"Try our . . ."

"Buy my . . ."

"Taste these . . ."

Most of this was not aimed at me, but at Bunny and Markie. The Deveels swarmed around them like . . . well, like Deveels smelling an easy profit. This is not to say that Guido and Nunzio weren't doing their jobs. If they hadn't been clearing a path for us, we wouldn't have been able to move at all. As it was, our progress was simply slowed to a crawl.

"Still think this was a good idea, High Roller?"

"Massha! If you . . ."

"Just asking. If you can think in this racket, though, you've got better concentration than I do."

She was right, but I wasn't about to admit it. I just kept staring forward as we walked, tracking the activity around me out of the corners of my eyes without turning my head.

"Skeevie! Can I have . . ."

"No."

"Look at . . ."

"No."

"Couldn't we . . ."

"No!"

Bunny was getting to be a pain. She seemed to want everything in sight. Fortunately, I had developed the perfect defense. All I had to do was say "No!" to everything.

"Why did we go shopping if we aren't going to buy anything?"

"Well . . ."

So much for my perfect defense. Not to be stymied, I switched immediately to Plan B, which was simply to keep our purchases at a minimum. I didn't seem to be too successful at that, either, but I consoled myself by trying to imagine how much junk we would have gotten loaded down with if I hadn't been riding the brake.

Surprisingly enough, despite all of Aahz's dire predictions, Markie wasn't much trouble at all. I found her to be remarkably well mannered and obedient, and she never asked me to buy her anything. Instead, she contented herself with pointing out to Bunny the few booths that individual overlooked.

There weren't many.

My only salvation was that Bunny did not seem interested in the usual collection of whiz-bangs and wowers that most visitors to the Bazaar find irresistible. She was remarkably loyal to her prime passion—apparel. Hats, dresses, shoes, and accessories all had to pass her close scrutiny.

I'll admit that Bunny did not indulge in random purchases. She had a shrewd eye for fabric and construction, and better color sense than anyone

I have ever known. Aahz always said that Imps were flashy dressers, and I had secretly tried to pattern my own wardrobe after their example. However, one afternoon of shopping with Bunny was an education in itself. Imps have nothing on molls when it comes to clothes sense.

The more I watched Bunny peruse the fashions available at the Bazaar, the more self-conscious I became about my own appearance. Eventually, I found myself looking over a few items for myself, and from there it was a short step to buying.

In no time flat, we had a small mountain of packages to cart along with us. Bunny had stocked up on a couple of outfits that changed color with her mood, and was now wearing an intriguing blouse which had a transparent patch that migrated randomly around her torso. If the latter sounds distracting, it was. My own indulgences were few, but sufficient to add to the overall bulk of merchandise we had to transport.

Guido and Nunzio were exempt from package-carrying duties, and Massha flatly refused on the basis that being a large woman trying to maneuver through the Bazaar was difficult enough without trying to juggle packages at the same time. Realizing the "you break it, you bought it" policies of the Bazaar, I could scarcely argue with her cautious position.

The final resolution to our baggage problem was really quite simple. I flexed my magic powers a bit and levitated the whole kit and kaboodle. I don't normally like to flaunt my powers publicly, but I figured that this was a necessary exception to the rule. Of course, having our purchases floating along behind us was like having a lighthouse in tow; it drew the Deveels out of their stalls in droves.

To my surprise, I started to enjoy the situation. Humility and anonymity is well and good, but sometimes it's nice to be made a fuss over. Bunny hung on my arm and shoulder like a boneless falcon, cooing little endearments of appreciation . . . though the fact that I was willing to finance her purchases seemed to be making as much as or more of an impression on her than my minor display of magic.

"Can't say I think much of her taste in clothes," Massha murmured to me as we paused once more while Bunny darted into a nearby booth.

To say the least, I was not eager to get drawn into a discussion comparing the respective tastes in clothes of Bunny and my apprentice.

"Different body types look better in different styles," I said, as tactfully as I could.

"Yeah? And what style looks best on *my* body type?"

"In all honesty, Massha, I can't picture you dressing any differently than you do."

"Really? Say, thanks, Skeeve. A girl always likes to hear a few appreciative noises about how she looks."

I had narrowly sidestepped that booby-trap and cast about frantically for a new subject before the other interpretation of my statement occurred to her.

"Umm . . . hasn't Markie been well-behaved?"

"I'll say. I'll admit I was a little worried when you first brought her in, but she's been an angel. I don't think I've ever known a kid this patient and obedient."

"Undemanding, too," I said. "I've been thinking of getting her something while we're out, but I'm having trouble coming up with anything appropriate. The Bazaar isn't big on toy shops."

"Are you kidding? It's one big toy shop!"

"Massha . . ."

"Okay, okay. So they're mostly toys for adults. Let me think. How old is she, anyway?"

"I'm not really sure. She said she was in the third grade at Elementary School . . . even though she calls it Elemental School . . . so that would make her . . ."

I realized that Massha was staring at me in wide-eyed horror.

"Elemental School!?"

"That's what she called it. Cute, huh? Why, what does . . ."

My apprentice interrupted me by grabbing my arm so hard that it hurt. "Skeeve. We've got to get her back home . . . QUICK!!"

"But I don't see . . ."

"I'll explain later! Just get her and go! I'll round up Bunny and get her back, but you've got to get moving!"

To say the least, I found her manner puzzling. I had never seen Massha so upset. This was obviously not the time for questions, though, so I looked around for Markie.

She was standing, fists clenched, glaring at a tent with a closed flap.

All of a sudden everyone was getting uptight. First Massha, and now Markie.

"What's with the kid?" I said, tapping Guido on the shoulder.

"Bunny's in trying on some peek-a-boo nighties, and the owner chased Markie out," my bodyguard explained. "She don't like it much, but she'll get over it. It's part of bein' a kid, I guess."

"I see. Well, I was just going to take her back home anyway. Could one of you stay with . . ."

"SKEEVE! STOP HER!!"

Massha was shouting at me. I was turning toward her to see what she was talking about when it happened, so I didn't see all the details.

There was a sudden WHOOSH followed by the sounds of ripping canvas, wood splintering, and assorted screams and curses.

I whipped my head back around, and my jaw dropped in astonishment.

The booth that Bunny was in was in tatters. The entire stock of the place was sailing off over the Bazaar, as was what was left of the tent. Bunny was trying to cover herself with her hands and screaming her head off. The proprietor, a particularly greasy-looking Deveel, was also screaming his head off, but his emotions were being vented in our general direction instead of at the world in general.

I would say it was a major dilemma except for one thing. The displays on either side of Bunny's tent and for two rows behind it were in a similar state. *That* is a major dilemma, making the destruction of a single booth pale in comparison.

A voice sprang into my head, drowning out the clamor of the enraged merchants. "If you break it, you bought it!" the voice said, and it spoke with a Devan accent.

"What happened?" I gasped, though whether to myself or to the gods, I wasn't sure.

Massha answered.

"What happened was Markie!" she said grimly. "She blew her cork and summoned up an air elemental . . . you know, like you learn to do at *Elemental* School? It appears that when the kid throws a tantrum, she's going to do it with magic!"

My mind grasped the meaning of her words instantly, just as fast as it leaped on to the next plateau. Aahz! I wasn't sure which was going to be worse: breaking the news to Aahz, or telling him how much it had cost us to learn about it!

# Chapter VII

*"There's a time to fight, and
a time to hide out!"*
**B. Cassidy**

I'VE heard that when some people get depressed, they retire to their neighborhood bar and tell their troubles to a sympathetic bartender. The problem with the Bazaar at Deva (a problem I had never noticed before) is that there are no sympathetic bartenders!

Consequently, I had to settle for the next best thing and holed up in the Yellow Crescent Inn.

Now, a fast-food joint may seem to you to be a poor substitute for a bar. It is. This particular fast-food joint, however, is owned and managed by my only friend at the Bazaar who isn't living with me. This last part was especially important at the moment, since I didn't think I was apt to get much sympathy in my own home.

Gus is a gargoyle, but despite his fierce appearance he's one of the friendliest beings I've ever met. He's helped Aahz and me out on some of our more dubious assignments, so he's less inclined to ask "How did you get yourself into this?" than most. Usually, he's more interested in "How do you get out of it?"

"How did you get yourself into this one?" he said, shaking his head.

Well, nobody's perfect . . . especially friends.

"I *told* you, Gus. One lousy card game where I expected to lose. If I had known it was going to backfire like this, so help me I would have folded every hand!"

"You see, there's your problem," the gargoyle said, flashing a grin toothier than normal. "Instead of sitting in and losing, you'd be better off not sitting in at all!"

I rewarded his sound advice by rolling my eyes.

"It's all hypothetical anyway. What's done is done. The question is, 'What do I do now?' "

"Not so fast. Let's stick with the card game for a minute. Why did you sit in if you were expecting to lose?"

"Look. Can we drop the card game? I was wrong. Okay? Is that what you want to hear?"

"No-o-o," Gus said slowly. "I still want to hear why you went in the first place. Humor me."

I stared at him for a moment, but he seemed perfectly serious.

I shrugged. "The Geek sent me an invitation. Frankly, it was quite flattering to get one. I just thought it would be sociable to . . ."

"Stop!" the gargoyle interrupted, raising his hand. "There's your problem."

"What is?"

"Trying to be sociable. What's the matter? Aren't your current round of friends good enough for you?"

That made me a little bit nervous. I was having enough problems without having Gus get his nose out of joint.

"It isn't that, Gus. Really. The whole crew—yourself included—is closer to me than my family ever was. It's just . . . I don't know . . ."

". . . you want to be liked. Right?"

"Yeah. I guess that's it."

"And that's your problem!"

That one threw me.

"I don't get it," I admitted.

The gargoyle sighed, then ducked behind the counter. "Have another milkshake," he said, shoving one toward me. "This might take a while, but I'll try to explain."

I like to think it's a sign of my growing savoir-faire that I now enjoy strawberry milkshakes. When I first visited the Bazaar, I rejected them out of hand because they looked like pink swamp muck. I was now moderately addicted to them, though I still wouldn't eat the food here. Then again, maybe it was a sign of something else completely if I thought a taste for strawberry milkshakes was a sign of savoir-faire!

"Look, Skeeve," Gus began, sipping at a milkshake of his own, "you're a nice guy . . . one of the nicest I've ever known. You go out of your way to 'do the right thing' . . . to be nice to people. The key phrase there is 'go out of your way.' You're in a 'trouble-heavy' profession anyway. Nobody hires a magician because things are going well. Then you add to that your chosen lifestyle. Because you want to be liked, you place yourself in situations you wouldn't go near if it was for your own personal satisfaction. Case in point: the card game. If you had been out for personal gain, i.e., wealth, you wouldn't have gone near it, since you don't know the game. But you wanted to be friendly, so you went expecting to lose. That's not normal, and it resulted in a not-normal outcome, to wit, Markie. That's why you get into trouble."

I chewed my lip slightly as I thought over what he was saying.

"So if I want to stay out of trouble, I've got to stop being a nice guy? I'm not sure I can do that, Gus."

"Neither am I," the gargoyle agreed cheerfully. "What's more, if you could, I don't think I or any of your other friends would like you any more. I don't even think you'd like yourself."

"Then why are you recommending that I change?"

"I'm not! I'm just pointing out that it's the way you are, not any outside circumstances, that keeps getting you into trouble. In short, since you aren't going to change, get used to being in trouble. It's going to be your constant state for a long while."

I found myself massaging my forehead again.

"Thanks, Gus," I said. "I knew I could count on you to cheer me up."

"Don't knock it. Now you can focus on solving your current problem instead of wasting time wondering why it exists."

"Funny. I thought I was doing just that. Someone *else* wanted to talk about what was causing my problems."

My sarcasm didn't faze the gargoyle in the least.

"Right," he nodded. "That brings us to your current problem."

"Now you're talking. What do you think I should do, Gus?"

"Beats me. I'd say you've got a real dilemma on your hands."

I closed my eyes as my headache hammered anew.

"I don't know what I'd do without you, Gus."

"Hey. Don't mention it. What are friends for? Whoops! Here comes Tananda!"

The other disadvantage to holing up at the Yellow Crescent Inn, besides the fact that it isn't a bar, is that it's located right across the street from my home. This is not good for someone who's trying to avoid his house-mates.

Fortunately, this was one situation I could handle with relative ease.

"Don't tell her I'm here, Gus," I instructed.

"But . . ."

Not waiting to hear the rest of his protest, I grabbed my milkshake, slipped into a chair at a nearby table, and set to work with a fast disguise spell. By the time Tananda hit the door, the only one she could see in the place besides Gus was a potbellied Deveel sipping on a strawberry milkshake.

"Hi, Gus!" she sang. "Have you seen Skeeve around?"

"He . . . aahh . . . was in earlier." The gargoyle carefully avoided the lie.

"Oh, well. I guess I'll just have to leave without saying goodbye to him, then. Too bad. We weren't on particularly good terms the last time I saw him."

"You're leaving?"

Gus said it before the words burst out of my own mouth, saving me from blowing my disguise.

"Yeah. I figure it's about time I moved on."

"I . . . umm . . . have been hearing some strange things about my neighbors, but I've never been sure how much to believe," the gargoyle said thoughtfully. "This sudden departure wouldn't have anything to do with the new moll that's been foisted off on Skeeve, would it?"

"Bunny? Naw. I'll admit I was a bit out of sorts when I first heard about it, but Chumley explained the whole thing to me."

"Then what's the problem?"

Gus was doing a terrific job of beating me to my lines. As long as he kept it up, I'd be able to get all my questions answered without revealing myself.

It had occurred to me to confront Tananda directly as soon as I heard what she was up to, but then I realized that this was a rare chance to hear her thoughts when she didn't think I was around.

"Well, it's something Markie said . . ."

Markie again. I definitely owed Aahz an apology.

". . . She made some crack about her daddy, that's Skeeve, letting me live there, and it got me to thinking. Things have been nice these last couple years . . . almost too nice. Since we haven't had to worry about overhead, Chumley and I haven't been working much. More important, we haven't been working at working. It's too easy to hang around the place and wait for something to come to us."

"Getting fat and lazy, huh?" Gus grinned.

"Something like that. Now, you know me, Gus. I've always been footloose and fancy free. Ready to follow a job or a whim at the drop of a hat. If anyone had suggested to me that I should settle down, I would have punched their lights out. Now all of a sudden, I've got a permanent address and family . . . family beyond Chumley, I mean. I hadn't realized how domestic I was getting until Skeeve showed up with Markie. A kid, even. When I first saw her, my first thought was that it would be nice to have a kid around the place! Now I ask you, Gus, does that sound like me?"

"No, it doesn't."

The gargoyle's voice was so quiet I scarcely recognized it as his.

"Right then I saw the handwriting on the wall. If I don't start moving again, I'm going to take root . . . permanently. You know, the worst thing is that I don't really want to go. That's the scariest part of all."

"I don't think Aahz or Skeeve want you to go either."

"Now don't you start on me, Gus. This is hard enough for me as it is. Like I said, they're family, but they're stifling me. I've got to get away, even if it's only for a little while, or I'm going to lose a part of me . . . forever."

"Well, if you've made up your mind . . . good luck."

"Thanks, Gus. I'll be in touch from time to time. Keep an eye on the boys in case they buy more trouble than they can sell."

"I don't think you have to worry about Chumley. He's pretty level-headed."

"Chumley's not the one I'm worried about."

I thought that was going to be her parting shot, but she paused with one hand on the door.

"You know, it's probably just as well that I couldn't find Skeeve. I'm not sure I could have stuck to my guns in a face-to-face . . . but then again, maybe that's why I was looking for him."

I could feel Gus's eyes on me as she slipped out.

"I suppose it's pointless to ask why you didn't say something, *Mister* Skeeve."

Even though I had worried earlier about getting Gus angry with me, somehow it didn't matter anymore.

"At first it was curiosity," I said, letting my disguise slip away. "Then, I didn't want to embarrass her."

"And at the end there? When she flat-out said that you could talk her out of going? Why didn't you speak up then? Do you *want* her to disappear?"

I couldn't even manage a spark of anger. "You know better than that, Gus," I said quietly. "You're hurting and lashing out at whoever's handy, which happens to be me. I didn't try to get her to stay for the same reason you didn't try harder. She feels we're stifling her, and if she wants out, it'd be pretty small of us to try to keep her for our own sakes, wouldn't it?"

There was prolonged silence, which was fine by me. I didn't feel much like talking anymore.

Rising, I started for the door.

"You were looking the other way when she left," the gargoyle said. "You might like to know there were tears in her eyes."

"Mine too," I replied without turning. "That's why I was looking the other way."

# Chapter VIII

*"What did I do wrong?"*
**Lear, Rex**

**W**ITH a heavy heart, I headed back home. I was no longer worried about Aahz yelling at me. If anything, I was rather hoping he would. If he did, I decided that for a change I wouldn't even argue back. In short, I felt terrible and was in the mood to do a little penance.

Sliding through the tent flap, I cocked an ear and listened for Aahz. Actually, I was a little surprised that I couldn't hear him from the street, but I was sure I would be able to locate his position in the house with no difficulty. As I've said before, my partner has no problem expressing his moods, particularly anger.

The house was silent.

From the lack of reverberations and/or falling plaster, I assumed that Aahz was out . . . probably looking for me with blood in his eye. I debated going out to look for him, but decided that it would be better to wait right here. He'd be back eventually, so I headed for the garden to make myself comfortable until he showed up.

What I call the garden is actually our courtyard. It has a fountain and an abundance of plants, so I tend to think of it as a piece of the outdoors rather than as an enclosed area. I had been spending more and more time there lately, especially when I wanted time to think. It reminded me of some of the quieter spots I would find from time to time back when I was living on my own in the woods . . . back before I met Garkin, and, through him, Aahz.

That memory led me to ponder a curious point: Were there other successful beings, like myself, who used their new prosperity to recreate the setting or atmosphere of their pre-success days? If so, it made for a curious cycle.

I was so preoccupied with this thought as I entered the garden that I almost missed the fact that I wasn't alone. Someone else was using my retreat . . . specifically, Aahz.

He was sitting on one of the stone benches, chin in his hands and elbows on his knees, staring blankly into the water as it flowed through the fountain.

To say the least, I was surprised. Aahz has never been the meditative type, particularly in times of crisis. He's more the "beat on someone or something until the problem goes away" type. Still, here he was, not agitated, not pacing, just sitting and staring. It was enough out of character for him to unnerve me completely.

"Umm . . . Hi, Aahz," I said hesitantly.

"Hello, Skeeve," he replied without looking around.

I waited for a few moments for him to say something else. He didn't. Finally I sat down on the bench next to him and stared at the water myself a bit.

We sat that way for a while, neither of us saying anything. The trickling water began to have a tranquilizing, hypnotic effect on me, and I found my mind starting to relax and drift.

"It's been quite a day, hasn't it, partner?"

My mind reflexively recoiled into a full defensive posture before it dawned on me that Aahz was still speaking quietly.

"Y . . . Yes."

I waited, but he seemed off in his own thoughts again. My nerves shot, I decided to take the initiative.

"Look, Aahz. About Markie . . ."

"Yes?"

"I knew about the Elemental School thing. She told me on the way back from the Geek's. I just didn't know enough to realize it was important."

"I know," Aahz sighed, not looking at me. "I hadn't bothered to teach you about elemental magic . . . just like I hadn't taught you about dragon poker."

No explosion! I was starting to get a little worried about my partner.

"Aren't you upset?"

"Of course I'm upset," he said, favoring me with a fleeting glimpse of bared teeth, a barely recognizable smile. "Do you think I'm always this jovial?"

"I mean, aren't you mad?"

"Oh, I'm past 'mad.' I'm all the way to 'thoughtful.' "

I arrived at the startling conclusion that I liked it better when Aahz was shouting and unreasonable. *That* I knew how to deal with. This latest mood of his was a total unknown.

"What are you thinking about?"

"Parenthood."

"Parenthood?"

"Yeah. You know, that state of total responsibility for another being? Well, at least, that's the theory."

I wasn't sure I was following this at all.

"Aahz? Are you trying to say you feel responsible for what happened with Markie because you hadn't taught me more about magic and poker?"

"Yes. No. I don't know."

"But that's silly!"

"I know," he replied, with his first honest grin since I had entered the garden. "That's what got me thinking about parenthood."

I abandoned any hope of following his logic.

"You'll have to explain it to me, Aahz. I'm a little slow today."

He straightened up a bit, draping one arm around my shoulders.

"I'll try, but it isn't easy," he said in a tone that was almost conversational. "You see, regardless of what I said when I was ranting at you about how much of a problem Markie was going to be, it's been a long time since I was a parent. I've been sitting here, trying to remember what it was like. What's so surprising to me is the realization that I've never really stopped. Nobody does."

I started to shift uncomfortably.

"Hear me out. For once I'm trying to share some of my hard-won lessons with you without shouting. Forget the theories of parenthood! What it's really all about is taking pride in things you can never be sure you had a hand in, and accepting the responsibility and guilt for things you either didn't know or had no control over. Actually, it's a lot more complicated than that, but that's the bare bones of the matter."

"You don't make it sound particularly attractive," I observed.

"In a lot of ways, it isn't. Your kid expects you to know everything . . . to be able to answer any question he asks and, more important, to provide a logical explanation of what is essentially an illogical world. Soci-

ety, on the other hand, expects you to train your kid in everything necessary for them to become a successful, responsible member of the community . . . even if you aren't yourself. The problem is that you aren't the
only source of input for the kid. Friends, schools, and other adults are all
supplying other opinions, many of which you don't agree with. That
means that if your kid succeeds, you don't really know if it was because of
or in spite of your influence. On the other hand, if the kid goes bad, you
always wonder if there was something else you could have said or done or
done differently that could have salvaged things before they hit the wall."

His hand tightened slightly on my shoulder, but I don't think he did it
consciously.

"Now, I wasn't a particularly good parent . . . which I like to think
places me in the majority. I didn't interact much with my kids. Business
was always a good excuse, but the truth was that I was glad to let someone
else handle their upbringing as much as possible. I can see now that it was
because I was afraid that if I tried to do it myself, that in my ignorance and
uncertainty I would make some terrible mistake. The end result was that
some of the kids turned out okay, some of them . . . let's say less than
okay. What I was left with was a nagging feeling that I could have done
better. That I could have—should have—made more of a difference."

He released his hold on my shoulders and stood up.

"Which brings us to you."

I wasn't sure if I should feel uncomfortable because he was focusing
on me, or glad because he was pacing again.

"I've never consciously thought of you as a son, but in hindsight I
realize that a lot of how I've treated you has been driven by my lingering
guilt from parenthood. In you, I had another chance to mold someone
. . . to give all the advice I felt I should have given my own kids. If at
times I've seemed to overreact when things didn't go well, it's because deep
inside I saw it as a personal failure. I mean, this was my second chance. A
time to show how much I had learned from my earlier perceived failures,
and you know what? Now I'm giving it my full attention and my best shot,
and things are *still* going wrong!"

This was doing nothing to brighten my mood. On top of everything
else, now I had the distinct feeling I had somehow let Aahz down.

"I don't think you can say it's your fault, Aahz. I mean, you've tried
hard and been more patient with me than anyone I've ever known. Nobody can teach someone else everything, even if they could remember
what should be taught. I've got a certain saturation point. After that, I'm
not going to learn anything new until I've digested what I've got. Even
then, I've got to be honest and say there are some things I don't believe no

matter how often you tell me. I've just got to find out for myself. A craftsman can't blame his skill if he has defective material."

"That's just what I've been thinking," Aahz nodded. "I can't keep blaming myself for everything. It's very astute of you to have figured this out at your age . . . without going through what I have."

"It's no big thing to figure out that I'm a dummy," I said bitterly. "I've known it all along."

Suddenly, I felt myself being lifted into the air. I looked past Aahz's hand, which was gripping my shirt by the collar, down the length of his arm, and into his yellow eyes.

"Wrong lesson!" he snarled, sounding much like his old self. "What you're supposed to be learning isn't that you're dumb. You're not, and if you were listening, I just complimented you on that fact."

"Then what . . ." I managed, with what little air I had left.

"The point is that what's happened in the past isn't *my* fault, just like what's happening now isn't *your* fault!"

"Aaggh . . . urk . . ." was my swift rebuttal.

"Oh! Sorry."

My feet hit the floor and air flooded back into my lungs.

"All a parent, *any* parent, can do is give it their best shot, right or wrong." Aahz continued as if there had been no interruption. "The actual outcome rests on so many variables, no single person can assume responsibility, blame, or praise for whatever happens. That's important for me to remember in my dealings with you . . . and for you to remember in your dealings with Markie. It's not your fault!"

"It isn't?"

"That's right. We both have strong paternal streaks in us, though I don't know where you got yours from, but all we can do is our best. We've got to remember not to try to shoulder the blame for what other people do . . . like Tananda."

That sobered me up again. "You know about that, huh?"

"Yeah. She told me to tell you goodbye if she didn't see you, but I guess you already know."

I simply nodded, unable to speak.

"I was already worried about how you were going to react to the problems with Markie, and when Tananda left I knew you were going to take it hard. I've been trying to find a way to show you that you aren't alone. Right or wrong, what you're feeling has been around for a long time."

"Thanks, Aahz."

"Has it helped at all?"

I thought for a moment.

"A bit."

My partner heaved another sigh.

"Well," he said, "I tried. That's what's important . . . I think."

"Cheerio, chaps. How's every little thing?"

I glanced up to find Chumley striding toward us, beaming merrily. "Oh. Hi, Chumley."

"I thought you'd like to know," the troll announced, "I think I've figured out a way to charge the damage Markie caused this afternoon back to the Mob as a business expense!"

"That's swell, Chumley," Aahz said dully.

"Yeah. Terrific."

" 'Allo, 'allo?" he said, cocking his head at us. "Any time the two biggest hustlers at the Bazaar fail to get excited over money, there's got to be something wrong. Out with it now. What's troubling you?"

"Do you want to tell him, Aahz?"

"Well . . ."

"I say, this wouldn't be about little sister leaving the nest, would it? Oh, there's a giggle."

"You know?" I blinked.

"I can see you're all broken up over it," Aahz said in a dangerous tone.

"Tish tosh!" the troll exclaimed. "I don't see where it's anything to get upset about. Tananda's just settling things in her mind, is all. She's found that she likes something that goes against her self-image. It might take a few days, but eventually she'll figure out that it's not the end of the world. Everybody goes through it. It's called 'growing up.' If anything, I think it's bloody marvelous that she's finally having to learn that things don't stay the same forever."

"You do?" I was suddenly starting to feel better.

"Certainly. Why, in just the time we've been chumming around together, Aahz has changed, you've changed, so have I, though I don't tend to show it as dramatically as you two or little sister. You blokes have just got a bad case of the guilts. Poppycock! You can't take the blame for everything, you know."

"That's good advice," I said, standing up and stretching. "Why can't you ever give me good advice like that, partner?"

"Cause any fool can see it without being told," Aahz snarled, but there was a twinkle in his eye. "The problem is that Pervects aren't just any fool."

"Quite right," Chumley grinned. "Now how about joining me in a little Happy Hour spot of wine while I tell you how clever I am at saving you money."

"I'd rather you impressed us with a solution to our baby-sitting problems," my partner said grimly, heading for the lounge.

I followed in their wake, strangely happy. Things were back to normal . . . or as normal as they ever get around here. Between us, I was sure we could find a positive course of action. I mean, after all, how much trouble could one little girl . . .

That thought crumbled in front of an image of elemental-blown tents.

I resolved to do more listening than talking in the upcoming war council.

# Chapter IX

*"They never let you live it down.
One little mistake!"*

**Nero**

RELAXING over drinks with Aahz and Chumley, I felt the tensions and depressions of the day slipping away. It was nice to know that when things really got tough, I had friends to help me solve my problems, however complex or apparently hopeless.

"Well, guys," I said, pouring another round of wine for everyone. "Any ideas as to what we should do?"

"Beats me," Chumley said, toying with his goblet.

"I still think it's *your* problem," Aahz announced, leaning back in his chair and grinning evilly. "I mean, after all, you got into it without our help."

Like I said, it's great to have friends.

"I can't say I go along with that, Aahz old boy," the troll said with a wave. "Although I'll admit it's tempting. The unfortunate reality is that as long as we're living and working as closely as we are, his problems are our problems, don't you know?"

As much as I appreciated the fact that Chumley's logic was moving them closer to lending me assistance, I felt the need to defend myself a little.

"I'd like to think it's a two-way street, Aahz. I've gotten dragged into a few of *your* problems as well."

He started to snap back, then pursed his lips and returned his attention to his wine. "I'll avoid comparing lists of how often which of us has gotten us in how much trouble and simply concede the point. I guess that's part of what a partnership is all about. Sorry if I seem a little snorky from time to time, but I've never had a partner before. It takes getting used to."

"I say! Well said, Aahz!" Chumley applauded. "You know, you're getting more civilized every day."

"Let's not get too carried away just yet. How about you, Chumley? You and your sister have helped us out often enough, but I don't recall either of *you* bringing your problems home with you. Isn't that a little lopsided?"

"I've always figured it's our way of kicking in on the rent," the troll said casually. "If our problems ever start interfering with your work, then I'll figure we've overstayed our welcome."

This came as a total surprise to me. I realized with a start that I was usually so busy with my own life and problems that I never got around to asking much about the work Chumley and Tananda were doing.

"Whoa up a minute here," I said. "Are you two having problems I don't know about?"

"Well, it isn't all beer and skittles," the troll grimaced briefly. "The subject at hand, however, is *your* problems. There's nothing on my plate that has a higher priority just now, so let's get to work on the latest crisis, shall we? I suggest we all put on our thinking caps and brainstorm a little. Let's just stare at the ceiling and each toss out ideas as they occur to us."

I made myself a little promise to return to the subject of Tananda and Chumley's problems at a later date, then joined the others in staring thoughtfully at the ceiling.

Time crawled along, and no one said anything.

"Well, so much for brainstorming," Aahz said, reaching for the wine again. "I'll admit I'm coming up blank."

"Perhaps it would help if we started by defining the problem," Chumley urged. "Now, as I see it, we have two problems: Markie and Bunny. We're going to have trouble figuring out what to do about Bunny until we find out what Don Bruce has up his sleeve, and we've got to come up with a way to keep Markie from totally disrupting our lives until her father comes to pick her up."

"*If* he picks her up," my partner corrected helpfully.

"I'll admit, I still don't know how you did so well in that game to end up with Markie in the first place," the troll said, cocking one outsized eye at me and ignoring Aahz.

"Dumb luck . . . with the emphasis on *dumb.*"

"That's not the way I heard it," Chumley smirked. "Whatever your method was, it was successful enough to make you the talk of the Bazaar."

"What!?" Aahz said, sitting up in his chair again.

"You would hear it yourself if you weren't spending all your time sulking in your room," the troll winked. "When I went out after little sister today, it seemed that all I was hearing about was the new dragon poker champion of Deva. Everybody's talking about the game, or what they've heard about the game. I suspect they're embellishing upon the facts, from some of the descriptions of the hands, but there are those who are taking it all as gospel."

I remembered then that when the game broke up, the other players had been very enthusiastic about my playing. At the time, I had been worried about the secret of my night out reaching Aahz (which, you'll recall, it did before I got home). The troubles with Markie and Bunny had occupied my mind and time ever since, so I hadn't stopped to think of other potential repercussions of the game gossip. Now, however . . .

Aahz was out of his seat, pacing back and forth.

"Chumley, if what you're saying is true . . . are you following this, partner?"

"Too bloody well," I growled.

That got my partner to pause momentarily to roll his eyes.

"Watch yourself," he warned. "You're starting to talk like Chumley now."

"You want I should talk like Guido instead, know what I mean?"

"I don't understand," the troll interrupted. "Is something amiss?"

"We don't have two problems," Aahz announced. "We've got *three!* Markie, Bunny, *and* the rumor mill!"

"Gossip? How can that be a problem?"

"Think it through, Chumley," I said. "All I need right now is to have a bunch of hotshot dragon poker players hunting me up to see if I'm as good as everybody says."

"That's only part of it, partner," Aahz added. "This could hurt our business and public images as well."

I closed my eyes and sighed.

"Spell it out for me, Aahz. I'm still learning, remember?"

"Well, we already know your reputation at magic has been growing fast . . . almost too fast. The competition hates you because you're taking all the prime assignments. No big deal! Professional jealousy is the price of success in any field. There comes a time, however, when you can get too big too fast. Then it isn't just your rivals you worry about. Everybody wants you taken down a peg or two if for no other reason than to convince themselves that your success is abnormal . . . that they don't have to feel bad for not measuring up."

He paused to stare at me hard.

"I'm afraid this dragon poker thing just might push you into the second category. A lot of beings excel here at the Bazaar, but they're only noted in one field. The Geek, for example, is a recognized figure among the gamblers, but he doesn't have any reputation to speak of as a magician or merchant. People can accept that . . . work hard and you rise toward the top of your group. You, on the other hand, have just made a strong showing in a second profession. I'm afraid there's going to be some backlash."

"Backlash?" I echoed weakly.

"It's like I've been trying to tell you: people aren't going to want you to get too much above them. At the very least they might start boycotting our business. At most . . . well, there are ways of sabotaging other people's success."

"You mean they're going to . . ."

"That's enough!" Chumley declared, slapping his palm down on the table loudly.

It suddenly occurred to me that I had never seen Chumley mad. It also occurred to me that I was glad our furniture was strong enough to withstand even Aahz's tirades. If not, the troll would have destroyed the table just stopping the conversation.

"Now listen up, both of you!" he ordered, leveling a gnarled finger at us. "I think the current crisis has gone to your heads. You two are overreacting . . . snapping at shadows! I'll admit we've got some problems, but we've handled worse. This is no time to get panicky."

"But . . ."

"Hear me out, Aahz. I've listened to you bellow often enough."

I opened my mouth to make a witty comment, then, for once, thought better of it.

"Markie is a potential disaster, but the key word there is *potential.* She's a good kid who will do what we say . . . *if* we learn to watch what we say to her. The same goes for Bunny. She's smart as a whip and . . ."

"Bunny?" I blurted, forgetting myself for a moment.

"Yes, Bunny. It's been a long time since there's been anyone around here I could discuss literature and theater with. She's really quite intelligent if you bother to talk to her."

"We *are* talking about the same Bunny, aren't we?" Aahz murmured.

"The one who comes across dumb as a stone," Chumley confirmed grimly. "Just remember how *I* come across when I'm putting on my Big Crunch act . . . but we're wandering. The subject is problems, and I maintain with a little coaching Bunny won't be one."

He paused to glare at us.

"As to the rumor of Skeeve's abilities at dragon poker, I've never in my life heard anyone get as alarmed as you, Aahz. Sure, there are negative sides to any rumor, but you have to get pretty extreme to do the projections that have been voiced just now."

"Hey, Boss!" Guido called, sticking his head in the door. "The Geek's here to see you."

"I'll handle this," Aahz said, heading for the reception area. "You stay here and listen to what Chumley has to say. He's probably right. I have been edgy lately . . . for some unknown reason."

"If I am right, then you should hear it, too," the troll called after him.

"Talk to me, Chumley," I said. "That's probably the closest you'll ever hear to an apology from Aahz, anyway."

"Quite right. Where was I? Oh, yes. Even if Aahz's appraisal of the reaction to your success is correct, it shouldn't have too much impact on your work. The small fry may go to other magicians, but you've been trying to cut down on unimportant jobs anyway. When someone is *really* in trouble, they're going to want the best available magician working on it . . . and right now, that means you."

I thought about what he was saying, weighing it carefully in my mind.

"Even if Aahz is just a little right," I said, "I'm not wild about having any ill feeling generated about me at the Bazaar. Admiration I don't mind, but envy makes me uneasy."

"Now that you'll just have to get used to," the troll laughed, clapping a hand lightly on my shoulder. "Whether you know it or not, that's been building for some time . . . long before this dragon poker thing came up. You've got a lot going for you, Skeeve, and as long as you do, there will be blokes who envy it."

"So you really think the dragon poker rumors are harmless?"

"Quite right. Really, what harm can come from idle gossip?"

"You know, Chumley, you aren't wrong very often. But when you miss, you really miss."

We looked up to find Aahz leaning in the doorway.

"What's wrong, Aahz? You look like someone just served you water when you were expecting wine."

My partner didn't even smile at my attempted humor.

"Worse than that," he said. "That was the Geek downstairs."

"We know. What did he want?"

"I was hoping he had come to pick up Markie for her father. . . ."
Aahz's voice trailed off to nothing.

"I take it he didn't?" I prompted.

"No, he didn't. In fact, the subject never came up."

Almost without thinking, my partner's hand groped for his oversized
goblet of wine.

"He had an invitation . . . no, make that a challenge. The Sen-Sen
Ante Kid has heard about Skeeve here. He wants a showdown match of
head-to-head dragon poker. The Geek is making the arrangements."

# Chapter X

*"A spoonful of sugar helps the medicine go down!"*
**L. Borgia**

"**J**UST let the energy flow."

"That's easy for you to say!"

"Did I stutter?"

"You know, Hot Stuff, maybe it would be better if I . . ."

"Quit talking and concentrate, Massha."

"You started it."

"And I'm finishing it. Focus on the candle!"

If some of that sounds vaguely familiar, it should. It's the old "light the candle" game. Theoretically, it builds a student's confidence. In actuality, it's a pain in the butt. Apprentices hate the candle drill. I did when I was an apprentice. It's a lot more fun when you're on the teaching end.

"Come on, Skeeve. I'm getting too old to learn this stuff."

"And you're getting older the longer you stall, *apprentice*. Remember, you came to me to learn magic. Just because we've gotten distracted from time to time doesn't mean I've forgotten completely. Now light the candle."

She turned her attention to the exercise again with a mutter I chose to ignore.

I had been thinking hard about my conversations with Aahz and Chumley. The whole question of what to do about the challenge from the

Kid was touchy enough that for once I decided to seek the counsel of my advisors before making a commitment I might later regret. Wiser heads than mine were addressing the dilemma at this very moment. Unfortunately, aforesaid wiser heads were in total disagreement as to what course of action to follow.

Aahz was in favor of refusing the match, while Chumley insisted that a refusal would only inflame the situation. He maintained that the only sane way out would be to face the Kid and lose (no one seriously thought I would have a chance in such a game), thereby getting me off the hot seat once and for all. The main problem with that solution was that it involved voluntarily giving up a substantial amount of money . . . and Aahz wouldn't hear of it.

As the battle raged on, I thought about the earlier portions of our conversations. I thought about parenthood and responsibility. Then I went looking for Massha.

When we first met, Massha was holding down a job as court magician for one of the city-states in the dimension of Jahk . . . that's right. Where they hold the Big Game every year. The problem was that she didn't really know any magic. She was what is known in the field as a mechanic, and all her powers were purchased across the counter in the form of rings, pendants, and other magical devices. After she saw us strut our stuff in the Big Game, she decided to try to learn some of the non-mechanical variety of magic . . . and for some unknown reason picked or picked on me to provide her with lessons.

Now, to say the least, I had never thought of Massha as a daughter, but she was my apprentice and therefore a responsibility I had accepted. Unfortunately, I had dodged that responsibility more often than not for the very reasons Aahz had listed: I was unsure of my own abilities and therefore afraid of making a mistake. What I hadn't done was give it my best shot, win or lose. That realization sparked me into a new resolve that if anything happened to Massha in the future, it wouldn't be because I hadn't at least tried to teach her what she asked.

I was also aware that I wanted to learn more about any problems Chumley and Tananda were having, as well as getting a better fix on just who or what Bunny was. At this moment, however, Tananda was absent and Chumley was arguing with Aahz, putting that objective on hold. Bunny was around somewhere, but given a choice between her and Massha, I opted for addressing old obligations before plunging into new ones. Ergo, I rousted out Massha for a long-overdue magic lesson.

"It's just not working, Skeeve. I told you I can't do it."

She sank back in her chair dejected and scowled at the floor. Curious, I reached over and felt the candle wick. It wasn't even warm.

"Not bad," I lied. "You're showing some improvement."

"Don't kid a kidder." Massha grimaced. "I'm not getting anywhere."

"Could you light it with one of your rings?"

She spread her fingers and made a quick inventory. "Sure. This little trinket right here could do the job, but that's not the point."

"Bear with me. How does it work? Or, more important, how does it feel when it works?"

She gave a quick shrug.

"There's nothing to it. You see, this circle around the stone here moves, and I rotate it according to how tight a beam I want. Pressing the back of the ring activates it, so all I have to do is aim it and relax. The ring does all the work."

"That's it!" I exclaimed, snapping my fingers.

"What's it?"

"Never mind. Keep going. How does it feel?"

"Well," she frowned thoughtfully, "It sort of tingles. It's like I was a hose and there was water rushing through me and out the ring."

"Bingo!"

"What's that supposed to mean?"

"Listen, Massha. Listen closely."

I was speaking carefully now, trying hard to contain my excitement over what I hoped was a major breakthrough.

"Our problem with teaching you non-mechanical magic is that you don't believe in it! I mean, you know that it exists and all, but you don't believe that you can do it. You're working hard at overcoming that every time you try to cast a spell, and that's the problem: You try. . . . You work hard. You know you've got to believe, so you work hard at overcoming your disbelief every time you . . ."

"Yeah. So?"

"It means you tense up instead of relaxing the way you do when you're working your rings. Tensing blocks the flow of the energies, so you end up with less power at your disposal than you have when you're just walking around. The idea of casting a spell isn't to tense up, it's to relax . . . if anything, it's an exercise in forced relaxation."

My apprentice bit at her lower lip. "I don't know. That sounds too easy."

"On the one hand it's easy. Viewed a different way, one of the hardest things to do is relax on cue, especially if there's a crisis raging around you at the time."

"So all I have to do is relax?" she asked skeptically.

"Remember that 'hose' feeling you get when you use the ring? That's the energies being channeled through you and focused on your objective. If you pinch off a hose, how much water gets through?"

"I guess that makes sense."

"Try it . . . now. Reach out your hand and focus on the candle wick as if you were going to use your ring, only don't activate it. Just tell yourself that the ring is working and relax."

She started to say something, then changed her mind. Instead, she drew a deep breath, blew it out, then pointed a finger at the candle.

"Just relax," I urged softly. "Let the energies flow."

"But . . ."

"Don't talk. Keep your mind on the candle and hear me like I'm talking from a long way off."

Obediently, she focused on the candle.

"Feel the flow of the energies . . . just like when you're using the ring. Relax some more. Feel how the flow increases? Now, without tensing up, tighten that flow down to a narrow beam and aim it at the wick."

I was concentrating on Massha so much I almost missed it. A small glow of light started to form on the candle wick.

"That's it," I said, fighting to keep my voice calm. "Now . . ."

"Daddy! Guido says . . ."

"Ssshh!!!" I hissed. "Not now, Markie! We're trying to light the candle."

She paused in the doorway and cocked her head quizzically.

"Oh, that's easy!" she beamed suddenly and raised her head.

"MARKIE!! DON'T . . ."

But I was too late.

There was a sudden flash of light in the room, and the candle lit. Well, it didn't exactly light, it melted like a bag of water when you take away the bag. So did the candle holder. The table lit, though . . . briefly. At least one corner of it did. It flared for a moment, then the fire died as abruptly as it had appeared. What was left was a charred quarter-circle of tabletop where the corner used to be. That and a table leg standing alone like a burnt-out torch. The fire had hit so fast and smooth the leg didn't even topple over.

I don't remember reaching for Markie, but somehow I had her by the shoulders shaking her.

"WHAT DID YOU DO THAT FOR??" I said in my best paternal tones.

"You . . . you said . . . you wanted the . . . candle lit."

*"That's* lighting a candle?!?"

"I still have a little trouble with control . . . but my teacher says I'm doing better."

I realized I was having a little trouble with control, too. I stopped shaking her and tried to calm myself. This effort was aided by the fact that I noticed that Markie's lip was quivering and she was blinking her eyes rapidly. It suddenly dawned on me that she was about to cry. I decided that, not knowing what would happen when she cried, I would do my best to stay ignorant by heading her off at the pass.

"Umm . . . that was a Fire Elemental, right? Did you learn that at Elemental School?"

Getting someone to talk often serves to stave off tears . . . at least, it had always worked on me.

"Y . . . Yes," she said meekly. "At Elemental School, we learn Fire for starters."

"It's . . . ummm . . . very impressive. Look, I'm sorry if I barked at you, Markie, but you see, I didn't just want the candle lit. I wanted Massha to light it. It was part of her magic lesson."

"I didn't know that."

"I know. I didn't think to tell you. That's why I'm apologizing. What happened here was my fault. Okay?"

She nodded her head, exaggerating the motion until it looked like she had a broken neck. It was an interesting illusion, one that I vastly preferred to the idea of her crying . . . especially in the mood I was in. The thought of Markie with a broken neck . . .

"Aahh . . . you *did* interrupt Massha's lesson, though," I said, forcing the other concept from my mind. "Don't you think it would be nice if you apologized to her?"

"That's a great idea, Daddy," she beamed. "I'll do that the next time I see her. Okay?"

That's when I realized my apprentice had slipped out of the room.

\* \* \*

"What do you think you're doing, Massha?"

Leaning casually in the doorway of Massha's bedroom, I realized my voice lacked the intimidating power of Aahz's, but it's the only voice I've got.

"What does it look like I'm doing?" she snarled, carrying a massive armload of clothes from her closet to dump on the bed.

"I'd say, offhand, that it looks like you're packing. The question is, why?"

"People usually pack because it's the easiest way to carry their things when they travel. Less wear and tear on the wardrobe."

Suddenly, I was weary of the banter. Heaving a sigh, I moved in front of her, blocking her path.

"No more games, Massha. Okay? Tell me straight out, why are you leaving? Don't you owe your teacher that much at least?"

She turned away, busying herself with something on her dresser.

"C'mon, Skeeve," she said in a tone so low I could barely hear it. "You saw what happened downstairs."

"I saw you on the verge of making a major breakthrough in your lessons, if that's what you mean. If Markie hadn't come in, you would have had the candle lit in another few seconds."

"Big deal!"

She spun to face me, and I could see that she was trying not to cry. There seemed to be a lot of that going around.

"Excuse me, Skeeve, but big fat hairy deal. So I can light a candle. So what?! After years of study, Massha can light a candle . . . and a little girl can blow the end off the table without even trying! What does that make me? A magician? Ha ha! What a joke."

"Massha, *I* can't do what Markie did downstairs . . . or what she did in the Bazaar either, for that matter. I told you when you first approached me to be my apprentice exactly how little magic I knew. I'm still learning, though . . . and in the meantime we're still holding our own in the magic business . . . and that's here at the Bazaar. The Magic Capital of the dimensions."

That seemed to settle her a bit, but not much.

"Tell me honestly, Hot Stuff," she said, pursing her lips. "How good do you think I could ever be with magic . . . really?"

"I don't know. I'd like to think that with work and practice you could be better than you are now, though. That's really all any of us can hope for."

"You may be right Skeeve, and it's a good thought. The fact still remains that in the meantime, I'll always be small potatoes around here . . . magically, of course. The way things are going, I'm destined to be a hanger-on. A leech. You and Aahz are nice guys, and you'd never throw me out, but I can't think of one good reason why I should stay."

"I can."

My head came around so fast I was in momentary danger of whiplash. Framed in the doorway was . . .

"TANANDA!"

"In the flesh," she said with a wink. "But that's not the subject here. Massha, I can't speak for long-term conditions, but I've got one good reason why you shouldn't leave just now. It's the same reason I'm back."

"What's that?"

"It involves the Great Skeeve here. C'mon downstairs. I'm going to brief everybody at once at a war council. We've got a full-blown crisis on our hands."

# Chapter XI

*"I believe we're under attack."*
**Col. Travis**

ONE of the rooms in our extra-dimensional palace had a large oval table in it surrounded by chairs. When we moved in, we dubbed it the Conference Room, since there didn't seem to be any other practical use for it. We never used it for conferences, mind you, but it's always nice to have a conference room.

Tonight, however, it was packed to capacity. Apparently Tananda had rounded up the whole household, including Markie and Bunny, before locating Massha and me, and everyone was already seated as we walked in.

"Can we get started now?" Aahz asked caustically. "I *do* have other things to do, you know."

"Really?" Chumley sneered. "Like what?"

"Like talking to the Geek about that invitation," my partner shot back.

"Without talking to your partner first?"

"I didn't say I was going to refuse or accept. I just want to talk to him about . . ."

"Can we table the argument for the moment?" I interrupted. "I want to hear what Tananda has to say."

"Thanks, Skeeve," she said, flashing me a quick smile before dropping back into her solemn manner. "I guess you all know I was moving out of here. Well, poking around the Bazaar, I heard a rumor that's changed my mind. If it's true, we're all going to have our hands full dealing with it."

She paused, but no one else said anything. For a change, we were all giving her our undivided attention.

"I guess I should drop the shoe first, then we can all go on from there. The talk on the street is that someone's hired the Ax to do a number on Skeeve."

There was a few heartbeats of silence; then the room exploded.

"Why should anyone . . ."

"Who's hired the Ax?"

"Where did you hear . . ."

"Hold it! HOLD IT!" Tananda shouted, holding up her hands for silence. "I can only answer one question at a time . . . but I'll warn you in advance, I don't have that many answers to start with."

"Who's hired him?" Aahz demanded, seizing first position.

"The way I heard it, a group of magicians here at the Bazaar is none too happy with Skeeve's success. They feel he's taking all the choice assignments these days . . . getting all the glory work. What they've done is pool their money so they can hire the Ax to do what they're all afraid to do themselves . . . namely, deal with Skeeve."

"Do you hear that, Chumley? Still think I'm being melodramatic?"

"Shut up, Aahz. Where'd you hear this, little sister?"

"Remember Vic? The little vampire that relocated here from Limbo? Well, he's opened his own magic practice here at the Bazaar. It seems that he was approached to contribute to the fund. He's new enough here that he didn't know any of them by name, but they claim to have the support of nearly a dozen of the smalltime magicians."

"Why didn't he warn us as soon as he heard?"

"He's trying to stay neutral. He didn't contribute, but he also didn't want to be the one to blow the whistle to Skeeve. The only reason he said anything to me was that he was afraid that anyone close to Skeeve might get caught in the crossfire. I must admit, he seems to have a rather exaggerated idea of how much Skeeve here can handle on his own."

"Can I ask a question?" I said grimly. "As the intended victim?"

"Sure, Skeeve. Ask away."

"Who's the Ax?"

At least half the heads at the table swiveled toward me while the faces attached to them dropped their jaws.

"You're kidding!"

"Don't you know who . . ."

"Aahz, didn't you teach him any . . ."

"Whoa! Hold it!" I shouted over the clamor. "I can only take so much of this informative babbling at one time. Aahz! As my friend, partner, and sometimes mentor, could you deign to tell me in simple terms who the Ax is?"

"Nobody knows."

I closed my eyes and gave my head a small shake in an effort to clear my ears. After all this "Gee, why don't you know that?" brouhaha, I could swear he said . . .

"He's right, handsome," Tananda chimed in. "The Ax's real identity is one of the most closely guarded secrets in all the dimensions. That's why he's so effective at what he does."

"That may be true," I nodded. "But from the reaction in this room when you dropped the name, I'd guess that somebody knows *something* about him. Now, let me rephrase the question. If you don't know *who* the Ax is, could someone enlighten me as to *what* he is?"

"The Ax is the greatest Character Assassin in all the dimensions," Aahz said with a snarl. "He works freelance and charges fees that make ours look like pocket change. Once the Ax is on your tail, though, you might as well kiss it goodbye. He's ruined more careers than five stock-market crashes. Haven't you ever heard the expression 'take the ax to someone'? Well, that's where it comes from."

I felt that all-too-familiar "down elevator" sensation in my stomach. "How does he do it?"

"It varies," my partner shrugged. "He tailor-makes his attack depending on the assignment. The only constant is that whatever you were when he started, you're not when he's done."

"I wish you'd quit saying 'you' all the time. I'm not dead yet."

"Sorry, partner. Figure of speech."

"Well, that's just swell!" Guido exploded. "How're Nunzio 'n' me supposed to guard the Boss when we don't know what's comin' at him?"

"You don't," Aahz shot back. "This is out of your category, Guido. We're talking about character assassination, not a physical attack. It's not in your job description."

"Izzat so!" Nunzio said in his squeaky voice. "Don Bruce says we should guard him. I don't remember him sayin' anything about physical or non-physical attacks. Right, Guido?"

"That's right! If the Boss has got someone after his scalp, guardin' him is our job . . . if that's all right with you, MISTER Aahz!"

"I wouldn't trust you two to guard a fish head, much less my partner!" Aahz roared, surging to his feet.

"Stop it, Aahz!" Tananda ordered, kicking my partner's chair so that it cut his legs out from under him and plopped him back into his seat. "If we're up against the Ax, we're going to need all the help we can get. Let's stop bickering about the 'who' and concentrate on the 'how.' Okay? We're all scared, but that doesn't mean we should turn on each other when it's the Ax that's our target."

That cooled everybody down for the moment. There were a few glares and mutters exchanged, but at least the volume level dropped to where I could be heard.

"I think you're all overlooking something," I said quietly.

"What's that?" Tananda blinked.

"Aahz came close a minute ago. This is my problem . . . and it's not really in any of your job descriptions. We're all friends, and there are business ties between Aahz and me, as well as Guido and Nunzio, but we're talking about reputations here. If I get hit, and everyone seems to be betting against me right now, anyone standing close to me is going to get mud splashed on them, too. It seems to me that the best course of action is for the rest of you to pull back, or, better still, for me to move out and present a solo target. That way, we're only running the risk of having one career ruined . . . mine. I got where I am by standing on your shoulders. If I can't maintain it on my own, well, maybe it wasn't much of a career to start with."

The whole room was staring at me as I lurched to a halt.

"You know, Skeeve old boy," Chumley said, clearing his throat, "As much as I like you, sometimes it's difficult to remember just how intelligent you are."

"I'll say," Tananda snarled. "That's about the dumbest . . . Wait a minute! Does this have anything to do with my leaving?"

"A bit," I admitted. "And Massha leaving and Aahz's talking about responsibility, and . . ."

"Stop right there!" Aahz ordered, holding up his hand. "Let's talk about responsibility, *partner*. It's funny that *I* should have to lecture *you* about this, but there are all sorts of responsibilities. One of the ones that I've learned about from you is the responsibility to one's friends: helping them out when they're in trouble, *and* letting them help you in return. I haven't forgotten how you came into a strange dimension to bust me out of prison after I'd refused your help in the first place; or how you signed us on to play in the Big Game to bail Tananda out after she was caught thieving; or how you insisted that Don Bruce assign Guido and Nunzio here to you when they were in line for disciplinary action after botching their assignment for the Mob. I haven't forgotten it, and I'll bet they haven't either, even if you have. Now, I suggest you shut up about job descriptions and let your friends help you . . . *partner.*"

"A-bloody-men." Chumley nodded.

"You could have left me with the Geek for the slavers," Markie said thoughtfully, in a surprisingly adult voice.

"So, now that that's settled," my partner said, rubbing his hands together, "let's get to work. My buddy Guido here has raised a good point. How do we defend Skeeve when we don't know how or when the Ax will strike?"

We hadn't really settled it, and Aahz wasn't about to give me a chance to point it out. I was just as glad, though, since I really didn't know what to say.

"All we can do is be on the lookout for anyone or anything strange showing up." Tananda shrugged.

"Like a showdown match of dragon poker with the Sen-Sen Ante Kid," Chumley said, staring into the distance.

"What's that?"

"You missed it, little sister. It seems that our boy Skeeve has drawn the attention of the king of dragon poker. He wants a head-to-head showdown match, and he wants it soon."

"Don't look at me like that, Chumley." Aahz grimaced. "I'm changing my vote. If we want to preserve Skeeve's reputation, there's no way he can refuse the challenge. *Now* I'm willing to admit it'll be money well spent."

"My daddy can beat anybody at dragon poker," Markie declared loyally.

"Your daddy can get his brains beaten out royally," my partner corrected gently. "I just hope we can teach him enough between now and game time that he can lose gracefully."

"I don't like it," Tananda growled. "It's too convenient. Somehow this game has the Ax's fingerprints all over it."

"You're probably right," Aahz sighed. "But there's not much else we can do except accept the challenge and try to make the best of a bad situation."

"Bite the bullet and play the cards we're dealt. Eh, Aahz?" I murmured.

I thought I had spoken quietly, but everyone around the table winced, including Markie. They might be loyal enough to risk their lives and careers defending me, but they weren't going to laugh at my jokes.

"Wait a minute!" Nunzio squeaked. "Do you think there's a chance that the Kid is actually the Ax?"

"Low probability," Bunny said, speaking for the first time in the meeting. "Someone like the Ax has to work a low profile. The Sen-Sen Ante Kid is too noticeable. If he were a character assassin, people would notice in no time flat. Besides, when he wins, nobody thinks it's because his opponents are disreputable . . . it's because the Kid is good. No, I figure the Ax has got to be like the purloined letter . . . he can hide in plain sight. Figure the last person you'd suspect, and you'll be getting close to his real identity."

The conversation swirled on around me, but I didn't listen very closely. For some reason, a thought had occurred to me while Bunny was talking. We had all been referring to the Ax as a "he," but if no one knew his real identity, he could just as easily be a "she." If anything, men were much less defensive and more inclined to brag about the details of their careers when they were with a woman.

Bunny was a woman. She had also appeared suddenly on our doorstep right around the time the Ax was supposed to be getting his assignment. We already knew that she was smarter than she let on . . . words like "purloined" didn't go with the vacant stare she so carefully cultivated. What better place for the Ax to strike from than the inside?

I decided that I should have a little chat with my moll as soon as the opportunity presented itself.

# Chapter XII

*"No one should hide their true self
behind a false face."*
**L. Chaney**

IT was with a certain amount of trepidation that I approached Bunny's bedroom. In case you haven't noticed, my experience with women is rather limited . . . like to the fingers of one hand limited.

Tananda, Massha, Luanna, Queen Hemlock, and now Bunny were the only adult females I had ever had to deal with, and thus far my track record was less than glowing. I had had a crush on Tananda for a while, but now she was more of a big sister to me. Massha was . . . well, Massha. I guess if anything I saw her as a kid sister, someone to be protected and sometimes cuddled. I've never really understood her open admiration of me, but it had stood firm through some of my most embarrassing mishaps and made it easy for me to confide in her. Even though I still thought of Luanna as my one true love, I had only spoken to her on four occasions, and after our last exchange I wasn't sure there would ever be a fifth meeting. The only relationship I had had with a woman which was more disastrous than my attempt at love was the one I had had with Queen Hemlock. She might not shoot me on sight, but there was no doubt in anyone's mind that she would like to . . . and she's the one who wanted to marry me!

Of course, none of the women I had dealt with so far was anything like Bunny, though whether this was good or bad I wasn't entirely sure. The fact still remained, however, that I was going to have to learn more about her, for two reasons: first, if she was going to be a resident of our household, I wanted to get a better fix on where she was coming from so I could treat her as something other than a mad aunt in the cellar; and second, if she was the Ax, the sooner I found out, the better. Unfortunately, the only way I could think of to obtain the necessary information was to talk to her.

I raised my hand, hesitated for a moment, then rapped on her door. It occurred to me that, even though I had never been in front of a firing squad, now I knew how it felt.

"Who is it?"

"It's Skeeve, Bunny. Have you got a minute?"

The door flew open and Bunny was there, grabbing my arm and pulling me inside. She was dressed in a slinky jumpsuit with the neck unlaced past her navel, which was a great relief to me. When I called on Queen Hemlock in her bedroom, she had received me in the altogether.

"Geez! It's good to see you. I was startin' to think you weren't ever comin' by!"

With a double-jointed shift of her hips she bumped the door shut, while her hands flew to the lacings in her outfit. So much for being relieved.

"If you just give me a second, hon, I'll be all set to go. You kinda caught me unprepared, and . . ."

"Bunny, could you just knock it off for a while? Huh?"

For some reason the events of the last few days suddenly rested heavy on my shoulders, and I just wasn't in the mood for games.

She stared at me with eyes as big as a Pervect's bar bill, but her hands ceased their activity. "What's the matter, Skeevie? Don't you like me?"

"I really don't know, Bunny," I said heavily. "You've never really given me a chance, have you?"

She drew in a sharp breath and started to retort angrily. Then she hesitated and looked away suddenly, licking her lips nervously.

"I . . . I don't know what you mean. Didn't I come to your room and try to be friendly?"

"I think you *do* know what I mean," I pressed, sensing a weakening in her defenses. "Every time we see each other, you're hitting me in the face with your 'sex-kitten' routine. I never know whether to run or applaud, but neither action is particularly conducive to getting to know you."

"Don't knock it," she said. "It's a great little bit. It's gotten me this far, hasn't it? Besides, isn't that what men want from a girl?"

"I don't."

"Really?"

There was a none-too-gentle mockery in her voice. She took a deep breath and pulled her shoulders back. "So tell me, what *does* cross your mind when I do this?"

Regardless of what impression I may have left on you from my earlier exploits, I do think fast. Fast enough to censor my first three thoughts before answering.

"Mostly discomfort," I said truthfully. "It's impressive, all right, but I get the feeling I should do something about it and I'm not sure I'm up to it."

She smiled triumphantly and let her breath out, easing the tension across her chest and my mind. Of the two, I think my mind needed it more.

"You have just hit on the secret of the sex kittens. It's not that you don't like it. There's just too much of it for you to be sure you can handle it."

"I'm not sure I follow you."

"Men like to brag and strut a lot, but they've got egos as brittle as spun glass. If a girl calls their bluff, comes at them like a seething volcano that can't be put out, men get scared. Instead of fanning a gentle feminine ember, they're faced with a forest fire, so they take their wind elsewhere. Oh, they keep us around to impress people. 'Look at the tigress I've tamed,' and all that. But when we're alone they usually keep their distance. I'll bet a moll sees less actual action than your average coed . . . except our pay scale is a lot better."

That made me think. On the one hand, she had called my reaction pretty close. Her roaring come-on *had* scared me a bit . . . well, a lot. Still, there was the other hand.

"It sounds like you don't think very much of men," I observed.

"Hey! Don't get me wrong. They're a lot better than the alternatives. I just got a little sick of listening to the same old lines over and over and decided to turn the tables on 'em. That's all."

"That wasn't what I meant. A second ago you said 'That's what men want from a girl.' It may be true, and I won't try to argue the point. It's uncomfortably close to 'That's *all* men want from a girl,' though, and that I *will* argue."

She scowled thoughtfully and chewed her lower lip. "I guess that *is* over-generalizing a bit," she admitted.

"Good."

"It's more accurate to say 'That's all men want from a *beautiful* girl.' "

"Bunny . . ."

"No, you listen to me, Skeeve. This is one subject I've had a lot more experience at than you have. It's fine to talk about minds when you look like Massha. But when you grow up looking good like I did—no brag, just a statement of fact—it's one long string of men hitting on you. If they're interested in your mind, I'd say they need a crash course in anatomy!"

In the course of our friendship, I had had many long chats with Massha about what it meant to a woman to be less than attractive. However, this was the first time I had ever been made to realize that beauty might be something less than an asset.

"I don't recall 'hitting on you,' Bunny."

"Okay, okay. Maybe I *have* taken to counterpunching before someone else starts. There's been enough of a pattern that I think I'm justified in jumping to conclusions. As I recall, you were a little preoccupied when we met. How would you have reacted if we ran into each other casually in a bar?"

That wasn't difficult at all to imagine . . . unfortunately.

"Touche!" I acknowledged. "Let me just toss one thought at you, Bunny. Then I'll yield to your experience. The question of sex is going to hang in the air over *any* male-female encounter until it's resolved. I think it lingers from pre-civilization days when survival of the species hinged on propagation. It's strongest when encountering a member of the opposite sex one finds attractive . . . such as a beautiful woman, or, I believe the phrase is, a 'hunk.' Part of civilization, though I don't know how many other people think of it this way, is setting rules and laws to help settle that question quickly: siblings, parents, and people under age or married to someone else are off limits . . . well, usually, but you get my point. Theoretically, this allows people to spend less time sniffing at each other and more time getting on with other endeavors . . . like art or business. I'm not sure it's an improvement, mind you, but it has brought us a long way."

"That's an interesting theory, Skeeve," Bunny said thoughtfully. "Where'd you hear it?"

"I made it up," I admitted.

"I'll have to mull that one over for a while. Even if you're right, though, what does it prove?"

"Well, I guess I'm trying to say that I think you're focusing too much on the existence of the question. Each time it comes up, resolve it and move on to other things. Specifically, I think we can resolve the question between us right now. As far as I'm concerned, the answer is no, or at least not for a long time. If we can agree on that, I'd like to move on to other things . . . like getting to know you better."

"I'd say that sounds like a pass, if you weren't saying 'no' in the same breath. Maybe I have been a little hypersensitive on the subject. Okay. Agreed. Let's try it as friends."

She stuck out her hand, and I shook it solemnly. In the back of my mind was a twinge of guilt. Now that I had gotten her to relax her guard, I was going to try to pump her for information.

"What would you like to know?"

"Well, except for the fact that you're smarter than you let on and that you're Don Bruce's niece, I really don't know much about you at all!"

"Whoops," she giggled, "You weren't even supposed to know about the niece part."

It was a much nicer giggle than her usual brain-jarring squeal.

"Let's start there, then. I understand your uncle doesn't approve of your career choice."

"You can say that again. He had a profession all picked out for me, put me through school and everything. The trouble was that he didn't bother to check with me. Frankly, I'd rather do anything else than what he had in mind."

"What was that?"

"He wanted me to be an accountant."

My mind flashed back to my old nemesis J. R. Grimble back at Possiltum. Trying to picture Bunny in his place was more than my imagination could manage.

"Umm . . . I suppose accounting is okay work. I can see why Don Bruce didn't want you to follow his footsteps into a life of crime."

Bunny cocked a skeptical eyebrow at me. "If you believe that, you don't know much about accounting."

"Whatever. It does occur to me that there are more choices for one's livelihood than being an accountant or being a moll."

"I don't want to set you off again," she smirked, "but my looks were working against me. Most legitimate businessmen were afraid that if they hired me their wives, or partners, or board of directors, or staff would think they were putting a mistress on the payroll. After a while I decided to go with the flow and go into a field where being attractive was a requirement instead of a handicap. If I'm guilty of anything, it's laziness."

"I don't know," I said, shaking my head. "I'll admit I don't think much of your career choice."

"Oh, yeah? Well, before you start sitting in moral judgment, let me tell you . . ."

"Whoa! Time out!" I interrupted. "What I meant was there isn't much of a future in it. Nothing personal, but nobody stays young and good-looking forever. From what I hear, your job doesn't have much of a retirement plan."

"None of the Mob jobs do," she shrugged. "It pays the bills while I'm looking for something better."

Now we were getting somewhere.

"Speaking of the Mob, Bunny, I'll admit this Ax thing has me worried. Do you know offhand if the Mob ever handles character assassination? Maybe I could talk to someone and get some advice."

"I don't think they do. It's a little subtle for them. Still, I've never known Uncle Bruce to turn down any kind of work if the profit was high enough."

It occurred to me that that was a fairly evasive no-answer. I decided to try again.

"Speaking of your uncle, do you have any idea why he picked you for this assignment?"

There was the barest pause before she answered.

"No. I don't."

I had survived the Geek's dragon poker game watching other people, and I'm fairly good at it. To me, that hesitation was a dead giveaway. Bunny knew why she was here, she just wasn't telling.

As if she had read my thoughts, a startled look came over her face.

"Hey! It just dawned on me. Do you think I'm the Ax? Believe me, Skeeve, I'm not. Really!"

She was very sincere and very believable. Of course, if I were the Ax, that's exactly what I would say and how I would say it.

# Chapter XIII

*"Your Majesty should pay attention
to his appearance."*
**H. C. Andersen**

**T**HERE are many words to describe the next day's outing into the Bazaar. Unfortunately, none of them are "calm," "quiet," or "relaxing." Words like "zoo," "circus," and "chaos" spring much more readily to mind.

It started before we even left our base . . . specifically, over whether or not we should go out at all.

Aahz and Massha maintained that we should go to ground until things blew over, on the theory that it would provide the fewest opportunities for the Ax to attack. Guido and Nunzio sided with them, adding their own colorful phrases to the proceedings. "Going to the mattresses" was one of their favorites, an expression which never ceased to conjure intriguing images to my mind. Like I told Bunny, I'm not *totally* pure.

Tananda and Chumley took the other side, arguing that the best defense is a solid offense. Staying inside, they argued, would only make us sitting ducks. The only sane thing to do would be to get out and try to determine just what the Ax was going to try. Markie and Bunny chimed in supporting the brother-sister team, though I suspect it was more from a desire to see more of the Bazaar.

After staying neutral and listening for over an hour while the two sides went at each other, I finally cast my vote . . . in favor of going out. Strangely enough, my reasons aligned most closely with those of Bunny and Markie: while I was more than a little afraid of going out and being a moving target, I was even more afraid of being cooped up inside with my own team while they got progressively more nervous and short-tempered with each other.

No sooner was that resolved than a new argument erupted, this time over who was going along. Obviously, everyone wanted to go. Just as obviously, if everybody did, we would look like exactly what we were: a strike force looking for trouble. I somehow didn't think this would assist our efforts to preserve my reputation.

After another hour of name-calling, we came up with a compromise. We would all go. For discretion as well as strategic advantage, however, it was decided that part of the team would go in disguise. That is, in addition to making our party look smaller than it really was, it would also allow our teammates to watch from a short distance and, more important, listen to what was being said around us in the Bazaar. Aahz, Tananda, Chumley, Massha, and Nunzio would serve as our scouts and reserve, while Markie, Bunny, Guido, and I would act as the bait . . . a role I liked less the more I thought about it.

Thus it was that we finally set out on our morning stroll . . . early in the afternoon.

On the surface the Bazaar was unchanged, but it didn't take long before I began to notice some subtle differences. I had gotten so used to maintaining disguise spells that I could keep our five colleagues incognito without it eating into my concentration . . . which was just as well, because there was a lot to concentrate on.

Apparently word of our last shopping venture had spread, and the reaction among the Deveel merchants to our appearance in the stalls was mixed and extreme. Some of the displays closed abruptly as we approached, while others rushed to meet us. There were, of course, those who took a neutral stance, neither closing nor meeting us halfway, but rather watching us carefully as we looked over their wares. Wherever we went, however, I noticed a distinct lack of enthusiasm for the favorite Bazaar pastime of haggling. Prices were either declared firm or counteroffers stacked up with minimum verbiage. It seems that, while they still wanted our money, the Deveels weren't eager to prolong contact with us.

I wasn't sure exactly how to handle the situation. I could take advantage of their nervousness and drive some shameless bargains, or grit my teeth and pay more than I thought the items were worth. The trouble was that neither course would do much to improve my image in the eyes of the merchants or erase the memory of our last outing.

Of course, my life being what it is, there were distractions.

After our talk, Bunny had decided that we were friends and attacked her new role with the same enthusiasm she brought to playing a vamp. She still clung to my arm, mind you, and from a distance probably still looked like a moll. Her attention, however, was now centered on me instead of on herself.

Today she had decided to voice her opinion of my wardrobe.

"Really, Skeeve. We've *got* to get you some decent clothes."

She had somehow managed to get rid of her nasal voice as well as whatever it was she had always been chewing on. Maybe there was a connection there.

"What's wrong with what I'm wearing?"

I had on what I considered to be one of my spiffier outfits. The stripes on the pants were two inches wide and alternated yellow and light green, while the tunic was a brilliant red and purple paisley number.

"I wouldn't know where to start," she said, wrinkling her nose. "Let's just say it's a bit on the garish side."

"You didn't say anything about my clothes before."

"Right. Before. As in 'before we decided to be friends.' Molls don't stay employed by telling their men how tacky they dress. Sometimes I think one of the qualifications for having a decorative lady on your arm is to have no or negative clothes sense."

"Of course, I don't have much firsthand knowledge, but aren't there a few molls who dress a little flamboyantly themselves?" I said archly.

"True. But I'll bet if you checked into it, they're wearing outfits their men bought for them to dress up in. When we went shopping, you let me do the selecting and just picked up the bill. A lot of men figure if they're paying the fare, they should have the final say as to what their baby-doll wears. Let's face it, molls have to pay attention to how they look because their jobs depend on it. A girl who dresses like a sack of potatoes doesn't find work as a moll."

"So you're saying I dress like a sack of potatoes?"

"If a sack looked like you, it would knock the eyes out of the potatoes."

I groaned my appreciation. Heck, if no one was going to laugh at my jokes, why should I laugh at theirs? Of course, I filed her comment away for future use if the occasion should arise.

"Seriously though, Skeeve, your problem is that you dress like a kid. You've got some nice pieces in your wardrobe, but nobody's bothered to show you how to wear them. Bright outfits are nice, but you've got to balance them. Wearing a pattern with a muted solid accents the pattern. Wearing a pattern with a pattern is trouble, unless you really know what you're doing. More often than not, the patterns end up fighting each other . . . and if they're in two different colors you've got an all-out war. Your clothes should call attention to you, not to themselves."

Despite my indignation, I found myself being drawn into what she was saying. If there's one thing I've learned in my various adventures, it's that you take information where you find it.

"Let's see if I'm following you, Bunny. What you're saying is that just buying nice items, especially ones that catch my eye, isn't enough. I've got to watch how they go together . . . try to build a coordinated total. Right?"

"That's part of it," she nodded. "But I think we'd better go back to step one for a moment if we're going to educate you right. First, you've got to decide on the image you want to project. Your clothes make a statement about you, but you've got to know what that statement should be. Now, bankers depend on people trusting them with their money, so they dress conservatively to give the impression of dependability. No one will give their money to a banker who looks like he spends his afternoons playing the ponies. At the other end of the scale, you have the professional entertainers. They make their money getting people to look at them, so their outfits are usually flashy and flamboyant."

This was fascinating. Bunny wasn't telling me a thing I hadn't seen for myself, but she was defining patterns that hadn't registered on me before. Suddenly the whole clothes thing was starting to make sense.

"So what kind of image do I project?"

"Well, since you ask, right now you look like one of two things: either someone who's so rich and successful that he doesn't have to care what other people think, or like a kid who doesn't know how to dress. Here at the Bazaar, they know you're successful, so the merchants jump to the first conclusion and drag out every gaudy item they haven't been able to unload on anyone else and figure if they price it high enough, you'll go for it."

"A sucker or a fool," I murmured. "I don't really know what image I want, but it isn't either of those."

"Try this one on for size. You're a magician for hire, right? You want to look well off so your clients know you're good at what you do, but not so rich that they'll think you're overcharging them. You don't want to go too conservative, because in part they're buying into the mystique of magic, but if you go too flashy you'll look like a sideshow charlatan. In short, I think your best bet is to try for 'quiet power.' Someone who is apart from the workaday crowd, but who is so sure of himself that he doesn't have to openly try for attention."

"How do I look like that?"

"That's where Bunny comes in," she said with a wink. "If we're agreed on the end, I'll find the means. Follow me."

With that, she led me off into one of the most incredible shopping sprees I've ever taken part in. She insisted that I change into the first outfit we bought: a light blue open-necked shirt with cream-colored slacks and a matching neck scarf. Markie protested that she had liked the pretty clothes better, but as we made our way from stall to stall, I noticed a change in the manner of the proprietors. They still seemed a little nervous about our presence, but they were bringing out a completely different array of clothes for our examination, and several of them complimented me on what I was wearing . . . something that had never happened before.

I must admit I was a little surprised at how much some of these "simple and quiet" items cost, but Bunny assured me that the fabric and the workmanship justified the price.

"I don't understand it," I quipped at one point. "I thought that accountants were all tightfisted, and here you are: the ultimate consumer."

"You don't see me reaching for *my* bankroll, do you?" she purred back. "Accountants can deal with necessary expenses, as long as it's someone else's money. Our main job is to get you maximum purchase power for your hard-earned cash."

And so it went. When I had time to think, it occurred to me that if Bunny *was* the Ax, she was working awfully hard to make me look good. I was still trying to figure out how this could fit into a diabolical plan when I felt a nudge at my elbow. Glancing around, I found Aahz standing next to me.

Now, when I throw my disguise spell, I still see the person as they normally are. That's why I started nervously before I remembered that to anyone else at the Bazaar he looked like a fellow shopper exchanging a few words.

"Nice outfit, partner," he said. "It looks like your little playmate is doing some serious work on your wardrobe."

"Thanks, Aahz. Do you really like it?"

"Sure. There *is* one little item you might add to your list before we head for home."

"What's that?"

"About five decks of cards. While he might be impressed by your new image, I think it'll make a bigger impact on the Kid if you spend a little time learning how to play dragon poker before you square off with him."

That popped my bubble in a hurry. Aahz was right. Clothes and the Ax aside, there was one thing I was going to have to face up to soon, and that was a showdown with the best dragon poker player in all the dimensions.

# Chapter XIV

*"Sometimes luck isn't enough."*
**L. Luciano**

**"O**GRE'S high, Skeeve. Your bet."

"Oh! Umm . . . I'll go ten."

"Bump you ten."

"Out."

"Twenty to me? I'll go twenty on top of that."

"Call."

By now, you should know that sound. That's right. Dragon poker in full gallop. This time, however, it was a friendly game between Aahz, Tananda, Chumley, and me. Of course, I'm using the phrase "friendly" rather loosely here.

Aside from occasional shouting matches, I had never been in a fight with these three before. That is, when there had been trouble, we formed our circle with the horns out, not in. For the first time I found myself on the opposite side of a conflict from my colleagues, and I wasn't enjoying it at all. Realizing this was just a game, and a practice game at that, I was suddenly very glad I didn't have to face any one of them in a real life-and-death situation.

The banter was still there, but there was an edge on it. There was a cloud of tension over the table as the players focused on each other like circling predators. It had been there at the game at the Even-Odds, but then I was expecting it. One doesn't expect support or sympathy from total strangers in a card game. The trouble was that these three who were my closest friends were turning out to be total strangers when the chips were down . . . if you'll pardon the expression.

"I think you're bluffing, big brother. Up another forty."

I gulped and pushed another stack of my diminishing pile of chips into the pot.

"Call."

"You got me," the troll shrugged. "Out."

"Well, Skeeve. That leaves you and me. I've got an elf-high flush."

She displayed her hand and looked at me expectantly. I turned my hole cards over with what I hoped was a confident flourish.

Silence reigned as everyone bent forward to stare at my hand.

"Skeeve, this is garbage," Tananda said at last. "Aahz folded a better hand than this without his hole cards. I had you beat on the board."

"What she's trying to say, partner," Aahz smirked, "is that you should have either folded or raised. Calling the bet when the cards she has showing beat your hand is just tossing away money."

"Okay, okay! I get the point."

"Do you? You've still got about fifty chips there. Are you sure you don't want to wait until you've lost those, too? Or maybe we should redivide the chips and start over . . . *again.*"

"Lighten up, Aahz," Tananda ordered. "Skeeve had a system that had worked for him before. Why shouldn't he want to try it out before being forcefed something new?"

What they were referring to was my original resistance to taking lessons in dragon poker. I had pretty much decided to handle the upcoming game the same way I had played the game at the Even-Odds rather than try to crash-learn the rules. After some discussion (read: argument) it was agreed that we should play a demonstration game so that I could show my coaches how well my system worked.

Well, I showed them.

I could read Aahz pretty well, possibly because I knew him so intimately. Chumley and Tananda, though, threw me for a loop. I was unable to pick up any sort of giveaway clues in their speech or manner, nor could I manage to detect any apparent relationship between their betting and what they were holding. In a depressingly short period of time I had been cleaned out of my starting allotment of chips. Then we divvied the stacks up again and started over . . . with the same results. We were now closing in on the end of the third round, and I was ready to throw in the towel.

As much as I would have liked to tell myself that I was having a bad run of cards or that we had played too few hands to set the patterns, the horrible truth was that I was simply outclassed. I mean, usually I could spot if a player had a good hand. Then the question was "how good," or more specifically, if his was better than mine. Of course, the same went for weak hands. I depended on being able to detect a player who was betting a hand that needed development or if he was simply betting that the other hand in the round would develop worse than his. In this "demonstration game," however, I was caught flatfooted again and again. Too many times a hand that I had figured for guts-nothing turned out to be a powerhouse.

To say the least, it was depressing. These were players who wouldn't dream of challenging the Sen-Sen Ante Kid themselves, and they were cleaning my clock without half trying.

"I know when I'm licked, Aahz," I said. "Even if it does take me a little longer than most. I'm ready to take those lessons you offered . . . if you still think it will do any good."

"Sure it will, partner. At the very least, I don't think it can hurt your game, if tonight's been an accurate sample."

Trust a Pervect to know just what to say to cheer you up.

"Come on, Aahz old boy," Chumley interrupted. "Skeeve here is doing the best he can. He's just trying to hang on in a bad situation . . . like we all do. Let's not make it any rougher for him. Hmmm?"

"I suppose you're right."

"And watch comments like that when Markie's around," Tananda put in. "She's got a bad case of hero-worship for her new daddy, and we need him as an authority figure to keep her in line."

"Speaking of Markie," my partner grimaced, peering around, "where is our portable disaster area?"

The tail end of our shopping expedition had not gone well. Markie's mood seemed to deteriorate as the day wore on. Twice we were saved from total disaster only by timely intervention by our spotters when she started to get particularly upset. Not wishing to push our luck, I called a halt to the excursion, which almost triggered another tantrum from my young ward. I wondered if our parents had ever had shopping trips cut short by a cranky child.

"She's off somewhere with Bunny and the bodyguards. I thought this session would be rough enough without the added distraction of Markie cheering for her daddy."

"Good call," Chumley said. "Well, enough chitchat. Shall we have at it?"

"Right!" Aahz declared, rubbing his hands together as he leaned forward. "Now, the first thing we have to do is tighten up your betting strategy. If you keep . . ."

"Umm . . . Aren't you getting a little ahead of yourself, Aahz?" Tananda interrupted.

"How so?"

"Don't you think it would be nice if we taught him the sequence of hands first? It's a lot easier to bet when you know whether or not your hand is any good."

"Oh. Yeah. Of course."

"Let me handle this part, Aahz," the troll volunteered. "Now then, Skeeve. The ascending sequence of hands is as follows:

High Card

One Pair

Two Pair

Three Of A Kind

Three Pair

Full House (Three Of A Kind plus a Pair)

Four Of A Kind

Flush

Straight (those last two are ranked higher and reversed because of the sixth card)

Full Belly (two sets of Three Of A Kind)

Full Dragon (Four Of a Kind plus a Pair)

Straight Flush

Have you got that?"

Half an hour later, I could almost get through the list without referring to my crib sheet. By that time, my teachers' enthusiasm was noticeably dimmed. I decided to push on to the next lesson before I lost them completely.

"Close enough," I declared. "I can bone up on these on my own time. Where do we go from here? How much should I bet on which hands?"

"Not so fast," Aahz said. "First, you've got to finish learning about the hands."

"You mean there are more? I thought . . ."

"No. You've got all the hands . . . or will have, with a little practice. Now you've got to learn about *conditional modifiers.*"

"Conditional modifiers?" I echoed weakly.

"Sure. Without 'em, dragon poker would be just another straightforward game. Are you starting to see why I didn't want to take the time before to teach you?"

I nodded silently, staring at my list of card hands that I somehow had a feeling was about to become more complex.

"Cheer up, Skeeve," Chumley said gaily, clapping me on the shoulder. "This is going to be easier than if we were trying to teach you the whole game."

"It is?" I blinked, perking up slightly.

"Sure. You see, the conditional modifiers depend on certain variables, like the day of the week, the number of players, chair position, things like that. Now since this match is prearranged, we know what most of those variables will be. For example, there will only be the two of you playing, and as the challenged party you have your choice of chairs . . . pick the one facing south, incidentally."

"What my big brother is trying to say in his own clumsy way," Tananda interrupted by squeezing my arm softly, "is that you don't have to learn *all* the conditional modifiers. Just the ones that will be in effect for your game with the Kid."

"Oh. I get it. Thanks, Chumley. That makes me feel a lot better."

"Right-o. There can't be more than a dozen or two that will be pertinent."

The relief I had been feeling turned cold inside me. "Two dozen conditional modifiers?"

"C'mon, big brother. There aren't that many."

"I was going to say I thought he was underestimating," Aahz grinned.

"Well, let's bloody well count them off and see."

"Red dragons will be wild on even-numbered hands. . . ."

". . . But unicorns will be wild all evening. . . ."

". . . The corps-a-corps hand will be invalid all night, that's why we didn't bother to list it, partner. . . ."

". . . Once a night, a player can change the suit of one of his up cards. . . ."

". . . Every five hands, the sequence of cards is reversed, so the low cards are high and vice versa. . . ."

". . . Threes will be dead all night and treated as blank cards. . . ."

". . . And once a four-of-a-kind is played, that card value is also dead. . . ."

". . . Unless it's a wild card, then it simply ceases to be wild and can be played normally. . . ."

". . . If there's a ten showing in the first two face-up cards in each hand, then sevens will be dead. . . ."

". . . Unless there is a second ten showing, then it cancels the first. . . ."

". . . Of course, if the first card turned face up in a round is an Ogre, the round will be played with an extra hole card, four face up and five face down. . . ."

". . . A natural hand beats a hand of equal value built with wild cards. . . ."

"Hey—that's not a conditional modifier. That's a regular rule."

"It will still be in effect, won't it? Some of the conditional modifiers nullify standing rules, so I thought we should . . ."

"ARE YOU PUTTING ME ON?!!"

The conversation stopped on a dime as my coaches turned to stare at me.

"I mean, this is a joke. Right?"

"No, partner," Aahz said carefully. "This is what dragon poker is all about. Like Chumley said, just be thankful you're only playing one night and get to learn the abbreviated list."

"But how am I supposed to stand a chance in this game? I'm not even going to be able to remember all the rules."

An awkward silence came over the table.

"I . . . uhh . . . think you've missed the point, Skeeve," Tananda said at last. "You don't stand a chance. The Kid is the best there is. There's no way you can learn enough in a few days or a few years to even give him a run for his money. All we're trying to do is teach you enough so that you won't embarrass yourself—as in ruin the reputation of the Great Skeeve—while he whittles away at your stake. You've got to at least *look* like you know what you're doing. Otherwise you come across as a fool who doesn't know enough to know how little he knows."

I thought about that for a few.

"Doesn't that description actually fit me to a 'T'?"

"If so, let's keep it in the family. Okay?" my partner winked, punching me playfully on the shoulder. "Cheer up, Skeeve. In some ways it should be fun. There's nothing like competing in a game without the pressure to win to let you role-play to the hilt."

"Sure, Aahz."

"Okay, so let's get back to it. Just listen this time around. We'll go over it again slower later so you can write it all down."

With that, they launched into it again.

I listened with half an ear, all the while examining my feelings. I had gone into the first game at the Even-Odds expecting to lose, but I had been viewing that as a social evening. It was beyond my abilities to kid myself into believing this match with the Kid was going to be social. As much as I respected the views of my advisors, I was having a lot of trouble accepting the idea that I would help my reputation by losing. They were right, though, that I couldn't gracefully refuse the challenge. If I didn't stand a chance of winning, then the only option left was to lose gracefully. Right?

Try as I might, though, I couldn't still a little voice in the back of my mind that kept telling me that the ideal solution would be to take the Kid to the cleaners. Of course, that was impossible. Right? Right?

# Chapter XV

*"I need all the friends I can get."*
**Quasimodo**

**W**HILE my life may seem convoluted and depressing at times, at least there is one being who never turns from me in my hours of need.

"Gleep!"

I've never understood how a dragon's tongue can be slimy and sandpapery at the same time, but it is. Well, at least the one belonging to *my* dragon is.

"Down, fella . . . dow . . . hey! C'mon, Gleep. Stop it!"

"Gleep!" my pet declared as he deftly dodged my hands and left one more slimy trail across my face.

Obedient to a fault. They say you can judge a man's leadership ability by how well he handles animals.

"Darn it, Gleep! This is serious!"

I've often tried to convince Aahz that my dragon actually understands what I say. Whether that was the case here or if he was just sensitive to my tone, Gleep sank back on his haunches and cocked his head attentively.

"That's better," I sighed, daring to breathe through my nose again. Dragons have notoriously bad breath (hence the expression "dragon mouth"), and my pet's displays of affection had the unfortunate side effect of making me feel more than slightly faint. Of course, even breathing through my mouth, I could still taste it.

"You see, I've got a problem . . . well, several problems, and I thought maybe talking them out without being interrupted might . . ."

"Gleep!"

The tongue flicked out again, this time catching me with my mouth open. While I love my pet, there are times I wish he were . . . smaller. Times like this . . . and when I have to clean out his litter box.

"You want I should lean on the dragon for you, Boss?"

I looked around and discovered Nunzio sitting on one of the garden benches.

"Oh. Hi, Nunzio. What are you doing here? I thought you and Guido usually made yourself scarce when I was exercising Gleep."

"That's usually," the bodyguard shrugged. "My cousin and me, we talked it over and decided with this Ax fella on the loose that one of us should stick with you all the time, know what I mean? Right now it's my shift, and I'll be hangin' tight . . . no matter what you're doin'."

"I appreciate that, but I don't think there's any danger of getting hit here. I already decided not to take Gleep outside until the coast is clear. No sense tempting fate."

That was at least partially true. What I had really decided was that I didn't want to give the Ax a chance to strike at me through my pet. Aahz already complained enough about having a dragon in residence without adding fuel to the fire. Of course, if my suspicions were correct and Bunny *was* the Ax . . .

"Better safe than sorry . . . and you didn't answer my question. You want I should lean on the dragon?"

Sometimes the logic of my bodyguards eluded me completely.

"No. I mean, why should you lean on Gleep? You look comfortable where you are."

Nunzio rolled his eyes. "I don't mean 'lean on him' like really lean on him. I mean, do you want me to bend him a little? You know, rough him up some. I stay outta things between you and your partner, but you shouldn't have to put up with that kind of guff from a dragon."

"He's just being friendly."

"Friendly, schmendly. From what I've seen, you're in more danger from getting knocked off by your own pet than by anyone else I've seen at the Bazaar. All I've ever asked is that you let me do my job. . . . I *am* supposed to be guardin' your body, ya' know. That's how my position got its lofty title."

Not for the first time, I was impressed by Nunzio's total devotion to his work. For a moment I was tempted to let him do what he wanted. At the last minute, though, an image flashed through my mind of my outsized bodyguard and my dragon going at it hammer and tongs in the middle of the garden.

"Umm . . . thanks, but I think I'll pass, Nunzio. Gleep can be a pain sometimes, but I kind of like him jumping all over me once in a while. It makes me feel loved. Besides, I wouldn't want to see him get hurt . . . or you either, for that matter."

"Jumpin' up on you is one thing. Doin' it when you don't want him to is sompin' else. Besides, I wouldn't hurt him. I'd just . . . here, let me show you!"

Before I could stop him, he was on his feet, taking a straddle-legged stance facing my dragon.

"C'mere, Gleep. C'mon, fella."

My pet's head snapped around, then he went bounding toward what he thought was a new playmate.

"Nunzio. I . . ."

Just as the dragon reached him, my bodyguard held out a hand, palm outward.

"Stop, Gleep! Sit! I said SIT!!"

What happened next I had to reconstruct later from replaying my memory, it happened so fast.

Nunzio's hand snaked out and closed over Gleep's snout. With a jerk he pulled the nose down until it was under my pet's head, then pushed up sharply.

In mid-stride the dragon's haunches dropped into a sitting position and he stopped, all the while batting his eyelashes in bewilderment.

"Now stay. Stay!!"

My bodyguard carefully opened his hand and stepped back, holding his palm flat in front of my pet's face.

Gleep quivered slightly but didn't budge from his sitting position.

"See, Boss? He'll mind," Nunzio called over his shoulder. "Ya just gotta be firm with him."

I suddenly realized my jaw was dangling somewhere around my knees. "What . . . that's incredible, Nunzio! How did you . . . what did you . . ."

"I guess you never knew," he grinned. "I used ta be an animal trainer . . . mostly the nasty ones for shows, know what I mean?"

"An animal trainer?"

"Yeah. It seemed like a logical extension of bein' a schoolteacher . . . only without the parents to worry about."

I had to sit down. Between the demonstration with Gleep and the sudden insight to his background, Nunzio had my brain on overload.

"An animal trainer *and* a schoolteacher."

"That's right. Say, you want I should work with your dragon some more now that he's quieted down?"

"No. Let him run for a while. This is supposed to be his exercise time."

"You're the Boss."

He turned toward Gleep and clapped his hands sharply. The dragon bounded backwards, then crouched close to the ground, ready to play.

"Get it, boy!"

Moving with surprising believability, the bodyguard scooped an imaginary ball from the ground and pretended to throw it to the far end of the garden.

Gleep spun around and sprinted off in the direction of the "throw," flattening a bench and two shrubs as he went.

"Simply amazing," I murmured.

"I didn't mean to butt in," Nunzio said, sinking into the seat beside me. "It just looked like you wanted to talk and your dragon wanted to frolic."

"It's all right. I'd rather talk to you, anyway."

I was moderately astounded to discover this was true. I'd always been a bit of a loner, but lately it seemed I not only was able to talk to people, I enjoyed it. I hoped it wouldn't seriously change my friendship with Gleep.

"Me? Sure, Boss. What did you want to talk about?"

"Oh, nothing special. I guess I just realized we've never really talked, just the two of us. Tell me, how do you like our operation here?"

"It's okay, I guess. Never really thought about it much. It's not your run-of-the-mill Mob operation, that much is for sure. You got some strange people hangin' around you . . . but they're nice. I'd give my right arm for any one of them, they're so nice. That's different right there. Most outfits, everybody's tryin' to get ahead . . . so they spend more time watchin' each other than they do scopin' the opposition. Here, everybody covers for each other instead of nudging the other guy out."

"Do you want to get ahead, Nunzio?"

"Yes and no, know what I mean? I don't want to be doin' the same thing the rest of my life, but I'm not pushy to get to the top. Actually, I kinda like workin' for someone else. I let them make the big decisions, then all I gotta do is figure out how to make my part happen."

"You certainly do your part around here," I nodded. "I never knew before how hard a bodyguard works."

"Really? Gee, it's good to hear you say that, Boss. Sometimes Guido and me, we feel like dead weight around here. Maybe that's why we work so hard to do our jobs. I never thought much about whether I do or don't like it here. I mean, I go where I'm assigned and do what I'm told, so it doesn't matter what I think. Right? What I do know, though, is that I'd be real sorry if I had to leave. Nobody's ever treated me like you and your crew do."

Nunzio might not be an intellectual giant or the swiftest wit I've known, but I found his simple honesty touching . . . not to mention the loyalty it implied.

"Well, you've got a job here as long as I've got anything to say about it." I assured him.

"Thanks, Boss. I was startin' to get a little tired of how the Mob operates, know what I mean?" That rang a bell in my mind.

"Speaking of that, Nunzio, do you think the Mob would ever get involved with something like this character assassination thing?"

The bodyguard's brow furrowed with the effort of thinking.

"Naw!" he said at last. "Mostly people pay us *not* to do things. If we do have to do a number on someone, it's usually to make an example of them and we do something flashy like burn down their house or break their legs. Who would know it if we wrecked their career? What Tananda was sayin' about the Ax was interesting, but it's just not our style."

"Not even for the right price?" I urged. "How much do you think it would take to get Don Bruce to send someone in here after us?"

"I dunno. I'd have to say at least . . . wait a minute! Are you askin' if Bunny's the Ax?"

"Well, she did . . ."

"Forget it, Boss. Even if she could handle the job, which I'm not too sure she could, Don Bruce would never send her after you. Heck, you're one of his favorite chieftains right now. You should hear him . . ."

Nunzio suddenly pressed his palms against his cheeks to make exaggerated jowls as he spoke. ". . . Dat Skeeve, he's really got it on the ball, know what I mean? Mercy! If I had a hundred like him I could take over dis whole organization."

His imitation of Don Bruce was so perfect I had to laugh.

"That's great, Nunzio. Has he ever seen you do that?"

"I'm still employed and breathin', aren't I?" he winked. "Seriously, though. You're barkin' up the wrong tree with Bunny. Believe me, you're the apple of her uncle's eye right now."

"I suppose you're right," I sighed. "If you are, though, it leaves me right back where I started. Who is the Ax and what can . . ."

"Hi guys! Is that a private conversation, or can anyone join?"

We glanced up to find Bunny and Markie entering the garden.

"C'mon over, Bunny!" I waved, nudging Nunzio slightly in the ribs. "We were just going to . . ."

GLEEP!!!"

Suddenly my dragon was in front of me. Crouching and tense, he didn't look playful at all. I had only seen him like this a couple of times before, and then . . .

"STOP IT, GLEEP! GLEEP!!!" I screamed, realizing too late what was about to happen.

Fortunately, Nunzio was quicker than I was. From his sitting position he threw himself forward in a body check against my pet's neck, just as the dragon let loose with a stream of fire. The flames leapt forward to harmlessly scorch a wall.

Bunny swept Markie behind her with one arm.

"Geez! What was . . ."

"I'll get him!" Markie cried, balling up her fists.

"MARKIE!! STOP!!"

"But Daddy . . ."

"Just hold it. Okay? Nunzio?"

"I've got him, Boss," he called, both hands wrapped securely around Gleep's snout as the dragon struggled to get free.

"Bunny! You and Markie get inside! Now!!!"

The two of them hurried from sight, and I turned my attention to my pet.

Gleep seemed to have calmed down as fast as he had exploded, now that Bunny and Markie were gone. Nunzio was stroking his neck soothingly while staring at me in wide-eyed amazement.

"I dunno what happened there, Boss, but he seems okay now."

"What happened," I said grimly, "was Gleep trying to protect me from something or someone he saw as a threat."

"But Boss . . ."

"Look Nunzio, I know you mean well, but Gleep and I go back a long way. I trust his instincts more than I do my own judgment."

"But . . ."

"I want you to do two things right away. First, put Gleep back in his stable . . . I think he's had enough exercise for one day. Then get word to Don Bruce. I want to have a little talk with him about his 'present'!"

# Chapter XVI

*"I thought we were friends!"*
**Banquo**

"**I** tell you, partner, this is crazy!"

"Like heck it is!"

"Bunny can't be the Ax! She's a space cadet."

"That's what she'd like us to think. I found out different!"

"Really? How?"

"By . . . well, by talking to her."

I spotted the flaw in my logic as soon as I said it, and Aahz wasn't far behind.

"Skeeve," he said solemnly, "has it occurred to you that if she's the Ax and you're her target, that you would probably be the last person she would relax around? Do you really think you could trick her into giving away her I.Q. in a simple conversation?"

"Well . . . maybe she was being clever. It could be that it was her way of trying to throw us off the track."

My partner didn't say anything to that. He just cocked his head and raised one eyebrow *very* high.

"It *could* be," I repeated lamely.

"C'mon, Skeeve. Give."

"What?"

"Even you need more evidence than that before you go off half-cocked. What are you holding back?"

He had me. I was just afraid that he was going to find my real reason even less believable than the one I had already stated.

"Okay," I said with a sigh. "If you really want to know, what finally convinced me was that Gleep doesn't like her."

"Gleep? You mean that stupid dragon of yours? That Gleep?"

"Gleep isn't st . . ."

"Partner, your dragon doesn't like *me!* That doesn't make me the Ax!!"

"He's never tried to fry you, either!"

That one stopped him for a moment. "He did that? He really let fly at Bunny?"

"That's right. If Nunzio hadn't been there . . ."

As if summoned by the mention of his name, the bodyguard stuck his head into the room.

"Hey, Boss! Don Bruce is here."

"Show him in."

"I still think you're making a mistake," Aahz warned, leaning against a wall.

"Maybe," I said grimly. "With luck I'll get Don Bruce to confirm my suspicions before I show my cards."

"This I've got to see."

"There you are, Skeeve. The boys said you wanted to see me."

Don Bruce is the Mob's fairy godfather. I've never seen him dressed in anything that wasn't lavender, and today was no exception. His ensemble included shorts, sandals, a floppy brimmed hat, and a sports shirt with large dark purple flowers printed all over it. Maybe my wardrobe sessions with Bunny were making me overly sensitive on the subject of clothes, but his attire hardly seemed appropriate for one of the most powerful men in the Mob.

Even his dark glasses had violet lenses.

"You know, this is quite a place you got here. Never been here before, but I heard a lot about it in the yearly report. It doesn't look this big from the outside."

"We like to keep a low profile," I said.

"Yeah, I know. It's like I keep tellin' 'em back at Mob Central, you run a class operation. I like that. Makes us all look good."

I was starting to feel a little uncomfortable. The last thing I wanted to discuss with Don Bruce was our current operation.

"Like some wine?" Aahz chimed in, coming to my rescue.

"It's a little early, but why not? So! What is it you wanted to see me about?"

"It's about Bunny."

"Bunny? Oh yeah. How's she workin' out?"

Even if I hadn't already been suspicious, Don Bruce's response would have seemed overly casual. Aahz caught it too, raising his eyebrow again as he poured the wine.

"I thought we should have a little chat about why you sent her here."

"What's to chat about? You needed a moll, and I figured . . ."

"I mean the *real* reason."

Our guest paused, glanced back and forth betweeen Aahz and me a couple of times, then shrugged his shoulders. "She told you, huh? Funny, I would have thought that was one secret she would have kept."

"Actually, I figured it out all by myself. In fact, when the subject came up, she denied it."

"Always said you were smart, Skeeve. Now I see you're smart enough to get me to admit to what you couldn't trick out of Bunny. Pretty good."

I shot a triumphant glance at Aahz, who was suddenly very busy with the wine. Despite my feeling of victory over having puzzled out the identity of the Ax, I was still more than a little annoyed.

"What I can't figure out," I said, "is why you tried it in the first place. I've always played it pretty straight with you."

At least Don Bruce had the grace to look embarrassed. "I know, I know. It seemed like a good idea at the time, is all. I was in a bit of a spot, and it seemed like a harmless way out."

"Harmless? Harmless! That's my whole life and career we're talking about."

"Hey! C'mon, Skeeve. Aren't you exaggerating a little bit there! I don't think . . ."

"Exaggerating??"

"Well, I still think you'd make a good husband for her . . ."

"Exaggerating? Aahz, are you listening to . . ."

As I turned to appeal to my partner, I noticed he was laughing so hard he was spilling the wine. Of all the reactions I might have expected from him, laughing wasn't . . .

Then it hit me.

"Husband?!?!?"

"Of course. Isn't that what we've been talkin' about?"

"Skeeve here thinks that your niece is the Ax and that you turned her loose on him to destroy his career," my partner managed between gasps.

"The Ax???"

"HUSBAND????"

"Are you crazy??"

"One of us is!!"

"How about both?" Aahz grinned, stepping between us. "Wine, anyone?"

"But he said . . ."

"What about . . ."

"Gentlemen, gentlemen. It's clear that communications have gotten a little fouled up between the two of you. I suggest you each take some wine and we'll start all over again from the top."

Almost mechanically, we both reached for the wine, eyeing each other all the while like angry cats.

"Very good," my partner nodded. "Now then, Don Bruce, as the visiting team I believe you have first serve."

"What's this about the Ax!?!" the mobster demanded, leaning forward so suddenly half the wine sloshed out of his glass.

"You know who the Ax is??"

"I know *what* he is! The question is, what does he have to do with you and Bunny?"

"We've heard recently that someone's hired the Ax to do a number on Skeeve," Aahz supplied.

". . . Right about the same time Bunny showed up," I added.

"And that's supposed to make her the Ax?"

"Well, there *has* been some trouble since she arrived."

"Like what?"

"Welll . . . Tananda left because of things that were said when she found out that Bunny was in my bedroom one morning."

"Tananda? The same Tananda that said 'Hi' to me when I walked in here today?"

"She . . . ummm . . . came back."

"I see. What else?"

"She scared off my girlfriend."

"Girlfriend? You got a girlfriend?"

"Well, not exactly . . . but I might have had one if Bunny wasn't here."

"Uh-huh. Aahz, haven't you ever told him the 'bird in the hand' story?"

"I try, but he isn't big on listening."

I can always count on my partner to rally to my defense in times of crisis.

"What else?"

"Ummm . . ."

"Tell him!" Aahz smiled.

"Tell me what?"

"My dragon doesn't like her."

"I'm not surprised. She's never gotten along with animals . . . at least the four-footed kind. I don't see where that makes her the Ax, though."

"It's . . . it's just that on top of the other evidence . . ."

My voice trailed off in front of Don Bruce's stony stare.

"You know, Skeeve," he said at last. "As much as I like you, there are times, like now, I wish you was on the other side of the law. If the D.A.s put together a case like you do, we could cut our bribe budget by ninety percent, and our attorney's fees by a hundred percent!"

"But . . ."

"Now listen close, 'cause I'm only goin' to go over this once. You're the representative for the Mob, and *me*, here at the Bazaar. If you look bad, then we look bad. Got it? What possible sense would it make for us to hire someone to make you, and *us*, look bad?"

On the ropes, I glanced at Aahz for support.

"That was going to be the next question *I* was going to ask, partner." Terrific.

"Well," Don Bruce announced, standing up. "If that's settled, I guess I can go now."

"Not so fast," my partner smiled, holding up a hand. "There's still the matter of the question that Skeeve asked: if Bunny isn't the Ax, what's she doing here? What was that you were saying about a husband?"

The mobster sank back into his chair and reached for his wine, all the while avoiding my eyes.

"I'm not gettin' any younger," he said. "Some day I'm goin' to retire, and I thought I should maybe start lookin' around for a replacement. It's always nice to have 'em in the family . . . the real family, I mean, and since I got an unmarried niece . . ."

"Whoa! Wait a minute," Aahz interrupted. "Are you saying that you're considering Skeeve as your eventual replacement in the Mob?"

"It's a possibility. Why not? Like I said, he runs a class operation and he's smart . . . at least I used to think so."

"Don Bruce I . . . I don't know what to say," I said honestly.

"Then don't say nothin'!" he responded grimly. "Whatever's goin' to happen is a long way off. That's why I didn't say anything to you direct. I'm not ready to retire yet."

"Oh." I didn't know whether to feel disappointment or relief.

"About Bunny?" my partner prompted.

The mobster shrugged. "What's to say that hasn't already been said? She's my niece, he's one of my favorite chieftains. I thought it would be a good idea to put 'em close to each other and see if anything happened."

"I . . . I don't know," I said thoughtfully. "I mean, Bunny's nice enough . . . especially now that I know she isn't the Ax. I just don't think I'm ready to get married yet."

"Didn't say you were," Don Bruce shrugged. "Don't get me wrong, Skeeve. I'm not tryin' to push you into this. I know it'll take time. Like I said, I just fixed it so you two could meet and see if anything develops . . . that's all. If it works out, fine. If it doesn't, also fine. I'm not about to try to force things or kid myself that you two will make a pair if you won't. If nothing else, you've got a pretty good accountant while you find out . . . and from lookin' over your financial figures you could use one."

"Izzat so?"

He had finally tweaked Aahz close to home . . . or his wallet, which in his case is the same thing.

"What's wrong with our finances? We're doing okay."

"Okay isn't soarin'. You boys got no plan. The way I see it, you've spent so much time livin' hand-to-mouth you've never learned what to do with money except stack it and spend it. Bunny can show you how to make your money work for you."

Aahz rubbed his chin thoughtfully. It was interesting to see my partner caught between pride and greed.

"I dunno," he said at last. "It sounds good, and we'll probably look into it eventually, but we're a little tight right now."

"The way I hear it, you're tight all the time," Don Bruce commented drily.

"No. I mean right now we're *really* tight for finances. We've got a lot of capital tied up in the big game tonight."

"Big game? What big game?"

"Skeeve is going head to head with the Sen-Sen Ante Kid at dragon poker tonight. It's a challenge match."

"That's why I wanted to talk to you about Bunny," I said. "Since I thought she was the Ax, I didn't want her around to cause trouble at the game."

"Why didn't anybody tell me about this game?" Don Bruce demanded. "It wasn't in your report!"

"It's come up since then."

"What are the stakes?"

I looked at Aahz. I had been so busy trying to learn how dragon poker was played that I had never gotten around to asking about the stakes.

For some reason, my partner suddenly looked uncomfortable.

"Table stakes," he said.

"Table stakes?" I frowned. "What's that?"

I half-expected him to tell me he'd explain later, but instead he addressed the subject with surprising enthusiasm.

"In a table stakes game each of you starts with a certain amount of money. Then you play until one of you is out of chips, or . . ."

"I know what table stakes are," Don Bruce interrupted. "What I want to know is how much you're playing for."

Aahz hesitated, then shrugged. "A quarter of a million each."

"A QUARTER OF A MILLION???"

I hadn't hit that note since my voice changed.

"Didn't you know?" the mobster scowled.

"We hadn't told him," my partner sighed. "I was afraid that if he knew what the stakes were, he'd clutch. We were just going to give him the stack of chips to play without telling him how much they were worth."

"A quarter of a million?" I repeated, a little hoarser this time.

"See?" Aahz grinned. "You're clutching."

"But, Aahz, do we *have* a quarter of a million to spare?"

My partner's grin faded and he started avoiding my eyes.

"I can answer that one, Skeeve," Don Bruce said. *"No one* has a quarter of a million to spare. Even if you've got it, you don't have it to spare, know what I mean?"

"It's not going to take *all* our money," Aahz said slowly. "The others have chipped in out of their savings, too: Tananda, Chumley, Massha, even Guido and Nunzio. We've all got a piece of the action."

"Us too," the mobster declared. "Put the Mob down for half."

I'm not sure who was more surprised, Aahz or me. But Aahz recovered first.

"That's nice of you, Don Bruce, but you don't understand what's really happening here. Skeeve here is a rank beginner at the game. He had one lucky night, and by the time the rumor mill got through with it, he had drawn a challenge from the Kid. He can't refuse without looking foolish, and with the Ax on the loose we can't afford any bad press we can avoid. That's why we're pooling our money, so Skeeve can go in there and lose gracefully. The actual outcome is preordained. The Kid's going to eat him alive."

". . . And maybe you weren't listening earlier," the mobster shot back. "If Skeeve looks bad, we look bad. The Mob backs its people, especially when it comes to public image. Win or lose, we're in for half, okay?"

"If you say so," Aahz shrugged.

". . . And try to save me a couple seats. I'm gonna want to see my boy in action—firsthand."

"It'll cost!"

"Did I ask? Just . . ."

I wasn't really listening to the conversation any more. I hadn't realized before just how solidly my friends were behind me.

A quarter of a million . . .

Right then something solidified in my mind that had been hovering there for several days now. Whatever the others thought, I was going to try my best to win this game!

# Chapter XVII

*"Shut up and deal!"*
**F.D.R.**

THERE was an aura of expectation over the Bazaar that night as we set out for the Even-Odds. At first I thought I was just seeing things differently because of my anticipation and nervousness. As we walked, however, it became more and more apparent that it was not simply my imagination.

Not a single vendor or shop shill approached us, not a Deveel hailed us with a proposed bargain. On the contrary, as we proceeded along the aisles, conversation and business ground to a halt as everyone turned to watch us pass. A few called out their wishes of "good luck" or friendly gibes about seeing me after the game, but for the most part they simply stared in silent fascination.

If I had ever had any doubts as to the existence or extent of the rumor mill and grapevine at the Bazaar, that night put them to rest forever. Everybody and I mean *everybody* knew who I was, where I was going, and what was waiting for me.

In some ways it was fun. I've noted earlier that I generally kept a low profile in the immediate neighborhood and have gotten used to walking around unnoticed. My recent shopping trips had gained me a certain notoriety, but it was nothing compared to this. Tonight, I was a full-blown celebrity! Realizing the uncertainty of the game's outcome, I decided to seize the moment and play my part to the hilt.

To a certain degree it was easy. We already made quite a procession. Guido and Nunzio were decked out in their working clothes of trenchcoats and weapons and preceded us, clearing a path through the gawkers. Tananda and Chumley brought up the rear looking positively grim as they eyeballed anyone who seemed to be edging too close. Aahz was walking just ahead of me, carrying our stake money in two large bags. If anyone entertained the thought of intercepting us for the money, all they had to do was look at Aahz's swagger and the gleam in his yellow eyes, and they would suddenly decide there were easier ways to get rich . . . like wrestling dragons or panning for gold in a swamp.

We had left Markie back at our place over her loud and indignant protests. I had stood firm, though. This game was going to be rough enough without having her around as a distraction. Massha had volunteered to stay with her, claiming she was far too nervous about the game to enjoy watching it anyway.

Bunny was decked out in a clinging outfit in brilliant white and hung on my arm like I was the most important thing in her life. More than a few envious eyes darted from her to me and back again.

No one was kidding anyone, though, as to who the center of attention was. You guessed it. Me! After all, I was the one on my way to lock horns with the legendary Sen-Sen Ante Kid on his own terrain . . . a card table. Bunny had chosen my clothes for me, and I was resplendent in a dark maroon open-necked shirt with light charcoal gray slacks and vest. I felt and looked like a million . . . well, make that a quarter of a million. If I was going to have my head handed to me tonight, I was at least going to be able to accept it in style . . . which was the whole point of this exercise, anyway.

I didn't even try to match Aahz's strut, knowing I would only suffer by comparison. Instead, I contented myself with maintaining a slow, measured, dignified pace as I nodded and waved at the well-wishers. The idea was to exude unhurried confidence. In actuality, it made me feel like I was on the way to the gallows, but I did my best to hide it and keep smiling.

The crowds got progressively thicker as we neared the Even-Odds, and I realized with some astonishment that this was because of the game. Those without the clout or the money to get space inside were loitering around the area in hopes of being one of the first to hear about the game's outcome. I had known that gambling was big at the Bazaar, but I never thought it was *this* popular.

The assemblage melted away before us, clearing a path to the door. I

began to recognize faces in the crowd, people I knew. There was Gus
waving enthusiastically at me, and over there . . .

"Vic!"

I veered from our straight line and the whole procession ground to a
halt.

"Hi, Skeeve!" the vampire smiled, clapping me on the shoulder.
"Good luck tonight!"

"I'm going to need it!" I confided. "Seriously, though, I've been
meaning to stop by and thank you for your warning about the Ax."

Vic's face fell. "You might have trouble finding me. I'm about to lose
my office."

"Really? Is business that bad?"

"Worse. There's an awful lot of competition here."

"Well, tell you what. Why don't you stop by my place tomorrow and
we'll talk. Maybe we can work out a small loan or maybe even subcontract
some assignments until you're established."

"Gee. Thanks, Skeeve!"

A sudden inspiration hit me. "Come by around noon. We'll do
lunch!"

It seemed like a really good idea to me. I wondered why businessmen
hadn't thought of talking out ideas over lunch before! For some reason, Vic
winced before returning my smile.

"Lunch it is," he said.

"Umm . . . I hate to interrupt, partner, but you *do* have an appointment you're supposed to be at."

"Right, Aahz. Vic! Tomorrow!"

With that, I allowed myself to be ushered into the Even-Odds.

A ripple of applause broke out as I entered the main bar and gaming
room, and I barely caught myself from turning to look behind me. For me
or against me, the people were here to watch the game and if nothing else
were grateful to me for providing the evening's entertainment.

Terrific. I was about to risk a quarter of a million in gold so that folks
wouldn't have to watch summer reruns.

The club had been rearranged since the last time I was there. One
card table stood alone in the center of the room, while scores of people
lined the walls. While the crowd outside might have been larger, the group
inside the club made up with clout what they lacked in numbers. While I
didn't begin to recognize everyone, the ones I did spot led me to believe
that the 'Who's Who' of Deva was assembled to watch the game. Hay-ner,
my landlord and leader of the Devan Chamber of Commerce was there

along with his usual clutch of cronies. He nodded politely when our eyes met, but I suspected he was really hoping to see me lose.

Don Bruce was there as promised, and raised his hands over his head, clenched them together, and gave them a brief shake, smiling all the while. I guessed it was some sign of encouragement. At the very least, I hoped I wasn't being hailed with some secret Mob death sign. Of course, that didn't occur to me until after I had waved back.

"Skeeve. SKEEVE! Have you got a moment?"

I glanced around to find the Geek standing at my elbow.

"Sure, Geek," I shrugged. "What can I do for you?"

The Deveel seemed extremely nervous, his complexion several shades off its normal hue. "I . . . you can promise not to hold a grudge. I promise you that tonight was none of my doing. All I did was make the arrangements after the Kid issued the challenge. I didn't give him your name . . . honest."

To say the least, I found his attitude surprising.

"Sure, Geek. I never thought you . . ."

"If I had known it would lead to this, I never would have invited you to my game in the first place, much less . . ."

I was suddenly very alert.

"Wait a minute, Geek! What are you talking about?"

"You're outclassed!" the Deveel explained, glancing around fearfully. "You don't stand a chance against the Kid. I just want you to understand, if you lose all your money tonight, that I didn't mean to set you up. I don't want you or your crew looking for me with blood in your respective eyes."

Now, as you know, I knew that I was outclassed. What intrigued me was that the Geek knew it, too.

"Geek, I think we'd better . . ."

A loud burst of applause and cheers interrupted me. By the time I got through craning my neck to see what was going on, the Geek had disappeared into the crowd. With that discussion closed, I turned my attention again to the subject at hand.

"Who's that?" I said, nodding toward the figure that had just entered the club.

Aahz slid a comforting arm around my shoulders.

"That's him. That's the Sen-Sen Ante Kid."

"THAT'S the Kid???!!"

The man in the door was enormous, he was huge . . . that is to say, he was Massha's size. For some reason, I had been expecting someone closer to my own age. This character, though, was something else.

He was totally hairless, no beard, no eyebrows, and completely bald.

His skin was light blue in color, and that combined with his fat and wrinkles gave the overall impression of a half-deflated blue bowling ball. His eyes were extremely dark, however, and glittered slightly as they fixed on me.

"That's the Kid?" I repeated.

Aahz shrugged. "He's had the title for a long time."

The man-mountain had two bags with him which looked very similar to the ones Aahz had carried for us. He handed them casually to one of the onlookers.

"Cash me in!" he ordered in a booming voice. "I hear there's a game here tonight."

For some reason, this brought a loud round of laughter and applause from the audience. I didn't think it was all that funny, but I smiled politely. The Kid's eyes noted my lack of enthusiasm and glittered with increased ferocity.

"You must be the Great Skeeve."

His voice was a dangerous purr, but it still reverberated off the walls. He moved toward me with a surprisingly light tread, holding out his hand in welcome.

The crowd seemed to hold its breath.

". . . And you must be the one they call the Sen-Sen Ante Kid," I responded, abandoning my hand into his grip.

Again I was surprised . . . this time by the gentleness of his handshake.

"I just hope your magic isn't as good as your reputation."

"That's funny, I was just hoping your luck is as bad as your jokes."

I didn't mean to be offensive. The words just kind of slipped out before I could stop them.

The Kid's face froze.

I wished someone else would say something to change the subject, but the room echoed with deathly quiet.

Suddenly, my opponent threw his head back and laughed heartily. "I like that!" he declared. "You know, no one else has ever had the nerve to tell me my jokes stink. I'm starting to see where you had the guts to accept my little challenge."

The room came to life, everybody talking or laughing at the same time. I felt like I had just passed some kind of initiation ritual. A wave of relief broke over me . . . but it was tinged with something else. I found myself liking the Kid. Young or not, he was definitely not the boogey-man I had been expecting.

"Thanks, Kid," I said quietly, taking advantage of the cover noise. "I must admit, I appreciate someone else who can laugh at themselves. I have to do it so often myself."

"Ain't that the truth," he murmured back, glancing around to be sure no one else was listening in. "If you let it, all this stuff can go to your head. Say, would you like a drink or something before we get started?"

"That confident I'm not," I laughed. "I want to have a clear head when we square off."

"Suit yourself," he shrugged.

Before I could say anything else, he turned to the crowd and raised his voice again. "Can you keep it down?" he roared. "We're ready to play cards up here!"

Like magic, the noise stopped and all eyes turned to the two of us again.

I found myself wishing I had accepted the drink.

# Chapter XVIII

*"Cast your fate to the winds."*
**L. Bernstein**

**T**HE table was waiting for us. There were only two chairs with chips stacked neatly in front of them.

I had a sudden moment of panic when I realized I didn't know which chair was facing south, but Aahz came to my rescue. Darting out of the crowd, he pulled out one chair and held it for me to sit in. To the crowd it looked like a polite gesture, but my friends knew I had come dangerously close to changing the rules I had labored so hard to memorize.

"Cards!" the Kid ordered, holding out one hand as he eased into the chair facing me.

A new deck materialized in his hand. He examined it like a glass of fine wine, holding it up to the light to be sure the wrapping was intact and even sniffing the seal to be sure the factory glue was the same.

Satisfied, he offered the deck to me. I smiled and spread my hands to show I was satisfied. I mean, heck! If he hadn't found anything wrong, it was a cinch that I wouldn't be able to detect any foul play.

The gesture seemed to impress him though, and he gave me a small bow before opening the deck. Once the cards were out of the box, his pudgy fingers seemed to take on a life of their own. Moving swiftly, they removed the jokers and cast them aside, then began peeling cards off the deck two at a time, one from the top and one from the bottom.

Watching the process, I began to realize why his handshake had been so gentle. Large as they were, his fingers were graceful, delicate, and sensitive as they went about their task. These were not the hands of a rough laborer, or even a fighter. They existed to do one thing: to handle a deck of cards.

By now the deck had been rough mixed. The Kid scooped up the pile, squared it, then give it several quick shuffles. His moves were so precise he didn't even have to re-square the deck when he was done . . . just set it on the center of the table.

"Cut for deal?" he asked.

I repeated my earlier gesture. "Be my guest."

Even this seemed to impress the Kid . . . and the crowd. A low murmur rippled around the room as the pluses and minuses of my move were discussed. The truth of the matter was that after watching the Kid handle the deck, I was embarrassed to show my own lack of skill.

He reached for the deck, and the cards sprang to life again. With a hypnotic rhythm he began cutting the deck and riffing the cards together, all the while staring at me with unblinking eyes. I knew I was being psyched out, but was powerless to fight the effect.

"For the ante, shall we say one thousand?"

"Let's say five thousand," I returned.

The rhythm faltered. The Kid realized he had slipped and moved swiftly to cover it. Setting the cards aside for a moment, he reached for his chips.

"Five thousand it is," he said, tossing a handful into the center of the table. "And . . . my trademark."

A small white breath mint followed the chips into the pot.

I was counting out my own chips when something occurred to me.

"How much is that worth?" I said, pointing at the mint.

That surprised my opponent.

"What? The mint? One copper a roll. But you don't have to . . ."

Before he had finished speaking I added a small coin to my chips, pushed them into the center of the table, grabbed his mint, and popped it into my mouth.

This time the audience actually gasped before lapsing into silence. For several heartbeats there was no sound in the room except the mint crunching between my teeth. I almost regretted my bold move. The mint was incredibly strong.

Finally the Kid grinned.

"I see. You eat my luck, eh? Good. Very good. You'll find, though, that it takes more than that to disturb my game."

His tone was jovial, but his eyes darkened even more than they had been and his shuffling took on a sharper, more vengeful tone. I knew I had scored a hit.

I stole a glance at Aahz, who winked at me broadly.

"Cut!"

The deck was in front of me. Moving with forced nonchalance, I cut the deck roughly in half, then leaned back in my chair. While I tried to appear casual, inside I was crossing my fingers and toes and everything else crossable. I had devised my strategy on my own and hadn't discussed it with anyone . . . not even Aahz. Now we got to see how it worked.

One card . . . two cards . . . three cards came gliding across the table to me, face down. They slid to a stop neatly aligned, another tribute to the Kid's skill, and lay there like land mines.

I ignored them, waiting for the next card.

It came, coasting to a stop face up next to its brethren. It was the seven of diamonds and the Kid dealt himself . . .

The ten of diamonds. A ten!

The rules came back to me like a song I didn't want to remember. A ten face up meant my seven was dead . . . valueless.

"So much for eating my luck, eh?" the Kid chuckled, taking a quick glance at his hole cards. "My ten will go . . . five thousand."

". . . And up five."

The gasp from the crowd was louder this time . . . possibly because my coaches had joined in. I heard Aahz clear his throat noisily, but wouldn't look in his direction. The Kid was staring at me in undisguised surprise. Apparently he had either expected me to fold or call . . . possibly because that would have been the sane thing to do.

"You're awfully proud of that dead card," he said thoughtfully. "All right. I'll call. Pot's right."

Two more cards floated onto the table face up. I got a ten! The ten of clubs, to be specific. That canceled his ten and made my seven live again.

The Kid got the unicorn of hearts. Wild card! Now I had ten-seven high against his pair of tens showing.

Terrific.

"I won't try to kid you," my opponent smiled. "A pair of tens is worth . . . twenty thousand."

". . . And up twenty."

The Kid's smile faded. His eyes flicked quickly to my cards, then he nodded. "Call."

No comment. No witty banter. I had him thinking.

The next cards were en route. The three of hearts slid into my lineup. A dead card. Opposing it, the Kid got . . .

The ten of hearts!

I was now looking at three tens against my ten-seven high! For a moment my resolve wavered, but I shored it up again. I was in too far to change now.

The Kid was eyeing me thoughtfully. "I don't suppose you'd go thirty on that?" he said.

"I'll not only go it, I'll raise you thirty."

There were muffled exclamations of disbelief in the room . . . and some not so muffled. I recognized the voices of some of the latter.

The Kid just shook his head and pushed the appropriate number of chips into the pot without a word. The crowd lapsed into silence and craned their necks to see the next cards.

The dragon of spades to me, and the ogre of hearts to the Kid.

No apparent help for either hand . . . except that now the Kid had three hearts face up.

We both studied each other's cards for a few moments.

"I'll admit I can't figure out what you're betting, Skeeve," my opponent sighed. "But this hand's worth fifty."

". . . And up fifty."

Instead of responding, the Kid leaned back in his chair and stared at me.

"Check me on this," he said. "Either I've missed it completely, or you haven't looked at your hole cards yet."

"That's right."

The crowd started muttering again. At least some of them had missed that point.

"So you're betting blind?"

"Right."

". . . And raising me to boot."

I nodded.

"I don't get it. How do you expect to win?"

I regarded him for a moment before I answered. To say the least, I had the room's undivided attention.

"Kid, you're the best there is at dragon poker. You've spent years honing your skills to be the best, and nothing that happens here tonight is going to change that. Me, I'm lucky . . . if you can call it that. I got lucky one night, and that somehow earned me the chance to play this game with you tonight. That's why I'm betting the way I am."

The Kid shook his head. "Maybe I'm slow, but I still don't get it."

"In the long run, your skill would beat my luck. It always does. I figure the only chance I've got is to juice the betting on this one hand . . . go for broke. All the skill in the dimensions can't change the outcome of one hand. That's luck . . . which puts us on an equal footing."

My opponent digested this for a few moments, then threw back his head and gave a bark of laughter.

"I love it!" he crowed. "A half million pot riding on one hand. Skeeve, I like your style. Win or lose, it's been a pleasure matching wits with you."

"Thank you, Kid. I feel the same way."

"In the meantime, there's this hand to play. I hate to keep all these people hanging in suspense when we already know how the betting's going to go."

He swept the rest of his chips into the pot. "I'll call your raise and raise you back . . . thirty-five. That's the whole stake."

"Agreed," I said, pushing my chips out.

"Now let's see what we got," he winked, reaching for the deck.

The two of diamonds to me . . . the eight of clubs to the Kid . . . then one more card each face down.

The crowd pressed forward as my opponent peered at his last card.

"Skeeve," he said almost regretfully. "You had an interesting strategy there, but my hand's good . . . real good."

He flipped two of his down cards over.

"Full Dragon . . . four Ogres and a pair of tens."

"Nice hand," I acknowledged.

"Yeah. Right. Now let's see what you've got."

With as much poise as I could muster, I turned over my hole cards.

# Chapter XIX

*"Can't you take a joke?"*
T. Eulenspiegel

**M**ASSHA looked up from her book and bonbons as we trooped through the door.

"That was quick," she said. "How did it go?"

"Hi, Massha. Where's Markie?"

"Upstairs in her room. After the second time she tried to sneak out, I sent her to bed and took up sentry duty here by the door. What happened at the game?"

"Well, I still say you were wrong," Aahz growled. "Of all the dumb stunts you've pulled . . ."

"C'mon, partner. What's done is done. Okay? You're just mad because I didn't check with you first."

"That's the least of . . ."

"WILL SOMEBODY TELL ME WHAT HAPPENED?"

"What? Oh. Sorry, Massha. I won. Aahz here is upset because . . ."

I was suddenly swept up in a gargantuan hug and kiss as my apprentice expressed her delight at the news.

"I'll say he won. In one hand he won," Tananda grinned. "Never seen anything like it."

"Three unicorns and the six of clubs in the hole," Aahz raged. "Three wild cards, which, when used with the once-a-night suit shift rule on the seven of diamonds, yields . . ."

"A straight-bloody-flush!" Chumley sang. "Which took the Kid's Full Dragon and the largest pot that's ever been seen at the Bazaar."

"I knew you could do it, Daddy!" Markie shrieked, emerging from her hiding spot on the stairs.

So much for sending her to bed early.

"I wish you could have seen the Kid's face, Massha," the troll continued merrily. "I'll bet he wishes now that he carries antacids instead of breath mints."

"You should have seen the crowd. They're going to be talking about this one for years!"

Massha finally let me down and held up a hand.

"Hold it! Wait a minute! I get the feeling I've missed a lap here somewhere. Hot Stuff here won. Right? As in walked away with all the marbles?"

The brother and sister team nodded vigorously. I just tried to get my breath back.

"So how come Green and Scaly is breathing smoke? I should think he'd be leading the cheering."

"BECAUSE HE GAVE THE MONEY AWAY! THAT'S WHY!!!"

"Yes. That would explain it." Massha nodded thoughtfully.

"C'mon, Aahz! I didn't *give* it away."

As I've discovered before, it's a lot easier to find your breath when you're under attack.

"Whoa! Wait!" my apprentice said, stepping between us. "Before you two get started again, talk to Massha. Remember, I'm the one who wasn't there."

"Well, the Kid and I got to talking after the game. He's really a nice guy, and I found out that he had pretty much been betting everything he had . . ."

"That's what he *claimed*," Aahz snorted. "I think he was making a play for our sympathies."

". . . and I got to thinking. I had worked hard to be sure that both the Kid's and my reputations would be intact, no matter how the game came out. What I really wanted to do was to retire from the dragon poker circuit and let *him* take on all the hotshot challengers . . ."

"That much I'll agree with."

"Aahz! Just let him tell it. Okay?"

". . . But he couldn't keep playing if he was broke, which would leave me as the logical target for the up-and-comings, so I let him keep the quarter of a million he had lost . . ."

"See! SEE!!! What did I tell you?"

". . . as a LOAN so he could use it as a stake in future games. . . ."

"That's when I knew he had . . . a loan??"

I grinned at my partner.

"Uh-huh. As in 'put your money to work for you instead of stacking it,' a concept I believe you found very interesting when it was first broached. Of course, you had already gone off half-cocked and stomped away before we got to that part."

Any sarcasm I had managed to load into my voice was lost on Aahz, which is not surprising when you realize we were talking about money.

"A loan, eh?" he said thoughtfully. "What were the terms?"

"Tell him, Bunny."

"BUNNY??"

"Hey! You weren't there, remember? I decided to see what our accountant could do. Bunny?"

"Well, I've never dealt with stake money before, no pun intended, so I had to kind of feel my way along. I think I got us a pretty good arrangement, though."

"Which was . . ."

"Until the Kid pays us back . . . and it's got to be paid back in full, no partial payments, we get half his winnings."

"Hmmm," my partner murmured. "Not bad."

"If you can think of anything else I should have asked for, I'm open to . . ."

"If he could think of anything else," I said, winking at her, "you can believe he would have roared it out by now. You did great, Bunny."

"Gee. Thanks, Skeeve."

"Now then, if someone would be so kind as to break out the wine, I feel like celebrating."

"Of course, Boss, you realize that now a lot of people know that you've got a lot of cash on hand," Guido pointed out, edging close to me. "As soon as Nunzio gets back, I think we'd better take a look at beefin' up security on the place, know what I mean?"

"Where is Nunzio, anyway?" Massha said, peering around.

"He'll be along in a bit," I smiled. "I had a little errand for him after the game."

"Well, here's to you, Skeeve!" Chumley called, lifting his goblet aloft. "After all our worrying about whether your reputation could survive a match with the Kid, I dare say you came out of it well ahead of where you were before."

"That's right," his sister giggled. "I wonder what the Ax thinks about what happened."

That was the cue I had been waiting for. I took a deep breath and a deeper drink of wine, then assumed my most casual manner.

"Why bother speculating, Tananda? Why not ask direct?"

"What's that, Skeeve?"

"I said, why not ask the Ax directly? After all, she's in the room right now."

The gaiety of the mood vanished in an eyeblink as everybody stared at me.

"Partner," Aahz murmured, "I thought we settled this when we talked to Don Bruce."

I cut him off with the wave of a hand.

"As a matter of fact, I'm a little curious about what the Ax is thinking myself. Why don't you tell us . . . Markie?"

My young ward squirmed under the room's combined gaze.

"But, Daddy . . . I don't . . . you . . . oh, heck! You figured it out, huh?"

"Uh-huh." I nodded, not feeling at all triumphant.

She heaved a great sigh. "Oh, well. I was about to throw in the towel anyway. I had just hoped I could beat a retreat before my cover was blown. If you don't mind, I'd like to join you in some of that wine now."

"Help yourself."

"MARKIE?!?"

Aahz had finally recovered enough to make noise. Of course, it comes reflexively to him. The others were still working on it.

"Don't let the little-girl looks fool you, Aahz," she winked. "Folks are small and soft on my dimension. In the right clothes, it's easy to pass yourself off as being younger than you really are . . . lots younger."

"But . . . but . . ."

"Think about it for a minute, Aahz," I said. "You had all the pieces the first day. Kids, particularly little girls, are embarrassing at best, trouble at worst. The trick is that you *expect* them to be trouble, so you don't even consider the possibility that what they're doing could be premeditated and planned."

I paused to take a sip of wine, and for once no one interrupted me with questions.

"If you look back on it, most of the problems we've been having have originated directly or indirectly from Markie. She mouthed off about

Bunny being in my bed to get Tananda upset, and when that didn't work she made a few digs about her living here free that got her thinking about leaving . . . just like she deliberately made Massha look bad in the middle of her magic lesson for the same reason, to get her to leave."

"Almost worked, too," my apprentice observed thoughtfully.

"The business in the Bazaar was no accident, either," I continued. "All she had to do was wait for the right opportunity to pretend to get mad so we wouldn't suspect she was blasting things deliberately. If you recall, she even tried to convince me that I didn't need to take dragon poker lessons."

"Of course," Markie put in, "that's not easy to do when people think you're a kid."

"The biggest clue was Gleep. I thought he was trying to protect me from Bunny, but it was Markie he was really after. I keep telling you that he's smarter than you think."

"Remind me to apologize to your dragon," Aahz said, still staring at Markie.

"It was a good plan," she sighed. "Ninety-nine percent of the time it would have worked. The problem was that everyone underestimated you, Skeeve . . . you and your friends. I didn't think you'd have enough money to pay off the irate merchants after I did a number on their displays, and your friends . . ."

She shook her head slowly.

"Usually if word gets out that I'm on assignment, it makes my work easier. The target's associates bail out to keep from getting hit in the crossfire, and trying to get them to stay or come back only makes things worse. Part of sinking someone's career is cutting them off from their support network."

She raised her wine in a mock toast to me.

"Your friends wouldn't run . . . or if they did, they wouldn't stay gone once they heard you were in trouble. That's when I started to have second thoughts about this assignment. I mean, there are some careers that shouldn't be scuttled, and I think yours is one of them. You can take that as a compliment . . . it's meant as one. That's why I was about to call it quits anyway. I realized my heart just wasn't in my work this time around."

She set down her wine and stood up.

"Well, I guess that's that. I'll go upstairs and pack now. Make you a deal. If you all promise not to tell anyone who the famous Ax is, I'll spread the word that you're so invincible that even the Ax couldn't trip you up. Okay?"

Watching her leave the room, I realized with some surprise that I would miss her. Despite what Aahz had said, it had been kind of nice having a kid around the place.

"That's it?" my partner frowned. "You're just going to let her walk?"

"I was the target. I figure it was my call. Besides, she didn't do any real damage. As Chumley pointed out a second ago, we're further ahead than we were when she arrived."

"Of course, there's the matter of the damages we had to pay for her little magic display at the Bazaar."

For once, I was ahead of my partner when it came to money.

"I haven't forgotten that, Aahz. I just figure to recoup the loss from another source. You see, what finally tipped me off was . . . wait. Here they are now."

Nunzio was just coming into the room, dragging the Geek with him.

"Hello, Skeeve," the Deveel said, squirming in my bodyguard's grasp. "Your . . . ah, associate here says you wanted to see me?"

"He tried to sneak out after I told him, Boss," Nunzio squeaked. "That's what took me so long."

"Hello, Geek," I purred. "Have a seat. I want to have a little chat with you about a card game."

"C'mon, Skeeve. I already told you . . ."

"Sit!"

The Geek dropped into the indicated chair like gravity had suddenly trebled. I had borrowed the tone of voice from Nunzio's dragon-training demonstration. It worked.

"What the Geek was starting to say," I explained, turning to Aahz, "is that before the game tonight he warned me that I was overmatched and asked me not to have any hard feelings . . . that the game with the Kid wasn't his idea."

"That's right," the Deveel interjected. "Word just got out and . . ."

"What I'm curious about, however, is how he knew I was out-classed."

I smiled at the Geek, trying to show my teeth the way Aahz does. "You see, I don't want to talk about tonight's game. I was hoping you could give us a little more information about the *other* game . . . you know, the one where I won Markie?"

The Deveel glanced nervously around the group of assembled scowls.

"I . . . I don't know what you mean."

"Let me make it easy for you. At this point I figure the game had to be rigged. That's the only way you would know in advance what a weak dragon poker player I am. Somehow you were throwing hands my way to be sure I won big, big enough to include Markie. I'm just curious how you did it without triggering the magic or telepathy monitors."

The Geek seemed to shrink a little in his chair. When he spoke, his voice was so low we could barely hear him.

"Marked cards," he said.

The room exploded.

"MARKED CARDS??"

"But how . . ."

"Wouldn't that . . ."

I waved them back to silence.

"It makes sense. Think about it," I instructed. "Specifically, think back to our trip to Limbo. Remember how hard it was to disguise ourselves without using magic? Everybody at the Bazaar gets so used to things being done magically, they forget there are non-magical ways to do the same things . . . like false beards, or marked cards."

The Geek was on his feet now.

"You can't hold that against me! So someone else paid me to throw the game your way. Heck, I should think you'd be happy. You came out ahead, didn't you? What's to be mad about?"

"I'll bet if I try real hard I could think of something."

"Look, if it's revenge you want, you already got it. I lost a bundle tonight betting against you. You want blood, I'm bleeding!"

The Deveel was sweating visibly now. Then again, he's always been a little nervous around me for some reason.

"Relax, Geek. I'm not going to hurt you. If anything, I'm going to help you . . . just like you helped me."

"Yeah?" he said suspiciously.

"You say you're short of cash, we'll fix it."

"What!!??" Aahz roared, but Tananda poked him in the ribs and he subsided into sullen silence.

"Bunny?"

"Yeah, Skeeve?"

"First thing tomorrow I want you to run over to the Even-Odds. Go over the books, take inventory, and come up with a fair price for the place."

The Geek blinked.

"My club? But I . . ."

". . . Then draw up an agreement for us to take it off the Geek's hands . . . at half the price you arrive at."

"WHAT!!??" the Deveel screeched, forgetting his fear. "Why should I sell my club for . . ."

". . . More than it will be worth if the word gets out that you're running rigged games?" I finished for him. "Because you're a shrewd businessman, Geek. Besides, you need the money. Right?"

The Geek swallowed hard, then licked his lips before he spoke. "Right."

"How was that, Geek?" Aahz frowned. "I didn't quite hear you."

"I did," I said firmly. "Well, we won't keep you any longer, Geek. I know you'll want to get back to your club and clean up a bit. Otherwise we'll have to reduce the amount of our appraisal."

The Deveel started to snarl something, then thought better of it and slunk out into the night.

"Do you think that will make up for what we had to pay in damages, partner?" I said innocently.

"Skeeve, sometimes you amaze me," Aahz said, lifting his wine in a salute. "Now if there are no more surprises, I'm ready to party."

It was tempting, but I was on a roll and didn't want to let the moment slip away.

"There *is* one more thing," I announced. "Now that we've taken care of the Ax and the Kid, I think we should address the major problem that's come up . . . while everyone is here."

"Major problem?" my partner scowled. "What's that?"

Taking a deep breath, I went for it.

# Chapter XX

*"So what else is new?"*
**W. Cronkite**

THE whole crew was staring at me as I rolled my goblet of wine back and forth in my hand, trying to decide where to start.

"If I've seemed a little distracted during this latest crisis," I said at last, "it's because I've been wrestling with another problem that's come to my attention . . . a big one. So big that, in my mind, the other stuff took a lower priority."

"Whatever you're talking about, partner," Aahz frowned, "I've missed it."

"You just said it, Aahz. The magic word is 'partner.' Things have been going real well for you and me, but we aren't the only ones in this household. When we were talking to Chumley and he said that his life wasn't all beer and skittles, it took me a while to puzzle out what he was talking about, but it finally came clear."

I looked at the troll.

"Business is off for you, isn't it, Chumley?"

"Well, I don't like to complain . . ."

"I know, but maybe you should once in a while. I had never stopped to think about it before, but you've been getting fewer and fewer assignments since you moved in with us, haven't you?"

"Is that true, Chumley?" Aahz said. "I never noticed . . ."

"No one's noticed because the attention has always been on us, Aahz. The Aahz and Skeeve team has been taking priority over everything and everyone else. We've been so busy living up to our big-name image that we've missed what it's doing to our colleagues, the ones who have to a large extent been responsible for our success."

"Oh, come now, Skeeve old boy," Chumley laughed uneasily. "I think you're exaggerating a bit there."

"Am I? Your business is off, and so is Tananda's. I hate to say it, but she was right when she left, we are stifling her with our current setup. Guido and Nunzio knock themselves out trying to be super-bodyguards because they're afraid we'll decide we don't really need them and send them packing. Even Massha thinks of herself as a non-contributing team member. Bunny's our newest arrival, and she tried to tell me that the only way she could help us is as an ornament!"

"I feel better about that after tonight, Skeeve," Bunny corrected. "Between negotiating with the Kid and getting the assignment to price out the Even-Odds, I think I can do something for you besides breathe heavy."

"Exactly!" I nodded. "That's what's giving me the courage to propose the plan I've cooked up."

"Plan? What plan?"

"That's what I wanted to talk to you about, Aahz. Actually, what I wanted to talk to all of you about. What we're dealing with in this household isn't really a partnership . . . it's a company. Everybody in this room contributes to the success of our group as a whole, and I think it's about time we restructured our setup to reflect that. What we really need is a system where all of us have a say as to what's going on. Then clients will be able to approach us as a group, and we quote prices, hand out assignments or subcontract, and share the profits as a group. That's my proposal, for what it's worth. What do the rest of you think?"

The silence stretched on until I started to wonder if they were trying to think of a tactful way to tell me I belonged in a rubber room.

"I don't know, Skeeve," Aahz said at last.

"What aren't you sure of?" I urged.

"I don't know if we should call ourselves Magic, Inc., or Chaos, Ltd."

"Magic, Inc., has already been used," Tananda argued. "Besides, I think the name should be a little more dignified and formal."

"You do that, then the clients are goin' to be surprised when they actually see us, know what I mean?" Guido put in. "We ain't exactly dignified and formal ourselves."

I leaned back in my chair and took a deep breath. If that was their only concern, my idea was at least deemed worthy of consideration.

Massha caught my eye and winked.

I toasted her back, feeling justifiably smug.

"Does this company accept new applicants?"

We all turned to find Markie in the door, suitcase in her hand.

"I don't think I have to tell you all about my qualifications," she continued, "but I admire this group and would be proud to be a part of it."

The crew exchanged glances.

"Well, Markie . . ."

"It's still nebulous . . ."

"You've got the Elemental stuff down cold . . ."

"What do you think, Skeeve?" Aahz said. "You're the one who's usually big on recruiting old enemies."

"No," I said firmly.

They were all looking at me again.

"Sorry to sound so overbearing right after claiming I wanted everybody to have a say in things," I continued, "but if Markie's in, I'm out."

"What's the problem, Skeeve?" Markie frowned. "I thought we were still on pretty good terms."

"We are," I nodded. "I'm not mad at you. I won't work against your career or hit you or hold a grudge. You were just doing your job."

I raised my head and our eyes met.

"I just can't go along with how you work, is all. You say you admire our group—well, the glue that holds us together is trust. The way you operate is to get people to trust you, then betray it. Even if you stayed loyal to our group, I don't think I want to be associated in business with someone who thinks that's the way to turn a profit."

I stopped there, and no one else raised a voice to contradict me.

Markie picked up her suitcase and started for the door. At the last moment, though, she turned back to me and I could see tears in her eyes.

"I can't argue with what you're saying, Skeeve," she said, "but I can't help wishing you had settled for hitting me and let me join."

There was total silence as she made her departure.

"The young lady has raised a valid point," Chumley said at last. "What is our position on new members?"

"If we're open, I'd like to put Vic's name up for consideration," Massha chimed in.

"First we've got to decide if we need anyone else," Tananda corrected.

"That raises the whole question of free-lance vs. exclusive contracts," Nunzio said. "I don't think that it's realistic to have all our shares equal."

"I've been doodling up a plan on just that point, Nunzio," Bunny called, waving the napkin she had been scribbling on. "If you can hold on for a few minutes, I'll have something to propose officially."

As interested as I was in the proceedings, I had trouble concentrating on what was being said. For some reason, Markie's face kept crowding into my mind.

Sure, what I said was rough, but it was necessary. If you're going to run a business or a team, you've got to set a standard and adhere to it. There's no room for sentimentality. I had done the right thing, hadn't I? Hadn't I?

# M.Y.T.H. INC. LINK

---

# Author's Introduction

The series of books loosely referred to throughout the known dimensions as **The Myth Adventures of Aahz and Skeeve** has been growing steadily in popularity since they premiered back in 1978. (Actually, you probably don't have to be told this, as you are already holding a volume in your hands. The ones who need to be informed are those who would never *dream* of picking up a fantasy book . . . like that guy browsing through mysteries, or your roommate. So what you want to do is tap them on the shoulder or over the head, and . . .)

Excuse me! I tend to get excited and digress when there's the smell of money in the air . . . especially if it's moving away. Where was I?

Books . . . growing in popularity . . . oh, yes!

The question I am asked most often as a writer is not "Where do you get your ideas?", but rather, "Is there going to be another Myth book?" The answer, for a while anyway, is a definite "Yes!" After completing **Little Myth Marker** I signed a contract with Donning/Starblaze for an additional six books, of which this is the first. While we're still "discussing" if they will be written at the rate of one or two a year, it *is* sure at this point that the series will be around for a while.

I realized after completing the manuscript for this volume that the title might be unclear to the casual reader. This is a terrible thing to realize so close to publication, particularly since the book has already been promoted under that title, so it's too late to change it. In desperation, I'm resorting to the cheap device of an author's intro to attempt to clarify things.

#7 is titled **M.Y.T.H. Inc. Link** because it marks a definite change in the series from the first six and therefore "links" the beginning of the series to what comes after. (Cute, eh? Confusing, but cute.) Unfortunately, most of the changes involve the writer, and, as such, may not be readily apparent to the reader. In a vain attempt to alleviate that situation, I thought I would take advantage of this breaking point in the series to give the reader a little insight into the mind of a writer and how a series, specifically this one, comes to exist. If you couldn't care less, feel free to skip directly into the main body of the book (as the rest of this introduction contains nothing you need to read) and (hopefully) enjoy it.

Writers not only "live" what they write, they occasionally use that fact to regulate their actual lives. That is, if they are feeling "down," sometimes writing something "up" can improve their mood. This was how the first Myth book came into existence.

At the time (1976) I was writing my first novel, **Cold Cash War** for St. Martin's Press. That particular book is a grim little number about corporate wars, and contains occasional scenes that can only be described as grisly. Wounded mercenaries burying themselves while still alive to rob the other side of the body count and executives arranging to have their rivals shot down in the streets were the norm in that universe. It was an interesting project, and, as it was my first, I could really get wrapped up in it. Unfortunately, I was still working full time at a nine-to-five job and had a wife and two kids. It was unfortunate in that I discovered that if I wrote **Cold Cash** for too many nights at a stretch, I'd start looking at my fellow office workers, not to mention passersby on the sidewalk and my own family, as targets or attackers. This is not the best condition to ensure one's continued mental health.

I decided I needed another writing project to use as a break for **Cold Cash** (if you just stop writing, you never get back to it!), preferably something a bit lighter. To that end, I started building the idea for my next book.

Being a fan of Conan and Kane and that crowd, I had always wanted to try my hand at Heroic Fantasy, and this seemed like as good a time as any. The field had been getting increasingly solemn and grandiose, and to my eye was long overdue for a good lampooning. (Anything or anyone who falls into the trap of taking themselves too seriously is fair game for this, and, fortunately for writers such as myself, there is no shortage of targets these days.)

First, I needed a main character. Since Heroic Fantasy was already loaded with brawny barbarian swordsmen hunting wizards, I decided to go to the opposite extreme and do my story from the point of view of a magician. To keep it interesting, he had to be fairly incompetent . . . say, maybe an apprentice. It's always helpful to give your lead character an associate or sidekick. This allows you to use dialogue to impart information to the reader without resorting to lengthy introspection. For a confidant to a magician . . . why not a demon? To contrast personalities, I'd have to make him as snorky and unpleasant as my lead is nice.

Right about here, fate took a hand. I have always been a fan of the Bob Hope/Bing Crosby "Road" movies, and it turned out that at the same time I was tinkering with these new characters, there was a weeklong festival of the entire set of those films on television. Of course, as a dedicated writer working on a book with a deadline, I was immune to such temptation, right? If you believe that, you have a lot to learn about writers . . . or at least *this* writer. Each evening found me camped in front of the idiot tube to catch one more round of the particular brand of insanity those movies abound in. To combat the guilts of feeling *totally* irresponsible, I kept a notepad on my lap so I could "work on character development" during the commercials. Trying to switch moods back and forth between the "Road" movies and **Cold Cash** was impossible, so it made more sense to be futzing around with *my* comedy while watching theirs. In the process, the bantering swindlers whose plans always land them in inordinate amounts of trouble wandered off the screen and onto my notepad . . . and the characters of Aahz and Skeeve started to take shape.

By the time **Cold Cash** was done, I was ready to present Aahz and Skeeve as a proposal for my next book. When I mentioned this to my agent, however, I discovered there was a minor detail I had overlooked. "Humor doesn't sell!" I was told. "We're trying to get your career launched right now, and you need a really strong book to follow **Cold Cash!** Got anything else?" This attitude startled me, but it was easily confirmed. A brief glance at a year's worth of *Publishers Weekly* showed that indeed, unless you were Erma Bombeck with a national following via a syndicated column, humor simply did not show on the best-seller lists. Consequently, I went with another project, **The Bug Wars,** and relegated the Aahz and Skeeve proposal to a bottom drawer.

There it remained while I spent roughly a year working on **The Bug Wars.** Then one evening in late 1977 my phone rang. It was Kelly Freas, the artist who had done the cover painting for the issue of *Analog* in which an excerpt of **Cold Cash** had been published, and a longtime friend from the convention circuit. He explained that he was starting a new line of books (Starblaze) with a Virginia-based publishing house (Donning) and was currently soliciting submissions. Did I have any unpublished manuscripts lying around? Needless to say, I was flattered, but I had to admit the only thing I had ready for submission was a humor presentation . . .

and he wouldn't want that, would he? There was a noticeable hesitation; then he suggested I send it in so he could take a look at it.

In an impressively short time, he got back to me with his reaction: He liked the characters and the setting, but felt the story was weak. If I thought I could come up with another story line, he'd cut me a contract. Being as greedy and prone to flattery as the next person, I agreed. When I discovered he needed it "just as soon as possible so that it can be one of our premiere titles," I was a bit less confident, but said I would give it my best shot. What the heck, I was on a roll.

To give you an idea of how much I had gotten caught up in the momentum of the deal, it wasn't until then that I realized none of this had been cleared with my agent. With a certain degree of abashed trepidation, I phoned my agent and explained the situation. There was a weighty pause, then he agreed. "I can see where you'd want to do a favor for an old buddy," he said, "and you might as well give him something that isn't going to go anywhere." I always thrive on encouragement.

So, I had characters, a setting, a contract, but no story. Facing an ASAP deadline and pressured by my agent to "finish it off quick and get back to serious writing," I resorted to a time-honored resource for writers under pressure . . . I stole a story line! Actually, I rationalized it rather neatly. This book is a parody, right? Why not take a "done to death" story line and do it one more time with the tongue-in-cheek respect it deserves? (This was the start of a pattern, but more about that later. . . .)

With a sort of preordained story line and characters I already knew like they were family, the writing went fairly quickly. To be precise, I wrote the thing front to back in five weeks while working full-time days. As an added bonus, I tossed in chapter quotes. After all, the books I was parodying usually had chapter quotes for songs or characters invented by the author for just that purpose, so why not do the same for mine? (When the book became a series, I found out "why not!" If you do it in the first volume, the readers expect it in subsequent volumes. It's a lot harder to come up with 120 cute quotes than it is to invent 20! I often spend more time on the *##!! quotes than I do writing the book!)

The manuscript went in and was accepted without a hitch. (There are certain advantages to dealing with artists who are editors. They tend to leave your writing alone!) The problem which arose was, of all things, on the title. I had always had problems titling books, and this one had been no exception. What I had finally come up with was **The Demon And I.** Doesn't make it, Kelly said. I promised to try to think of an alternative. Three weeks later, press time for the catalog was upon us, and I was still trying to think of a better title. On the day of the noon deadline, I was sitting on the phone with Kelly at 11:45, still trying to come up with a title. **Demon on Square One?** How about **Demon at Large?** Better, but not funny.

Funny . . . funny . . . My mind started darting over lines and movie titles from classic comedy. What do you think of **Another Fine Mess?** Hmmm . . . Kelly put down the phone and bounced the title off his wife, Polly, whose taste exceeds the sum of ours combined. He was back in a moment. Did I say **Another Fine Mess,** or **Another Fine** *Myth?* I confirmed the former. Another conference. Well, it wasn't red-hot, but it seemed to be the best we had to come up with. They'd go with that.

Three hours later (and that much closer to sundown, when I normally start thinking), my brain started to turn over like a car engine on a cold morning. **Another Fine Myth . . . Hit or Myth . . . Myth-Conceptions!** I hurriedly grabbed the phone and called Kelly back.

On the off chance he wanted to buy another book with these characters, I explained, and definitely if there was a possibility of turning it into a series, the "Myth" bit could come in handy to tie the titles together! In fact, it was a natural to use **Myth-Conceptions** as a title for the first book, and hold **Another Fine Myth** for the sequel! How solid was that noon deadline?

It turned out the noon deadline had been real. (A sure sign of an inexperienced editor. The real pros *never* tell you the truth about when they need a manuscript or title, just to allow time for the wayward creative minds to miss the supposed deadline and still hit the real deadline!) He did, however, like the idea. While we couldn't change the title from **Another Fine Mess** to **Myth-Conceptions,** we could change it to **Another Fine Myth** and claim a typo in the catalog! We'd just hold the **Myth-Conceptions** title for the second one . . . we *were* talking about doing a second one, weren't we? Whoops!

So the series was launched. Over the years, Donning kept contracting them from me, usually one at a time, and I kept swiping plots to parody. The mad magician out to take over the world, the select force against an army, the master heist, the big game, the war against organized crime . . . all the old familiar chestnuts (which I follow avidly myself) were dragged out and run over one more time. Some strange things happened along the way, however.

I had promised myself from the beginning that Skeeve would grow and develop as the series continued. This would theoretically keep me from falling into the trap of telling the same story and using the same gags over and over again. Rereading the manuscripts as they piled up, however, I began to realize how much of my own growth and development was easing onto the pages. Since I started writing the Myth series, I have been raising (or, more accurately, assisting in raising between books) two children of my own, and experiencing all the trials and doubts that go with parenthood. I went from being a full-time cost accountant with a regular paycheck to a full-time writer with a spastic cash flow, and hence became even more concerned with money than I had been when it was plentiful. I tried to start a corporation of my own, only to have it fold within the first six months. With the success of the books, I even experienced the heady sensation of being a minor celebrity and having total strangers recognize my name. All these experiences and more became a part of Skeeve's development and the evolution of his relationship with his rat-pack of friends. Because of this, the friends themselves began to take on new life and dimensions until they began crowding in on the central story of Skeeve.

This brings us to **M.Y.T.H. Inc. Link.** (Remember? I started out telling you about that? It's the book you're starting right now.) In this volume the readers get a chance to see the Myth universe and, more importantly, Skeeve through eyes other than those belonging to the central character. Lest the diehard Skeeve fans panic, let me hasten to assure them I haven't finished with Skeeve's viewpoint . . . not by a long shot! In the upcoming volumes, however, the Skeeve-narrated volumes will have the regular "Myth" titles, and those from other viewpoints will be designated by the "M.Y.T.H. Inc." label. This particular volume has sections of both, hence the "Link" between old and new formats. Get it? Oh well, maybe it will become clearer after you read this one.

The other major change which is occurring is that with the contractual assurance that there will be future volumes, I can work a larger canvas as a storyteller (yes, that is a mixed metaphor) than I was able to when planning one book at a time. Not every story element has to be resolved within a single book, and setups for future stories and situations can be seeded in. Among other things, this means that I will probably be moving away from the predictable "old plot parodies" I have been indulging in in the past, and creating situations and tales unique to the Myth universe and its inhabitants.

(If that sounds like you'll have to buy every volume to stay abreast of what's happening, it's not entirely accidental. I've learned a lot from co-editing **Thieves' World**®, too!)

The new path I have chosen for *Myth* and myself is extremely challenging to an author, but one I feel is a necessary option to either shutting the series down or "cranking out one more of the same." There are those in both the book and comic industries who insist that series readers rapidly become addicted to the status quo, and will protest or rebel against any attempt to change it. I can only hope the loyal *Myth* readers find the new directions as enjoyable and intriguing as I do. If not, tough! This is the way it's going to be for at least five more books.

While I can occasionally sound very uncaring and set in my ways, like any author I am always curious about reader reactions . . . particularly when instituting a major pattern change. In case you weren't aware of it, you can always write me (or any author, assuming they're alive) in care of the publisher. If you'd like a larger forum in which to air your feelings, there's always the Myth-Adventures Fan Club (P.O. Box 95, Sutter, CA 95982 (blatant plug!) with their quarterly publication.

In closing, I would like to sincerely thank all the *Myth* readers for their loyalty and interest over the years. All your letters are read (even if I don't get a chance to answer them all) and deeply appreciated. After all the earlier warnings from my (ex-) agent and the lack of interest from other publishers, the appearance of the *Myth* books on genre and chain-store best-seller lists has not only increased my stature in the field to where I am now offered the six-book contracts that allow me to experiment with new concepts, but combined with the popularity of Piers Anthony's **Xanth** books has forced publishers to review their attitudes toward humorous fantasy. The door has been opened for a new wave of talented writers, whose efforts are even now available on the stands. For these hitherto unrecognized humorists as well as for myself and the *Myth* gang, again, I thank you.

—Robert Lynn Asprin
Ann Arbor, 1986

# Chapter I

*"Petty crime is the scourge
of business today."*
**D. Lorean**

I actually liked our new office facilities better than the old. Even though Aahz had argued hard to keep the Even-Odds as a bar (read "money-making venture"), the rest of us ganged up on him and insisted that since we had an extra building it would make more sense to remodel it into offices than to keep trying to do business out of our home. I mean, who really needs a lot of strangers traipsing in and out of your private life all the time? That practice had already landed us in trouble once, and the memory of that escapade was what finally convinced my old mentor to go along with the plan.

Of course, remodeling was more of a hassle than I had expected, even after getting one of the local religious temples to do the carpentry. Even working cheap they were more expensive than I had imagined, and the hours they kept . . . but I digress.

I had a large office now, with a desk, "in" basket, Day-Timers Scheduler, visitor chairs, the whole nine yards. As I said, I liked it a lot. What I didn't like was the title that went with it . . . to wit, President.

That's right. Everybody insisted that since incorporating our merry band of misfits was my idea, I was the logical choice for titular head of the organization. Even Aahz betrayed me, proclaiming it was a great idea, though to my eye he was hiding a snicker when he said it. If I had known my suggestion would lead to this, believe me I would have kept my mouth shut.

Don't get me wrong, the crew is great! If I were going to lead a group, I couldn't ask for a nicer, more loyal bunch than the one currently at my disposal. Of course, there might be those who would argue the point with me. A trollop, a troll, two gangsters, a moll, and a Pervert . . . excuse me, Pervect . . . an overweight vamp, and a baby dragon might not seem like the ideal team to the average person. They didn't to me when I first met them. Still, they've been unswerving in their support of me over the years, and together we've piled up an impressive track record. No, I'd rather stick with the rat-pack I know, however strange, than trust my fate to anyone else, no matter how qualified they might seem. If anything, from time to time I wonder what they think of me and wish I could peek inside their heads to learn their opinions. Whatever they think, they stick around . . . and that's what counts.

It isn't the crew that makes me edgy . . . it's the title. You see, as long as I can remember, I've always thought that being a leader was the equivalent of walking around with a large bulls-eye painted on your back. Basically the job involves holding the bag for a lot of people instead of just for yourself. If anything goes wrong, you end up being to blame. Even if someone else perpetrated the foul-up, as the leader you're responsible. On the off chance things go right, all you really feel is guilty for taking the credit for someone else's work. All in all, it seems to me to be a no-win, thankless position, one that I would much rather delegate to someone else while I had fun in the field. Unfortunately, everyone else seemed to have the same basic opinion, and as the least experienced member of the crew I was less adept at coming up with reasons to dodge the slot than the others. Consequently, I became the President of M.Y.T.H. Inc. (That's Magical Young Trouble-shooting Heroes. Don't blame me. I didn't come up with the name), an association of magicians and trouble-shooters dedicated to simultaneously helping others and making money.

Our base of operations was the Bazaar at Deva, a well-known rendez-vous for magic dealing that was the crossroads of the dimensions. As might be imagined, in an environment like that, there was never a shortage of work.

\* \* \*

I had barely gotten settled for the morning when there was a light rap on the door of my office and Bunny stuck her head in.

"Busy, Boss?"

"Well . . ."

She was gone before I could finish formulating a vague answer. This wasn't unusual. Bunny acted as my secretary and always knew more about what I had on the docket than I did. Her inquiries as to my schedule were usually made out of politeness or to check to be sure I wasn't doing something undignified before ushering a client into the office.

"The Great Skeeve will see you now," she said, gesturing grandly to her charge. "In the future, I'd suggest you make an appointment so you won't be kept waiting."

The Deveel Bunny was introducing seemed a bit slimy, even for a Deveel. His bright red complexion was covered with unhealthy-looking pink blotches, and his face was contorted into a permanent leer, which he directed at Bunny's back as she left the room.

Now, there's no denying that Bunny's one of the more attractive females I've ever met, but there was something unwholesome about the attention this dude was giving her. With an effort, I tried to quell the growing dislike I was feeling toward the Deveel. A client was a client, and we were in business to help people in trouble, not make moral judgments on them.

"Can I help you?" I said, keeping my voice polite.

That brought the Deveel's attention back to me, and he extended a hand across the desk.

"So you're the Great Skeeve, eh? Pleased to meet you. Been hearing some good things about your work. Say, you really got a great setup. I especially like that little number you got working as a receptionist. Might even try to hire her away from you. The girl's obviously loaded with talent."

Looking at his leer and wink, I somehow couldn't bring myself to shake his hand.

"Bunny is my administrative assistant," I said carefully. "She is also a stockholder in the company. She earns her position with her skills, not with her looks."

"I bet she does," the Deveel winked again. "I'd love to get a sample of those skills someday."

That did it.

"How about right now?" I smiled, then raised my voice slightly. "Bunny? Could you come in here for a moment?"

She appeared almost at once, ignoring the Deveel's leer as she moved to my desk.

"Yes, sir?"

"Bunny, you forgot to brief me on this client. Who is he?"

She arched one eyebrow and shot a sideways glance at the Deveel. We rarely did our briefings in front of clients. Our eyes met again and I gave her a small nod to confirm my request.

"His name is Bane," she said with a shrug. "He's known to run a small shop here at the Bazaar selling small novelty magic items. His annual take from that operation is in the low six figures."

"Hey! That's pretty good," the Deveel grinned.

Bunny continued as if she hadn't heard.

"He also has secret ownership of three other businesses, and partial ownership of a dozen more. Most notable is a magic factory which supplies shops in this and other dimensions. It's located in a sub-dimension accessible through the office of his shop, and employs several hundred workers. The estimated take from that factory alone is in the mid seven figure range annually."

The Deveel had stopped leering.

"How did you know all that?" he demanded. "That's supposed to be secret!"

"He also fancies himself to be a lady-killer, but there is little evidence to support his claim. The female companions he is seen in public with are paid for their company, and none have lasted more than a week. It seems they feel the money is insufficient for enduring his revolting personality. Foodwise, he has a weakness for broccoli."

I turned a neutral smile on the deflated Deveel.

". . . And *that*, sir, is the talent that earns Bunny her job. Did you enjoy your sample?"

"She's wrong about the broccoli," Bane said weakly. "I hate broccoli."

I raised an eyebrow at Bunny, who winked back at me.

"Noted," she said. "Will there be anything else, Boss?"

"Stick around, Bunny. I'll probably need your help quoting Mr. Bane a price for our services . . . that is, if he ever gets around to telling us what his problem is."

That brought the Deveel out of his shocked trance.

"I'll tell you what the problem is! Miss Bunny here was dead right when she said my magic factory is my prize holding. The trouble is that someone's robbing me blind! I'm losing a fortune to pilferage!"

"What percentage loss?" Bunny said, suddenly attentive.

"Pushing fourteen percent . . . up from six last year."

"Are we talking retail or cost value?"

"Cost."

"What's your actual volume loss?"

"Less than eight percent. They know exactly what items to go after . . . small, but expensive."

I sat back and tried to look wise. They had lost me completely about two laps into the conversation, but Bunny seemed to know what she was doing, so I gave her her head.

"Everybody I've sent in to investigate gets tagged as a company spy before they even sit down," Bane was saying. "Now, the word I get is that your crew has some contacts in organized crime, and I was figuring . . ."

He let his voice trail off, then shrugged as if he was embarrassed to complete the thought.

Bunny looked over at me, and I could tell she was trying to hide a smile. She was the niece of Don Bruce, the Mob's Fairy Godfather, and it always amused her to encounter the near-superstitious awe outsiders felt toward her uncle's organization.

"I think we can help you," I said carefully. "Of course, it will cost."

"How much?" Bane countered, settling back for what was acknowledged throughout the dimensions as a Deveel's specialty . . . haggling.

In response, Bunny scribbled something quickly on her notepad, then tore the sheet off and handed it to Bane.

The Deveel glanced at it and blanched a light pink.

"WHAT!! That's robbery and you know it!"

"Not when you consider what the losses are costing you," Bunny said sweetly. "Tell you what. If you'd rather, we'll take a few points in your factory . . . say, half the percentage reduction in pilferage once we take the case?"

Bane went from pink to a volcanic red in the space of a few heartbeats.

"All right! It's a deal . . . at the original offer!"

I nodded slightly.

"Fine. I'll assign a couple of agents to it immediately."

"Wait a minute! I'm paying prices like these and I'm not even getting the services of the head honcho? What are you trying to pull here? I want . . ."

"The Great Skeeve stands behind every M.Y.T.H. Inc. contract," Bunny interrupted. "If you wish to contract his personal services, the price would be substantially higher . . . like, say, controlling interest?"

"All right, all right! I get the message!" the Deveel said. "Send in your agents. They just better be good, that's all. At these rates, I expect results!"

With that, he slammed out of the office, leaving Bunny and me alone.

"How much *did* you charge him?"

"Just our usual fees."

"Really?"

"Well . . . I did add in a small premium 'cause I didn't like him. Any objections?"

"No. Just curious is all."

"Say, Boss. Would you mind including me in this assignment? It shouldn't take too long, and this one's got me a little curious."

"Okay . . . but not as lead operative. I want to be able to pull you back here if things get hairy in the office. Let your partner run the show."

"No problem. Who are you teaming me with?"

I leaned back in my chair and smiled.

"Can't you guess? The client wants organized crime, he *gets* organized crime!"

# Guido's Tale

"Guido, are you *sure* you've got your instructions right?"

That is Bunny talkin'. For some reason the Boss has deemed it wise to delegate to me her company for this job. Now this is okay with me, as Bunny is more than enjoyable to look at and a swell head to boot, which is to say she is smarter than me, which is a thing I do not say about many people, guys or dolls.

The only trepidation with which I view this pairin' is that as swell as she is, Bunny also has a marked tendency to nag whenever a job is on. This is because she is handicapped with a problem, which is that she has her cap set for the Boss. Now we are all aware of this, for it was apparent as the nose on your face from the day they first encountered. Even the Boss could see this, which is sayin' sumpin', for while I admire the Boss as an organizer, he is a little thick between the ears when it comes to skirts. To show you what I mean, once he was aware that Bunny did indeed entertain notions on his bod, his response was to half faint from the nervousness. This is from a guy I've watched take on vampires and werewolf types, not to mention Don Bruce himself, without so much as battin' an eye. Like I say, dolls is not his strong suit.

Anyway, I was talkin' about Bunny and her problem. She finally managed to convince the Boss that she wasn't really tryin' to pair up with him, but was just interested in furtherin' her career as a business type. Now this was a blatant lie, and we all knew it . . . even though it seems to have fooled the Boss. Even that green bum, Aahz, could see what

Bunny was up to. (This surprised me a bit, for I always thought his main talent was makin' loud noises.) All that Bunny was doin' was switchin' from one come-on to another. Her overall motivational goal has never changed.

The unfortunate circumstance of this is that instead of wooin' the Boss with her bod, which as I have said is outstandin', she is now tryin' to win his admiration with what a sharp cookie she is. This should not be overly difficult, as Bunny is one shrewd operator, but like all dolls she feels she has limited time in which to accomplish her objective before her looks run out, so she is tryin' extra hard to make sure the Boss notices her.

This unfortunately can make her a real headache in the posterior regions to work with. She is so afraid that someone else will mess up her performance record that she can drive a skilled worker such as myself up a proverbial tree with her nervous double-check chatter. Still, she is a swell doll and we are all pullin' for her, so we put up with it.

"Yes, Bunny," I sez.

" 'Yes, Bunny' what?"

"Yes, Bunny, I'm sure I got my instructions right."

"Then repeat them back to me."

"Why?"

"Guido!"

When Bunny gets that tone in her voice, there is little else to do but to humor her. This is in part because part of my job is to be supportive to my teammate when on an assignment, but also because Bunny has a mean left hook when she feels you are givin' her grief. My cousin Nunzio chanced to discover this fact one time before he was informed that she was Don Bruce's niece, and as he has a jaw like an anvil against which I have had occasion to injure my fist with noticeable results, I have no desire to confirm for myself the strength of the blow with which she decked him. Consequently I decided to comply with her rather annoying request.

"The Boss wants us to find out how the goods of a particular establishment is successfully wanderin' off the premises without detection," I sez. "To that end I am to intermingle with the workers as one of them to see if I can determine how this is bein' accomplished."

"And . . ." she sez, givin' me the hairy eyeball.

". . . And you are to do the same, only with the office types. At the end of a week we are to regroup in order that we may compare observations and see if we are perhaps barkin' up the wrong tree."

"And . . ." she sez again, lookin' a trifle agitated.

At this point I commence to grow a trifle nervous, for while she is

obviously expectin' me to continue in my oration, I have run out of instructions to reiterate.

". . . And . . . ummm . . ." I sez, tryin' to think of what I have
overlooked.

". . . And not to start any trouble!" she finishes, lookin' at me hard-
like. "Right?"

"Yeah. Sure, Bunny."

"Say it!"

". . . And not to start any trouble."

\* \* \*

Now I am more than a little hurt that Bunny feels it is necessary to
bring this point to my attention so forceful like, as in my opinion it is not
in my nature to start trouble under any circumstances. Both Nunzio and
me go out of our way to avoid any unnecessary disputes of a violent
nature, and only bestir ourselves to bring such difficulties to a halt once
they are thrust upon us. I do not, however, bring my injured feelings to
Bunny's attention as I know she is a swell person who would not deliberately inflict such wounds upon the self-image of a delicate person such as
myself. She is merely nervous as to the successful completion of the pending job, as I have previously orated, and would only feel bad if I were to let
on how callous and heartless she was behavin'. There are many in my line
of work who display similar signs of nervousness when preparin' for a
major assignment. I once worked with a guy what had a tendency to fidget
with a sharp knife when waitin' for a job to commence, usually on the bods
of his fellow caperers. One can only be understandin' of the motivationals
of such types and not take offense at their personal foibles when the heat is
on. This is one of the secrets to success learned early on by us executive
types. Be that as it may, I am forced to admit I am more than a little
relieved when it is time for the job to begin, allowin' me to part company
with Bunny for a while.

As a worker type, I report to work much earlier than is required for
office types like Bunny. Why this is I am not sure, but it is one of those
inescapable inequities with which life is fraught . . . like your line always
bein' the longest when they are broken down by alphabet.

To prepare for my undercover maneuverin's, I have abandoned my
normally spiffy threads in order to dress more appropriate for the worker
types with which I am to intermingle. This is the only part of the assignment which causes me any discomfort. You see, the more successful a
worker type is, the more he dresses like a skid-row bum or a rag heap, so

that he looks like he is either ready to roll in the mud or has just been rolled himself, which is in direct contradiction to what I learned in business college.

For those of you to whom this last tidbit of knowledge comes as a surprise, I would hasten to point out that I have indeed attended higher learnin' institutes, as that is the only way to obtain the master's type degree that I possess. If perchance you wonder, as some do, why a person with such credentials should choose the line of work that I have to pursue, my reasons are twofold: Firstus, I am a social type who perfers workin' with people; and second, I find my sensitive nature is repelled by the ruthlessness necessitated by bein' an upper management type. I simply do not have it in me to mess up people's lives with layoffs and plant shutdowns and the like. Rather, I find it far more sociable to break an occasional leg or two or perhaps rearrange a face a little than to live with the more long-term damage inflicted by upper management for the good of their respective companies. Therefore, as I am indeed presented with the enviable position of havin' a choice in career paths, I have traditionally opted to be an order taker rather than an order giver. It's a cleaner way to make a livin'.

So anyway, I report for work bright and early and am shown around the plant before commencin' my actual duties. Let me tell you I am impressed by this set-up like I have seldom been impressed by nothin' before. It is like Santa's North Pole elf sweatshop done up proper.

When I was in grad school, I used to read a lot of comics. Most particularly I was taken by the ads they used to carry therein for X-Ray Glasses and Whoopie Cushions and such, which I was unfortunately never able to afford as I was not an untypical student and therefore had less money than your average eight-year-old. Walkin' into the plant, however, I suddenly realized that this particular set of indulgences had not truly passed me by as I had feared.

The place was gargantuous, by which I mean it was really big, and jammed from wall to wall to ceilin' with conveyor belts and vats and stacks of materials and boxes labeled in languages I am not privileged to recognize, as well as large numbers of worker types strollin' around checkin' gauges and pushin' carts and otherwise engaged in the sorts of activities one does when the doors are open and there's a chance that the management types might come by on their way to the coffee machine and look in to see what you're doin'. What was even more impressive was the goods in production. At a glance I could see that as an admirer of cheap junk gimmicks, I had indeed died and gone to pig heaven. It was my guess, however uneducated, that what I had found was the major supplier for those ads which I earlier referenced, as well as most of the peddlers in the Bazaar who cater to the tourist trade.

Now right away I can see what the problem is, as most of the goods bein' produced are of a small and portable nature, and who could resist waltzin' off with a few samples in their pockets? Merchandise of this nature would be enough to tempt a saint, of which I seriously doubt the majority of the work force is made up of.

At the time I think that this will make my job substantially easier than anticipated. It is my reasonin' that all I need do is figure out how I myself would liberate a few choice items, then watch to see who is doin' the same. Of course, I figure it will behoove me to test my proposed system myself so as to see if it really can be done in such a manner, and at the same time acquire a little bonus or two I can gloat about in front of Nunzio.

First, however, I had to concentrate on establishin' myself as a good worker so that no one would suspect that I was there for anythin' else other than makin' an honest wage.

The job I was assigned to first was simple enough for a person of my skills and dexterity. All I had to do was sprinkle a dab of Pixie Dust on each Magic Floating Coaster as it came down the line. The major challenge seemed to be to be sure to apply as little as possible, as Pixie Dust is expensive even at bulk rates and one definitely does not want to give the customer more than they paid for.

With this in mind, I set to work . . . only to discover that the job was actually far more complex than I had originally perceived. You see, the Pixie Dust is kept in a large bag, which floats because that is what the Pixie Dust within does. The first trick is to keep the bag from floatin' away while one is workin' with it, which is actually harder than it sounds because the Pixie Dust is almost strong enough to float the bag *and* whoever is attemptin' to hold it down. There is a safety line attached to the bag as an anchor, but it holds the bag too high to work with. Consequently one must wrestle with the bag while applyin' the Pixie Dust, a feat which is not unlike tryin' to hold a large beach ball under water while doin' needle-point, and only rely on the safety line to haul the bag down into position again should it get away, which it often does. One might ask whyfore the line is not made shorter to hold the bag in the proper position and thereby make the job simpler. I suppose it is the same reason that working-type mothers will drown their children at birth if they feel there is the slightest chance they will grow up to be production engineers.

The other problem I encountered was one which I am surprised no one saw fit to warn me about. That is that when one works with Pixie

Dust, it must be remembered that it floats, and therefore pours up instead of down.

When first I attempted to sprinkle a little Pixie Dust on a Magic Floating Coaster, I was puzzled as to why the coaster would not subsequently float. On the chance that I had not applied a sufficient quantity of the substance in question, I added some more . . . and then a little more, not realizin' that it was floatin' up toward the ceilin' instead of down onto the coaster. Unfortunately, I was bent over the coaster at the time, as I was tryin' to keep the bag from floatin' away, and unbeknownst to me the dust was sprinklin' onto me rather than the coaster in question. The first admissible evidence I had that things was goin' awry was when I noticed that my feet were no longer in contact with the floor and that indeed I had become as buoyant as the bag which I was tryin' to hold down. Fortuitously, my grip is firm enough to crumble bricks so I managed to maintain my hold on the bag and eventually pull myself down the safety line instead of floatin' to the ceilin' in independent flight. Further, I was able to brush the Pixie Dust off my clothes so as to maintain my groundward orientation as well as my dignity.

The only thing which was not understandable about this passing incident was the uninvolvement of the other worker types. Not only had they not come over to assist me in my moment of misfortune, they had also refrained from making rude and uproarious noises at my predicament. This second point in particular I concerned myself with as bein' unusual, as worker types are notorious jokesters and unlikely to pass up such an obvious opportunity for low amusement.

The reason for this did indeed become crystalline when we finally broke for lunch.

I was just settlin' in to enjoy my midday repast, and chanced to ask the worker type seated next to me to pass me a napkin from the receptice by him as it was not within my reach. Instead of goin' along with this request as one would expect any civilized person to do, this joker mouths off to the effect that he won't give the time of day to any company spy, much less a napkin. Now if there is one thing I will not tolerate it is bein' called a fink, especially when I happen to be workin' as one. I therefore deem it necessary to show this individual the error of his assumptions by bendin' him a little in my most calm, friendly manner. Just when I think we are startin' to communicate, I notice that someone is beatin' me across the back with a chair. This does nothin' to improve my mood, as I am already annoyed to begin with, so I prop the Mouth against a nearby wall with one hand, thereby freein' the other which I then use to snag the other cretin as he winds up for another swing. I am just beginnin' to warm up to

my work when I hear a low whistle of warnin' from the crowd which has
naturally gathered to watch our discussion, and I look around to see one of
the foremen ambling over to see what the commotion's about.

Now foremen are perhaps the lowest form of management, as they are
usually turncoat worker types, and this one proves to be no exception to
the norm. Without so much as a how-do-you-do, he commences to demand to know what's goin' on and who started it anyway. As has been
noted, I already had my wind up and was seriously considerin' whether or
not to simply expand our discussion group to include the foreman when I
remember how nervous Bunny was and consider the difficulty I would
have explainin' the situation to her if I were to suffer termination the first
day on the job for roughin' up a management type. Consequently I shift
my grip from my two dance partners to my temper and proceed to explain
to the foreman that no one has started anythin' as indeed nothin' is happenin' . . . that my colleagues chanced to fall down and I was simply
helpin' them to their feet is all.

My explanations can be very convincing, as any jury can tell you, and
the foreman decides to accept this one without question, somehow
overlookin' the fact that I had helped the Mouth to his feet with such
enthusiasm that his feet were not touchin' the floor when the proceedin's
were halted. Perhaps he attributed this phenomenon to the Pixie Dust
which was so fond of levitatin' anything in the plant that wasn't tied down.
Whatever the reason, he buys the story and wanders off, leavin' me to
share my lunch with my two colleagues whose lunch has somehow gotten
tromped on during playtime.

Apparently, my display of masculine-type prowess has convinced everyone that I am indeed not a company spy, for the two guys which
jumped me in such an unprofessional manner is now very eager to chat on
the friendliest of terms. The one I have been referrin' to as the Mouth
turns out to be named Roxie, and his chair-swingin' buddy is Sion. Right
away we hit it off as they seem to be regular-type guys, even if they can't
throw a punch to save their own skins, and it seems we share a lot of
common interests . . . like skirts and an occasional bet on the ponies. Of
course, they are immediately advanced to the top of my list of suspects, as
anyone who thinks like me is also likely to have little regard for respectin'
the privacy rights of other people's property.

The other thing they tell me before we return to our respective tasks is
that the Pixie Dust job I am doin' is really a chump chore reserved for new
worker types what don't know enough to argue with their assignments. It
is suggested that I have a few words with the foreman, as he has obviously
been impressed with my demeanor, and see if I can't get some work more

in keepin' with my obvious talents. I am naturally grateful for this advice, and pursue their suggestion without further delay.

The foreman does indeed listen to my words, and sends me off to a new station for the balance of the day. Upon arrivin' at the scene of my reassignment, however, it occurs to me that perhaps I would have been wiser to keep my big yap in a closed position.

My new job really stinks . . . and I mean to tell you this is meant as literal as possible. All I had to do, see, was stand at the end of a conveyor belt and inspect the end product as it came off the line. Now, when I say "end product," this is also meant to be interpreted very literal-like. The quicker of you have doubtlessly perceived by now the product to which I am referrin', but for the benefit of the slower readers and sober editors, I will clarify my allusions.

What I am inspectin' is rubber Doggie Doodle, which comes in three sizes: Embarrassing, Disgusting, and Unbelievable. This is not, of course, how they are labeled, but rather how I choose to refer to them after a mere few moments' exposure. Now since, as I have mentioned before, this is a class operation, it is to be expected that our product has to be noticeably different than similar offerin's on the market. It is unfortunate that as the Final Inspector, I must deal with the finished product, which means before it goes into the boxes, but after the "Realistic, Life-like Aroma that Actually Sticks to Your Hands" is added.

It is also unfortunate that I am unable to locate either the foreman or the two jokers who had advised me for the rest of the afternoon. Of course, I am not permitted the luxury of a prolonged search, as the conveyor belt continues to move whether the inspector is inspectin' or not, and in no time at all the work begins to pile up. As I am not particularly handy with a shovel, I deem it wisest to continue workin' and save our discussion for a later, more private time.

Now mind you, the work doesn't really bother me all that much. One of the chores me and Nunzio toss coins over back home is cleanin' up after the Boss's dragon, and after that, Doggie Doodle really looks like a bit of an understatement, if you know what I mean. If anything, this causes me to chuckle a bit as I work, for while I am on assignment Nunzio must do the honors all by himself, so by comparison my end of the stick looks pretty clean. Then too, the fact that Roxie and Sion is now playin' tricks on me is a sign that I am indeed bein' accepted as one of the worker types, which will make my job considerably easier.

The only real problem I have with my assignment is that, considerin' the product with which I am workin', I feel it would be unwise to test the security-type precautions when I leave work that night. Even if I wished to liberate a few samples, which I was not particularly desirous of doin' since as I have noted we already have lots at home of a far superior quality, the "Realistic, Life-like Aroma that Really Sticks to Your Hands" would negate its passin' unnoticed by even the densest security-type guard.

As it turns out, this was a blessin' incognito. When closin' time finally rolls around, I discover that it would not be as easy to sneak stuff out of this plant as I had originally perceived. Everything the worker types took out of the plant with 'em was given the once and twice over by hard-eyed types who definitely knew what they were doin', and while we didn't have to go through a strip search, we did have to walk one at a time through a series of alarm systems that used a variety of rays to frisk us for objects and substances belongin' to the company. As it was, I almost got into trouble because there were still lingerin' specks of Pixie Dust on me from my morning duties, but Roxie stepped forward and explained things to the guards that was rapidly gatherin' and they settled for reclaimin' the Pixie Dust without things gettin' too personal.

This settled things between me and Roxie for the Doggie Doodle joke, and after I bounced Sion against a wall a few times to show my appreciation for his part in the prank, we all went off in search of some unprintable diversions.

Now if this last bit seems, perchance, a little shallow to you, you must first consider the whole situational before renderin' your verdict. I think it's been referenced before that the factory under investigation is located in one of those unlisted dimensions the Deveels specialize in. As the only way into this dimension from the Bazaar is through the owner's front-type operation, and as he is not wild about the notion of hundreds of worker types traipsin' through his office each shift, part of the contract for workin' in said factory is that one has to agree to stay in this unlisted dimension for a week at a time. To this end, the owner has provided rooms for the worker types, but as he is cheap even for a Deveel, each room is shared by bein's workin' different shifts. That is to say, you only have your room for one shift, and the rest of the time you're either workin' or hangin' out. Just so's we don't get bored between workin' and sleepin', the owner has also provided a variety of bars, restaurants, movies, and video joints for our amusement, all of which cost but can be charged back against our paychecks. If this seems like a bit of a closed economy to you, I would hasten to remind you that no one has ever accused the Deveels of bein' dumb when it comes to turnin' a profit. Anyway, all of this is to explain why it is that I am forced to go carousin' with Roxie and Sion instead of retirin' to my room to re-read the classics as would be my normal bent.

Now to be truthful with you, this carryin' on is not nearly so bad as I am lettin' on. It is simply that it is embarrassin' to my carefully maintained image to admit how really dull these evenings was, so's I reflexively sort of try to build them up more than I should. I mean, you'd think that off hours with a bunch of guys what work at a magic joke and novelty factory would be a barrel of laughs. You know, more fun than callin' in phony heist tips to the cops. Well, they surprised me by contentin' themselves to drinkin' and gamblin' and maybe a fistfight or two for their amusements . . . like I say, the same old borin' stuff any good-natured bunch of guys does. Mostly what they do is sit around and gripe about the work at the plant and how underpaid they are . . . which I do not pay much attention to as there is not a worker type alive that does not indulge in this particular pastime. In no time flat I determines that nobody in the work force is well enough versed in the finer points of non-backer entrepreneurmanship, which is to say crime, to converse with me on my own level. This is not surprisin' in this age of specialization, but it does mean I don't get nobody to talk to.

What I am gettin', though, is depressed . . . a feelin' which continues to grow as the week rolls on. It is not the work or the company of the worker types which is erodin' at my morale, but rather the diminishin' possibility of puttin' a wrap on this job.

It seems the more I observe in my undercover-type investigation, the more puzzled I become as to how the pilferage is bein' accomplished. The better I get to know my fellow worker types, the more I am convinced that they are not involved in any such goin's on, even in a marginal manner. This is not to say that they are lackin' in the smarts department, as they are easily as quick on the uptake as anyone I ever worked with in school or the business. Rather, I am makin' a tribute to the tightness of the plant security which must necessarily be penetrated in order to perpetrate such an activity.

As I have earlier said, this is an age of specialization, and none of the worker types I meet have adequately applied themselves to be able to hold a candle to me in my particular field of endeavor. Now realizin' that after a week of intense schemin', I have not yet come up with a plan for samplin' the merchandise that I feel has enough of a chance of succeedin' as to make it worthwhile to try, I cannot convince myself that the security can be cracked by any amateur, however talented.

Considerin' this, I am edgin' closer to the unpleasant conclusion that not only is it long odds against us findin' a fast answer, there is a chance we might not be able to crack this case at all. Such thoughts cause me great anxieties, which lead to depression as I am as success-oriented as the next person.

My mood truly bottoms out at the end of the week, specifically when I am presented with my paycheck. Now, I am not countin' on the money I earn as a worker type, as I am already bein' well subsidized by the Boss. Nonetheless I am surprised to see the amount my week's worth of toil has actually brought me. To be truthful, I have again yielded to the temptation of understatement. I was not surprised, I was shocked . . . which is not a good thing for, as anyone in the Mob can tell you, when I am shocked I tend to express the unsettlement of my nerves physically.

The fact that I am not needin' the money in question means that I was only a little shocked, so it only took three of my fellow worker types to pull me off the payroll type what slipped me the bad news. Of course, by that time I had also been hit by a couple of tranquilizer darts which I am told is standard issue for most companies in the Bazaar to ease personnel relations. If, perchance, your company does not already follow this policy, I heartily give it my recommend, as it certainly saves depreciation on your payroll types and therefore minimizes the expense of trainin' new ones.

Anyway, once I am calmed down to a point where I am merely tossin' furniture and the payroll type has recomposed himself, which is to say he has received sufficient first aid to talk, he explains the realities of life to me. Not only has the cost of the aforementioned carousin' been deducted from my earnin's, but also charges for my room which, realizin' the figure quoted only represents a third of the take on that facility, puts it several notches above the poshest resort it has ever been my decadent pleasure to patronize. Also there is an itemized bill for every bit or scrap of waste that has occurred at my duty station durin' the week, down to the last speck of Pixie Dust. Normally I would be curious as to how this accountin' was done, as it indicates a work force in the plant even more efficient than the security types which have been keepin' me at bay, but at the time I was too busy bein' outraged at bein' charged retail instead of cost for the materials lost.

All that keeps me from truly expressin' my opinion of the situation is that Roxie explains that I am not bein' singled out for special treatment, but that this is indeed a plant-wide policy which all the worker types must suffer. He also points out that the cost of the first aid for the payroll type is gonna be charged against my paycheck, and that what I have left will not be sufficient for me to indulge myself in another go 'round.

Thus it is that I am doubly disheartened when I hook up with Bunny for our weekly meetin' and debriefin', bein' as how I am not only a failure but a poor failure which is the worst kind to be.

"Guido, what's wrong?" she sez when we meet. "You look terrible!"

As I have said, Bunny is a swell head, but she is still a skirt, which means she has an unerring instinct for what to say to pick a guy up when he's under the weather.

"I am depressed," I sez, since she wasn't around when I explained it to you. "The workin' conditions at the plant are terrible, especially considerin' the pay we aren't gettin'."

At this, Bunny rolls her eyes and groans to express her sympathy.

"Oh, Guido! You're talking just like a . . . what is it that you call them? Oh, yes. Just like a worker type."

"That's 'cause I *am* a worker type!"

This earns me the hairy eyeball.

"No, you're not," she sez real hard-like. "You're an executive for M.Y.T.H. Inc. here on an investigation. Now quit being negative and let's talk about the job."

It occurs to me that she has a truly unusual concept of how to avoid negative thinkin'.

"Suit yourself," I sez, givin' her my best careless shrug like I usually save for court performances. "As far as the job goes, I am truly at a dead end. After a week I have discovered nothin' and don't have the foggiest where to look next."

"Good!" she sez, breakin' into a smile which could melt an iceberg, of which there are very few at the Bazaar with which I could test my hyperbole. Naturally I am surprised.

"Perhaps my small-but-normally-accurate ears are deceivin' me, Bunny. Did I understand you to say that it's a good thing that I am gettin' nowhere in my investigations?"

"That's right. You see, I think I'm on to something at my end, and if you're coming up empty in the plant, maybe you can help me with my theories! Now here's what I want you to do."

\* \* \*

Followin' Bunny's suggestion, I start out the next week by bracin' the foreman to reassign me to work in the warehouse on inventory. At first he is reluctant as he does not like worker types tellin' him his job, but after I point out to him how small the hospitalization benefits provided by the owner really are, he becomes far more reasonable.

All I have to do to give Bunny the support she requests is to double-check the materials comin' into the plant, and send her an extra copy of each day's tally in the inter-office mail. This pleases me immensely, as it is not only easy work, it also gives me substantial amounts of free time with which I can pursue a project of my own.

You see, I am still more than a little steamed over the hatchet job which was performed upon my paycheck. I therefore take it upon myself to commence conductin' my own unofficial survey as to workin' conditions around the plant, and since my eye has the benefit of business school trainin', which most of the workin' types have not bothered with, it becomes rapidly apparent that the situational stinks worse than the Doggie Doodle did.

Just as an example, the plant has made a practice of hirin' all sorts of bein's, many of which is extremely difficult to describe without gettin' vulgar. Now this is not surprisin' considerin' the Bazaar is the main source for their recruitin', but it makes for some teeth-grindin' inequalities in the pay scales.

Before the wrong idea is given, let me elucidate for a moment on the point of view I am comin' from. I personally don't care much who or what is workin' next to me as long as they can carry their share of the job. You will notice I have not even mentioned that Roxie is bright orange and Sion is mauve, as I feel this has nothin' to do with my assessment of their personalities or their abilities. I will admit to bein' a little uneasy around bein's what got more arms or legs than I do, but this is more a professional reaction, since should the occasion arise that we might have a difference of opinion, my fightin' style is intended for opposition what can throw the same number of punches and kicks per side as I can, and a few extra fists can make a big difference. But, as I say, this is more a professional wariness than any judgment on their overall worth as bein's. I only mention this on the off chance that some of my remarks about strange bein's might be taken as bein' pergerdous, a rap of which I have never been convicted. I am not that sort of person.

As I was sayin', though, the plant has lots of strange bein's workin' the line. The indignity of the situation, however, is that even though they got these extra arms and in some cases is doin' the work of several worker types, they is gettin' paid the same as anyone else. While to some this might seem unfair to the ones bein' so exploited, I see it as a threat to the worker types with the usual count of arms and legs, as it will obviously save the company significant cost if they can hire as many of the former as possible, whilst layin' off a disproportionate number of the latter.

Another inequality I observe concerns the security types which I have been unable to circumvent. Now this has been a source of curiosity to me since I first arrived at the plant, since it doesn't take an accountin' whiz to figure out that if the plant is payin' the security types what they're worth, their cost should be substantially more than would seem economically wise. I chance across the answer one time when I happen to eavesdrop on a couple off-duty lunchin' security types who are gripin' about their jobs. It seems that they are underpaid as much as us workin' types, despite the fact that they are safeguardin' stuff worth millions! While this is doubtlessly unfair, I do not include it in my notes because I have found that it is not only not unusual, but is actually customary for plants or societies to under-pay their guardian types. I suppose that as bonkers as it seems, this is in actuality the way things should be. If guardian types made a decent wage, then criminal types like me would go into that line of work as it has better hours and better retirement benefits than the career path I am currently pursuin', and if there was no crime there would be no need for guardian types and we would all end up unemployed. Viewin' it that way, the status quo is probably for the best.

Anyway, I continues to keep my eyes and ears open until I feel I have gathered sufficient injustices to make my point, then I wait for the right moment to present my findin's. This proves to be no great test of my patience, since, as I have noted, the worker types love to gripe about their jobs and tonight proves to be no exception to this rule.

"What do you think, Guido?" Roxie sez, turnin' to me. "Do the guys workin' the Dribble Toilets have it worse than the ones workin' the Bat-tery-Operated Whoopie Cushions?"

I make a big show of thinkin' hard before I give my answer.

"I think," I sez carefully, "that if brains was dynamite, the whole plant wouldn't have the powder to blow its nose."

It takes him a minute to get my drift, but when he does, his eyes go real mean.

"What's that supposed to mean?"

"I mean I've been sittin' here listenin' to you guys bellyache for nearly two weeks now, and ain't none of youse heard a thing that's goin' on."

"All right, Mr. Doggie Doodle, if you're so smart why don't you tell all of us who have been workin' here for years what it is you've learned in a whole two weeks."

I choose to ignore the Doggie Doodle crack, as there are now several tables of worker types listenin' to our conversation and I'm afraid I'll lose their attention if I take the time to bust Roxie's head.

"Youse guys spend all your time arguin' about who's gettin' honked the worst, and in the meantime you're missin' the point. The point is that you're *all* gettin' the Purple Shaft."

With that I commences to itemize a dozen or so of the more reprehen-sible examples of the exploitation of worker types I have noted in my investigation. By the time I am done, the whole bar is listenin', and there is an ugly murmur goin' around.

"All right, Guido. You've made your point," Roxie sez, tryin' to take another swallow of his drink before he realizes that it's empty. "So what are we supposed to do about it? We don't set company policy."

I shows him the smile that makes witnesses lose their memories.

"We don't set company policy, but we *do* decide whether or not we're gonna work for the wages offered in the conditions provided."

At this, Roxie lights up like he just won the lottery.

"That's right!" he sez. "They control the plant, but without us workers there won't be no Doggie Doodle to ship!"

The crowd is gettin' pretty worked up now, and there's a lot of drink buyin' and back slappin' goin' on when someone just has to raise a discouragin' word.

"So what's to stop 'em from just hiring a new work force if we hold out?"

That is Sion talkin'. As you may have noticed, he don't mouth off near as much as Roxie does, but when he opens up, the other worker types are inclined to listen. This time is no exception, and the room starts to quiet down as the worker types try to focus on this new problem.

"C'mon, Sion," Roxie sez, tryin' to laugh it off. "What idiots would work for these wages under these conditions?"

"Roxie, *we've* been doing just that for years! I don't think they'll have any more trouble finding a new work force than they had finding the old one."

I decided it was time I took a hand in the proceedin's.

"There are a few things you are overlookin', Sion," I sez. "First off, it will take time to hire and train a new work force, and durin' that time the plant ain't producin' Doggie Doodle to sell, which means the owner is losin' money which he does not like to do."

Sion just shrugged at that one.

"True enough, but he'd probably rather take the short-term loss of a shutdown than the long-term expense of giving us higher wages."

"Which brings up the other thing you're overlookin'."

"Which is?"

"There is one intolerable workin' condition a new work force would have to endure that we haven't . . . to wit, us! We don't have to get past us to come to work each mornin', and whilst the security types are aces at guardin' a plant, it is my best appraisal that they would not be able to provide bodyguard service for an entire new work force."

This seemed to satisfy the objection in question, and we then got down to workin' out the details, for while from the outside it may seem simple to organize a labor movement, there is much to be planned before anythin' can actually be set into motion. The other two shifts had to be brought on board and a list of demands agreed upon, not to mention the buildin' of a contingency fund in case the other side wanted to try starvin' us out.

A lot of the guys wanted me to run the thing, but I felt I could not accept in clear consciousness and successfully proposed Roxie for the position. The alibi I gave is that the worker types should be represented by someone who has more than two weeks' experience on the job, but in reality I wasn't sure how much longer I had before the Boss pulled me back to my normal duties and I did not want the movement to flounder from havin' its leader disappear sudden like. The chore I did volunteer for was givin' lessons in how to handle any outsiders the plant tried to hire, as most of the current worker types did not know a sawed-off pool cue from a tire iron when it came to labor negotiations.

Between workin' in the warehouse and helpin' with the movement, I was so busy I almost missed my weekly meetin' with Bunny. Fortuitously I remembered, which is a good thing as Bunny is a doll and no doll likes to be forgotten.

"Hi, Babe!" I sez, givin' her one of my seediest winks. "How's it goin'?"

"Well, you're sure in a chipper mood," she sez, grinnin' back at me. "I thought I'd have good news for you, but I guess you already heard."

"Heard? Heard what?"

"The assignment's over. I've cracked the case."

Now this causes me a little guilt and embarrassment, as I have not thought about our assignment for days, but I cover for it by actin' enthusiastic instead.

"No foolin'? You found out how the stuff is bein' liberated?"

"Well, actually it turns out to be a case of embezzlement, not pilferage. One of the Deveels in Accounting was tinkering with the receiving records and paying for more than was coming in at the shipping dock."

"Bunny," I sez, "try to remember that my degree is not in accounting. Could you perhaps try to enlighten me in baby talk so's I can understand the nature of the heist?"

"Okay. When we buy the raw materials, each shipment is counted and a tally sent to Accounting. That tally determines how much we pay to our supplier, as well as alerting us as to how much raw material there is in inventory. Now our embezzler had a deal going with the suppliers to bill us for more material than we actually received. He would rig the receiving tallies to tie out to the overage, pay the supplier for goods they never shipped, then split the extra money with them. The trouble was that since the same numbers were used for the inventories, the records showed that there were more goods in inventory than were actually there, so when the plant came up short, the owner thought the employees were stealing from him. The missing goods weren't being pilfered, they were never in the plant at all!"

I gave a low whistle of appreciation.

"That's great, Bunny! The Boss'll be real proud of you when he hears."

That actually made her blush a little.

"I didn't do it all by myself, you know. I wouldn't have been able to prove anything if you hadn't been feeding me duplicate records on the side."

"A mere trifling," I sez expansively. "I for one am goin' to make sure the Boss knows just what a gem he has workin' for him so's you get your just esteem in his eyes."

"Thanks, Guido," she sez, layin' a hand on my arm. "I try to impress him, but sometimes I think . . ."

She breaks off and looks away, and it occurs to me that she is about to commence leakin' at the eyes. In an effort to avert this occurrence which will undoubtedly embarrass us both, I wrench the conversation back to our original topic.

"So what are they goin' to do with this bum now that you caught him?"

"Nothing."

"Say what?"

"No, that's not right. He's going to get a promotion."

"Get outta here!"

She turns back, and I can see she's now got an impish grin on, which is a welcome change.

"Really. It turns out he's the owner's brother-in-law. The owner is so impressed with the smarts it took to set up this scam that he's giving the little creep a higher position in the organization. I guess he wants him stealing for the company instead of from it."

It takes me several moments to realize that my normally agile mouth is stuck in the open position.

"So where does that leave us?" I manage at last.

"With a successful investigation under our belts along with a fat bonus for resolving the thing so fast. I've got a hunch, though, that part of that bonus is gag money to ensure we don't spread it around that the owner was being flimflammed by his own brother-in-law."

Now I am indeed glad that we have resolved the pilferage assignment without implicatin' any of the worker types I have been buddies with, but at the same time I am realizin' that with the job over, I will not be around to help them out when the Doggie Doodle hits the fan.

"Well, that's that, I guess. We'd better report in to the Boss and see what's been happenin' while we've been gone."

"Is something wrong, Guido? You seem a little down."

"Aaah! It's nothin', Bunny. Just thinkin' that I'll miss some of the guys back at the plant, is all."

"Maybe not," she sez, real mysterious like.

Now it's my turn to give her the hairy eyeball.

"Now, Bunny," I sez, "if you've got sumpin' up your sleeve other than lint, I would suggest you share it with me. You know I am not good when it comes to surprises."

"Well, I was going to wait until we got back home, but I suppose it won't hurt to give you a preview."

She looks around like there might be someone listenin' in, then hunches forward so I can hear her whisper.

"I picked up a rumor back at the plant office that there may be a union forming at the magic factory. I'm going to suggest to Skeeve that we do a little prospecting . . . you know, put in a bid. Can you imagine what we could charge for breaking up a union?"

I develop a sudden interest in the ceiling.

"Uh, Bunny?" I sez. "I know you want to impress the Boss with how good you are at findin' work for us, but I think in the longer run that it would be in the best interests of M.Y.T.H. Inc. to pass on this particular caper."

"But why? The owner stands to lose ten times as much if a union forms than he was dropping to embezzlement. We could make a real killing here. He already knows our work."

In response, I lean back and give her a slow smile.

"When it comes to makin' a killin', Bunny, I would advise you not to try to teach your grandmother, which in this case is me, how to steal sheep. Furthermore, there are times when it is wisest not to let the client know too much about your work . . . and trust me, Bunny, this is one such time!"

# Chapter II

*"It all hinges on your
definition of 'a good time'!"*
**L. Borgia**

" . . . **A**N outside agitator and a union organizer! And to think I was paying him to slit my throat!!"

I somehow managed to keep a straight face, which was harder than it sounds.

"Actually, Mr. Bane, I was paying him to help uncover the source of your inventory leak, which he did, and you were paying him to work in your factory, which he also did. I'm not sure exactly what it is that you're complaining about."

For a moment I thought the Deveel was going to come across the desk at my throat.

"What I'm complaining about is that your so-called agent organized a union in my factory that's costing me a bundle!"

"There's no proof he was involved. . . ."

"So how come his name comes up every time. . . ."

". . . And even if he was, I'm not sure what concern it is of mine. I run a business, Mr. Bane, with employees, not slaves. What they do on their off hours is their affair, not mine."

"But he was acting as your agent!!!"

". . . To investigate the pilferage problem, which, I'm told, has been settled."

As we were speaking, Chumley poked his head into my office, saw what was going on, and came in all the way, shifting to his big bad troll persona as he did. In case you are wondering, I was working without a receptionist at the time, having deemed it wise to have both Bunny and Guido lie low for a while after finding out what had *really* happened on their last assignment. As an additional precaution, I had insisted that they hide out separately, since I was afraid that Bunny would kill Guido if they were alone within an arm's reach of each other. For some reason my secretary seemed to take Guido's labor activities very personally.

". . . Now, if you'll excuse me, Mr. Bane, I'm rather busy at the moment. If you wish to pursue the matter further, I suggest you take it up with Big Crunch here. He usually handles the complaints for our company."

The Deveel started to speak angrily as he glanced behind him, then did a double-take and swallowed whatever it was he was about to say as his gaze went up . . . and up! As I can testify from firsthand experience, trolls can look very large when viewed from up close.

"Little Deveel want to fight with Big Crunch? Crunch likes to fight!"

Bane pinked slightly, then turned back to me.

"Now look, Sk . . . Mr. Skeeve. All that's in the past, right? What say we talk about what your outfit can do to help me with this labor thing."

I leaned back in my chair and put my hand behind my head.

"Not interested, Mr. Bane. Labor disputes are not our forte. If you'd like a little free advice, though, I'd advise you to settle. Prolonged strikes can be very costly."

The Deveel started to bare his teeth, then glanced at Chumley again and twisted it into a smile. In fact, he didn't say another word until he reached the door, and even then he spoke with careful respect.

"Um . . . if it ain't asking too much, could you send this Guido around, just to say hi to the workers? What with him disappearing the way he did, there are some who are saying that I had him terminated. It might make things a little easier for me in the negotiations."

"I'll ask him . . . next time I see him."

The Deveel nodded his thanks and left.

"Bit of a sticky wicket, eh, Skeeve?" Chumley said, relaxing back into his normal self.

"Just another satisfied customer of M.Y.T.H. Inc. stopping by to express his gratitude," I sighed. "Remind me not to send Guido out on assignment again without *very* explicit instructions. Hmmmm?"

"How about a muzzle and leash?"

I shook my head and sat forward in my chair again, glancing over the paperwork that seemed to breed on my desk whenever Bunny was away.

"Enough of that. What can I do for you, Chumley?"

"Hmm? Oh, nothing, really. I was just looking for little sister to see if she wanted to join me for lunch. Has she been about?"

"Tananda? As a matter of fact, I just sent her out on an assignment. Sorry."

"No matter. What kind of work are you giving the old girl, anyway?"

"Oh, nothing big," I said, rummaging through the paper for the letter I had been reading when Bane burst in. "Just a little collection job a few dimensions over."

"ARE YOU OUT OF YOUR BLOODY MIND??!!!"

Chumley was suddenly leaning over my desk, his two moon eyes of different sizes scant inches from my own. It occurred to me that I had never seen the troll really angry. Upon viewing it, I sincerely hoped I would never see it again. That is, of course, assuming I could survive the first time.

"Whoa! Chumley! Calm! What's wrong?"

"YOU SENT HER OUT ON A COLLECTION JOB ALONE?"

"She should be all right," I said hastily. "It sounded like a pretty calm mission. In fact, that's why I sent her instead of one of our heavy hitters . . . I thought the job called for finesse, not muscle. Besides, Tananda can take care of herself pretty well."

The troll groaned and let his head fall forward until it thudded on my desk. He stayed that way for a few moments, breathing deeply, before he spoke.

"Skeeve . . . Skeeve . . . Skeeve. I keep forgetting how new you are to our little family."

This was starting to get me worried.

"C'mon, Chumley, what's wrong? Tananda will be okay, won't she?"

The troll raised his head to look at me.

"Skeeve, you don't realize . . . we all relax around you, but you never see us when you aren't around."

Terrific.

"Look, Chumley. Your logic is as enviable as ever, but can't you just say what the problem is? If you think Tananda's in danger . . ."

"SHE'S NOT THE ONE I'M WORRIED ABOUT!"

With visible effort, Chumley composed himself.

"Skeeve . . . let me try to explain. Little sister is a wonderful person, and I truly love and admire her, but she has a tendency to . . . overreact under pressure. Mum always said it was her competitive reaction to having an older brother who could tear things apart without trying, but some of the people she's worked with tend to simply describe it as a mean streak. In a nutshell, though, Tananda has a bigger flair for wanton destruction than I do . . . or anyone else I've ever met. Now, if this job you're describing calls for finesse . . ."

He broke off and shook his head.

"No," he said with a ring of finality to his voice. "There's no other way to handle it. I'll just have to catch up with her and try to keep her from getting too out of hand. Which dimension did you say she was headed for again?"

The direct question finally snapped me out of the mind-freeze his explanation had put me in.

"Really, Chumley. Aren't you exaggerating just a little? I mean, how much trouble could she cause?"

The troll sighed.

"Ever hear of a dimension called Rinasp?"

"Can't say that I have."

"That's because there's no one there anymore. That's the last place little sister went on a collection job."

"I've got the name of the dimension here somewhere!" I said, diving into my paperwork with newfound desperation.

# Chumley's Tale

Dash it all to blazes anyway! You'd think by now that Skeeve would have the sense to look a bit before he leaped . . . especially when his leaping tends to involve others as it does! If he thinks that Tananda can't . . . If he can't figure out that even I don't . . . Well, he has no idea of the way our Mum raised us, is all I've got to say.

Of course, one cannot expect wonders from a Klahd raised by a Pervert, can one . . . hmmm?? Well, Chumley old boy, time to muddle through one more time, what?

I must admit this latest collection assignment for Tananda had me worried. At her best little sister tends to lack tact, and lately . . .

As near as I can tell, there was bad blood building between her and Bunny. They had never really hit it off well, but things had gotten noticeably sticky since Don Bruce's niece set her cap for Skeeve. Not that little sister had any designs on the lad herself, mind you. If anything, her feelings toward him are more sisterly than anything else . . . Lord help him. Rather it seems that it's Bunny's tactics that are setting Tananda's teeth on edge.

You see, what with Bunny trying to be so spit-spot efficient on the job to impress Skeeve, little sister has gotten it into her head that it's making *her* look bad professionally. Tananda has always been exceedingly proud of her looks and her work, and what with Bunny strutting around the office going on about how well the last assignment went, she feels a wee bit threatened on both counts. As near as I could tell, she was bound and determined to prove that what she had picked up in the Guttersnipe Survival School was more than a match for the education Bunny had acquired at whatever finishing school the Mob had sent her to. Combined with her normal tendency for over-exuberance, it boded ill for whoever it was she was out to collect from.

I was also underwhelmed by the setting for this pending disaster. I mean, really, what kind of name is Arcadia for a dimension? It sounds like one of those confounded video parlors. I probably would have been hard-pressed to even find it if I hadn't gotten directions along with the name. The coordinates dropped me at the edge of a town, and since they were the same ones little sister had used, I could only assume I wasn't far behind her.

At first viewing, Arcadia seemed pleasant enough; one might almost be tempted to call it quaint—the kind of quiet, sleepy place where one could relax and feel at home. For some reason, I found myself fervently hoping it would be the same when we left.

My casual inspection of the surroundings was cut short by a hail from nearby.

"Welcome to Arcadia, Stranger. Can I offer you a cool glass of juice?"

The source of this greeting was a rather gnomish old man who was perched on the seat of a tricycle vending cart. He seemed to take my appearance, both my physical makeup and my presence at this time and place, so casually I almost replied before remembering that I had a front to maintain. It's a bit of a bother, but I've found no one will hire a well-mannered troll.

"Good! Good! Crunch thirsty!"

With my best guttural growl, I grabbed two of the offered glasses and popped them in my mouth, rolling my eyes as I chewed happily. It's a good bit . . . one that seldom fails to take folks aback. The gnome, however, never batted an eye.

"Don't think I've seen you before, Stranger. What brings you to Arcadia?"

I decided to abandon any further efforts at intimidating him and instead got right to the point.

"Crunch looking for friend. Seen little woman . . . so high . . . with green hair?"

"As a matter of fact, she was just by a little bit ago. She a friend of yours?"

I nodded my head vigorously and showed my fangs.

"Crunch likes little woman. Pulled thorn from Crunch's foot once. Where little woman go?"

"Well, she asked me where the police station was, then took off in that direction . . . that way."

An awfully nice chap, really. I decided I could afford to unbend a little.

"Crunch thanks nice man. If nice man needs strong friend, call Crunch, okay?"

"Sure thing. And if I can help you any more, just give a holler."

I left then before we got too chummy. I mean, there are precious few people who will be civil, much less nice, to a troll, and I was afraid of getting more interested in continuing my conversation with him than with finding Tananda. For the good of Arcadia, that would never do.

As it was, I guess my little chat had taken longer than I had realized, for when I found Tananda she was sitting dejectedly on the steps of the police station, her business inside apparently already concluded. Things must have gone better than I had dared hope, as she was not incarcerated, and the building was still standing.

"What ho, little sister," I called, as cheerily as I could manage. "You look a little down at the mouth. Problems?"

"Oh. Hi . . . Chumley? What are you doing here?"

Fortunately, I had anticipated this question and had my answer well rehearsed.

"Just taking a bit of a holiday. I promised Aahz I would stop by this dimension and check out a few potential investments, and when Skeeve said you were here as well, I thought I would stop by and see how you were doing."

"That can be summarized in one word," she said, resting her chin in her hands once more. "Lousy."

"Run into a spot of trouble? Come, come. Tell big brother all about it."

She gave a little shrug.

"There's not all that much to tell. I'm here on a collection assignment, so I thought I'd check with the local gendarmes to see if this guy had a record or if they knew where he was."

"And . . ." I prompted.

"Well, they know who he is all right. It seems he's a wealthy philanthropist . . . has given millions for civic improvements, helps the poor, that kind of stuff."

I scratched my head and frowned.

"Doesn't sound like the sort of chap to leave a bill unpaid, does he?"

"The real problem is going to be how to check it out. It seems he's also a bit of a recluse. No one's seen him for years."

I could see why she was depressed. It didn't sound like the kind of chore that could be finished in record time, which is, of course, what she wanted to do to make a good showing.

"Could be a bit of a sticky wicket. Who is this chap, anyway?"

"The name is Hoos. Sounds like something out of Dr. Seuss, doesn't it?"

"Actually, it sounds like a bank."

"How's that again?"

Instead of repeating myself, I simply pointed. Across the street and three doors down was a building prominently labeled Hoos National Bank.

Tananda was on her feet and moving in a flash.

"Thanks, Chumley. This may not be so bad after all."

"Don't forget. We're terribly close to the police station," I cautioned, hurrying to keep up.

"What do you mean, 'we'?" she said, stopping abruptly. "This is *my* assignment, big brother, so don't interfere or get underfoot. Capish?"

Realizing I was here to try to keep her out of trouble, I thought it ill-advised to start a brawl with Tananda in the middle of a public street, much less in front of a police station.

"Perish the thought. I just thought I'd tag along . . . as an observer. You know I love watching you work. Besides, as Mums always said, 'You can never tell when a friendly witness can come in handy.' "

I'm not sure if my words assured her, or if she simply accepted that a confirming report wouldn't hurt, but she grunted silently and headed into the bank.

The place was pretty standard for a bank: tellers' cages, tables for filling out deposit or withdrawal slips, etc. The only thing that was at all noteworthy was a special window for Inter-Dimensional Currency Exchange, which to me indicated that they did more demon business than might be expected for such an out-of-the-way dimension. I was going to point this out to Tananda, but she apparently had plans of her own. Without so much as a glance at the windows, she marched up to the manager's office.

"May I help you, Miss?" the twitty-looking fellow seated there said with a notable lack of sincerity.

"Yes. I'd like to see Mr. Hoos."

That got us a long, slow once-over with the weak eyes, his gaze lingering on me for several extra beats. I did my best to look innocent . . . which is not that easy to do for a troll.

"I'm afraid that's quite impossible," he said at last, returning his attention to the work on his desk.

I could sense Tananda fighting with her temper and mentally crossed my fingers.

"It's extremely urgent."

The eyes flicked our way again, and he set his pencil down with a visible sigh.

"Then perhaps you'd better deal with me."

"I have some information for Mr. Hoos, but I think he'd want to hear it personally."

"That's your opinion. If, after hearing it, I agree, then you might be allowed to repeat it to Mr. Hoos."

Stalemate.

Tananda seemed to recognize this as well.

"Well, I don't want to start a panic, but I have it on good authority that this bank is going to be robbed."

I was a little surprised by this, though I did my best not to show it. The bank manager, however, seemed to take it in stride.

"I'm afraid you're mistaken, young lady," he said with a tight smile.

"My sources are seldom wrong," she insisted.

"You're new to Arcadia, aren't you?"

"Well . . ."

"Once you've learned your way around, you'll realize that there isn't a criminal in the dimension who would steal from Mr. Hoos, much less try to rob his bank."

This Hoos chap was starting to sound like quite a fellow. Little sister, however, was not so easily deterred.

"What about a criminal from another dimension? Someone who isn't so impressed with Mr. Hoos?"

The manager raised an eyebrow.

"Like who, for example?"

"Well . . . what if I and my friend here decided to . . ."

That was as far as she got.

For all his stuffiness, I had to admit the manager was good. I didn't see him move or signal, but suddenly the bank was filled with armed guards. For some reason, their attention seemed to be centered on us.

I nudged Tananda, but she waved me off irritably.

". . . Of course, that was simply a 'what if.' "

"Of course," the manager smiled, without humor. "I believe our business is concluded. Good day."

"But . . ."

"I said 'Good day.' "

With that he returned to his work, ignoring us completely.

It would have been bordering on lunacy to try to take on the whole room full of guards. I was therefore startled to realize little sister was starting to contemplate that very action. As casually as I could, I started whistling Gilbert and Sullivan's "A Policeman's Lot Is Not a Happy One" as a gentle reminder of the police station not half a block away. Tananda gave me a look that would curdle cream, but she got the message and we left without further ado.

"Now what, little sister?" I said, as tactfully as I could manage.

"Isn't it obvious?"

I thought about that for a few moments.

"No," I admitted frankly. "Seems to me you've come up against a dead end."

"Then you weren't listening in there," she said, giving me one of her smug grins. "The manager gave me a big clue for where to try next."

". . . And that was?"

"Don't you remember he said no criminal would rob this Hoos guy?"

"Quite. So?"

". . . So if there's a criminal connection here, I should be able to get some information out of the underworld."

That sounded a tad ominous to me, but I have long since learned not to argue with Tananda when she gets her mind set on something. Instead, I decided to try a different approach.

"Not to be a noodge," I noodged, "but how do you propose to find said underworld? They don't exactly list in the yellow pages, you know."

Her pace slowed noticeably.

"That's a problem," she admitted. "Still, there must be a way to get information around . . ."

"Can I offer you a glass of cold juice, Miss?"

It was my friend from the morning with his vending cart. A part of me wanted to wave him off, as interrupting little sister in mid-scheme is not the healthiest of pastimes, but I couldn't think of a way to do it without breaking character. Tananda surprised me, however. Instead of removing his head at the waist for breaking into her thought process, she turned her most dazzling smile on him.

"Well, hi there!" she purred. "Say, I never did get a chance to thank you for giving me directions to the police station this morning."

Now, little sister's smiles can be devastating to the nervous system of anyone of the male gender, and this individual was no exception.

"Don't mention it," he flushed. "If there's anything else I can do to be of assistance . . ."

"Oh, there is one teensy-tiny favor you could do for me."

Her eyelashes fluttered like mad, and the vendor melted visibly.

"Name it."

"Wellll . . . could you tell me where I could find a hardened criminal or five? You see, I'm new here and don't know a soul I could ask."

I thought this was a little tacky and fully expected the vendor to refuse the information in a misdirected attempt to shelter the pretty girl from evil influences. The old boy seemed to take it in stride, however.

"Criminals, eh?" he said, rubbing his chin. "Haven't had much dealings with that sort for a while. When I did, though, they could usually be found down at the Suspended Sentence."

"The what?"

"The Suspended Sentence. It's a combination tavern/inn. The owner opened it after getting off a pretty sticky trial. It seems the judge wasn't wrong in letting him go, since he's gone straight, as far as I can tell, but there's a bad element that hangs out there. I think they figure some of the good luck might rub off on them."

Tananda punched me lightly in the ribs and winked.

"Well, that sounds like my next stop. Where'd you say this place was, old timer?"

"Just a couple of blocks down the street there, then turn left up the alley. You can't miss it."

"Hey, thanks. You've been a big help, really."

"Don't mention it. Sure you wouldn't like some juice?"

"Maybe later. Right now I'm in a hurry."

The old man shook his head at her retreating back.

"That's the trouble with folks today. Everybody's in such a hurry. Don't you agree, big fella?"

Again I found myself torn between entering a conversation with this likable chap and watching over little sister. As always, family loyalty won out.

"Ahh . . . Big Crunch in hurry too. Will talk with little man later."

"Sure. Anytime. I'm usually around."

He waved goodbye, and I waved back as I hurried after Tananda.

Little sister seemed quite preoccupied when I caught up with her, so I deemed it wisest to keep silent as I fell in beside her. I assumed she was planning out her next move . . . at least, until she spoke.

"Tell me, big brother," she said, without looking at me. "What do you think of Bunny?"

Now Mums didn't raise any stupid children. Just Tananda and me. It didn't take any great mental gymnastics to figure out that perhaps this was not the best time to sing great praises of little sister's rival. Still, I would feel less than truthful, not to mention a little disloyal, if I gave false testimony when queried directly.

"Um . . . well, there's no denying she's attractive."

Tananda nodded her agreement.

". . . In a cheap, shallow sort of way, I suppose," she acknowledged.

"Of course," I said carefully, "she does have a little problem with overachievement."

"A *little* problem! Chumley, you have a positive talent for understatement. Bunny's one of the pushiest bitches I know."

I was suddenly quite glad I had not verbalized my thought comparing Bunny's overachievement problem with little sister's. I somehow doubted Tananda was including herself in her inventory of pushy bitches. Still, there was one more point I wanted to test the ice with.

"Then again, her performance may be influenced by her infatuation with Skeeve."

At this, Tananda lashed out with her hand at a signpost we were passing, which took on a noticeable tilt. Though she isn't as strong as yours truly, little sister still packs a wallop . . . especially when she's mad.

"That's the part that really grinds me," she snarled. "If she thinks she can just waltz in out of left field and take over Skeeve . . . I was about to say she'd have to do it over my dead body, but it might give her ideas. I don't really want to have tasters munching on my food before I enjoy it. She's got another think coming, is all I've got to say!"

I gave her my longest innocent stare.

"Why, little sister!" I said. "You sound positively jealous. I had no idea you entertained any romantic designs on Skeeve yourself."

That slowed her pace a tad.

"Well, I don't, really. It's just that . . . blast it, Chumley, we helped raise Skeeve and make him what he is today. You'd think he could do better than some primping gold digger from Mobdom."

"And just what is he? Hmmm?"

Tananda shot me a look.

"I'm not sure I follow you there, big brother."

"Take a good look at what it is we've raised. Right now Skeeve is one of the hottest, most successful magician/businessmen in the Bazaar. Who exactly do you expect him to take up with for female companionship? Massha? A scullery maid? Maybe one of the vendors or come-on girls?"

"Well, no."

I had a full head of steam now. Tananda and I rarely talk seriously, and when we do it usually involves her dressing me down for some indiscretion or other. I wasn't about to let her slip away on this one.

"Of course Skeeve is going to start drawing attention from some pretty high-powered husband hunters. Whether we like it or not, the lad's growing up . . . and others are bound to notice, even if you haven't. In all honesty, little sister, if you met him today for the first time instead of having known him for years, wouldn't you find him a tempting morsel?"

"He's still a little young for me, but I see your point . . . and I don't tumble for just anybody."

"Since when?" I said, but I said it very quietly.

Tananda gave me a hard look, and for a moment I thought she had heard me.

"To hear you talk," she frowned, "I'd almost think you were in favor of a Bunny/Skeeve match-up."

"Her or somebody like her. Face it, little sister, the lad isn't likely to tie onto some nice, polite, 'girl-next-door' sort with his current life-style . . . and if he managed to, the rest of us would eat her alive in crackerjack time."

Tananda's pace slowed to almost a standstill.

"You mean that hanging around with us is ruining Skeeve's social life? Is that what you're trying to say?"

I wanted to take her by her shoulders and shake her, but even my gentlest shakes can be rather violent and I didn't want to get arrested for an attempted mugging. Instead, I settled for facing her with my sternest expression.

"Now, don't go all maudlin on me. What I'm trying to say is that Skeeve is used to associating with heavy hitters, so it's going to take a tougher-than-average lady fair to be comfortable around him, and vice versa. He'd be miserable with someone like that Luanna person."

"What's wrong with Luanna?"

I shrugged and resumed our stroll, forcing Tananda to keep up.

"Oh, she's pretty enough, I suppose. But she's a small-time swindler who's so shortsighted she'd sell him out at the first hint of trouble. In short, she'd be an anchor around his neck who would keep him from climbing and potentially drag him down. If we're going to fix the lad up with a swindler, she should at least be a big-league swindler . . . like, say, a certain someone we know who has the Mob for a dowry."

That at least got a laugh out of Tananda, and I knew we had weathered the storm.

"Chumley, you're incredible! And I thought women were manipulative matchmakers. I never realized it before, but you're a bit of a snob, big brother."

"Think yew," I said in my best clipped accent. "I accept that observation with pride . . . when I consider the alternatives. I feel everyone would prefer to be snobs if they ever really had the choice."

"Why are we stopping?"

"Well, if we're done deciding Master Skeeve's future for the moment, I believe we have a spot of business to attend to."

She looked where I was pointing and found we were indeed standing in front of a dubious-looking establishment, embellished with a faded sign which proclaimed it to be the Suspended Sentence. The windows that weren't painted over were broken or gone completely, revealing a darkened interior. It might have been an abandoned building if it weren't for the definite sounds of conversation and laughter issuing forth from within.

Tananda started forward, then halted in her tracks.

"Wait a minute, big brother. What did you mean, 'we'?"

"Well, I thought that since I was here, I'd just . . ."

"Wrong," she said firmly. "This is still my assignment, Chumley, and I'm quite capable of handling it by myself."

"Oh, I wouldn't breathe a word."

"No, you'd just loom over everybody with that snaggletoothed grin of yours and intimidate them into cooperating with me. Well, you can just wait out here while I go in alone. I'll do my own intimidating, if you don't mind."

This was exactly the sort of thing I was afraid of.

"It would be less brutal if I were along," I argued weakly.

"Why, big brother," she said with a wink. "A little brutality never bothered me. I thought you knew that."

Outflanked and outmaneuvered, I had no choice but to lean against the wall and watch as she marched into the tavern.

"Oh, I know, little sister," I sighed. "Believe me, I know."

Though forbidden to take active part in the proceedings, I was understandably curious and kept one ear cocked to try to ascertain what was happening from the sound effects. I didn't have long to wait.

The undercurrent of conversation we had noted earlier ceased abruptly as Tananda made her entrance. A pregnant pause followed, then there was a murmured comment prompting a sharp bark of laughter.

I closed my eyes.

What happened next was so preordained as to be choreographed. I recognized little sister's voice raised in query, answered by another laugh. Then came the unmistakable sound of furniture breaking. No, that's not quite right. Actually, the noise indicated the furniture was being smashed, as it swung quickly and forcefully until an immovable object was encountered . . . like a head, for example.

The outcries were louder now, ranging from indignation to anger, punctuated by breaking glass and other such cacophonies. Years of hanging around with Tananda had trained my ear, so I amused myself by trying to catalogue the damage by its sound.

That was a table going over. . . .

. . . Another chair. . . .

. . . A mirror (wonder how she missed the glasses?). . . .

. . . That was definitely a bone breaking. . . .

. . . Someone's head hitting the bar, the side, I think. . . .

. . . *There* go the glasses. . . .

A body hurtled through the plate-glass window next to me and bounced once on the sidewalk before coming to a halt in a limp heap . . . a fairly good-sized one, too.

Unless I was mistaken, little sister was resorting to magic in this brawl or else she wouldn't have gotten that extra bounce on a horizontal throw. Either that or she was *really* annoyed! I debated whether or not to chide her for breaking our unwritten rules regarding no magic in barroom brawls, but decided to let it slide. On the off chance that she was simply overly perturbed, such comment would only invite retaliation, and Tananda can be quite a handful even when she isn't steaming.

By this time, the din inside had ceased and an ominous stillness prevailed. I figured it was jolly well time I checked things out, so I edged my way along the wall and peeked through the door.

With the exception of one lonely chair which seemed to have escaped unscathed, the place was a wreck with everything in splinters or tatters. Bodies, limp or moaning, were strewn casually about the wreckage, giving the overall effect of a battlefield after a hard fight . . . which, of course, it was.

The only surprising element in the scene was Tananda. Instead of proudly surveying the carnage, as was her normal habit, she was leaning against the bar chatting quietly with the bartender. This puzzle was rapidly solved, as the individual in question glanced up and saw my rather distinctive features in the doorway.

"Hey, Chumley! Come join us in a drink to my long-overdue remodeling."

Tananda glanced my way sharply, then nodded her approval.

"Come on in, big brother. You'll never guess who owns this dive."

"I think I just figured it out, actually," I said, helping myself to a drink from a broken bottle that was perched on the bar. "Hello, Weasel. Bit of a ways from your normal prowl grounds, aren't you?"

"Not anymore," he shrugged. "This is home sweet home these days. Can't think of anyplace else I've been that would let me operate as a respectable businessman."

Tananda gagged slightly on her drink.

"A respectable businessman? C'mon, Weasel. This is Tananda and Chumley you're talking to. How long have we known you? I don't believe you've had an honest thought that whole time."

Weasel shook his head sadly.

"Look around you, sweetheart. This is my place . . . or at least it used to be. Been running it fair and square for some time now. It may not be as exciting as my old life-style, but it's easily as profitable since I never lose any time in the slammer."

Little sister was opening her mouth to make another snide remark when I elbowed her in the ribs. While I'm not above a bit of larceny myself from time to time, I figured that if Weasel genuinely wanted to go straight, the least we could do is not give him a hard time about it.

"So tell me, old chap," I said. "What brought about this amazing reform? A good woman or a bad caper?"

"Neither, actually. The way it was, see, was that I was framed . . . no, really, this time. I hadn't done a thing, but all the evidence had me pegged for being guilty as sin. I thought I had really had it, but this guy pops up and backs me hard. I mean, he springs for a really good mouthpiece, and when the jury finds me guilty anyway, he talks to the judge and gets me a suspended sentence. As if that weren't enough, after I'm loose again, he spots me the cash I need to start this place . . . a nice no-interest loan. 'Pay it back when you can,' he sez. I'll tell you, I ain't never had anybody believe in me like that before. Kinda made me think things over about how I was always saying that I had to be a crook 'cause no one

would give me a fair shake. Well, sir, I decided to give the honest life a try
. . . and haven't regretted it yet."

"This mysterious benefactor you mentioned . . . his name wouldn't
happen to be Hoos, would it?"

"That's right, Chumley. Easily the finest man I've ever met. You see,
I'm not the only one he's helped out. Most of the people in this dimension
have had some kind of hand up from him at one time or another. I'm not
surprised you've heard of him."

Tananda trotted out her best smile.

"That brings us to why I'm here, Weasel. I'm trying to find this Hoos
character, and so far the locals haven't been very helpful. Can you give me
an introduction, or at least point me in a direction?"

The smile that had been on Weasel's face disappeared as if he had just
been told he was left out of a rich uncle's will. His eyes lost their focus, and
he licked his lips nervously.

"Sorry, Tananda," he said. "Can't help you there."

"Wait a minute, old buddy." Tananda's smile was a little forced now.
"You must know where to find him. Where do you make your payments
on this place?"

"Made the last payment half a year ago. Now if you'll excuse
me . . ."

Tananda had him by the sleeve before he could take a step.

"You're holding out on me, Weasel," she snarled, abandoning any
attempt at sweetness. "Now either you tell me where I can find this Hoos
character or I'll . . ."

"You'll what? Wreck the place? You're a little late there, sweetheart.
You want the last chair, be my guest. It doesn't match the rest of the decor
now, anyway."

From little sister's expression, I was pretty sure what she was thinking
of destroying wasn't the chair, so I thought I'd better get my oar in before
things got completely out of hand.

"If you don't mind my asking, old chap, is there any particular reason
you're being so obstinate over a simple request?"

Tananda gave me one of her "stay out of this" looks, but Weasel
didn't seem to mind the interruption.

"Are you kidding?" he said. "Maybe you weren't listening, but I owe
this guy . . . a lot more than just paying back a loan. He gave me a
chance to start over when everybody else had written me off. I'm supposed
to show my appreciation by setting a couple of goons on his trail?"

"Goons?"

She said it very softly, but I don't think anyone in the room mistook

Tananda's meaning. In fact, a few of her earlier playmates who were still conscious started crawling toward the door in an effort to put more distance between themselves and the pending explosion.

Weasel, however, remained uncowed.

"Yeah, goons. What happened in here a few minutes ago? An ice-cream social?"

"He's got you there, little sister."

That brought her head around with a snap.

"Shut up, Chumley!" she snarled. "This is my assignment. Remember?"

"Wouldn't have it any other way. I do think Weasel has a point, though. You really don't give the impression of someone who wants a peaceful chat."

At first I thought she was going to go for my throat. Then she took a deep breath and blew it out slowly.

"Point taken," she said, releasing her grip. "Weasel, I really just want to talk to this guy Hoos. No rough stuff, I promise."

The bartender pursed his lips.

"I don't know, Tananda. I'd like to believe you. I suppose if Chumley says it's on the up-and-up . . ."

That did it. Tananda spun on her heel and headed for the door.

"If it takes Chumley's say-so, then forget it. Okay? I'll do this my way, without help, even if it kills someone."

"Hey, don't go away mad," Weasel called after her. "Tell you what I'll do. When the police ask what happened here, I'll keep your name out of it, okay? I'll just play dumb and collect from the insurance. It'll kill my rates, but . . ."

"Don't ruin your new record on my account. Total up the damages and I'll cover the cost personally."

With that she slammed out into the street, cutting off any further conversation.

"Is she kidding?" Weasel said. "It's gonna cost a bundle to fix this place up again."

"I really don't know, old boy. She's really mad, but by the same token, she's mad enough that I wouldn't cross her. If I were you, I'd start totaling up the damages. Eh, what?"

"I hear that," he nodded. "Well, you'd better get after her before she gets into trouble. Sorry to be such a hard case, but . . ."

"Tut, tut," I waved. "You've been more than generous, all things considered. Well, cheerio."

I had expected to have to repeat my earlier performance of catching up with little sister, but instead I found her sitting on the curb just outside the bar. Now, she's not one to cry, either from anger or frustration, but seeing her there with her shoulders hunched and her chin in her hands, I realized that this might be one of those rare times.

"I say, you're really taking this quite hard, aren't you?" I said, as gently as I could.

She didn't look around.

"It's just that . . . oh, pook! Weasel's right, and so are you. I've been charging around like a bull in a china shop, and all that's been accomplished is that even my friends won't help me out. Bunny'll never let me forget it if I can't even pull off a simple collection assignment."

Squatting beside her, I put a reassuring arm around her shoulders.

"I think that may be your problem, little sister. You're trying so hard to set a speed record to impress Bunny that you're rushing things . . . even for you. Now, I suggest that we retire someplace and think things through a bit, hmmm? Forget about getting the job done fast and just concentrate on getting it done."

That perked her up a bit, and she even managed a weak smile.

"Okay," she said. "Even though I still want to handle this on my own, I suppose there's nothing wrong with using you for a consultant since you're here. What I really feel like right now is a stiff drink to settle me down. I don't suppose you've spotted anyplace besides the Suspended Sentence where we could . . . ."

"Care for a glass of juice?"

We looked up to find the old boy with his vending cart smiling down on us. For a moment I was afraid that Tananda would snap at him, but she gave him a grin that was far more sincere than her earlier smile.

"Thanks, but I had something stronger in mind. And while we're on the subject of thanks, I appreciate the information you gave me earlier . . . the second time, that is. I guess I was in too much of a hurry before to remember my manners."

"Don't mention it. It seems like most folks are in a hurry these days. Me, I always felt you should take your time and enjoy things. We've all got so little time, the least we should do is savor what time we have."

Tananda smiled at him with genuine warmth instead of her usual manipulative heat.

"That's good advice," she said. "I'll try to remember it. Come on, Chumley. We've got some planning to do . . . slow and careful planning, that is."

"Well, just holler if I can be of any help."

"Thanks, but what we really need is someone who can put us in touch with Mr. Hoos. I don't suppose you'd happen to know where I could find him?"

"Oh, that's easy."

"It is?"

I think we said it simultaneously. It was that kind of a surprise.

"Sure. Just stand up, blink three times, and he'll be right here."

That sounded a bit balmy to me, and for the first time I started doubting the old boy's sanity. Little sister, however, seemed to take him seriously. She was on her feet in the blink of an eye, blinking furiously.

"Well?" she said, peering around.

"Please to meet you, Missy. My name's Hoos. What's yours?"

We gaped at him . . . it seemed to be the logical thing to do at the time.

"You!?" Tananda managed at last. "Why didn't you say something before?"

"Didn't know until now it was me you were looking for."

It was really none of my business, but I had to ask.

"Just out of curiosity, why was it necessary for little sister to blink three times?"

As I spoke, I realized I had forgotten to use my Big Crunch speech patterns. Hoos didn't seem to notice.

"Wasn't, really. It's just you've been working so hard to find me, I thought I should throw in a little something to keep the meeting from being too anticlimactic. So, what can I do for you?"

There was a gleam of mischievousness in the old boy's eye that led me to believe he wasn't as daft as he would like people to believe. Tananda missed it, though, as she fumbled a battered sheet of paper out of her tunic.

"Mr. Hoos," she said briskly, "I'm here representing a client who claims you owe him money on this old account. I was wondering when he could expect payment, or if you would like to set up a schedule for regular submissions?"

Hoos took the paper from her and studied it casually.

"Well, I'll be . . . I could have sworn I wrote him a check on this the next day."

"He did say something about a check being returned," Tananda conceded.

"Must of held onto it until I closed out. Darn! I thought I had covered everything."

"You closed out the account with the bank?"

Hoos winked at her.

"No, I closed out the bank. That was back when I was consolidating my holdings."

"Oh. Well, as I was saying, if you'd like to set up a payment schedule . . ."

He waved a hand at her and opened the top of his vending cart. From my height advantage, I could see that the bottom of it was filled with gold coins.

"Why don't we just settle up now?" he said. "I've got a little cold cash with me . . . get it? Cold cash? Let's see, you'll be wanting some interest on that . . ."

"MR. HOOS!"

We turned to find the bank manager striding rapidly toward us.

"I thought we agreed that you'd handle all your transactions through the bank! Carrying cash is an open invitation to the criminal element, remember?"

"What kind of a shakedown is going on here?" Weasel demanded, emerging from the door behind us. "This sure doesn't look like a friendly chat to me!"

A crowd was starting to form around us as people on the street drifted over and shopkeepers emerged from their stores. None of them looked particularly happy . . . or friendly.

"I know you want to handle this yourself, little sister," I murmured. "Would you mind if I at least showed my fangs to back some of this rabble off a ways? I want to get out of here alive, too."

"NOW JUST HOLD ON, *EVERYBODY!*"

Hoos was standing on the seat of his vending cart holding up restraining hands to the mob.

"This little lady has a legitimate bill she's collecting for. That's all. Now just ease off and go back to whatever you were doing. Can't a man do a little business in private any more?"

That seemed to placate most of the onlookers, and they began to disperse slowly. Weasel and the bank manager didn't budge.

"Let me see that bill," the manager demanded. "Do you recall incurring this debt, Mr. Hoos?"

"Yes, I recall incurring this debt, Mr. Hoos," Hoos said, mimicking the manager's voice. "Now, if you don't mind, I'll just pay it and the matter will be settled."

"Well, this is most irregular. I don't know why they didn't simply follow regular channels and present their claim at the bank."

"We *did* stop by the bank," Tananda snapped. "All we got was a runaround."

The manager peered at her.

"Oh, yes. I remember," he drawled. "What I don't recall is your saying anything about submitting a claim for payment. There was some mention made of a bank robbery, though. Wasn't there?"

"You *were* moving a bit fast there, little sister," I chided gently.

"You mean to say you were working legit, Tananda?" Weasel chimed in. "Why didn't you say so in the first place?"

"I did! What's going on here, anyway, Weasel?"

"Mr. Hoos is a very rich man," the bank manager said. "He is also quite generous . . . sometimes too generous for his own good."

"It's my money, ain't it?" Hoos retorted. "Now, where were we? Oh, yes."

He started shoveling handfuls of coins into a paper bag.

". . . We were talking about interest on this bill. What do you think would cover the trouble I've caused missing payment the way I did?"

"See what we mean?" Weasel said. "Mr. Hoos, any interest due should have been set at the time of the debt. Paying any more would be just giving your money away."

The bank manager gave us a weak excuse for an understanding smile.

"As you can see, many of us in this dimension who owe our good fortune to Mr. Hoos have taken it upon ourselves to protect him from unnecessary expense . . . not to mention from those who would seek to take advantage of his generosity."

". . . After you've benefited from that generosity yourself," I added innocently.

That got a cackle of laughter out of Hoos.

"That's right, Big Fella," he said. "Don't think too harshly of the boys, though. There's nothing quite as honest as a reformed criminal. Would you like me to tell you what the manager here was doing before I bailed him out?"

"I'd rather you didn't," the manager huffed, but there was a pleading note in his voice.

I saw that mischievous glint in the old boy's eyes again and found myself wondering for the first time who had *really* framed Weasel just before he decided to reform. I think little sister caught it too.

"I don't think any interest will be necessary, Mr. Hoos," she said, taking the bag from him. "I'm sure my client will be happy with the payment as is."

"Are you sure? Can't I give you a little something for your trouble?"

"Sorry. Company policy doesn't allow its agents to take tips. Weasel, you'll send me a bill for the damages to your place?"

"You got it, sweetheart," the bartender waved.

"There, now," Hoos said, reaching into his cart. "I can cover that expense for you, at least."

Tananda shook her head.

"It's baked into our operating budget. Really, Mr. Hoos, I'm already working legit. I really don't need any extra boosts. C'mon, Chumley. It's time we were going."

Waving goodbye to the others, I took my place beside her as she started the gyrations to blip us through to our home base on Deva.

"Perhaps I shouldn't mention it, little sister," I said softly, "but unless my eye for damage has deserted me completely, isn't that bill going to come to more than our company's share of the collection?"

"I said I'd cover it personally, and I will," she murmured back. "The important thing is that I've completed this assignment in record time . . . and if you say anything to Bunny about the damages, I'll make you wish you had never been born. Do we understand each other, big brother?"

# Chapter III

*"It's all a matter of taste."*
**B. Midler**

**"I** really have to compliment you, dear. It never ceases to amaze me how much you do with so little."

That was Bunny's comment following Tananda's report on her last assignment. I had asked her to sit in to take notes, and I had to admit she had been extremely attentive while Tananda was speaking . . . which was more than I managed to do. From the report, the assignment was so routine as to be dull, though I personally wanted to hear Chumley's side of it before I made any final judgments on that score. That particular troll, however, was nowhere to be found . . . a fact which made me more than a little suspicious. Bunny was as efficient as ever, though, covering for my wandering thoughts by providing compliments of her own.

"Why, thank you, Bunny," Tananda purred back. "It really means a lot to me to hear you say that, realizing how much you know about operating with minimal resources."

It occurred to me that it was nice that these two were getting along as well as they did. Our operation could be a real mess if the two of them took to feuding.

It also occurred to me that there were an awful lot of teeth showing for what was supposed to be a friendly meeting. I decided it was time to move on to other subjects before things got *too* friendly.

"Things have been pretty quiet around here while you've been gone, Tananda," I said. "Not much new at all. How about it, Bunny? Any new prospects we should know about?"

Bunny made a big show of consulting her note pad. Right away, this alerted me. You see, I know that Bunny keeps flawless notes in her head, and the only time she consults her pad is when she's stalling for time trying to decide whether or not to bring something to my attention. I may be slow, but I *do* learn.

"Welll . . ." she said slowly. "The only thing I show at all is an appointment with somebody named Hysterium."

"Hysterium? Why does that name sound familiar? Wait a minute. Didn't I see a letter from him about a week back?"

"That's right. He's a land speculator and developer who's been trying to get in to see you for some time now."

"That shouldn't be a problem. What time is the appointment for?"

Bunny was staring at her notes again.

"Actually, I was thinking of postponing the meeting, if not canceling it altogether," she said.

"Why would we want to do that?"

I was annoyed, but curious. I really wasn't wild about Bunny trying to make my decisions for me. Still, she had a good head for business, and if this guy made her hesitate, I wanted to know why.

"It's like I was trying to tell you before, Skeeve. Your time is valuable. You can't just give it away to any fruitcake who wants an appointment."

". . . And you figure this guy's a fruitcake?"

"He must be," she shrugged. "What he wants to talk about simply isn't our kind of work. As near as I've been able to make out, he wants us to serve as interior decorators."

That brought Tananda into the conversation.

"You're kidding. Interior decorators?"

Bunny actually giggled and turned to Tananda conspiratorially.

"That's right. It seems he started building a motel complex counting on the fact that his would be the only lodging available in the area. Since he's started construction, though, four others have either announced their intentions to build or have started construction themselves . . . right on his doorstep. Of course, since his original plan didn't include any competition, the design is more utilitarian than decorative. It's going to make his place look real shabby by comparison, and he's afraid of losing his shirt."

"That's bad," Tananda winced. "So what does he want us to do about it?"

"Well, apparently our outfit is getting a bit of a rep for being miracle workers . . . you know, 'If you're really up against a wall, call THEM!'? Anyway, he wants us to come up with an alternate design or a gimmick or something to catch people's attention so that his place will fill up before the competition rents out room one."

"Us? The man must be crazy."

"Crazy or desperate," Bunny nodded. "I know we'd have to be crazy to take the job."

I waited until they were done laughing before I ventured my opinion.

"I think we should take it," I said at last.

I suddenly had their undivided attention.

"Really? Why should we do that?"

I steepled my fingers and tried to look wise.

"First off, there's the fee . . . which, if I remember the letter correctly, was substantial even by our standards. Then again, there's the very point you were raising: we've never done anything like this before. It'll give us a chance to try something new . . . diversify instead of staying in a rut doing the same types of jobs over and over again. Finally . . ."

I gave them both a lazy smile.

". . . As you said, it's an impossible job, so we won't guarantee results. That means if we fail, it's what's expected, but if we succeed, we're heroes. The beauty of it is that either way we collect our fee."

The women exchanged quick glances, and for a moment I thought they were going to suggest that I take an extended vacation . . . like, say, at a rest home.

"Actually," Bunny said slowly, "I did have a course in interior decorating once in college. I suppose I could give it a shot. It might be fun designing a place on someone else's money."

"But, dear," Tananda put in, "you're so valuable here at the office. Since there's no guaranteed success on this one, it might be better if I took it on and left you free for more important assignments."

Bunny started to say something in return, then glanced at me and seemed to change her mind.

"I suppose if your heart's set on it, there's no reason we couldn't *both* work on it together. Right, Skeeve?"

Now *that* had to be the dumbest idea I had heard all day. Even if the two of them were getting along fine now, I was sure that if they started butting heads over design ideas, any hope of friendship would go right out the window.

Fortunately, I had a solution.

"Sorry," I said carefully, "I actually hadn't planned on using either one of you on this assignment."

That hung in the air for a few moments. Then Tananda cleared her throat.

"If you don't mind my asking, if you aren't going to use either of us, who are you giving the assignment to?"

I came around my desk and perched on the edge so I could speak more personally.

"The way I see it, the new design will have to be attention-getting, a real showstopper. Now when it comes to eye-catching displays, I think we've got just the person on our staff."

# Massha's Tale

"Are you *sure* the Great Skeeve sent you?"

Now I'll tell ya, folks, I'm used to people overreactin' to me, but this guy Hysterium seemed to be gettin' a little out a hand. I mean, Deveels are supposed to be used to dealin' with all sorts of folks without battin' an eye. Still, he was the client, and business is business.

"What ya sees is what ya gets, Cute, Rich, and Desperate."

It never hurts ta spread a little sugar around, but this time the customer just wasn't buyin'.

"*The* Great Skeeve? The one who runs M.Y.T.H. Inc.?"

This was startin' ta get redundant, so I decided it was time ta put a stop to it once and for all. I heaved a big sigh . . . which, I'll tell you, on me is really something.

"Tell ya what . . . Hysterium, is it? Never was much good with *names.* If you want I'll go back and tell the Prez that you decided not to avail yourself of our services. Hmmm?"

All of a sudden, he got a lot more appreciative of what he was gettin'.

"No! I mean, that won't be necessary. You . . . weren't quite what I was expecting, is all. So you're agents of M.Y.T.H. Inc., eh? What did you say your names were again?"

I don't know what he was expecting, but I was willin' ta believe we weren't it . . . at least, I wasn't. Even when I'm just lazin' around I can be quite an eyeful, and today I decked myself out to the nines just ta be sure to make an impression. Of course, in my case it's more like out to the nineties.

No one has ever called me petite . . . not even when I was born. In fact, the nurses took ta calling my mom the "Oooh-Ahh Bird," even though I didn't get the joke until I was older. The fact of the matter is, folks, that I'm larger than large . . . somewhere between huge and "Oh, my God," leaning just a teensy bit toward the latter. Now I figure when you're my size there's no way to hide it, so you might as well flaunt it . . . and, believe me, I've become an expert on flauntin' it.

Take for example my chosen attire for the day. Now a lot of girls moan that unless you got a perfect figure, you can't wear a bare midriff outfit. Well, I've proven over and over again that that just isn't so, and today was no exception. The top was a bright lime green with purple piping, which was a nice contrast to the orange-and-red-striped bottoms. While I feel there's nothing wrong with going barefoot, I found these darling turquoise harem slippers and couldn't resist addin' them to the ensemble. Of course, with that much color on the bod, a girl can't neglect her makeup. I was usin' violet lipstick accented by mauve eye shadow and screaming yellow nail polish, with just a touch of rouge to hide the fact that I'm not gettin' any younger. I'd thought of dyein' my hair electric blue instead of its normal orange, but decided I'd stick with the natural look.

Now, some folks ask where I find outfits like that. Well, if ya can keep a secret, I have a lot of 'em made especially for me. Face it, ya don't find clothes like these on the rack . . . or if ya do, they never fit right. Be sure ta keep that a secret, though. The designers I patronize *insist* that no one ever find out . . . probably afraid they'll get swamped with orders. They never put their labels in my clothes for the same reason. Even though I've promised not to breathe a word to anybody, they're afraid someone might find out by accident . . . or was that *in* an accident? Whatever.

Oh, yes. I was also wearin' more than my normal allocation of jewelry, which, for anyone who knows me, means quite a lot. Ta save time, I won't try to list the whole inventory here. Just realize I was wearin' multiples of everything: necklaces, dangle bracelets, ankle bangles, earrings, nose rings . . . I went especially heavy on rings, seein' as how this was for work. You see, not only are my rings a substantial part of my magical arsenal, Mom always said it wasn't ladylike to wear brass knuckles, and my rings give me the same edge in a fight, with style thrown in for good measure.

Anyway, I really didn't blame the client for bein' a little overwhelmed when we walked in. Even though he bounced back pretty well, all things considered, I think it took the two of us ta prove ta him just how desperate he really was.

"Well, I'm Massha," I said, "and my partner over there is Vic."

Hysterium nearly fell over his desk in his eagerness to shake Vic's hand. My partner was dressed stylishly, if sedately by my standards, in a leisure suit with a turtleneck and ankle-high boots. His whole outfit was in soft earth tones, and it was clear the Deveel had him pegged as the normal member of the twosome. Call it a mischievous streak, but I just couldn't let it stand at that.

"Actually, Vic isn't one of our regular staff. He's a free-lancer we bring in occasionally as a specialist."

"A specialist?" Hysterium noted, still shakin' Vic's hand. "Are you an interior decorator?"

My partner gave him a tight smile.

"No, I'm more of a night-life specialist. That's why I'm wearing these sunglasses. I'm very sensitive to the light."

"Night life? I'm not sure I understand."

I hid a little smile and looked at the ceiling.

"What Vic here is tryin' to say," I told the Deveel, as casually as I could, "is that he's a vampire."

Hysterium let go of the hand he had been pumpin' like it had bitten him.

"A vampire?!"

Vic smiled at him again, this time lettin' his outsized canines show.

"That's right. Why? Have you got something against vampires?"

The client started edgin' away across the office.

"No! It's just that I never . . . No. It's fine by me. Really."

"Well, now that that's settled," I said, takin' command of the situation again, "let's get down to business. If I understand it right, you've got a white elephant on your hands here and we're supposed to turn it into a gold mine by the first of the month."

Hysterium was gingerly seatin' himself behind his desk again.

"I . . . Yes. I guess you could summarize the situation that way. We're scheduled to be ready to open in three weeks."

". . . And what kind of budget have we got to pull this miracle off with?" Vic said, abandoning his "looming vampire" bit to lean casually against the wall.

"Budget?"

"You know, Big Plunger. As in 'money'?" I urged. "We know what our fees are. How much are you willin' to sink into decorations and advertisin' to launch this place properly?"

"Oh, that. I think I've got the figures here someplace. Of course, I'll be working with you on this."

He started rummagin' through the papers on his desk.

"Wrong again, High Roller," I said firmly. "You're going to turn everything over to us and take a three-week vacation."

The Deveel's rummagin' became a nervous fidget. I was startin' ta see how he got his name.

"But . . . I thought I'd be overseeing things. It *is* my project, after all."

"You thought wrong, Mister," Vic said. "For the next three weeks it's *our* project."

"Don't you want my input and ideas?"

Fortunately, Vic and I had talked this out on the way over, so I knew just what to say.

"Let me put it to you this way, Hysterium," I said. "If you had any ideas you thought would work, you'd be tryin' them yourself instead of hirin' us. Now, three weeks isn't a heck of a lot of time, and we can't waste any of it arguin' with you over every little point. The only way to be sure you don't yield to the temptation of kibitzin' and stay out from underfoot is for you not ta be here. Understand? Now make up your mind. Either you let us do the job without interference, or you do it yourself and we call it quits right now."

The Deveel deflated slightly. It's always a pleasure doin' business with desperate people.

"Don't you at least need me to sign the checks?" he asked weakly.

"Not if you contact the bank and tell 'em we're cleared to handle the funds," I smiled.

"While you're at it," Vic suggested, "let the contractor know we'll be making a few changes in the finishing work his crew will be doing. Say that we'll meet him here first thing in the morning to go over the changes. Of course, we'll need to see the blueprints right away."

Hysterium straightened up a little at that, glancin' quickly from one of us to the other.

"Can you at least let me in on your plans? It sounds like you have something specific in mind."

"Not really, Sugar," I winked. "We're just clearin' the decks so we can work. The marchin' orders are to turn a third-rate overnight hotel into the biggest tourist trap Deva has ever seen. Now will you get movin' so we can get started?"

* * *

It took us quite a while to go over the blueprints. You see, buildin' things had never been a big interest of mine, so it took a while to understand what all the lines and notes meant. Fortunately, Vic had studied a bit of architecture at one point when he was thinkin' of givin' up magic, so he could explain a lot of it to me . . . or at least enough so I could follow what he was talkin' about.

"Let's face it, Massha," he said at last, leanin' back in his chair. "No matter how long we stare at the drawings, they aren't going to change. What he's built here is a box full of rooms. The place has about as much personality as an actuary . . . which is to say, a little less than an accountant."

"You gotta admit, though," I observed, "the setup has a lot of space."

I could see why our client was nervous. The place was plain, but it was five floors of plain spread over a considerable hunk of land. There was a lot of extra land for expansion, which at the moment seemed unlikely. Hysterium had obviously sunk a bundle into puttin' this deal together, money he would never see again if nobody rented a room here.

"Tell me, Vic. Your home dimension is entertainment-oriented enough so that the competition for crowds has to be pretty heavy. What's packin' 'em in these days, anyway?"

The vampire frowned for a few moments as he thought over my question.

"Well, it depends on what kind of clientele you're after. You can go after the family groups or folks who have already retired. My favorite is the young professionals. They usually haven't started their families yet or are passing on them completely, which means they've got both money and time. For that set, clubs are always big. If I really wanted to pull crowds into a new place, I'd probably open a good disco."

"Now we're talkin'. Do you think you could put one together in three weeks?"

My partner shook his head and laughed.

"Hold on a second, Massha. I was just thinking out loud. Even if I could come up with a plan for a club, there's no room for it."

Now it was my turn ta laugh.

"Vic, honey, if there's one thing we've got it's room. Look here . . ."

I flipped the blueprints to the drawin's of the first floor.

". . . What if we knocked out the inside walls here on the ground level? That'd give us all the space we'd ever need for your disco."

"Too much space," the vampire said, studyin' the plans. "The key to one of these clubs is to keep it fairly small so people have to wait to get in.

Besides, I'm afraid if we knocked out *all* the internal walls, there wouldn't be enough support for the rest of the structure."

An idea was startin' ta form in my head.

"So try this. We keep the whole outer perimeter of rooms . . . turn 'em into shops or somethin'. That'll give extra support and cut back on your club space. And if that's still too big . . ."

"About four times too big."

"Uh huh. What would you say ta a casino? I haven't seen one yet that didn't draw tourists by the droves."

Vic expressed his admiration with a low whistle.

"You don't think small, do you? I'm surprised you aren't thinking of a way to make money off the grounds as well."

"I can't make up my mind between a golf course and an amusement park," I said. "That can wait for a while until we see how the rest of this works out."

Right about then, I noticed Vic babes had his cheaters off and was studyin' me. Now, I'm used to bein' stared at, but there was somethin' kinda unsettlin' about his expression that was outside the norm, if ya know what I mean. I waited for him ta speak his mind, but after a while the silence started gettin' to me.

"What're you lookin' at me that way for, Young and Bloodthirsty? Did I grow another head sudden-like when I wasn't lookin'?"

Instead of answerin' right away, he just kept starin' until I was thinkin' a bustin' him one just ta break the suspense.

"You know, Massha," he said finally, "for a so-called apprentice, you're pretty savvy. With the way you dress and talk it's easy to overlook, but there's quite a mind lurking behind all that mascara, isn't there?"

Now if there's one thing I have trouble handlin' it's praise . . . maybe 'cause I don't hear that much of it. To keep my embarrassment from bein' too noticeable, I did what I always do and ducked behind a laugh.

"Don't let the wrappin' fool ya, Fangs. Remember, I used ta be an independent before I signed on with Skeeve's gang. Magician for the city-state of Ta-hoe and then Veygus over on Jahk, that was me."

"Really? I didn't know that."

Just goes to show how rattled I was. I couldn't even remember how little Vic knew about our operation and the people in it.

"That was when I first ran into the Boy Wonder. He was in trouble then, too . . . in fact, Skeeve seems to have a knack for trouble. Remind me sometime to tell you about the spot he was in when I *did* join up."

"Why not now?" he said, leanin' back in his chair. "I'm not going anywhere, and there's no time like the present for learning more about one's business associates."

As you've probably noticed, I was eager to get off the spot, and talkin' about Skeeve seemed to be just the ticket I was lookin' for.

"Well, at the time his big green mentor had taken off for Perv, see . . . some kinda family problem. Anyway, the king puts the touch on Skeeve to stand in for him, supposedly so's his royalness could take a bit of a vacation . . . say, for a day or so. What the Man neglected to mention to our colleague was that his bride-to-be, a certain Queen Hemlock, was due ta show up expectin' ta tie the knot with whoever was warmin' the throne just then."

"Queen Hemlock?"

"Let me tell you, she was a real sweetheart. Probably would have ended up on the gallows at an early age if she hadn't been the daughter of a king. As it was, she ended up runnin' the richest kingdom in that dimension and was out to merge with the best military force around . . . which turned out to be the kingdom that Skeeve was babysittin'."

Vic frowned.

"If she was already in a position to buy anything she wanted, what did she need an army for?"

"For those doodads that *weren't* for sale. You see, we all have our little dreams. Hers was to rule the world. That was Queen Hemlock for you. The morals of a mink in heat and the humble aspirations of Genghis Khan."

"And the two of you stopped her?"

"To be truthful with you, Skeeve did. All I did was round up the king so we could put him back on the throne where he was supposed to be. Skeeve set 'em up with a pair of wedding rings that never come off which also link their lives. That meant if Queenie wanted to off Kingie and clear the path for a little world-conquering, she'd be slitting her own throat at the same time."

"Where'd he find those? I never heard of such a thing."

I gave him a chuckle and a wink.

"Neither has anyone else. What they got was some junk jewelry from a street vendor here at the Bazaar along with a fancy story concocted by one Skeeve the Great. What I'm sayin' is that he sold 'em a line of hooey, but it was enough to cool Hemlock's jets. Smooth move, wasn't it?"

Instead of joinin' in with my laughter, the vampire thought for a few moments, then shook his head.

"I don't get it," he said. "Now, don't mistake me . . . I think Skeeve's a swell guy and all that. It's just that from all I can find out, he doesn't use all that much magik, and what he does use is pretty weak stuff. So how has he built up an organization of top-flight talent around him like you and the others?"

"I'll tell ya, Vic, there's magik and there's magik. Skeeve has . . . how can I explain it? He may not be strong in the bibbity-bobbity-boo department, and he hasn't got the woman sense of a Quasimodo, but he's got enough heart for three normal folks."

I punched him lightly on the arm.

"Remember when I said he has a knack for gettin' into trouble? Well, the truth is that more often than not he's bailin' someone else out who really deserves to get what's comin' to 'em. In that Hemlock caper I was just tellin' you about, he could have headed for the horizon once he figured out that he'd been had. . . . but that would have left a whole kingdom without a leader, so he stuck it out. When I met him, he was workin' at gettin' Tananda loose after she got pinched tryin' ta steal a birthday present for Aahz. Heck, as I recall, the first time we crossed paths with you we were settin' up a jailbreak for his old mentor. That's Skeeve, if ya see what I mean. He's always gettin' in over his head tryin' ta do what he thinks is right, and a body gets the feelin' . . . I don't know, that if you stand beside him he just might be able to pull it off. Even if it don't work out, you feel you've been doin' somethin' good with your life instead of just hangin' in there for the old number one. Am I makin' any sense at all?"

"More than you know," Vic said. "If I'm understanding you properly, he sets a high personal standard, and consequently draws people to him who are impressed by the sincerity of his actions . . . who in turn try to match the proportionate output they perceive in him. It's an interesting theory. I'll have to think about it."

I couldn't help but notice that once old Fangs got wrapped up in somethin', he started soundin' more like a college prof than a night-lovin' partygoer. It made me a little curious, but since I don't like people tryin' to peek at more of me than I'm willin' to show, I decided to let it go.

"Speakin' a theories," I said, "we got one that isn't goin' to work itself out without a lotta pushin' from us."

The vampire stretched his arms and yawned.

"All right. I'll take care of the disco and the architect if you can start checking into the casino and the shops. Okay?"

I had to admit I was a little taken aback by his enthusiasm.

"You mean right now? It's pretty late."

He showed me his fangs in a little grin.

"For you, maybe. Us night people are just starting to wake up, which means it's just the right time for me to start scouting around for a band

and bar staff. Since we're on different missions anyway, though, I've got no problem if you want to catch a few Z's before you do your rounds. What say we meet here same time tomorrow for an update?"

\* \* \*

Now, folks, I may strut a bit and loud-talk even more, but I'll also be the first to admit that little Massha doesn't know everythin'. One of the many things I know next ta nothin' about is how ta run a casino. Considerin' this, it was easy ta see I was goin' ta require the services of an expert . . . in casinos, that is.

It took me a while to locate him, but I finally ran my mark to ground. He was slouched at a back table in a dingy bar, and from the look of him things hadn't been goin' real good. I was glad ta see that . . . not that I wished him ill, mind you; it just made my sales pitch a little easier.

"Hiya, Geek," I said, easin' up to his table. "Mind if I join ya?"

He blinked his eyes a couple times tryin' ta focus 'em before he realized that the person talkin' to him really was that big.

"Well, well, well. If it isn't one of the M.Y.T.H. Inc. hotshots. What brings you to this neck of the woods, Massha? Slumming?"

I pulled up a chair so's I could sit close to him. I mean, he hadn't said no, and that's about as close to an invitation as I usually get.

"I know you're busy, Geek, so I'll give it to ya straight. We're cookin' up a little deal and I'd like you to be a part of it. Interested?"

"Well, whaddaya know. After making me sell my club and putting me out on the street, the Great Skeeve has a deal for me. Isn't that just ducky!"

Now I may not know casinos, but I know drunk when I see it. Seein' as how it was just sunset, which for the Geek is like early morning, he was in pretty bad shape. The trouble was, I needed him sober. Normally I'd a taken him off someplace and let him sleep it off, but I was in a hurry. This called for drastic action.

Glancin' around the place to be sure there were no witnesses, I leaned forward, wrapped my arms around his neck, and gave him the biggest, juiciest kiss I knew. One of the other things I know more than a little about is kissin', and this particular sample lasted a fairly long time. When I felt him startin' ta struggle for air, I let go and leaned back.

"Wha . . . Who . . . Massha!" he said, gaspin' like a fish out of water. "What happened?"

I batted my eyelashes at him.

"I don't think I catch your drift, Big Red."

The Geek just sat there blinkin' for a few seconds, one hand on the top of his head like he was afraid it was goin' ta come off.

"I . . . I don't know," he managed at last. "I've been drunk for . . . what day is it? Never mind! . . . for a long time. Now all of a sudden I'm wide awake and stone cold sober. What happened? How long have you been here?"

I smiled ta myself and mentally accepted a pat on the back. My record was still intact. I've been told more times than you can count that nothin' sobers a body up as completely or as fast as a little hug and a kiss from Massha.

"Just long enough to catch the curtain goin' up," I said. "Now that we're all present and accounted for, though, I want ya ta listen close to a little proposition."

The Geek used ta be one of the biggest bookies at the Bazaar. At one point, he had his own club, called the Even-Odds. Of course, that was before Skeeve caught him usin' marked cards and suggested strongly that he sell us his club. I wasn't sure how the Prez would react to my cuttin' the Geek in on this new project, but he was the only one I could think of who had the necessary knowledge to set up a casino and was currently unemployed.

"I don't know, Massha," he said after I had explained the situation. "I mean, it sounds good . . . but a casino's a big operation. I'm not exactly rolling in investment capital right now."

"So start small and build. Look, Geek, the house is going ta be providin' the space and decor rent free. All you have ta do is set up security and round up some dealers to work the tables."

"Did you say 'rent free'?"

It occurred ta me that maybe I shouldn't have sobered him up quite so much. Now he was back ta thinkin' like a Deveel bookie.

"Well . . . practically. The way I figure it, the house will take a piece of the action, which means you'll only have ta pay rent if you lose money."

"That's no problem," the Geek said with a smile. "With the dealers I'm thinking of, there's no way we'll end up in the red."

Somehow, I didn't like the sound of that.

"I hope it goes without sayin' that we expect you ta run a clean operation, Geek," I warned. "I don't think the Great Skeeve would like ta be part of settin' up a crooked casino. Content yourself with the normal winnings the odds throw the house. Okay?"

"Massha! You wound me! Have I ever run anything but a clean game?"

I gave him a hard stare, and he had the decency to flush slightly.

"Only once that I know of," I said, "and if I recall correctly it was Skeeve who caught you at it that time. If I were you, I'd keep my nose clean . . . unless you want ta wake up some morning on a scratchy lily pad."

The Geek sat up a little straighter and lost his smug grin.

"Can he really do that?"

"It was just a figure of speech, but I think you catch my meanin'. Just remember, the only times you've lost money on your crew is when you got suckered into bettin' against us."

"That's true," the Deveel said with a thoughtful nod. "Speaking of Skeeve, are you sure there won't be a problem there? The last time I saw him we weren't on the best of terms."

"You worry about the casino and leave Skeeve ta me," I smiled confidently, hopin' I knew what I was talkin' about. "Anyway, Skeeve's not one ta hold a grudge. If memory serves me correctly, Aahz was all set ta tear your throat out that last meeting, and it was Skeeve who came up with the suggestion that let you off the hook with your skin intact."

"True enough," the Geek nodded. "The Kid's got class."

"Right. Oh! Say, speakin' a class, you might try to run down the Sen-Sen Ante Kid and offer him a permanent table of his own."

The Deveel cocked his head at me.

"No problem, but do you mind my asking why?"

"Well, the last time he was in the vicinity for that match-up with Skeeve, I got stuck baby-sitting that character assassin you fobbed off on us. That means I'm the only one a our team who didn't get a chance ta meet him . . . and, from what I hear, he's my kinda guy. Besides, he might appreciate settlin' down instead of hoppin' from game to game all the time. Aren't any of us gettin' any younger, ya know."

"Ain't that the truth," the Geek said with a grimace. "Say, that might not be such a bad idea. Having the best dragon poker player at the Bazaar as a permanent player at the casino would be a pretty good draw."

We talked a while more, but it was all detail stuff. The Geek was on board, and the casino was startin' ta take shape.

\* \* \*

Casinos may not be my forte, but nobody knows retail stores like yours truly. Bunny may be aces when it comes ta findin' class outfits at decent prices, and Tananda sure knows her weapons, but when it comes ta straight-at-ya, no-holds-barred shoppin', they both take a back seat ta Massha.

I had noticed this place long before the assignment came up, but it stuck in my mind so I thought I'd check it out. There were big "Going Out Of Business" and "Everything Must Go" sale signs all over the window, but they had been there for over a year, so I didn't pay 'em much heed.

For a storefront shop, the place was a disaster. Their stock could only be described as "stuff" . . . and that's bein' generous. There were T-shirts and ash trays and little dolls all mixed in with medications and magazines in no particular order. The shelves were crammed with a small selection of the cheap end of everything. They didn't have as many clothing items as a clothing store, as many hardware items as a hardware store . . . I could go on, but you get the point. If you wanted selection or quality in anything, you'd have ta go somewhere else. In short, it was just the sort of place I was lookin' for.

"Can I help you, lady?"

The proprietor was perched behind the counter on a stool readin' a newspaper. He didn't get up when he talked ta me, so I decided ta shake him up a little.

"Well, yes. I was thinkin' a buyin' a lot of . . . stuff. Can you give me some better prices if I buy in volume?"

That brought him out from behind the counter with a pad and pencil which had materialized out of thin air.

"Why, sure, lady. Always ready to deal. What was it you were thinking of?"

I took my time and looked around the place again.

"Actually, I was wonderin' if you could quote me a price on everything in the store."

"Everything? Did you say everything?"

"Everything . . . including your sweet adorable self."

"I don't understand, lady. Are you saying you want to buy my store?"

"Not the store, just what's in it. I'm thinkin' this place could do better in a new location. Truthfully now, how has business been going for you lately?"

The owner tossed his pad and pencil back onto the counter.

"Honestly? Not so hot. My main supplier for this junk just raised his prices . . . something about a new union in his factory. I either gotta raise my prices, which won't help, since this stuff is hard enough to move as it is, or go out of business, which I've seriously been considering."

I thought it would be best not to comment on the union he'd mentioned.

"You don't think a new location would help?"

"New location . . . big deal! This is the Bazaar at Deva, lady. One row of shops is like any other for pedestrian traffic. On any one of those rows you can find better stuff than I got to sell."

This was turnin' out ta be even better than I had hoped.

"Just suppose," I said, "just suppose the new location was in a hotel, and suppose that hotel had a casino and disco. That would give you a captive clientele, since nobody wants ta leave the building and wander around to find somethin' they can buy right where they are."

"A hotel and casino, eh? I dunno, though. Junk is still junk."

"Not if you had an exclusive to print the name of the place on every-thin' you sell. Junk with a name on it is souvenirs, and folks expect ta pay more for them. Right?"

The proprietor was startin' ta get excited.

"That's right! You got a place like this, lady? How much ya asking for rent?"

"Minimal, with a piece of the action goin' ta the house. How does that sound?"

"How much floor space do you have available? If I can expand, I can get a volume discount from my supplier and *still* raise my prices. Say, do you have a printer lined up yet?"

"Hadn't really thought about it."

"Good. I got a brother-in-law who does good work cheap . . . fast, too. How about a restaurant? All those folks gotta eat."

Now that was one that had slipped by both Vic and me.

"A restaurant?"

". . . 'Cause if you don't, I know a guy who's been looking to move his deli since they raised the rent on the place he's got."

I had a feelin' my problems with the storefronts was solved.

"Tell ya what, Well Connected. You pass the word ta the folks you think would fit into this deal, and I'll be back tomorrow with the floor plans. We can fight out who gets which space then."

\* \* \*

All in all, things went fairly smoothly carryin' out our plans for the revised hotel. It turned out, though, that for all our figurin' there was one detail we overlooked.

"We need a name!" Vic moaned for the hundredth time as he paced the office.

I looked up from where I was doodlin' on Hysterium's desk pad.

"What was he going to call it again?"

"The Hysterium Inn."

"Really, is it all that bad for a name?"

We looked at each other.

"Yes," we said at the same time.

"We could come up with a better name in our sleep."

"Terrific, Vic. What have you got?"

"Beg pardon?"

"The name. You said you could come up with a better one in your sleep."

"I said *we* could come up with a better name in our sleep. This is supposed to be a team, you know."

I shrugged helplessly.

"I'm not asleep."

"We need a name!" my teammate moaned for the hundred and first time.

"Look on the bright side, Fangs. At least we don't have ta overcome an established advertisin' campaign."

The vampire plopped into a chair.

"You can say that again," he growled. "I don't believe how cheap that Deveel is. He was going to open without any advertising at all!"

"Zero competition, remember? If you're figurin' on bein' the only game in town, you don't have ta advertise."

"Well, I think we can kiss the idea of bringing this job in under budget goodbye," Vic said grimly. "Sorry, Massha. I know how hard you've worked cutting corners expense-wise."

"Forget it," I waved. "How do you figure we should promote this place, anyway?"

"The usual newspaper ads aren't going to be enough . . . even though we'll have to do them anyway. This close to opening, we're going to have to come up with something extra to get the word out."

"How about billboards?"

Vic scrunched up his face.

"I don't know, Massha. I don't think a couple of billboards will do it."

"I was thinkin' more like lotsa billboards . . . more like fifty of them blanketin' the area for a ten-mile radius."

". . . Widely spaced further out, and closer together the nearer you get," he added thoughtfully. "I like it! Of course, it'll cost."

"So I shave a little here and there on the decorations. We'd better get on those right away. Nothin' too classy, mind you. We don't want to scare anybody away. What we need is someone who does the signs for the Reptile Farms. That kinda excitement."

"I know just the guy," Vic said, scribblin' down a note. "That brings us back to our original problem."

"Right. We need a name."

The vampire's head came up with a snap.

"Hey! That's my line."

"Sorry."

"This is the pits, you know?"

"How about that? The Pitts?"

"No. How about the Funny Farm?"

"Uh-uh. The Snake Pit?"

"Will you get off pits?"

"Well, then, how about . . ."

\* \* \*

What we finally settled on was The Fun House. Our judgment was influenced a bit by the fact that I managed to locate a down-at-the-heels carnival. We let 'em set up on our grounds, and they gave us our pick of their displays for decorations.

The best of the lot was the outsized figures they had on top of their rides . . . and particularly The Fun House. These figures were of bein's from all over the dimensions and were animated to move their arms and heads while hidden speakers went "Ho Ho Ho" at passersby. I thought they were terrific and had them installed all over the outside of the hotel . . . except for the Fat Lady. Her I had installed in the men's john off the lobby.

Once we had that, the rest of the decorations fell into place. There wasn't much we could do to make the shape of the building excitin', so I had it painted with wide stripes . . . like a circus tent, only with more colors.

Vic did the disco, and it was a beaut. He did the whole place in black: floors, walls, ceiling, furniture, everything. He also attached chairs and tables to the walls and ceiling at different angles with life-sized dummies in evening attire. The overall effect was one of disorientation, so that when the band was goin' and the lights flashin', you weren't really sure which way was up. To add to the effect, the dance floor was slanted a bit and rotated slowly. It was like bein' suspended in space and bein' buffeted by cosmic winds and gravity at the same time. He even named the club "The Pit" in appreciation of me and to apologize for comin' down so hard on the name when I suggested it for the hotel.

The casino was all mine, and I decided ta go for broke. I found a

painter with a sense of humor, and we did the place in camouflage . . .
except instead of usin' greens and browns, we leaned heavy on the basic
colors in day-glo shades. For a crownin' touch, we spaced mirrors all
around the place, but we used the distortion mirrors from the carnival Fun
House. This not only gave the place the illusion of bein' larger, but when
the customers glanced at themselves in the mirrors, they had the same
kind of meltin' lines as the decor. It definitely raised questions in the mind
as to exactly which reality we were operatin' in.

Vic was afraid the impact of the whole operation was a bit bright, but
I argued that the whole idea was ta stand out from the crowd and let
people know we were there. I did, however, unbend enough to agree that
we should have Skeeve on hand for our meetin' with Hysterium the night
before our opening. I mean, negotiatin' never was my strong suit, and I
had no idea how the client was going to react to our rather innovative
ideas.

*  *  *

"You've ruined me! That's what you've done! Ruined me!"

That was our client speakin'. You may guess from the sound of it that
he was less than pleased with our work. When you realize that that was
how he was soundin' after we had spent an hour calmin' him down, you've
got an idea of exactly how unhappy he was.

"I'm not sure I understand what your problem is, Mr. Hysterium,"
Vic said. "If you have a complaint . . ."

"*A* complaint?" the Deveel shrieked. "I wouldn't know where to start!
What did you people think you were doing, anyway?"

"We were turnin' your dump into a profit-makin' hotel. That's what
we were supposed to do."

I was tryin' to stay out of this 'cause a my temper, but I had to get a
word or two in here somewhere.

"A hotel? A hotel? This isn't a hotel! What I left you with was a hotel!
What I came back to is a sideshow! And what do *you* mean by profitable?
All the rooms on the first floor are gone! That cuts my rental earnings by
twenty percent!"

"Twenty percent of an empty hotel is still nothing!" I shot back.

"Massha's right," Vic said, stepping between us. "We needed that
space for attractions to draw in some customers. Besides, everything we
put in there generates revenue for the hotel."

"Not if they don't sell anything!" Hysterium argued. "Have you been
in any of those places? Have you seen the junk they're selling? And the

prices . . . they're charging more for a cup of coffee in that club you put in than I'm used to paying for a whole meal!"

"Not everybody eats as cheap as you do," I muttered under my breath.

"What?"

"I said you stand ta clear a heap when they do . . . sell stuff to the customers, that is."

"But there aren't going to be any . . . Ohhh! I'm ruined!"

The Deveel sank into a chair and hid his face in his hands.

"Of course, if you had wanted design approval, you should have stayed around. As it was, Massha and Vic had no recourse but to use their own judgment."

That was Skeeve speakin' from his chair in the corner. So far, he hadn't done much more than listen to the rantings.

"Stayed around?" Hysterium's head came up with a snap. "They made me go! They said I'd have to trust them if I wanted to use your outfit's services."

"Precisely," Skeeve nodded, changin' tactics without batting an eye. "You wanted our services, you trusted us, and we serviced you. I don't see what the complaint is."

"What the complaint is, is that you charged me an arm and a leg . . . in advance . . . to put me out of business! If I had lost money on a regular hotel it would have been bad enough, but to lose money *and* be made a laughing stock to boot. . . ." There were tears formin' in the developer's eyes. "That was my wife's family money I invested. I could turn a profit if I only had the capital, I told them. Now . . ."

His voice broke and his head sank again.

"If that's the only problem, maybe we can work something out."

"Forget it! Cutting your fee wouldn't help. I need to make money, not lose less."

"Actually, I was thinking more of taking the hotel off your hands. Buying it outright."

I shot a glance at Skeeve. He was leanin' back in his chair studyin' the ceiling.

"Are you serious?" the Deveel said hopefully.

"Why not? That way you turn a profit of . . . say, fifteen percent over cost? . . . for the building and land, and making the place work, much less dealing with its reputation, will be our problem. That's what we agreed to do in the first place . . . sort of."

Hysterium was on his feet pumpin' Skeeve's hand almost before the Prez had stopped talkin'.

"I'll tell you, Skeeve . . . Mr. Skeeve . . . you're a real gent. This is terrific! Just when I thought . . . I can't tell you how much I appreciate . . ."

"Don't mention it," Skeeve said, retrievin' his hand. "Why don't you go on over to my office right now? My secretary is still there. Just explain everything to her, and she'll start drawing up the papers. I want to have a few words with my agents, then I'll be along to sign off on the deal."

"On my way," the Deveel waved. "Gee. I can't get over . . ."

"Now, you realize, of course, we don't have that kind of cash on hand. We'll have to give a down payment and arrange some kind of payment schedule."

"Fine. Fine. As long we get a contract guaranteeing my profit."

Then he was gone, leavin' us ta stare at each other in silence. Finally, Skeeve gathered us up with his eyes.

"The place is booked solid?" he said, confirmin' what we had told him in our debriefing.

". . . For three weeks, with a waiting list for cancellations," Vic confirmed. "We're taking reservations for as much as a year and a half in advance."

". . . And Hysterium doesn't know?"

"He never asked, and we never got the chance to tell him," I shrugged. "You saw how he was."

Skeeve nodded thoughtfully.

"That means, if my calculations are correct, we'll be able to pay him off in full in less than three months . . . not including the take from the casino and the shops."

He rose and stretched, then gave us a wink.

"C'mon, you two," he said. "I think I'll invest an arm and a leg and buy you both a drink!"

# Chapter IV

*"If you're too busy to help
your friends, you're too busy!"*
**L. Iacocca**

ACTUALLY, I wasn't all that wild over The Fun House. I mean, it was making us money hand over fist, but I somehow never figured on owning a hotel/casino. In particular, I didn't think it was a good idea to set the precedent of buying out dissatisfied customers, no matter how profitable the deal turned out to be. As it was, Hysterium's relatives (on his wife's side) were trying to get the deal invalidated on the basis that he must have been out of his mind, or at least not in his right mind, to sell such a lucrative business at the price he did. I wasn't particularly worried, as this was still the Bazaar at Deva, and if everyone who signed off on a bad deal here was declared insane, the economy would collapse.

The part that really bothered me about the deal was that it meant associating with the Geek again. In past dealings with him, he had consistently proven to be primarily concerned with lining his own pockets without much regard for anyone else, and I felt it was dangerous to place him in a position where he had such temptingly easy access to our money, or even a piece of it.

Still, I couldn't argue with Massha's logic in including him in the scheme, and at the time she approached him she had no idea he was going to end up reporting to us. Bunny assured me that she was personally auditing the financial reports for the casino that the Geek turned in along with our share of the take, but I found that in spite of that I tended to spend inordinate amounts of time studying the spreadsheets myself, half expecting to find some indication that he was somehow skimming a little off the top for his personal accounts.

That's what I was doing this particular afternoon, setting aside the countless letters and chores that were pressing on my time to take one more pass at auditing the Geek's financial reports. Bunny had told me once that a hefty percentage of accountants and financial analysts operated more out of spite than from any instinctive or learned insight. That is, rather than detecting that there's anything wrong from the figures they study, they single out some department that's been giving them grief or a manager who made snide comments about them at the company party, then go over their reports *very* carefully. She maintains that anyone's reports will come up flawed or suspicious if reviewed closely enough.

That may well be, if one is a skilled numbers cruncher. All I discovered was that prolonged periods of time spent staring at rows of little numbers are a pain . . . literally and figuratively. Specifically, after a few hours hunched over the reports, I was feeling cramps and stabbing pain: in my eyes, my neck, my back, and regions lower.

Leaning back to ease the strain and stretching a bit, my eye fell on the pencil I had tossed down on my desk from disgust and frustration. With a smirk, I reached out with my mind, grabbed it, and flipped it into the air. What do magicians do when they get bored or depressed? Tinker around with magik, natch!

Remember once upon a time when I used to sweat and groan to levitate a feather? Well, those days are long gone. Nothing like a few years of using the basics like levitation to save your skin to increase one's confidence . . . and, as Aahz always told me, confidence is the key to magik.

I took the pencil up to the ceiling, paused, then took it on a tour of the room, stopping cold at each corner to give it a right-angle turn. I realized I was humming a little tune under my breath as I put it through its paces, so I brought it down over the desk and started using it like a conductor's baton, cueing the drums and the horns as the tune built.

"Nice to see you're keeping your hand in."

I glanced over at the door, and discovered my old mentor leaning against the frame watching me work.

"Hi, Aahz," I said, keeping the pencil moving smoothly. "Well, things have been so busy I haven't had much time to practice, but I do still turn a spell now and then."

As offhand as I sounded, I was secretly very pleased that the pencil hadn't wavered when Aahz surprised me. Not breaking concentration on a spell, or, rather, maintaining a spell once concentration was broken, had been one of the harder lessons Aahz had taught me, and I thought I finally had it down pat. I only hoped he noticed.

"Got a few minutes for your old partner?"

"Sure, pull up a chair."

I decided it would be rude to keep playing with the pencil while I was talking to Aahz, so I brought it down to where I could pluck it smoothly from the air as I leaned forward. Aahz didn't seem to notice, though. He was craning his neck slightly to look at the papers scattered across my desk.

"What's all this?"

"Oh, just going over the financials from The Fun House. I still don't trust the Geek completely."

Aahz settled back in his chair and cocked his head at me.

"The Fun House, eh? Haven't really had a chance to talk with you much about that one. That was quite a coup you pulled off there."

I felt warmed and flattered by his comment. While we were technically equals . . . had been for some time . . . he was still my old teacher, and I couldn't help but react to praise from him.

"It seemed like the best route out of a bad situation," I said offhandedly.

"That's right," he nodded. "It's always easier to solve a problem by throwing money at it than by thinking your way out."

Suddenly this no longer sounded particularly complimentary. I felt my pride turning to defensiveness with the speed of a snuffed candle.

"I believe the financial returns to the company have more than justified the wisdom of the investment."

It sounded a little stuffy, even to me. I had noticed that more and more these days I was retreating into stuffiness for defense in situations where I used to whine about my inexperience or lack of working data.

"Well, I've never been one to complain about clearing a profit," Aahz said, flashing one of his ear-to-ear displays of teeth. "Even when it means acquiring a casino we neither want nor need."

This was definitely sounding like a lecture shaping up instead of a testimonial as to what a fine job I had been doing. While I could make time for a chat and would always take time for "atta boys," I was in no mood to have my shortcomings expounded upon.

"What's done is done, and hindsight is academic," I said briskly, cutting short the casino conversation. "What was it you wanted to see me about?"

I almost started fidgeting with the papers on my desk to press the point home that I was busy, but remembered in time that they were the casino financial reports . . . definitely *not* the way to draw conversation away from that particular subject.

"Oh, nothing much," Aahz shrugged. "I was just heading out on a little assignment and thought you might want to tag along."

"An assignment? I haven't given you an assignment."

I regretted the words as soon as I said them. Not only did they sound bureaucratic, they underscored the fact that I hadn't been finding any work for Aahz, despite our heavy work load.

My old mentor never batted an eye at the faux pas.

"It's not really an assignment. More a busman's holiday. I was going to do a little work on my own time. A favor for a friend who can't afford our normal fees."

I should have been suspicious right then. If I'm at all money-grubbing, it rubbed off from Aahz during our association. Anytime Aahz starts talking about giving something away that we could sell, like our time, I should know there's something afoot.

"Gee, Aahz, I don't think I could take the time. I've been really busy."

". . . Levitating pencils and checking for embezzlement of funds that are all gravy anyway?"

His attempt at an innocent smile was short enough of the mark to be a deliberate botch.

"C'mon, Aahz. That's not fair. I *have* been working hard. I just need a break once in a while. That's all."

"My point precisely," my partner said, springing his trap. "It's about time you got out of this office and out in the field before you become a permanent part of that chair. You don't want to get too far out of touch with the troops, you know, and this little chore is just the thing to remind you what it's like to be on assignment."

I could feel myself being outflanked the longer he talked. In desperation, I held up a hand.

"All right, all right. Tell me about it. Who is this friend of yours?"

"Actually, he's more of an acquaintance. You know him too. Remember Quigley?"

"Quigley? Demon hunter turned magician? That Quigley?"

Aahz nodded vigorously.

"That's the one. It seems he's got a problem he's not up to handling himself . . . which isn't surprising, somehow. I thought you might be interested in lending a hand, since we were the ones who set him up for it."

Check and mate.

"Okay, Aahz," I said, looking mournfully at the unfinished work on my desk. "Just let me clear a few things with Bunny, and I'll be right with you."

# Aahz's Tale

Jahk hadn't changed much from our last visit, but then these off-the-beaten-track dimensions seldom do. We were traveling in disguise, which we Pervects have gotten into the habit of doing when visiting a dimension we've been to before, and the Kid picked up the trick from me. You see, contrary to popular belief, Pervects don't like to fight _all_ the time, and the second time through a dimension we usually end up in a fight with anyone who recognizes us and figures they're better prepared than the first meeting. This only confirms the belief we hold on Perv that the rest of the dimensions are antisocial and we'd best swing first to get the surprise advantage, not to mention doing our best to discourage off-dimension visitors whenever possible. Our dimension is unpleasant enough without having strange riffraff drifting through stirring up trouble.

Of course, being a Pervect wasn't the only reason certain citizens of Jahk might want to hang our scalps out to dry. The last time we passed through here, we stirred things up pretty well with our surprise entry into their Big Game. As old and cynical as I may be, I have to smile when I think of the havoc we wreaked then.

"How long do you think this problem of Quigley's is going to take, Aahz?" Skeeve said, breaking into my wandering thoughts.

"I really don't know," I shrugged. "I imagine we'll have a better idea once he fills us in on exactly what the problem is."

The Kid stopped in his tracks and scowled at me.

"You mean you agreed to help without knowing what you were volunteering for? Then how did you know we set him up for it?"

Even though Skeeve's proved himself many times over to be a fast learner, there are still times when he can be dense to the point of being exasperating.

"What was Quigley doing when we first met him?"

"He was a demon hunter. Why?"

"And what's he doing now?"

"Last thing we heard, he was holding down a job as Court Magician for Ta-hoe."

"Now what do you suppose prompted him to take up magik for a living instead of sword-swinging?"

"Oh."

He looked a bit crestfallen for a few moments but rallied back gamely.

"I still think you should have found out what the problem was. Once we're in there, there's no telling how long it's going to take, and I can't be away from the office *too* long. I'm really busy these days."

"Well, then," I smiled, "we should probably be hooking up with him ASAP instead of standing here in the street arguing."

The Kid rolled his eyes melodramatically and set off marching down the road again.

Skeeve has changed a lot in the years I've worked with him. When we first met, he was a kid. Now, he's a young man . . . even though I still tend to think of him as "the Kid." Old habits die hard. He's grown from a gangly boy into a youth who has to shave . . . even though it's only necessary occasionally, so he tends to forget until Bunny reminds him. Even more astonishing is how much he's gained in confidence and poise to a point where he's acquired a certain amount of style. All in all, it's been interesting watching my young charge develop over the last few years. I just wish I felt better about the directions he's been developing in.

You see, Skeeve's most endearing trademark has always been that he cared for people . . . really cared. Whether it was his feeling for Garkin when his old teacher died, even though my colleague never really gave the Kid a fair shake as a student, or the lengths he went to to bolster Ajax's sagging ego when the old Archer was doubting his own value in a fight, Skeeve has always had an unerring ability to see the good in people and act accordingly. That's a lot of why I stuck around to work with him . . . as much to learn as to teach.

Lately, however, things seem to be changing. Ever since he has taken the slot as president of our corporation, Skeeve seems to be worrying more and more about business and less and less about people. The others may not have noticed it. Bunny and Tananda have been so busy trying to one-up each other they wouldn't notice if a brass band marched through the room, and Chumley's had his hands full just keeping them apart. Massha and the hoods are big on blind loyalty. They'd probably follow Skeeve right off a cliff without thinking twice or asking question one. Then again, they haven't known him as long or as well as I have and may simply think his current behavior is normal. To me, however, it represents a major change.

This whole casino purchase thing is just one example. The Skeeve I've known would have insisted that Hysterium know all the facts before signing the contract, or at least given him a more generous price for his efforts. Instead, we were treated to a display of opportunism that would make a hardened Deveel haggler envious.

Now, you all know that I have nothing against making a profit, especially a sinfully large one . . . but that's me. Skeeve is supposed to be the counterbalancing humanitarian. While I've been learning about people from him, I'm afraid he's been absorbing the wrong lessons from me . . . or the right one too well.

Anyway, that's why I didn't chuck Quigley's letter in the wastebasket when it got forwarded to us at the Bazaar. I figured it would give me some time alone with Skeeve to find out whether I was just being a Nervous Nelly, or if there was really something to worry about. So far, I was leaning toward the latter.

Fortunately, Quigley hadn't moved. As impatient as the Kid was being, I was afraid he'd back out of the whole deal if we had to take extra time just to run him down. Our knock was answered with a cautious eye appearing at the crack of the door as it opened slightly.

"Oh! I was hoping . . . that is, I was expecting . . . Can I help you gentlemen?"

We had seen the "old man" disguise before, so there was no doubt that it was really Quigley peering out at us.

"It's us, Quigley," the Kid said briskly before I could even say "Hi." "Will you let us in, or should we just go home?"

"Skeeve? Oh, thank goodness. Certainly . . . come right in."

I personally thought Skeeve was being a bit abrupt, and Quigley's fawning over him wasn't going to improve his manners at all.

"Sorry for the reception," the magician said, herding us inside, "but I was afraid it might be one of my creditors."

As he closed the door, Quigley let his disguise spell drop . . . too much effort to maintain, I guess. Viewing his true appearance, I was slightly shocked.

The years had not been kind to our old ally. There were strain marks etched deeply into his face that hadn't been there when we were here before. The place itself seemed the worse for wear. The walls needed painting badly . . . or at least washing, and the furnishings showed signs of being repaired instead of replaced.

"This place is a dump!" Skeeve observed with his newfound lack of diplomacy. "Really, Quigley. If you won't think of yourself, think of the profession. How are people supposed to respect magicians if they see one of them living like this?"

"Ease up, partner," I said softly. "We can't all own casinos. Some of us have had to live in broken-down shacks in the forest . . . or even sleep under trees on the open road."

That earned me a sharp glance, but Quigley intervened.

"No, Skeeve's right. All I can say is that I've tried. That's part of what's gotten me into this mess I'm in. I've overextended my credit trying to keep up a good front, and now it's catching up with me."

"Gee, Quigley, if that's your only problem we can take care of it in no time at all. We can arrange a quick consolidation loan to get the wolves off your back . . . with a slight interest charge, of course. Right, Aahz?"

The possibility of a fast resolution of the problem seemed to brighten Skeeve's mood immensely. I was almost tempted to go along with it, but I had the feeling there was more to the situation than was meeting the eye.

"I dunno, Skeeve. I think I'd like to hear a little more about exactly what the problem is, if it's all right with you."

"C'mon, Aahz. Let's just settle his accounts and split. If we hurry, we can be back at the office by lunch."

While I had tried to be patient, even promised myself to be, his wheedling tones finally got to me.

"Look, *Kid,*" I said, using the phrase deliberately. "If you're so all-fired eager to get back, then go! I'm going to give a shot at trying to solve the *real* problem here, if I can ever find out what it is, maybe even without just throwing money at it. Okay?"

It was a cheap shot, but Skeeve had been asking for it. For a minute I thought he was going to take me up on my suggestion and leave, but instead he sank onto a sofa and sulked. Terrific. I turned my back on him and switched my attention to Quigley.

It seemed funny after all these years to take the lead in what was essentially a "people" situation. Usually I handled the tactics . . . okay, and occasionally the money . . . and left the people-handling to Skeeve. It was his part of the partnership to keep my abrasive personality from alienating too many people, particularly our friends. With him off in a blue funk, however, the task fell to me, and I was badly out of practice. Heck, I'll be honest, I was never *in* practice for this sort of thing. Ironically, I found myself trying to think of what Skeeve would say and do at a time like this.

"So, Quigley," I said, trying to smile warmly, "what exactly seems to be the problem?"

He fidgeted uncomfortably.

"Well, it's a long story. I . . . I'm not sure where to begin."

I suddenly remembered that non-Pervects tend to get nervous at the sight of Pervect teeth and dumped the smile.

"Why don't you start at the beginning? How come you're having money problems? You seemed to be doing all right the last time we were here."

"That's when it started," he sighed, "the last time you were here. Remember how they used to settle who was going to be the government around here? With the Big Game?"

Actually I hadn't thought about it for years, but it was starting to come back to me as he talked.

"Uh-huh. The Big Game between Ta-hoe and Veygus each year would decide who would get the Trophy *and* be the capital for the next year."

Quigley nodded vaguely.

"Right. Well, that's all changed now. When you guys won the game and took off with the Trophy, it stood the whole five-hundred-year-old system on its ear. For a while there was a faction that maintained that since you had the Trophy in Possiltum, that's where the capital should be for a year. Fortunately, wiser heads won out."

It was nice to know that there were *some* hassles that passed us by. I noticed that in spite of himself, Skeeve had perked up and was listening as Quigley continued.

"What they finally decided was that a Common Council should run the government. The plan was put into action with equal representation from both city-states, and for the first time in five hundred years the government of the dimension stabilized."

It actually sounded like some good had come out of our madcap caper. That made me feel kind of good. Still . . .

"I don't get it, Quigley. How is that a problem?"

The magician gave a wry smirk.

"Think about it, Aahz. With the feud over between the two city-states, there was no reason to maintain two magicians. It was decided that one would do just fine."

"Whoops," I said.

" 'Whoops' is right. Massha was their first choice. She had served as magician for both city-states at one time or another, and, frankly, they were more impressed with her than with me . . . especially after I let their hostage demon escape at the Big Game. When they went to tell her, though, she had disappeared. That left them with me."

I found myself wondering if Massha had signed on as Skeeve's apprentice before or after she knew about the organizational change and Quigley getting the boot.

"She's working with us over on Deva," Skeeve commented, finally getting drawn into the conversation.

"Really? Well, I suppose it makes sense. After you've gone as far as you can go on the local level, it's only natural to graduate into the big time."

"I still don't see how you ended up behind the eight ball financially," I said, trying to steer the conversation back on course."

Quigley made a face.

"It's my contract. I ended up having to take a substantial pay cut under the new situation. My salary before was adequate, but nothing to cheer about. Now . . ."

His voice trailed off.

"I don't get it," Skeeve said. "How can you be making less money for serving two city-states than you made working for one?"

"Like I said, it's my contract. There are clauses in there I didn't even know about until the council hit me with them."

"What kind of clauses?" I frowned.

"Well, that the employer has the right to set my pay scale is the biggest one I remember. '. . . According to the need of the community,' and they pointed out that with no feud, my workload, and therefore my pay, should be reduced accordingly. Then there's the 'No Quit' clause . . ."

"The what?"

"The 'No Quit' clause. In short, it says that they can fire me, but I can't quit for the duration of my contract. If I leave, I have to pay my replacement, 'sub-contractor' I think they call it, myself . . . even if they pay him more than they were paying me. That's why I'm stuck here. I can't afford to quit. By the time I got done deducting someone else's wages out of whatever I was earning on my new job, I'd be making even less than I am now. I can't believe I could land a position making more than double what I'm currently earning. Not with my track record."

For a moment I thought Skeeve was going to offer him a position with our company, but instead he groaned and hid his face in his hands.

"Quig-ley! How could you sign a contract with those kind of terms in it? Heck, how could you sign *any* contract without knowing for sure what was in it?"

"Frankly, I was so happy to find work at all I didn't think to ask many questions."

". . . There's also the minor fact," I put in, "that when he was getting started in this game, he was all alone. He didn't have a teacher or a bunch of friends to look over his contracts or warn him off bad deals."

It was getting harder and harder to keep the Kid from getting too intolerant of other people's mistakes. Even that not-too-subtle admonishment only had partial success.

"Well, he could have asked me," he grumbled. "I could have at least spotted the major gaffes."

"As I recall," I tried again, staring at the ceiling, "at the time you were working as the Court Magician at Possiltum . . . without any kind of written agreement at all. Would *you* have come to you for contract advice?"

"All right, all right. I hear you, Aahz. So what is it you want me to do, Quigley?"

I caught the use of "me" instead of "us," but let it go for the time being.

"Well, it's a little late, but I'd like to take you up on your offer. I was hoping you could look over the contract and see if there's a way out of it. My time is almost up, but I'm afraid they're going to exercise their renewal option and I'll be stuck here for another three years."

"Don't tell me, let me guess," I winced. "It's their option whether or not to renew your contract. You have no say in the matter. Right?"

"Right. How did you know?"

"Lucky guess. I figured it went nicely with the 'No Quit' clause. And I thought slavery had been outlawed. . . ."

"Just exactly what are your duties these days, Quigley?"

Skeeve had been maintaining a thoughtful silence on the sofa until he interrupted me with his question.

"Not much, really," Quigley admitted. "More entertainment than anything else. As a matter of fact, I'm going to have to be leaving soon. I'm due to put on an appearance at the Game this afternoon."

"The Game?" I said. "They're still playing that?"

"Oh, certainly. It's still the major activity for entertainment and betting around here. They just don't play it for the Trophy, is all. It's been a much less emotional game since you guys trounced the locals, but they still get pretty worked up over it. I'll be putting on the after-Game entertainment. Nothing much, just a few . . ."

I glanced at him when he failed to finish his sentence, only to discover he was snoring quietly in his chair, sound asleep. Puzzled, I shifted my gaze to Skeeve.

"Sleep spell," he said with a wink. "I figured it was only appropriate. After all, I learned that spell on our last trip here after our friend here used it on Tananda."

"Don't you want to hear more about the contract we're supposed to be breaking for him, or at least take a look at it?"

"Don't need to. I've already heard enough to rough out a plan."

". . . And that is . . . ?"

His smile broadened.

"I'll give you a hint."

His features seemed to melt and shift . . . and I was looking at the "old man" disguise Quigley favored for his work.

"We don't want two Quigleys attending the game, do we? The way I see it, the best way to get him out of the contract is to take his place this afternoon."

I didn't like the sound of that.

"You're going to get him fired? Isn't that a bit drastic? I mean, how's it going to look on his resumé?"

"Look, Aahz," he snarled. "I was the one who wanted to take the easy out and buy him out of his troubles. Remember? *You're* the one who said there had to be another way. Well, I've got another way. Now are you coming, or do you just want me to tell you how it went after it's over?"

\* \* \*

The stadium was impressive no matter how you looked at it. Of course, any time you get nearly 100,000 people together all screaming for blood, it's bound to be impressive. I was just glad that this time they weren't screaming for *our* blood.

There was one bad moment, though. It seems that Quigley/Skeeve as a City-State Official got in free, whereas I, in disguise as an ordinary Joe, had to get a ticket to get past the fences. This was well and good, except that it meant we were separated for a bit. During that time, it suddenly dawned on me that if Skeeve got a little lax or wandered out of range, my disguise spell would disappear, revealing my true identity. As one of the team that trounced the locals and made off with their beloved Trophy, it occurred to me that there could be healthier pastimes than being suddenly exposed in the middle of thousands of hopped-up Game fans. Fortunately, I never had to find out for sure. Skeeve loitered about until I gained admission, and we pushed on together. It did give me pause, however, to realize how much I had grown to depend on the Kid's skills since losing my own powers.

Quigley/Skeeve was apparently well known, and many of the fans called to him as we entered the stadium proper. The salutations, however, were less than complimentary.

"Quigley! How's it going, you old fart?"

"Hey, Quigley! Are you going to do the same trick again?"

"Yeah! Maybe you can get it right this time!"

Each of these catcalls was, of course, accompanied by the proper "Haw, haw, haw!" brays, as can only be managed by fans who have started drinking days before in preparation for *their* role in the game. Maybe Quigley was used to this treatment, but it had been a long time since anyone had spoken to the Great Skeeve like that, and I noticed a dangerous glint developing in his eye that boded ill for whoever he finally decided to focus his demonstration on.

The Game itself was actually rather enjoyable. It was a lot more fun to watch when we weren't the ones getting our brains beaten out on the field. I found myself cheering for the occasional outstanding play and hooting the rare intervention of the officials, along with the rest of the crazed mob.

Quigley/Skeeve, on the other hand, maintained an ominous silence. I found this to be increasingly unnerving as the afternoon wore on. I knew him well enough to tell he was planning something. What I didn't know were the specifics of "what" and "when." Finally, as the end of the Game loomed close, I could contain myself no longer.

"Say, uh, Skeeve," I said, leaning close so he could hear me over the din of the crowd. "Have you got your plan worked out?"

He nodded without taking his eyes off the field.

"Mind telling me about it?"

"Well, remember how I got fired from Possiltum?" he said, glancing around to see if anyone was eavesdropping.

"Yeah. You told the King off. So?"

". . . So I don't see any reason why the same thing shouldn't work here. I don't imagine that City-State Officials are any less pompous or impressed with themselves than the monarch of a broken-down kingdom was."

That made sense. It was nice to see the Kid hadn't completely lost his feel for people.

"So what are you going to chew them out over? Their treatment of Quigley?"

He shook his head.

"Out of character," he said. "Quigley isn't the type to make a fuss over himself. No, I figured to make the fight the key issue."

"Fight? What fight?"

"The one that's about to break out on the field," Quigley/Skeeve grinned. "The way I see it, these two teams have been rivals for over five hundred years. I can't believe *all* their old grudges have been forgotten just because the government's changed."

"I dunno, partner. It's been a pretty clean game so far. Besides, it's already a rough contact sport. What's going to start a fight?"

"Most of the contact is around the ball . . . or cube, or whatever they call it. Never did get that straight. This late in the Game, all the players are hyped up but not thinking too clearly from butting heads all afternoon. Now watch close."

He leaned forward to hide his hands, as one finger stretched out and pointed at the field.

There were two particularly burly individuals who had been notably at each other's throats all day, to the delight of the crowd. At the moment, they were jogging slowly side by side along the edge of the main action of the field, watching for the ball/cube to bounce free. Suddenly, one player's arm lashed out in a vicious backhand that smashed into his rival's face, knocking his helmet off and sending him sprawling onto the turf. The move was so totally unexpected and unnecessary that the crowd was stunned into silence and immobility. Even the player who had thrown the punch looked surprised . . . which he undoubtedly was. Nothing like a little tightly focused levitation to make someone's limbs act unpredictably, unless they're expecting it and braced against the interference.

The only one who didn't seem immobilized by the move was the player who had been decked. Like I said, the actual players of the Game, unlike their out-of-shape fans, are built like brick walls—with roughly the same sense of humor. The felled player was on his feet with a bounce and launched himself at his supposed attacker. While that party was unsure about the magik that had momentarily seized his arm, he knew what to do about being pummeled, and in no time at all the two rivals were going at it hammer and tongs.

It might have worked, but apparently the teams took whatever truce had been called seriously. Amid the angry shouts from the stands and the referee's whistle, they piled on their respective teammates and pried them apart.

"Too bad, Skeeve," I said. "I thought you had them there."

When there was no response, I glanced at him. Brow furrowed slightly now, he was still working.

The player who had been attacked was free of his teammates. Though obviously still mad, he was under control as he bent to pick up his helmet. At his touch, however, the helmet took off through the air like a cannonball and slammed into the rival team member who had supposedly thrown the first punch. Now helmets in this game are equipped with either horns or points, and this one was no exception. The targeted player went down like a marionette with its strings cut, but not before losing a visible splatter of blood.

That did it.

At the sight of this new attack on their teammate, this time when the ball wasn't even in play, the fallen player's whole team went wild and headed for the now unhelmeted attacker . . . whose teammates in turn rallied to his defense.

Both benches emptied as the reserves came off the sidelines to join the fray . . . or started to. Before they had a chance to build up any speed, both sets of reserves were imprisoned by the glowing blue cages of magikal wards, an application I'll admit I had never thought of. Instead of the fresh teams from the benches, Quigley/Skeeve took the field.

I hadn't realized he had moved from my side until I saw him vault the low railing that separated the spectators from access to the playing field. The move was a bit spry for the "old man" guise he was using, but no one else seemed to notice.

It was a real pleasure to watch the Kid work . . . especially considering the fact that I taught him most of what he knows. I had to admit he had gotten pretty good over the years.

"STOP IT!! THAT'S ENOUGH!!" he roared. "I SAID, STOP IT!!!"

Still shouting, he waded into the players on the field who were locked in mortal combat. The ones who were standing he crumpled in their tracks with a gesture . . . a gesture which I realized was a simple sleep spell. The others he easily forced apart with judicious use of his levitational abilities. Two players who were grappling with each other he not only separated, but held aloft some twenty feet off the ground. As swiftly as it had started, the fight was stopped, and right handily, too.

As could have been predicted, no sooner had the dust settled than a troop of officious-looking individuals came storming out onto the field, making a beeline for Quigley/Skeeve. While I may have lost my powers, there's nothing wrong with my hearing, and I was easily able to listen in on the following exchange, unlike the restless fans in the stands around me.

"Quigley, you . . . How dare you interrupt the Game this way?"

"Game?" Quigley/Skeeve said coolly, folding his arms. "That wasn't a game, that was a fight . . . even though I can see how you could easily confuse the two."

"You have no right to . . . Put them down!"

This last was accompanied by a gesture at the suspended players. Skeeve didn't gesture, but the two players suddenly dropped to the turf with bone-jarring thuds that drew the same "Ooooo's" from the crowd as you get from a really good hit during actual play.

". . . As to my rights," Quigley/Skeeve intoned, not looking around, "I'm under contract to use my magikal powers to help keep the peace in Veygus and Ta-hoe. The way I see it, that includes stopping brawls when I happen across them . . . which I've just done. To that end, I'm declaring the Game over. The current score stands as final."

With that, the cage/wards began migrating toward their respective tunnels, herding the players within along with them. Needless to say, the crowd did not approve.

"You . . . you can't do that!" the official spokesman screamed over the rising tide of boos from the stands. "The most exciting plays happen in the last few minutes!"

As a final flourish, Quigley/Skeeve levitated the fallen players on the field down the tunnels after their teammates.

"I've done it," he said. "What's more, I intend to do it at every scheduling of this barbaric Game when things get out of hand. My contract is up for renewal soon, and I realized I've been a bit lax in my duties. Consequently, I thought I'd remind you of exactly what it is you're keeping on the payroll. If you don't like it, you can always fire me."

I smiled and shook my head in appreciation. I had to hand it to the Kid. If attacking the dimension's favorite pastime didn't get Quigley canned, I didn't know what would.

\* \* \*

"You shut down the Game?"

That was Quigley expressing his appreciation for Skeeve's help.

We were back at his place with our disguises off and the magician revived. Apparently our assistance wasn't quite what he had been expecting.

"It seemed like the surest way to get you out of your contract," Skeeve shrugged. "The locals seem rather attached to the Game."

"Attached to . . . I'm dead!" the magician cried with a groan. "I won't just get fired, I'll be lynched!"

The Kid was unmoved.

"Not to worry," he said. "You can always use a disguise spell to get away, or if it'll make you feel better, we'll give you an escort to . . ."

There was a knock on the door.

"Ah. Unless I miss my guess, that should be the Council now. Get the door, Quigley."

The magician hesitated and glanced around the room as if looking for a way to escape. Finally he sighed and trudged toward the door.

"Speaking of disguises, Skeeve . . ." I said.

"Oh, right. Sorry, Aahz."

With an absent-minded wave of his hand we were disguised again, this time in the appearances we used when we first arrived.

"Oh! Lord Magician. May we come in? There are certain matters we must . . . oh! I didn't realize you had guests."

It was indeed the Council. Right on schedule. I snuck a wink at Skeeve, who nodded in encouragement.

"These are . . . friends of mine," Quigley said lamely, as if he didn't quite believe it himself. "What was it you wanted to see me about?"

Several sets of uneasy eyes swept us.

"We . . . um . . . hoped to speak with you in private."

"We'll wait outside, Quigley," Skeeve said, getting to his feet. "Just holler if you need us."

\* \* \*

"Well, that's that," I sighed after the door closed behind us. "I wonder what Quigley's going to do for his next job?"

Skeeve leaned casually against the wall.

"I figure that's his problem," he said. "After all, he's the one who asked us to spring him from his contract. I assume he has something else lined up."

". . . And if he doesn't? Quigley's never been big in the planning-ahead department. It won't be easy for him to find work with a termination on his record."

"Like I said, that's his problem," Skeeve shrugged. "He can always . . ."

The door opened, and the Council trooped silently out. Quigley waited until they were clear, then beckoned us inside frantically.

"You'll never guess what happened," he said excitedly.

"You were fired, right?" Skeeve replied. "C'mon, Quigley, snap out of it. Remember us? We're the ones who set it up."

"No, I wasn't fired. Once they got over being mad, they were impressed by the show of magik I put on at the Game. They renewed my contract."

I found myself looking at Skeeve, who was in turn looking back at me. We held that pose for a few moments. Finally Skeeve heaved a sigh.

"Well," he said, "we'll just have to think of something else. Don't worry, Quigley. I haven't seen a contract yet that couldn't be broken."

"Ummm . . . actually, I'd rather you didn't."

That shook me a bit.

"Excuse me, Quigley. For a moment there I thought you said . . ."

"That's right. You see, the Council was impressed enough that they've given me a raise . . . a substantial raise. I don't think I'll be able to do better anywhere else, especially if they ask for a demonstration of my skills. There have been some changes in the contract, though, and I'd really appreciate it if you two could look it over and let me know what I'm in for."

*   *   *

"I'm sorry about that, Skeeve," I said as we trudged along. "All that work for nothing."

We had finally finished going over the contract with Quigley and were looking for a quiet spot to head back to Deva unobserved.

"Not really. We solved Quigley's problem for him, and that new contract is a definite improvement over the old one."

I had meant that he had done a lot of work for no pay, but decided not to push my luck by clarifying my statement.

"You kind of surprised me when we were talking outside," I admitted. "I half expected you to be figuring on recruiting Quigley for our crew, once he got free of his contract."

The Kid gave a harsh bark of laughter.

"Throw money at it again? Don't worry, Aahz. I'm not that crazy. I might have been willing to spot him a loan, but hire him? A no-talent, do-nothing like that? I run a tight ship at M.Y.T.H. Inc., and there's no room for deadwood . . . even if they are old friends. Speaking of the company, I wonder if there's any word about . . ."

He rambled on, talking about the work he was getting back to. I didn't listen too closely, though. Instead, I kept replaying something he had said in my mind.

"A no-talent do-nothing . . . no room for deadwood, even if they are old friends . . ."

A bit harsh, perhaps, but definitely food for thought.

# Chapter V

*"What fools these mortals be."*
**Smaug**

**I** never really realized how easy it was to buy something until I tried my hand at selling. I'm not talking about small, casual purchases here. I'm talking about something of size . . . like, say, a casino/hotel. Of course buying it had been simplified by the fact that the developer . . . what was his name? No matter . . . was desperate. Trying to offload it, however, was an entirely different matter.

Leaning back in my chair, I stared at the sea of paper on my desk, trying to mentally sort out the various offers, only to discover they were starting to run together in my head. I've noticed that happening more and more after midnight. With a muttered curse, I cast about for my notes.

"Working late, Skeeve?"

"What?" I said, glancing up. "Oh. Hi, Bunny. What are you doing here at this hour?"

"I could say I was worried about you, which I am, but truthfully I didn't even know you were still here till I saw the light on and poked my head in to check. No, I was just fetching a few things I had stored in my desk. Now, I can return the same question: what are *you* doing here?"

I stretched a bit as I answered, grateful for the break.

"Just trying to organize my thoughts on selling The Fun House. I'm going to have to make my recommendations to the Board as to which of these offers to accept when we discuss it at our monthly meeting."

She came around the desk and stood behind me, massaging the knots out of my shoulders. It felt wonderful.

"I don't see why you have to make a presentation to the Board at all," she said. "Why don't you just go ahead and make the decision unilaterally? You made the decision to sell without clearing it with anyone else."

Something in what she said had an ominous ring to it, but I was enjoying the backrub too much to pin it down just then.

"I made the decision unilaterally to open our door to offers . . . not to sell. The actual final call as to whether or not to sell, and which, if any, of the offers to accept, is up to the Board."

"Then if it's up to them, why are you killing yourself getting ready to make a pitch?"

I knew where she was coming from then. It was the old "you're working too hard" bit. It seemed like I was hearing that from everybody these days, or often enough that I could sing it from memory.

"Because I *really* want this motion to carry," I said, pulling away from her. "If there's going to be any opposition, I want to be sure I have my reasons and arguments down pat."

Bunny wandered back around the desk, hesitated, then plopped down into a chair.

"All right, then rehearse. Tell *me* why you want to sell, if you don't mind giving a preview."

I rose and began to pace, rubbing my lower lip as I organized my thoughts.

"Officially, I think it's necessary for two reasons. First, pretty soon now the novelty of the place is going to wear off, and when it does the crowds . . . and therefore our revenues . . . will decline. That will make it harder to sell than right now, when it's a hot spot. Second, the place is so successful it's going to generate imitators. From what I've been hearing at my 'businessman's lunches,' there are already several plans underway to construct or convert several of the nearby hotels into casinos. Again, it will dilute the market and lower our price if we wait too long."

Bunny listened attentively. When I was done, she nodded her head.

". . . And unofficially?"

"I beg your pardon?"

"You said, 'Officially, etc., etc.' That implies there are reasons you haven't mentioned."

That's when I realized how tired I was getting. A verbal slip like that could be costly in the wrong company. Still, Bunny was my confidential secretary. If I couldn't confide in her, I was in trouble.

"Unofficially, I'm doing it for Aahz."

"Aahz?"

"That's right. Remember him? My old partner? Well, when we were taking care of that little favor for Quigley, he kept needling me about The Fun House. There was a fairly constant stream of digs about 'throwing money at a problem' and how 'we never planned to run a casino' . . . stuff like that. I don't know why, but it's clear to me that the casino is a burr under his saddle, and if it will make him happy, I've got no problems dumping it. It just doesn't mean that much to me."

Bunny arched an eyebrow.

"So you're selling off the casino because you think it will make your old partner happy?"

"It's the best reason I can think of," I shrugged. "Bunny, he's been a combination father, teacher, coach, and Dutch uncle to me since Garkin was killed. I've lost track of the number of times he's saved my skin, usually by putting his own between me and whatever was incoming. With all I owe him, disposing of something that's bothering him seems a pretty small payback, but one I'll deliver without batting an eye."

"You might try to give him an assignment or two," she said, pursing her lips. "Maybe if he were a bit busier, he wouldn't have the time to brood and fault-find over the stuff you're doing without him."

I waited a heartbeat too long before laughing.

"Aahz is above petty jealousy, really," I said, wishing I was more sure of it myself. "Besides, I *am* trying to find an assignment for him. It's just that Perverts . . . excuse me, Pervects . . . aren't noted for their diplomacy in dealing with clients."

Not wishing to pursue the subject further, I gathered up a handful of proposals.

"Right now, I've got to go through these proposals a couple more times until I've got them straight in my mind."

"What's the problem? Just pick the best one and go with it."

I grimaced bitterly.

"It's not that easy. With some of these proposals, it's like comparing apples and oranges. One offers an ongoing percentage of profits . . . another is quoting a high purchase price, but wants to pay in installments . . . there are a handful that are offering stock in other businesses in addition to cash . . . it's just not that easy to decide which is actually the best offer."

"Maybe I can help," Bunny said, reaching for the stack of proposals. "I've had a fair amount of experience assessing offers."

I put my hand on the stack, intercepting her.

"Thanks for the offer, Bunny, but I'd rather do it myself. If I'm going to be president, I've got to learn to quit relying on others. The only way I'll learn to be self-reliant is to not indulge in depending on my staff."

She slowly withdrew her hand, her eyes searching mine as if she weren't sure she recognized me. I realized she was upset, but, reviewing what I had said, couldn't find anything wrong with my position. Too tired to sort it out just then, I decided to change the subject.

"While you're here, though, could you give me a quick briefing of what's on the dockets for tomorrow? I'd like to clear the decks to work on this stuff if I can."

Whatever was bothering her vanished as she became the efficient secretary again.

"The only thing that's pressing is assigning a team to a watchdog job. The client has a valuable shipment we're supposed to be guarding tomorrow night."

"Guard duty?" I frowned. "Isn't that a little low-class for our operation?"

"*I* thought so," she smiled sweetly, "but apparently you didn't when you committed us to it two weeks ago. A favor to one of your lunch buddies. Remember?"

"Oh. Right. Well, I think we can cover that one with Gleep. Send him over . . . and have Nunzio go along to keep an eye on him."

"All right."

She started to leave, but hesitated in the door.

"What about Aahz?"

I had already started to plunge into the proposals again and had to wrench my attention back to the conversation.

"What about him?"

"Nothing. Forget I asked."

There was no doubt about it. The staff was definitely starting to get a bit strange. Shaking my head, I addressed the proposals once more.

# Gleep's Tale

Inevitably, when conversing with my colleagues of the dragon set, and the subject of pets was raised, an argument would ensue as to the relative advantages and disadvantages of humans as pets. Traditionally, I have maintained a respectful silence during such sessions, being the youngest member in attendance and therefore obligated to learn from my elders. This should not, however, be taken as an indication that I lack opinions on the subject. I have numerous well-developed theories, which is the main reason I welcomed the chance to test them by acquiring a subject as young and yet as well-traveled as Skeeve was when I first encountered him. As my oration unfolds, you will note . . . but I'm getting ahead of myself. First things first is the order of business for organized and well-mannered organisms. I am the entity you have come to know in these volumes as . . .

"Gleep! C'mere, fella."

*That* is Nunzio. He is neither organized nor well-mannered. Consequently, as is so often the case when dealing with Skeeve and his rather dubious collection of associates, I chose to ignore him. Still, an interesting point has been raised, so I had probably best address it now before proceeding.

As was so rudely pointed out, I am known to this particular batch of humans, as well as to the readers of these volumes, simply as Gleep. For the sake of convenience, I will continue to identify myself to you by that name, thereby eliminating the frustrating task of attempting to instruct you in the pronunciation of my *real* name. Not only am I unsure you are physically able to reproduce the necessary sounds, but there is the fact that I have limited patience when it comes to dealing with humans. Then, too, it is customary for dragons to adopt aliases for these cross-phylum escapades. It saves embarrassment when the human chroniclers distort the facts when recording the incidents . . . which they invariably do.

If I seem noticeably more coherent than you would expect from my reputed one-word vocabulary, the reason is both simple and logical. First, I am still quite young for a dragon, and the vocal cords are one of the last things to develop in regard to our bodies. While I am quite able to converse and communicate with others of my species, I have another two hundred years before my voice is ready to attempt the particular combination of sounds and pitches necessary to converse extensively with humans in their own tongue.

As to my mental development, one must take into consideration the vast differences in our expected life-spans. A human is considered exceptional to survive for a hundred years, whereas dragons can live for thousands of years without being regarded as old by their friends and relations. The implications of this are too numerous to count, but the one which concerns us here is that, while I am perhaps young for a dragon, I am easily the oldest of those who affiliate themselves with Skeeve. Of course, humans tend to lack the breeding and upbringing of my kind, so they are far less inclined to heed the older and wiser heads in their midst, much less learn from them.

"Hey, Gleep! Can you hear me? Over here, boy."

I made a big show of nibbling on my foot as if troubled by an itch. Humans as a whole seem unable to grasp the subtleties of communication which would allow them to ascertain when they are being deliberately ignored, much less what it implies. Consequently, I have devised the technique of visibly demonstrating I am preoccupied when confronted with a particularly rude or ignorant statement or request. This not only serves to silence their yammerings, it slows the steady erosion of my nerves. To date, the technique yields about a twenty percent success ratio, which is significantly better than most tactics I have attempted. Unfortunately, this did not prove to be one of those twenty percenters.

"I'm talkin' ta *you*, Gleep. Now are ya gonna go where I tell ya or not?"

While I am waiting for my physical development to enable me to attempt the language of another species, I have serious doubts that Nunzio or Guido will master their *native* tongue, no matter how much time they are allowed. Somehow it reminds me of a tale one of my aunts used to tell about how she encountered a human in a faraway land and inquired if he were a native. "I ain't no native!" she was told. "I was born right here!" I quite agree with her that the only proper response when confronted by such logic was to eat him.

Nunzio was still carrying on in that squeaky little-boy voice of his which is so surprising when one first hears it, except now he had circled around behind me and was trying to push me in the direction he had indicated earlier. While he is impressively strong for a human, I outweighed him sufficiently that I was confident that there was no chance he could move me until I decided to cooperate. Still, his antics were annoying, and I briefly debated whether it was worth trying to improve his manners by belting him with my tail. I decided against it, of course. Even the strongest humans are dangerously frail and vulnerable, and I did not wish to distress Skeeve by damaging one of his playmates. A trauma like that could set my pet's training program back years.

Right about then I observed that Nunzio's breathing was becoming labored. Since he had already demonstrated his mental inflexibility, I grew concerned that he might suffer a heart attack before giving up his impossible task. Having just reminded myself of the undesirability of his untimely demise, I decided I would have to humor him.

Delaying just long enough for a leisurely yawn, I rose and ambled in the indicated direction . . . first sliding sideways a bit so that he fell on his face the next time he threw his weight against me. I reasoned that if he wasn't sturdy enough to survive a simple fall, then my pet was better off without his company.

Fortunately or un-, depending on your point of view, he scrambled rapidly to his feet and fell in step beside me as I walked.

"I want youse to familiarize yourself with the shipment which we are to be protectin'," he said, still breathing hard, "then wander around the place a little so's yer familiar with the layout."

This struck me as a particularly silly thing to do. I had sized up the shipment and the layout within moments of our arrival, and I had assumed that Nunzio had done the same. There simply wasn't all that much to analyze.

The warehouse was nothing more than a large room . . . four walls and a ceiling with rafters from which a scattered collection of lights poured down sufficiently inadequate light as to leave large pockets of shadows throughout the place. There was a small doorway in one wall, and a large sliding door in another, presumably leading to a loading dock. Except for the shipment piled in the center of the room, the place was empty.

The shipment itself consisted of a couple dozen boxes stacked on a wooden skid. From what my nose could ascertain, whatever was inside the boxes consisted of paper and ink. Why paper and ink should be valuable enough to warrant a guard I neither knew nor cared. Dragons do not have much use for paper . . . particularly paper money. Flammable currency is not our idea of a sound investment for a society. Still, someone must have felt the shipment to be of some worth, if not the human who had commissioned our services, then definitely the one dressed head to foot in black who was creeping around in the rafters.

All of this had become apparent to me as soon as we had entered the warehouse, so there was no reason to busy oneself with make-work additional checks. Nunzio, however, seemed bound and determined to prod me into rediscovering what I already knew. Even allowing for the fact that the human senses of sight, hearing, taste, touch, and smell are far below those of dragons, I was nonetheless appalled at how little he was able to detect on his own. Perhaps if he focused less of his attention on me and more on what was going on around us, he would have fared better. As it was, he was hopeless. If Skeeve was hoping that Nunzio would learn something from me, which was the only reason I could imagine for including him on the assignment, my pet was going to be sorely disappointed. Other than the fact that he seemed to try harder than most humans to interact positively with dragons, however crude and ignorant his attempts might be, I couldn't imagine why I was as tolerant of him as I was.

Whoever it was in the rafters was moving closer now. He might have been stealthy for a human, but my ears tracked him as easily as if he were banging two pots together as he came. While I was aware of his presence two steps through the door, I had been uncertain as to his intentions and therefore had been willing to be patient until sure whether he were simply an innocent bystander, or if he indeed entertained thoughts of larceny. His attempts to sneak up on us confirmed to me he was of the latter ilk, however incompetent he might be at it.

Trying to let Nunzio benefit from my abilities, I swiveled my head around and pointed at the intruder with my nose.

"Pay attention, Gleep!" my idiot charge said, jerking my muzzle down toward the boxes again. "This is what we're supposed to be guardin'. Understand?"

I understood that either humans were even slower to learn than the most critical dragons gave them credit for, which I was beginning to believe, or this particular specimen was brain-damaged, which was also a possibility. Rolling my eyes, I checked on the intruder again.

He was nearly above us now, his legs spread wide supporting his weight on two of the rafters. With careful deliberation, he removed something from within his sleeve, raised it to his mouth, and pointed it at us.

Part of the early training of any dragon is a series of lessons designed to impart a detailed knowledge of human weapons. This may sound strange for what is basically a peace-loving folk, but we consider it to be simple survival . . . such as humans instructing their young that bees sting or fire is hot. Regardless of our motivations, let it suffice to say that I was as cognizant of human weapons as any human, and considerably more so than any not in the military or other heroic vocations, and, as such, had no difficulty at all identifying the implement being directed at us as a blowgun.

Now, in addition to having better senses, dragons have armor which provides substantially more protection than humans enjoy from their skin. Consequently, I was relatively certain that whatever was set to emerge from the business end of the blowgun would not pose a threat to my well-being. It occurred to me, however, that the same could not be said for Nunzio, and, as I have said before, I have no qualms about going to some lengths to ensure my pet's peace of mind by protecting his associates.

Jerking my head free from Nunzio's grasp, I took quick aim and loosed a burst of #6 flame. Oh, yes. Dragons have various degrees of flame at their disposal, ranging from "toast a marshmallow" to "make a hole in rock." You might keep that in mind the next time you consider arguing with a dragon.

Within seconds of my extinguishing the pyrotechnics, a brief shower of black powder drifted down on us.

"Darn it, Gleep!" Nunzio said, brushing the powder from his clothes. "Don't do that again, hear me? Next time you might do more than knock some dust loose . . . and look at my clothes! Bad dragon!"

I had been around humans enough not to expect any thanks, but I found it annoying to be scolded for saving his life. With as much dignity as I could muster, which is considerable, I turned and sat with my back to him.

"GLEEP! UP, BOY! GOOD DRAGON! GOOD DRAGON!"

That was more like it. I turned to face him again, only to find him hopping around holding his foot. Not lacking in mental faculties, I was able to deduce that, in making my indignant gesture, I had succeeded in sitting on his lower extremities. It was unintentional, I assure you, as human feet are rather small and my excellent sense of touch does not extend to my posterior, but it did occur to me in hindsight (no pun intended) that it served him right.

"Look, you just sit there and I'll sit over here and we'll get along fine. Okay?"

He limped over to one of the cartons and sat down, alternately rubbing his foot and brushing his clothes off.

The powder was, of course, the remains of the late intruder/assassin. #6 flame has a tendency to have that effect on humans, which is why I used it. While human burial rights have always been a source of curiosity and puzzlement to me, I was fairly certain that they did not include having one's cremated remains brushed onto the floor or removed by a laundry service. Still, considering my difficulty in communicating a simple "look out" to Nunzio, I decided it would be too much effort to convey to him exactly what he was doing.

If my attitude toward killing a human seems a bit shocking in its casualness, remember that to dragons humans are an inferior species. You do not flinch from killing fleas to ensure the comfort of your dog or cat, regardless of what surviving fleas might think of your callous actions, and I do not hesitate to remove a bothersome human who might cause my pet distress by his actions. At least we dragons generally focus on individuals as opposed to the wholesale slaughter of species humans seem to accept as part of their daily life.

"You know, Gleep," Nunzio said, regarding me carefully, "after a

while in your company, even Guido's braggin' sounds good . . . but
don't tell him I said that."

"Gleep?"

That last sort of slipped out. As you may have noticed, I am sufficiently selfconscious about my one-word human vocabulary that I try to
rely on it as little as possible. The concept of my telling Guido anything,
however, startled me into the utterance.

"Now, don't take it so hard," Nunzio scowled, as always interpreting
my word wrong. "I didn't mean it. I'm just a little sore, is all."

I assumed he was referring to his foot. The human was feeling chatty,
however, and I soon learned otherwise.

"I just don't know what's goin' on lately, Gleep. Know what I mean?
On the paperwork things couldn't be goin' better, except lately everybody's
been actin' crazy. First the Boss buys a casino we built for somebody else,
then overnight he wants to sell it. Bunny and Tananda are goin' at each
other for a while, then all of a sudden Bunny's actin' quiet and depressed
and Tananda . . . did you know she wanted to borrow money from me
the other day? Right after she gets done with that collection job? I don't
know what she did with her commission or why she doesn't ask the Boss
for an advance or even what she needs the money for. Just 'Can you spot
me some cash, Nunzio? No questions asked?', and when I try to offer my
services as a confidential type, she sez 'In that case, forget it. I'll ask
someone else!' and leaves all huffy-like. I'll tell ya, Gleep, there's sumpin'
afoot, and I'm not sure I like it."

He was raising some fascinating points, points which I'll freely admit
had escaped my notice. While I had devoted a certain portion of my
intellect to deciphering the intricacies of human conduct, there was much
in the subtleties of their intraspecies relationships which eluded me . . .
particularly when it came to individuals other than Skeeve. Reflecting on
Nunzio's words, I realized that my pet had not been to see me much lately,
which was in itself a break in pattern. Usually he would make time to visit,
talking to me about the problems he had been facing and the self-doubts he
felt. I wondered if his increased absences were an offshoot of the phenomenon Nunzio was describing. It was food for thought, and something I
promised myself I would consider carefully at a later point. Right now,
there were more immediate matters demanding my attention . . . like the
people burrowing in under the floor.

It seemed that, in the final analysis, Nunzio was as inept as most
humans when it came to guard duty. They make a big show of alertness
and caution when they come on duty, but within a matter of hours they
are working harder at dealing with their boredom than in watching what-

ever it is they're supposed to be guarding. To be honest, the fact that dragons have longer lives may explain part of why we are so much better at staving off boredom. After a few hundred years, days, even weeks shrink to where they have no real time value at all. Even our very young have an attention span that lasts for months . . . sometimes years.

Whatever the reason, Nunzio continued to ramble on about his concerns with the status quo, apparently oblivious to the scratching and digging sounds that were making their way closer to our position. This time it wasn't simply my better hearing, for the noise was easily within the human range, though admittedly soft. By using *my* hearing, I could listen in on the conversations of the diggers.

"How much farther?"

"Sshhh! About ten feet more."

"Don't 'sshhh' me! Nobody can hear us."

"*I* can hear you! This tunnel isn't that big, ya know."

"What are you going to do with your share of the money after we steal the stuff?"

"First we gotta steal it. *Then* I'll worry about what to do with my share."

That was the part I had been waiting to hear. There had always been the chance they were simply sewer diggers or escaping convicts or something equally nonthreatening to our situation. As it was, though, they were fair game.

Rising from where I had been sitting, I moved quietly to where they were digging.

". . . unless Don Bruce wants to . . . Hey! Where are you goin'? Get back here!"

I ignored Nunzio's shouting and listened again. On target. I estimated about four feet down. With a mental smirk, I began jumping up and down, landing as heavily as I could.

"What are you doin'? Stop that! Hey, Gleep!"

The noise Nunzio was making was trivial compared to what was being said four feet down. When I mentioned earlier that I was too heavy for Nunzio to move unassisted, I was not meaning to imply that he was weak. The simple poundage of a dragon is a factor to be reckoned with even if it's dead, and if it's alive and thinking, you have real problems. I felt the floor giving way and hopped clear, relishing the sounds of muffled screams below.

"Jeez. Now look what you've done! You broke the floor!"

Again I had expected no thanks and received none. This did not concern me, as at the moment I was more interested in assessing the damage, or lack of damage, I had inflicted on this latest round of potential thieves.

The floor, or a portion of it, now sagged about a foot lower, leading me to conclude that either the tunnel below had not been very high, or that it had only partially collapsed. Either way, there were no more sounds emanating from that direction, which meant the thieves were either dead or had retreated emptyhanded. Having accomplished my objective of removing yet another threat to the shipment, I set my mind once again on more important things. Turning a deaf ear to Nunzio's ravings, I flopped down and pretended to sleep while I indulged in a bit of leisurely analysis.

Perhaps Nunzio was right. It was possible that my pet was reacting adversely to the change in his status from free-lance operator to the head of a corporation, much the same as tropical fish will suffer if the pH of the water in their aquarium is changed too suddenly. I was very much aware that an organism's environment consisted of much more than their physical surroundings . . . social atmosphere, for example, often influenced a human's well-being. If that were the case, then it behooved me to do something about it.

Exactly how I was to make the necessary adjustments would be a problem. Whenever possible, I tried to allow my pet free will. That is, I liked to give him the illusion of choosing his own course and associates without interference from me. Occasionally I would stray from this stance, such as when they brought that horrible Markie creature into our home, but for the most part it was an unshakeable policy. This meant that if I indeed decided that it was time to winnow out or remove any or all of Skeeve's current associates for his own good, it would have to be done in a manner which could not be traced to me. This would not only preserve the illusion that I was not interfering in his life, but also save him the angst which would be generated if he realized I was responsible for the elimination of one or more of his friends. Yes, this would require considerable thought and consideration.

"Here, fella. Want a treat?"

This last was uttered by a sleazy-looking Deveel as he held out a hand with a lump of some unidentifiable substance in it.

I realized with a guilty start that I had overindulged, sinking too far into my thoughts to maintain awareness of my surroundings. After the unkind thoughts I had entertained about Nunzio's attention span, this was an inexcusable lapse on my part. Ignoring the offered gift, I raised my head and cast about desperately to reassess the situation.

There were three of them: the one currently addressing me, and two others who were talking to Nunzio.

"I dunno," the latter was saying. "I didn't get any instructions about anyone pickin' up the shipment early."

Something was definitely amiss. From his words and manner, even Nunzio was suspicious . . . which meant the plot had to be pretty transparent.

"C'mon boy. Take the treat."

The Deveel facing me was starting to sound a little desperate, but I continued ignoring him and his offering. It was drugged, of course. Just because humans can't smell a wide range of chemicals, they assume that no one else can either. This one was no problem. I was more concerned as to whether or not Nunzio would require assistance.

"I can't help it if your paperwork is fouled up," the smaller Deveel with Nunzio snarled, with a good imitation of impatience. "I've got a schedule to keep. Look. Here's a copy of my authorization."

As Nunzio bent to look at the paper the Deveel was holding, the one standing behind him produced a club and swung it at his head. There was a sharp "CRACK" . . . but it was from the club breaking, not from Nunzio's head, the latter being, as I have noted, exceptionally dense.

"I'm sorry, I can't let you have the shipment," Nunzio said, handing the paper back to the short Deveel who took it without losing the astounded expression from his face. "This authorization is nothin' but a blank piece of paper."

He glanced over his shoulder at the larger Deveel who was standing there staring at his broken club.

"Be with you in a second, fella. Just as soon as we get this authorization thing cleared up."

I decided that he would be able to handle things in his own peculiar way and turned my attention to the Deveel with the drugged treat.

He was looking at the conversation across the room, his mouth hanging open in amazement. I noticed, however, that he had neglected to withdraw his hand.

There are those who hypothesize that dragons do not have a sense of humor. To prove that that is not the case, I offer this as a counterexample.

Unhinging my jaw slightly, I stretched out my neck and took the treat in my mouth. Actually, I took his hand in my mouth . . . all the way to the shoulder. This was not as hazardous as it sounds. I simply took care not to swallow and therefore avoided any dangerous effects which might be generated by the drugged treat.

The Deveel glanced back when he heard my jaws crash together, and we looked into each others' eyes from a considerably closer range than he had anticipated. For effect, I waggled my eyebrows at him. The eyebrows did it, and his eyes rolled up into his head as he slumped to the floor in a dead faint.

Funny, huh? So much for not having a sense of humor.

Relaxing my jaws, I withdrew my head leaving the treat and his arm intact, and checked Nunzio's situation again.

The larger Deveel was stretched out on the floor unconscious while Nunzio was holding the other by the lapels with one hand, leisurely slapping him forehand and backhand as he spoke.

"I oughtta turn youse over to da authorities! A clumsy hijack like this could give our profession a bad name. Know what I mean? Are you listenin' ta me? Now take your buddies and get outta here before I change my mind! And don't come back until you find some decent help!"

I had to admit that Nunzio had a certain degree of style . . . for a human. If he had been fortunate enough to be born with a brain, he might have been a dragon.

While he was busy throwing the latest batch of attackers out the door, I decided to do a little investigating. After three attempts to relieve us of our prize, though Nunzio was only aware of one of them, I was beginning to grow a bit suspicious. Even for as crime-prone a lot as humans tend to be, three attempts in that close succession was unusual, and I wanted to know more about what it was we were guarding.

The cases still smelled of paper and ink, but that seemed an inadequate reason for the attention it had been drawing. As casually as I could, I swatted one of the cases with my tail, caving it in. Apparently I had not been casual enough, for the sound brought Nunzio sprinting to my side.

"Now what are you doin'? Look! You ruined . . . Hey! Wait a minute!"

He stooped and picked up one of the objects that had spilled from the case and examined it closely. I snaked my head around so I could look over his shoulder.

"Do you know what dis is, Gleep?"

As a matter of fact, I didn't. From what I could see, all it was was some kind of picture book . . . and a shoddily made one at that. What it *didn't* look like was anything valuable. Certainly nothing that would warrant the kind of attention we had been getting.

Nunzio tossed the book back onto the floor and glanced around nervously.

"This is over my head," he murmured. "I can't . . . Gleep, you keep an eye on this stuff. I'll be right back. I've gotta get the Boss . . . and Guido! Yeah. He knows about this stuff."

Admittedly perplexed, I watched him go, then studied the book again.

Very strange. There was clearly something in this situation that was escaping my scrutiny.

I rubbed my nose a few times in a vain effort to clear it of the smell of ink, then hunkered down to await my pet's arrival.

\* \* \*

"Comic books?"

Skeeve was clearly as perplexed as I had been.

"The 'valuable shipment' we're guarding is comic books?"

"That's what I thought, Boss," Nunzio said. "Screwy, huh? What do you think, Guido?"

Guido was busy prying open another case. He scanned the books on top, then dug a few out from the bottom to confirm they were the same. Studying two of them intently, he gave out with a low whistle.

"You know what these are worth, Boss?"

Skeeve shrugged.

"I don't know how many of them are here, but I've seen them on sale around the Bazaar at three or four for a silver, so they can't be worth much."

"Excuse me for interruptin'," Guido said, "but I am not referrin' to yer everyday, run-of-the-mill comic. I am lookin' at these, which are a horse from a different stable."

"They are?" my pet frowned. "I mean . . . it is? I mean . . . these all look the same to me. What makes them special?"

"It is not easy to explain, but if you will lend me your ears I will attempt to further your education, Boss. You too, Nunzio."

Guido gathered up a handful of the books and sat on one of the cases.

"If you will examine the evidence before you, you will note that while all these comics are the same, which is to say they are copies of the same issue, they each have the number 'one' in a box on their cover. This indicates that it is the first issue of this particular title."

I refrained from peering at one of the books. If Guido said the indicator was there, it was probably there, and looking at it wouldn't change anything.

"Immediately that 'one' makes the comic more valuable, both to someone who is tryin' to obtain a complete set, and especially to a collector. Now, certain titles is more popular than others, which makes them particularly valuable, but more important are titles which have indeed grown in popularity since they made their first debutante. In that situational, there are more readers of the title currently than there were when it began, and the laws of supply and demand drive the price of a first-issue copy through the roof."

He gestured dramatically with one of the books.

"This particular title premiered several years ago and is currently hotter than the guy what swiped the crown jewels. What is more, the print run on the first issue was very small, makin' a first-issue copy exceedingly valuable . . . with the accent on 'exceedingly.' I have with my own eyes seen a beat-up copy of the comic you are currently holding on a dealer's table with an askin' price of a hundert-fifty gold on it. Mind you, I'm not sayin' he got it, but that's what he was askin'."

Now it was Skeeve's turn to whistle. I might have been tempted myself, but whistling is difficult with a forked tongue.

"If that's true, this shipment is worth a fortune. He's got enough of them here."

"That is indeed the puzzlement, Boss," Guido said, looking at the cases. "If my memory is not seriously in error, there were only two thousand copies of this issue printed . . . yet if all these cases are full of the same merchandise, there are considerably more copies than that in this shipment to which we are referrin'. How this could be I am uncertain, but the explanation which occurs to me is less than favorable to the owner."

"Forgeries!" Nunzio squeaked. "The guy's a multicolored paper hanger!"

"A multi . . . never mind!" Skeeve waved. "What good would forged comics be?"

"The same as any other forgery," Guido shrugged. "You pass 'em off as originals and split with the money before anyone's the wiser. In some way's it's better'n phony money, since it isn't as hard to duplicate comics and, as youse can see, they're worth more per pound. The paper's cheaper, too."

My pet surveyed the shipment.

"So we've been made unwitting accomplices to a comic-forging deal, eh?"

". . . And without even gettin' a piece of the action," Nunzio snarled.

"That wasn't what I was thinking about," Skeeve said, shaking his head. "I was thinking of all the collectors who are going to plunk down their money to get a genuine collector's item, only to have the bottom drop out of the market when it's discovered that it's been flooded with forgeries."

He rubbed his lower lip thoughtfully.

"I wonder how much my lunch buddy has insured this shipment for?"

"Probably not much, if at all," Guido supplied. "To do so would necessitate the fillin' out of documents declarin' the contents of said shipment, and any insurance type knowledgeable enough to give him full value would also know the discrepancy between the shipment count and what was originally printed. You see, Boss, the trouble with runnin' a fraud is that it requires runnin' additional frauds to cover for it, and eventually someone is bound to catch on."

Skeeve wasn't even listening by the time Guido finished his oration. He was busy rubbing the spot between my ears, a strange smile on his face.

"Well, I guess nobody wins all the time."

"What was that, Boss?"

My pet turned to face them.

"I said that M.Y.T.H. Inc. fumbled the ball this time. Sorry, Nunzio, but this one is going into the records as a botched assignment. I can only assure you that it will *not* be reflected on your next performance review."

"I don't get it," Nunzio frowned. "What went wrong?"

"Why, the fire, of course. You know, the fire that destroyed the entire shipment due to our inattentiveness and neglect? Terribly careless of us, wasn't it?"

"Fire? What fire?"

Skeeve stepped to one side and bowed to me, sweeping one hand toward the cases.

"Gleep? I believe this is your specialty?"

I waffled briefly between using a #4 or a #6, then said "to heck with it" and cut loose with a #9. It was a bit show-offy, I'll admit, but with Guido and Nunzio watching, not to mention my pet, it was pointless to spare the firepower.

They were impressed, which was not surprising, as #9 is quite impressive. There wasn't even any afterburn to put out, since by the time I shut down the old flamethrower, there was nothing left to burn.

For several moments we all stood staring at the charred spot on the warehouse floor.

"Wow!" Guido breathed at last.

"You can say that double for me," Nunzio nodded, slipping an arm around my neck. "Good dragon, Gleep. Good dragon."

"Well, gentlemen," Skeeve said, rubbing his hands together, "now that that's over I guess we can head . . . What's that?"

He pointed at the collapsed portion of the floor, noticing it for the first time.

"That?" Nunzio squeaked innocently. "Beats me, Boss. It was like that when we got here."

I didn't bother to return his wink, for I was already starting to retreat into heavy thought. I only hoped that in the final analysis I wouldn't decide that either Guido or Nunzio was an unsettling influence on my pet. Time would tell.

# Chapter VI

*"Not everything in life is funny."*
**R. L. Asprin**

$\mathbf{T}$HE crew seemed to be in high spirits as they gathered in my office for our monthly board meeting. Congratulations and jibes were exchanged in equal portions, as was the norm, and they began to settle in for what promised to be a marathon session.

I was glad *they* were in a good mood. It might make what I had to say a little easier, though I doubted it. I was still reeling from the one-two punch I had just received, and now it was my job to pass it on to them.

My own view of the pending session was a mixture of dread and impatience. Impatience finally dominated, and I called the meeting to order.

"I know you all came prepared to discuss the sale of The Fun House," I said, looking around at the team members sprawled hither and yon, "but something has come up that I think takes priority over that. If no one objects, I'll temporarily table the casino discussion in favor of new business."

That caused a bit of a stir and an exchange of puzzled glances and shrugs. Not wanting to be sidetracked by a round of questions or comments, I hurried on.

"There's an assignment . . . no, I can't call it that. There's no payment involved and no client. It's just something I think M.Y.T.H. should get involved in. I don't feel I can order anyone to take part . . . in fact, I don't even see putting it to a vote. It's got to be on an individual volunteer basis."

Tananda raised her hand. I nodded at her.

"Do we get to hear what it is? Or are we supposed to volunteer blind?"

I searched for the words for a moment, then gave up. Instead of speaking, I pushed the little oblong box that was on my desk toward her. She frowned at it, glanced at me, then picked it up and raised the lid.

One look inside was all it took for her to get the message. Sinking back in her seat, we locked eyes for a moment; then she shook her head and gave a low whistle.

"I say, is this a private horror, or can any number play?" Chumley grumbled from across the office.

In response, Tananda held up the box, tilting it so everyone could see the contents. Inside was a severed finger, a woman's finger, to be exact. It was wearing a particularly gaudy ring.

There was a long silence as the assemblage stared at the missive. Then Massha cleared her throat.

"How much for just the ring?" she quipped, but from the tone of her voice she wasn't expecting anyone to laugh.

Nobody did.

"I don't get it, Boss," Guido scowled. "Is this supposed to be a joke or sumpin'?"

"You and Nunzio weren't around for the big finale, Guido," I said. "Remember Queen Hemlock? Back on my home dimension of Klah?"

"Sure," he nodded. "She was an okay skirt . . . a little creepy, though."

"I guess it depended on which side of her favor you were on," Tananda commented wryly, tossing the box back onto the table.

I ignored her.

"Bunny, you weren't around for any of this, so . . ."

"I've picked up some of it talking to Chumley," she waved.

"Well, Queen Hemlock had an interesting plan she wanted to put into effect after she married Rodrick: to combine Possiltum's military strength with the wealth of her own kingdom of Impasse and fulfill her lifelong dream of conquering the world. Of course, she also planned to kill Rodrick if he opposed the idea."

I picked up the box and toyed with it idly.

"I thought I had stopped her by giving Rodrick wedding rings that they thought linked their lives, rings that wouldn't come off. The one in the box here is hers . . . of course, she had to cut off her finger to get rid of it. I hadn't anticipated that."

"I rather suspect she wanted her dream more than her finger," Chumley said with a grimace.

"So it would seem," I nodded. "Now she's on the loose, with an army we inadvertently supplied her with back when I was Court Magician of Possiltum. I'm not the greatest military appraiser around, but I don't think there's anything on Klah that can stop her . . . unless M.Y.T.H. Inc. takes a hand in the game."

"What I don't understand," Chumley said, "is why she informed us of the situation via that missive. Wouldn't she be better off unopposed?"

"Don't you know a challenge when you see one, big brother?" Tananda sighed. "Gauntlets are out of style, so she's giving us the finger."

"You all seem ta have a higher opinion of Queenie than I do," Massha spoke up. "Ta me, it looks more like an invitation to a trap. As I recall, old Hemlock wasn't too well disposed toward us when we split. For all we know, her plan may have already run its course . . . in which case we get to be the featured entertainment at the victory celebration."

That hadn't occurred to me. I seemed to be missing a lot lately.

"You may be right, Massha," I said. "Under the best of circumstances, I'm not sure there's anything that can be done. That's why I'm putting it up for discussion. It's my home dimension, and I was the one who contributed to the problem, so my judgment is biased. In many ways, it's a personal problem. I can't expect anyone else to . . ."

"You're talking it to death, Hot Stuff," Massha interrupted. "You're our peerless leader, for better or worse. Just go for it. We'll be right behind you."

I shook my head and held up a restraining hand.

"It's not that simple. First of all, I don't want this to be a group commitment where a dissenting individual has to be an exception or go along with something they don't agree with. That's why I was calling for individual volunteers . . . with no stigma attached to anyone who doesn't want to sign up. Second . . ."

This was the hard part. Taking a deep breath, I plunged into it.

"Second, I won't be along for this one. Something else has come up that takes priority over Queen Hemlock. Now, if she's not that important to me . . ."

"Whoa. Stop the music!" Tananda exclaimed. "I want to hear what this hot deal is you've got going on the side. What's more important to you than defending your own home dimension?"

I avoided her eyes.

"It's not a deal or a job, really. It . . . It's personal. Something I can't delegate. I've got to handle it myself."

"So tell us," she demanded, crossing her arms. "We're family. If nothing else, don't you think we have a right to know what the head man is going to be doing while we're off fighting a war for him?"

I had had a feeling I wouldn't be able to slip this by unnoticed. With a sigh, I dropped the other shoe.

"Look around the room," I said. "Notice anything missing?"

There was a pause as everyone complied. It took a distressingly long time for them to figure it out.

"Aahz!" Chumley said at last. "Aahz isn't here."

"Say, that's right," Massha blinked. "I thought the meeting was a little quiet. Where is old Green and Scaly?"

"Gone."

It took a moment for it to sink in. Then the team stared at each other in shocked silence.

"The note was on my desk this morning," I continued. "It's his letter of resignation from M.Y.T.H. Inc. Apparently he feels that without his powers he's deadwood . . . taking up space without earning his pay. He's packed up and gone, headed back to Perv."

I dropped the paper back on my desk.

"That's why I'm not going after Queen Hemlock myself. I'm going to Perv . . . after Aahz."

The room exploded.

"To Perv?"

"You've got to be kidding, Hot Stuff."

"But, Boss . . ."

"Skeeve, you can't . . ."

"I say, Skeeve. What if he won't come back?"

I homed in on that last comment. As usual, Chumley managed to hit the heart of the matter.

"If he won't come back . . . well, I'll have tried. I've got to at least talk to him. We've been together too long to let it go with a letter. I'm going to Perv to talk with him face to face . . . and I'm going alone."

A new wave of protest rose in the room, but I cut it off.

"When you go after Queen Hemlock . . . excuse me . . . *if* you go after Queen Hemlock, you're going to need all the manpower you can muster. It's bad enough that I can't be there; don't divide your strength more than it already is. Besides . . ."

My voice faltered a little here.

"This is my problem . . . I mean *really* my problem. I've been doing a lot of thinking since I read this note, and the problem is bigger than Aahz."

I swept the assemblage slowly with my eyes.

"I've gotten pretty wrapped up with being president lately. It's been hard to . . . I've been trying to justify the faith you all have in me by making the business go. In the process, it's gotten so I'm pretty sparse with my 'thank yous' and 'atta boys,' and I've all but lost contact with all of you outside of a business context. Aahz has been my best friend for years, and if he . . . Let's just say I'll be looking for myself as much as for Aahz."

There was dead silence as my oration ground to a halt. If I had been hoping for any protests over my analysis, I was playing to the wrong audience. Suddenly, I wanted the meeting to be over with.

I cleared my throat.

"I'm taking a leave of absence to find Aahz. No discussion is required or allowed. Now, the subject at hand is whether or not M.Y.T.H. Inc. is going to attempt to stop Queen Hemlock's assumed attempt to take over Klah. Are there any volunteers?"